The Chine

HER MINDER: BOOK TWO

THE CHINE

HER MINDER: BOOK TWO

Teddy Raye

Boscobel Books

Teddy Raye/Boscobel Books
118 Claridge Place
Belton, South Carolina 29627

Book Layout © 2016 BookDesignTemplates.com
Book Cover Design: Rusty Apper@mintvision
Book Cover Art: Patricia Sobral

The Chine – Her Minder: Book Two/ Teddy Raye. – 2nd ed.
ISBN 13: 978-0-9991642-2-8

This book is dedicated to the people who helped me to believe:

Pam Martin for her amazing editorial skills, encouragement and friendship. Thank you for not giving up on me, even when I was ready to give up on myself.

Murphy McCall, for being the inspiration and giving me the impetus to believe in Her Minder again. You started the whole ball rolling, babe, back in the day. Theresa, my angel, the owner of the biggest, sweetest most generous heart. Thank you for everything. Mike, The Good Doktor, for his advice and expertise in the kinkster world of BDSM.

Evan Harris, the God of Podcast and the soul of patience, who spent hours of his time bringing these characters to life for Audible. Rusty Apper, for amazing artistic skills and super support, not to mention a beautiful cover series and boundless enthusiasm- love you, mate! Patricia Sobral for creating beautiful artwork at the drop of a hat. Alan Rickman for The Voice. My Precious Muse, the real, true Dahlra. Thank you for reuniting with me.

I've often tried to teach my son that being a man, a good man, is being a man of peace who is capable of violence, judiciously applied, when needed.

~~Todd Hollingsworth

The sun watches what I do, but the moon knows all my secrets.

~~J M Wonderland

"Love seeketh not itself to please,
Nor for itself hath any care,
But for another gives its ease,
And builds a Heaven in Hell's despair."

So sung a little Clod of Clay
Trodden with the cattle's feet,
But a Pebble of the brook
Warbled out these metres meet:

"Love seeketh only self to please,
To bind another to its delight,
Joys in another's loss of ease,
And builds a Hell in Heaven's despite."
~~*William Blake, The Clod and The Pebble*

Flare up like a flame and make big shadows I can move in.
Let everything happen to you: beauty and terror.
Just keep going. No feeling is final.
Don't let yourself lose me...

Extinguish my eyes, I'll go on seeing you.
Seal my ears, I'll go on hearing you.
And without feet I can make my way to you,
Without a mouth I can swear your name.
Break off my arms, I'll take hold of you with my heart as with a hand.
Stop my heart, and my brain will start to beat.
And if you consume my brain with fire,
I'll feel you burn in every drop of my blood.
~~*Rilke's Book of Hours – Love Poems to God*

CHINE: /tʃaɪn/
Rhymes: -aɪn

From Middle English *chyne,* from Old French *eschine* (based on a blend of Latin spina 'spine' and a Germanic word meaning 'narrow piece', related to shin.) Also *chīnen* ("to crack, fissure, split"), from Old English *ċine, ċinu, ċīnan* ("to break into pieces, burst, crack; cleft, chink, gape, to grow in size'"), cognate to Old Saxon *kena.* Related to Dutch *keen,* also to chink.

Noun

The top of a ridge.
A steep-sided, deep, narrow ravine leading from the top of a cliff down to the sea. (Isle of Wight, Dorset)
The spine of an animal.
A sharp angle in the cross section of a hull.
The edge or rim of a cask, etc., formed by the projecting ends of the staves; the chamfered end of a stave.
The angle where the strakes of the bottom of a boat or ship meet the side.

Urban Dictionary

A mixture between chain and shrine.

The Passenger

April 1

April First. April-sodding-Fool's.

On a good day, driving a mini-cab was not exactly the most rewarding job in the world, but when these moronic oiks thought it was great fun to send a hard-working cabbie like Ralph Bhairam all over town just to find his pickup point was a public loo... Three of those he'd had already. *And* two giggly tarts had made him drive halfway to Brighton, then did a runner and skipped out on paying. God, people were work.

Ralph wanted to call it a night, but he needed the money. Those Uber bastards had spent the past eighteen months chiseling away at his patch. True, they had lost their license in the UK, but he was still struggling to reclaim control over his old ground. It would be another six months before he could stop worrying about paying the bills.

He pulled into the petrol station to pick up his Iron Bru and Twix, the cabbie's standard dinner. The young Pakistani shop clerk asked, "Busy tonight, Mister Ralph?" It was the same question he asked Ralph every night. Rather than embark on a potentially long and pointless conversation about the shite economy or the price of Iron Bru or the immature buggers who still thought pulling April Fool's day pranks on a bloke was fun, Ralph returned the stock question with his stock answer.

"Oh, about the usual." The clerk nodded sagely. Ralph imagined that as soon as he walked out, the kid would press some internal rewind button, and ask the next person who walked through the door the same question, in the same tone of voice. At the end of his shift, the clerk would send all of his customers' answers, including Ralph's, back to his alien superiors on the mothership for analysis.

And of course, there were times Ralph thought he might be cracking up from sheer boredom. *Occupational hazard, Sunshine.*

He slid into the driver's seat of his minicab. As he shook out a cigarette from a crumpled packet, the dispatcher's gruff voice sounded from his radio. "Car Seven, Car Seven, are you able to take a pickup from

Croydon?"

Depends on the location, he thought. There were some housing estates in South London he would not enter after dark, no matter how big a fare. He pressed the Send button. "Address?"

"20A Bond Gardens? That's somewhere around the flyover."

He knew the area; at least it was a real place and not a monument or something equally stupid. This might actually be a legit run. "Yeah, I'm on my way."

"You need to go to the door. Sounds like an elderly gentleman."

"Alright. On route."

Bond Gardens was an anonymous-looking block of apartments that backed onto the trading estates tucked under the flyover. Twenty-A was the ground floor flat down on the far end. As Ralph got out of his cab, the sound of music and voices coming from the Red Lion pub floated over the privet hedge on the next street but one. He longed for a pint, but knew better than to give into that wish; he could not afford to piss away his wages—not to mention losing his license on a drink-driving charge.

Ralph rang the bell at 20A, and waited. A form approached the glass door, its silhouette wavy and blurred in the mottled glass. "Yes?" The voice was quavering and high-pitched.

"Sterling Cab Service. You called for a car?"

"Oh, yes. One moment." The latch turned, and the door opened. Ralph found himself faced with an old man, stooped and stocky. Wispy, white hair, fine as candy floss, stood out in all directions around his small, round head. His forehead was covered in liver spots; his nose was a network of gin blossoms. He beckoned to Ralph with yellowed, tobacco-stained fingers. "Come in. I'm almost ready."

Ralph followed the old man down a narrow hall. The interior of the flat was dingy and damp. Discoloured curls of paper peeled from the walls like streamers. The faded checkerboard lino had been new somewhere around the time Chamberlain was Prime Minister. Overhead, a bare bulb provided greasy, yellow light, casting long shadows over the grime and neglect. The flat smelled of boiled cabbage and stale piss.

Think of the money, he reminded himself, watching the old man shuffle down the rabbit-warren hall. He turned abruptly and walked through one of the doorways, with Ralph close behind him. Pausing in the middle of the room, he tugged on a cord overhead, flooding the space with harsh light. Ralph stopped in his tracks, his breath knocked from his lungs in a gasp of shock.

"What the f—?"

The room was full of mannequins. Some were nude, some were dressed in tatty stockings and suspenders, some in formal wear, some in costumes. They were bald, or wore excessively long wigs. They lounged on the sagging sofa and perched on the arms of chairs; some were leaning against the nicotine-stained walls in casual poses. Heads devoid of any discernible facial features turned toward females with exaggeratedly made-up, haughty faces—leering men and smiling, doll-like children were propped against one another in the corner. A jumble of arms and legs and torsos poked out of the top of a plastic rubbish bin, like the branches of some strange, exotic tree. Weirdest of all, they were all looking expectantly toward the door, as if waiting for something or someone. The swaying light overhead made them look as if they were moving, breathing.

"Sweet baby Jesus and the orphans," Ralph muttered, trying to convince his skin not to crawl right off his bones.

The old man chuffed laughter, a wheezy, ghoulish sound, given the setting. "Like my collection, eh?" He tipped a wink Ralph found obscene.

"What the hell are you doing with all these?" He was unable to turn away from the creepy figures. He felt their painted eyes crawling over him, and he shuddered. "Look, mate, I don't know what game you think you're playing, but—"

"I know, I know, son." He gave Ralph's arm a clumsy pat. He repressed the impulse to push the old man away. "It's not everyone's cuppa, but the pay's good."

Leaving Ralph to puzzle over this cryptic statement, the old man produced a brown luggage tag and a biro. He bunched his knobbly, arthritic fingers around the pen, and sputtered the words *Model A230, 'DW'* on the tag. His handwriting was so shaky and cramped, Ralph could barely make out the letters.

That done, he headed over to the cracked naugahyde sofa in the middle of the room. Lying over the laps of several other dummies was one of those life-size sex dolls, covered head to toe in a black PVC catsuit, complete with a gimp mask. The old man grasped it by the neck and hauled it upright. "There we go, my dear." He tied the tag around the dummy's wrist, then picked it up and slung it over his shoulder. "I'll help you get it to the cab."

Ralph trailed behind the man as he stumped back down the hall and clumsily muscled his burden over the threshold, grunting with effort. When they reached the cab, Ralph opened the door, and the old geezer unceremoniously slung the dummy onto the back seat. It lolled into place with the boneless sprawl of a corpse.

"What am I supposed to do with it?"

The old man paused to catch his breath. He fumbled in the pocket of his shabby cardigan, wheezing. "Now, you'll need to take it to this address. Someone will be there. Bert's the name. He'll take it off your hands." He handed Ralph a folded piece of paper. It was grubby, the creases dark from handling. Ralph saw the address and huffed in anger.

"Alright, I know you think this is the funniest thing in the world, but—"

"I'm to pay you three times your fare, and a one-er bonus," the old man said matter-of-factly, pressing an open envelope into Ralph's hands.

Even without counting it, Ralph could tell it contained at least four times the rate to the destination, in addition to the extra ton. Every alarm bell he had ever cultivated in his time as a cabbie was clanging away like fucking Big Ben. "This *is* some kind of April Fool's joke, innit?"

The old man's watery eyes widened, then he burst into that witchety cackle that set Ralph's teeth on edge. "April Fool! That's a good one, and no mistake!" Still laughing, the old man touched his finger to his nose and winked. "No mistake." He sobered, and there was a thin, insistent edge to his voice. "Now, off you go. They're waitin' for ya. In Barnet, yeah?"

Ralph counted the money again. "Alright. Let him know I'm on my way."

"Good lad. Just pull up to the kerb and bib the horn. Bert'll be there." He limped back toward the flat, mopping his brow with a filthy handkerchief. When he reached the front stoop, he turned around and gave a cheery wave. Ralph did not return it.

He started the cab and told dispatch he would finish with this punter and call it a night. He did not mention the extra sponduliks, of course. His boss would want some kind of cut.

In the rearview mirror, Ralph could see the doll slouched over the seat, like a drunk sleeping off a hangover. He did not bother to repress a shudder. Still, if the old sod sent his little dolls to different parts of town with this kind of fare, he might prefer someone who did not ask too many questions. Hauling dummies all over London could become a nice little side-business...

"Let's just hope this Bert doesn't expect me to haul you inside the doors." The thought of touching it was repugnant. "God knows where you've been."

He started his meter and headed in the direction of Morden. SatNav predicted he was one hour and a bit from Barnet. He could not get there soon enough.

It was outside White City that Ralph heard the first noise from the back of his cab.

Christ. April Fool's Day.

CHAPTER ONE

Playing For Keeps

Two Months Earlier

When Elwess Talbert offered to share his home whenever they visited London, Sydney Chapin and her Minder, Dahlra Gar, considered it the perfect solution. Their first shared residence, the enormous terraced house in DeVere Gardens, was virtually empty now, and the increasingly regular commute to the city meant they needed a place that did not make them feel like two peas rolling around in a haunted tin can.

Never one to do things by half, Elwess had boasted his estate agent could sell the huge flat in a fortnight. At first, Sydney had laughed at his audacity; she was not laughing now. With no ongoing property chain to hold up the process, DeVere Gardens sold so quickly, they found themselves scrambling to get all the paperwork done in time for the new owners to start moving in before the end of January.

The last piece of furniture to go was the beautiful old bed in Sydney's room. It was now dismantled and on a moving van heading toward Elwess' Pelham Street home. As they took their final walk-through the flat, their footsteps echoing hollowly in the empty, high-ceilinged rooms, Sydney was glad to get out the door. Dahlra followed, shutting it behind him, and locked it for the last time. Staring up at DeVere's secretive facade, Sydney was surprised at the memories and emotions that surfaced as they took their leaving.

She thought of those awkward, early days, when every conversation was served with a generous helping of crème brûlée and recrimination, seasoned by her reluctance and resentment, his frustration and overcompensation. That rainy, autumn day she had foolishly locked herself out, too embarrassed and stubborn to call for help, and ended up soaked to the skin. She had been so ill, she nearly died of exposure. Dahlra had nursed her through it, and watched over her like a sentinel as she stumbled down that roughshod road to recovery. Living with the physical scars had been child's play compared to learning how to navigate the minefield in her head.

The look on Dahlra's face suggested he, too, was thinking of the past, when they struggled to find equilibrium in a situation neither could truly control. It was that look which convinced Sydney they had made the right decision; best to let the place go, and let someone else enjoy it, breathe their life force into it, make it a true home. The old ghosts were silent at last. They could no longer haunt them. Eighteen incredible months had passed since then. It was a new year, a new life, and one they would now in part share with Elwess.

It started off uneventfully, as most life-changing moments do, but Elwess' key would give them more than just a place to stay in London, and all the locks in the world could not confine the darkest parts of their former lives.

Once they were done with DeVere, they were free to prepare for the little assignment they had planned during Inigo's New Year's party, which Sydney had dryly christened, 'The Great sub Mission.' Since Valentine's Day would fall on a Sunday, it was decided that Sydney would drive from Maidenvine, their home in Windsor, down to London the Friday before. Dahlra was to meet them at The Library on Sunday evening, though why Sydney had to travel ahead on her own struck her as vaguely suspicious.

The two men spent a lot of time colluding by phone and email. As far as Elwess was concerned, the fourteenth of February could not come soon enough. He had appointed himself in charge of coordinating Sydney's leatherwear; he obtained her exact measurements, with special attention to her bust, hips and waist. He also requested her shoe size, thigh, calf and back measurements. When she asked why, Sydney was reminded that a proper submissive did not question her Dominant, but instead trusted his actions and his motives.

And since this soirée was all about being a proper sub, she did not push for details. Sydney had never been the type who tore the house apart looking for hidden Christmas presents; she certainly was not going to badger the man she loved into revealing whatever kinky surprise he and Elwess had dreamed up for Valentine's Day.

She also had the feeling Elwess might be planning some sort of Svengali voodoo shit on them, and told Dahlra as much. He had always viewed Elwess' behaviour with an indulgent amount of pragmatism, and encouraged her to do the same. They discussed it in bed on Thursday night. "I look at it from the standpoint of how much he absolutely adores you," explained Dahlra, "and how much he has given up for my benefit."

Sydney rose from the comfortable pillow that was his shoulder. "I'm not sure I follow you."

"I truly believe he would walk away from the entire lifestyle if you asked him."

"What?"

"I mean it. Elwess has changed over the years. He's found something he needs more than the things he wants. He'd do anything for you." Dahlra shifted so that they faced one another. "But as cold-blooded as it sounds, we have to look at the bigger picture. And plan accordingly."

That, Sydney could understand. During the New Year's party, Garnet Pinkerton, her old Agency partner, had made no secret of the fact he neither liked nor trusted Elwess. Sydney had defended Elwess at the time, but she had to admit one of Garnet's hypotheses had been right on the money.

Silverbirch, the case that had nearly cost Sydney her life, *was* ramping back up. What had started out as a sleazy, private club for the perverted rich and weekend warriors using human game for sport had evolved into an efficient organisation with powerful political and underworld contacts. The Agency had been assigned to investigate the organisation almost from the first moment it had surfaced.

It was a job tailor-made for Lightoller's network of operatives and intelligence, but from the off, something was amiss. Lines of communication were shut down; leads dead-ended, witnesses disappeared or lost their memory. The Agency found itself in a glass bubble where they were stone-walled and hamstrung at every turn. Wealthy and political fat cats pulled rank and called in favours; valuable time and resources were lost. It still baffled Sydney that such a penny-ante group like Silverbirch had so much pull in the rarefied halls of Parliament.

Worst of all, it became obvious it was an inside job. Vasily Gregorin, the agent whose life Sydney and her team saved from an assassination attempt on the night she and Dahlra first met, had viciously betrayed the Agency, then sold Sydney out to Silverbirch's business partners.

During what should have been a deep cover assignment, they had rumbled her, and she had ended up in the Cell, where Dahlra eventually orchestrated her escape.

Gregorin had paid for that betrayal with his life; Garnet Pinkerton had seen to that. Lightoller had lost his double, but so had Silverbirch. Shortly after Sydney returned to England, the body of Silverbirch's controller was found in the trunk of a car, surrounded by several bags of uncut heroin and almost three quarter of a million pounds in old readys. They were wrapped carelessly in plastic, and did not hold up to the amount of blood that had soaked into them from their owner's slashed throat. Other than that, the vehicle was clean of any evidence. The murderer was never found, and for a while, the organisation seemed to sputter and lose orbit. The investigation known as Operation Silverbirch was shelved, and the case grew cold.

Then, shortly before Lightoller called Sydney and asked her to do a bit of ad hoc consulting at the Ramcat Estate, the radar blipped with fresh activity. Word was that Silverbirch had a new controller, and the man at the helm was hungry. His ambitions were far-reaching; he was not content to merely front extreme kinksters and their warped morals when it came to safe, sane and consensual. Drugs, trafficking, guns, money laundering; he wanted to run with the big dogs now, and he was surrounding himself with a new set of shadowy, powerful supporters.

Agency analysts revealed that one of Silverbirch's most successful recruitment techniques was to blackmail and coerce its members, then ultimately threaten their loved ones. Everyone knew the hardest villain in the world could spit in the eye of God Himself, but if you wanted him whimpering and on his knees, you hit his family. Many of Silverbirch's top men were now compromised to the point where they had no choice but to remain, and they would do whatever it took to protect the organisation.

Just when it looked like Lightoller might get his chance to kick Silverbirch into touch, the information hemorrhage began anew. Covers were blown, raids were compromised or bungled with false intel, alibis were presented so ironclad you could not slip a fag paper between their arsecheeks. "Every sterile corridor resembles a swamp now," Garnet quipped.

And while it had not taken much persuasion to convince Inigo

Lightoller that Elwess was not the dangle who had been trickle-feeding Silverbirch, Sydney knew there was no guarantee the real mole would not strike at the Agency through Elwess. Gregorin had been all about the money; he was little more than a whore selling himself to the highest bidder. Like anyone of his ilk, it irritated Lightoller to have to pay an agent for his loyalty, but he was pragmatic enough to do it. Lightoller no longer held his agents so cheaply as to think they were faithful solely because of their love and respect for him.

What struck Sydney as more insidious was the feeling that this time, money was not the object. Something more personal might be at stake, and Elwess Talbert was exactly the kind of man Silverbirch would want in their little boy's club. Sydney could envision a time in the future when both Silverbirch and the Agency would vie for his affections. And while Elwess had always struck her as singularly ambiguous when it came to ethics, she sensed he had a least the workings of an inner moral compass. It was up to her and Dahlra to make sure he chose the right side. It all felt so manipulative, but Jesus—what didn't in this business?

"We'll just have to make sure Elwess finds wearing the white hat a much more attractive proposition..."

"Then he'll belong to us forever." Dahlra rolled over, pinning Sydney beneath him, and kissed her in that way that made her pretty much let him do whatever he wanted. "And together, we can keep you safe."

Sydney felt that fiery, protective instinct to hold him close. "My first priority is keep *you* safe," she whispered into his kiss. "Then we can work on saving the rest of the world."

Friday morning, Sydney kissed Dahlra goodbye, got in her Audi and pointed it toward London. In her rearview mirror, she could see him, standing on the steps, tall and relaxed and beautiful, waving goodbye. Watching his figure receding from view, she was suddenly struck by a feeling that stupidly felt like panic. Except for the rare occasion, she and Dahlra were virtually inseparable.

Relying on his capability, his easy company, his passion and his over-all protective tenderness had become the most natural thing in the world. True, there had been a time when she might have cheerfully maimed someone for the chance to be alone, but that was in the long-ago BD: Before Dahlra.

Now, as the miles placed a longer and longer distance between her and Maidenvine, it felt as if there was an invisible cord anchoring it to her heart. *Driving away from Dahlra feels like I'm driving out of my own skin.* Tension torqued across her forehead; for a moment, she felt as if she were coming down with a migraine. "Coming down with a case of the dumbass, more like," she muttered to herself. "He'll be with you in two days. Get a grip, Agent."

She had barely made it out of Windsor when she started to feel short of breath and slightly nauseous. Oh, great. She was having a frigging panic attack.

Blasting down the M25, Sydney dug her phone out of her purse and pressed a number on speed dial. It was answered in two rings, and the voice on the other end was warm and affectionate. "Hello, my girl. What did you forget?"

"I don't feel well."

"What's the matter?"

"Dunno. I just feel... strange."

There was the barest of hesitations. "Come home, then."

"No, it's... I'm just... aw, dammit. I'm just missing you."

"Oh, Sydney." Her name sounded musical in his mouth. "I miss you, too. But I'll be with you soon."

"Can't be soon enough." With a growl of frustration, she added, "I hate being such a wimp."

"You, a wimp? Never. Absence makes the heart grow fonder."

"I thought it was 'out of sight, out of mind.'"

"That's not possible." Now she heard concern. "If you're truly un-comfortable, come home. This is supposed to be a treat, not a trial. We can do this some other time. Or not at all."

Sydney seriously considered it. No, dammit. He had waved her off with a happy heart, and she should be excited to be on this roleplaying adventure. "Well, hell. No. We've been looking forward to this. I'm a grown up. It's time to put on the big-girl pants to prove it."

"Now that's an alluring image." He sounded so deadpan she laughed, and the iron grip of anxiety loosened.

"And don't you forget it. Oh, and that reminds me. If those Saturday girls at Waitrose flirt with you again, remind them I do have a license to kill. And no masturbating while I'm gone."

There was another hesitation, but this one had a different heft. "That almost sounds like a command, pet. Feeling a little Dominant, are we? One would almost think you're angling for a public spanking on Sunday."

"Stop that, or I will turn around."

She was rewarded with a rich laugh. "Hang up and drive, Temptation."

Elwess was carelessly leaning against his door when she arrived at the flat. He gave her a peck on the cheek before lifting her bags from the boot of the car. "I've just been on the phone with Dahlra. He wanted to know you arrived safely. Is everything okay?"

"Yeah, fine." Elwess was the last person she wanted to wimp out around; she would never hear the end of it.

She followed him into the bedroom he had designated as their home away from Maidenvine. It had originally been a plainly decorated guest room with magnolia walls and bland carpeting, but Elwess had given it a makeover. The mid-century modern furnishings had been replaced with the huge antique four-poster they had salvaged from DeVere Gardens. The walls were now painted a soft blue-grey; the bed linens were brocaded in the same colour with cocoa-brown accents. The carpet had been removed, and sheepskin rugs lay scattered over the hardwood oak floor.

Above the fireplace mantel, Sydney noticed a framed drawing of her and Dahlra, rendered in charcoal. The lines were sharp and energetically sketched, very stylised, but the likeness was unmistakable. It showed her nestled against Dahlra's shoulder; he had a protective arm around her waist and was looking down at her with a loving expression. She was looking straight at the artist, her lips parted, her eyes sultry and inviting. Sydney turned to Elwess, who had followed her gaze to the picture. "Did *you* do this?"

"You don't have to sound *so* surprised," he groused. "It's just a doodle. It turned out better than I expected."

She shook her head, marveling. "I'd say it was more than just a doodle. It's—it's amazing. I had no idea you could draw like that."

"I'm glad it meets with your approval."

"I'm serious. I also think Dahlra will try to sneak it back to Maiden-vine."

"It's yours if you want it. I'll make more. It's easy to be inspired with such a sexy Muse." His eyes raked over her body slowly, then rose to lock onto hers. She held his gaze, promising to stab herself in the leg if she blinked first.

Apparently Elwess was not interested in the game. He nodded toward her bag. "We have just enough time for a quick freshen up, but we have to be in Soho in fifteen minutes. You can call Dahlra while we drive."

"Why Soho?"

"Because that's where we need to go, and we need to go today because the shop will be closed tomorrow. Besides, Low Change doesn't like to be kept waiting, even if you *are* paying."

"Low Change?"

"My seamstress. She's the best in the business, even if she does treat her customers like shite."

Lo Chang was a short, myopic Asian woman with a cheese-grater voice that scraped out a combo of Pidgin English and South London drawl. She plied her trade off Little Newport Street in a dim, humid sweatshop that smelled of leather, starch, dye, and cigarette smoke.

"I made the garment you want, Ehress," she squawked. "You were more specific on this one than the others. Is she special or something?" She gave Sydney a look that made her feel anything but.

"Very special. A very special friend."

"Hmmph." Lo Chang produced a tape measure. "Take off your clothes, Miss *Special*."

Stripped down to her underwear, Sydney was roughly yanked this way and that as Lo Chang confirmed her measurements, glaring first at her notes, then at Elwess, as if she suspected him of passing bogus intel. "You should have told me to make the back higher. It's too late now. Hmm, too bad. She could be pretty except for her stripes. Too ugly to show off."

Shocked at her rudeness, Sydney felt torn between pulling her Glock and laughing at Chang's casual offensiveness.

Elwess growled, "Just bring me the bloody schmutter, Lo Chang. I didn't come here to be flattered all day."

"All right, hold your hosses. Jumped-up little scrote." She left the room, grumbling. Eventually, she returned with two large brown boxes, tied with string. She humped them up onto the warped formica counter with a grunt of effort. "These are the most expensive you ever buy. I hope she worth it."

"You have no idea," Sydney seethed. "But if you'd like a demo—"

"Mind your manners, Chang," Elwess warned. His dark eyes flashed a spark of irritation. "This is one of Europe's deadliest women."

She scoffed. "Deadly? I come from Shanghai. I know deadly—"

"And she will need more fetish wear in the coming months. When asked where to find the best seamstress in London, do you want her to mention your name, or Belladon's?"

Lo Chang's eyes narrowed. Then her wormy lips stretched into a sour grin full of yellowing teeth. "Master Ehress knows all Mistress is welcome here." She favoured Sydney with a lugubrious bow. "You tell your Mistress friends if they want the best, they come to Lo Chang."

While Sydney dressed, Elwess paid the woman an indecent amount of money in cash, collected the swag, and ushered her out of the stifling shop. As they walked back to the car, she said, "Elwess, it's not that I'm ungrateful, but what the hell did you just buy? I've known wedding dresses to cost less. You've really gone overboard."

"I knew exactly what it would cost and I bought it because it pleased me to. Think of it as a Valentine's gift."

Back at the flat, Sydney began to untie the first box, but Elwess pushed her hands away. "No, no. You'll try these on later. Let's have a drink first. You look like you could use one. You're carrying a lot of tension in your body."

He turned her around until she was facing away from him, and began massaging her tight shoulders. "Just relax, kitten. I don't always play the big bad wolf." His hands were warm and skilled, and her jangled nerves eased beneath his touch. As he worked his magic, he leaned in and murmured, "Better?"

She nodded tightly, and he kissed the side of her neck. "Before we have that drink, why don't you stop kidding yourself, and give Dahlra another call?"

With a final caress, he quietly left the room. Sydney could not get to her phone quickly enough.

They had been talking for over an hour, and if Sydney had been pressed to recall what they had actually discussed, she would have concluded the majority of it boiled down to *I miss you. I wish you were here. I'm miserable without you, and I'm freaking out because I'm being such a pussy about it.*

"I'm not happy with you right now."

"Why, Sydney?"

She shifted restlessly on the bed. She was used to sinking into a particular sweet spot in their mattress, and she could not find it in this one. "I was independent. Now I've regressed back to a teenager mooning over my date for the Senior Prom. Garnet would eat my lunch if he knew how I was behaving."

"From what I understand, Garnet is just as reliant on his Minder, and that's from the horse's mouth. It's perfectly normal."

"You've conditioned me to fall apart without you. I've turned into a baby. That's not normal. It's embarrassing. "

Dahlra poured comfort into every word. "My darling girl, you are the bravest, toughest person I know. So you miss me; it's not a character flaw, is it? People feel sad when they aren't with the person they love."

"Then I love you a lot."

"You don't know how I love hearing you say that."

"I'm actually close to tears here."

"You're not the only one. I'm rattling around this monstrosity of a house like a marble in a jar. I hate this place when you're not in it. I think I'll get a little drunk tonight to help me sleep."

"Oh, don't do that. Just take a long bath and pretend I'm with you. That's what I plan on doing." She looked around the bedroom and sighed. "Tell me you love me."

"I love you so much, I'm like a child missing his mother." He sounded so wistful Sydney seriously considered grabbing her car keys.

"If I were there—"

"If you were here right now, I would build a fire in our bedroom, and I would take you to bed and pull you into my lap. I would fondle and tease your lovely, tender nipples with my fingers, and when they were so tight and aching for my touch, I'd suck and nip at them until you were moaning, until you were begging for more." He no longer sounded wistful. He sounded like every woman's wet dream.

Sydney could hear her heavy breathing feeding back through the phone. "I think someone's getting aroused," he purred. "Are you wet for me, little girl?"

Bloody hell, was she ever. "Yes, sir."

"What are you doing about it? Tell me."

"I'm playing with my nipples."

"Oh, yes. Make them rock hard for me."

"Oh, God." Her voice was slurry; her body hot and cold and empty. "I wish you were here."

"I am. I'm with you now." He sounded dark and wicked. "I can see you. You're wet and slick and you taste like melting sugar."

She dipped her hand into the waistband of her jeans, and swirled her fingers in the moisture between her legs. Impulsively, she licked her fingers. "I'm touching myself. I'm tasting myself." She was primed and ready now. This was not something she could just switch off, not with Dahlra Gar purring in her ear.

"Close your eyes, and pretend it's my fingers teasing you, pleasuring you until you're ready to come. You're so beautiful when you're coming for me." She was moaning with every breath now. Her entire body went rigid, holding, holding, holding... "That's it. You're close, I can tell. Let go for me..."

She barely had time to rollover and cry out her orgasm into the pillow. In duet with his crooning encouragement, it seemed to go on for days. Sydney fell back, trying to catch her breath. Her clothes were a tangled mess; the phone hot against her sweaty face. It was a long while before she could speak.

"That... whoa. That was my first phone sex. And it was brilliant."

He laughed breathlessly. "Mine too, actually."

"Well, if you ever get bored with the medical profession, there's always a promising career in voice porn."

"I'll keep that in mind. But if you truly expect me to obey your 'no masturbation' rule, I'd better stop for now. This has got rather intense, and I'm afraid my cock is very much looking around for you."

She could not help but smile. "If I were there, I'd kneel at your feet, and unbutton your trousers, and take your sweet, hard hot cock in my—"

"Enough, girl! I'm only human." His sigh ended with a pained laugh. "Do you feel any better?"

"A little. Not one hundred percent, but it definitely took the edge off. I think I can sleep now."

"Good. I'm going for a cold shower and a bottle of wine."

Sydney thought longingly of the large tub at Maidenvine. "I wish I'd never agreed to come down early. Call me tomorrow?"

"Of course. But if you need to, call me. Anytime." He hesitated. "Would you like me to ask Elwess to sleep with you?"

That both surprised and discomfited her. "I'm not sure that would be wise, given my overall horniness. It might give him ideas."

"Hmm. As if he needs any encouragement. But in all seriousness, I'm concerned. You're in a textbook-prime situation for nightmares. I'll have a word with him if you like."

"Are you sure?"

"He won't cross the boundaries. Oh, he'll want to, but he won't. If I ordered him to watch over you all night, he'd make the Palace Guard look like slackers. And I would feel better, knowing you're not fighting the nightmares alone."

As Sydney prepared to retire for the night, there was a light knock on the door. Elwess let himself in. "I've just rung off with Dahlra. I understand he had a word with you about sleeping arrangements." His expression could not have been more inscrutable.

"Well, you know how protective he is, and when I have nightmares..."

"You're not always able to wake yourself. I know." He stood calmly, watching her, his stance more open, more Dominant. He did not look like he planned to take no for an answer. For all Sydney had seen and done with this man, there was a lot more going on in that brain of his that she still did not quite understand.

Still, if Dahlra trusted his motives, so could she. "Knowing you're here might help me to relax enough to sleep," she admitted at last.

Together they climbed into bed, and Sydney switched off the bedside lamp. "Goodnight, Elwess."

His voice was as deep and enveloping as the darkness. "Goodnight, kitten."

Lying in her old DeVere Gardens bed, so familiar and yet so foreign, Sydney thought of Dahlra, and a rush of longing threatened to overwhelm her. *I want to go home.*

The bed shifted; she jumped slightly as Elwess rolled over and wrapped his arm around her. His words reverberated against her back. "I know I'm no substitute for him, but I'll be here if you need me." A gentle kiss was placed on her shoulder, and he settled against her, a warm weight that rested the length of her body. "And that's not just tonight. It's for as long as you want me."

By Saturday afternoon, Sydney was on edge and grouchy. Her concentration was patchy; she could not focus long enough to sit still, much less carry on a coherent conversation. Her restlessness would have been amusing had it not been for her discomfort. Nevertheless, she tried to show a modicum of discipline, and only called Dahlra three times.

Elwess entered her bedroom that evening and casually draped himself in a chair. "You're going to pace a trench in my floor, you know. Crickey, I've seen some subdrop in my time, but you take the ginger biscuit, girl."

"Sundrop?"

"Sub. Drop. Sometimes when a sub is separated from her Dominant, she experiences a 'drop,' a feeling of being abandoned or alone. Some subs get very depressed or anxious. It's perfectly normal."

Sydney paced. "There's that word normal again."

"Pardon?"

"Nothing. If this is normal, it sucks. It feels awful. PMT is more enjoyable than this."

"It'll pass. What did you expect? You've lived in one another's pockets for almost two years. Did you honestly think you wouldn't have some reaction to separation?" His eyes narrowed, and he announced triumphantly, "Ah. You've never been in love with anyone before, have you?"

Caught beneath the weight of his stare, Sydney accepted the truth of it. "At first, it scared the hell out of me. It felt like I was showing weakness, or some such shit. Like loving Dahlra made me less of an agent, or less tough, or less... *me*. I don't know. It sounds stupid when I say it out loud."

"Vulnerability isn't stupid. It *is* scary. That's why I avoided it at all costs." Elwess laughed, but it sounded hollow. "That is, until the day you waltzed into The Chine, wearing nothing but a pair of leather boots and the love of my best friend. Haven't been the same since."

"Maybe *you've* been suffering from subdrop." He shot her a searching look but did not say anything. "I mean, you don't sound too happy about it. Somehow I feel like we're responsible for that unhappiness."

"No one is responsible for me except me, Sydney. But that's what happens when you let a little vulnerability seep in. Dahlra once told me only brave people allow themselves to be vulnerable."

Sydney thought of the steady, trusting love and devotion Dahlra brought to every aspect of their lives, and fought to absorb the emotion that threatened to spiral her down into the floor. "He's always been so brave in the ways that count."

"Dahlra's a good man. Almost an innocent."

"He is, bless his heart." She sobered. "Not like us."

Elwess shook his head with slow deliberation. "No. We know all the dirty deeds men do, because we've seen and done them all. We've lived in the shadows, you and me. And whether you like it or not, you're attracted to it."

That bothered her a bit. "No. No, I fight against it, Elwess."

That primal, hard arrogance returned. "You *live* in it, Sydney. And that's why we get on so well. You love Dahlra, but you *know* me. Dahlra and I balance one another out. He's good and kind and caring." He sneered. "I'm mad, bad and dangerous to know."

"Not to mention modest."

He made a moue of acquiescence. "I am what I am. I want you for the same reason you want me. We like the danger in the dark. But we also want to feel the light on our faces. That's Dahlra: he's our sun. And I'm not ashamed to admit that he's changed me. I taught him how to use his talents; he taught me how to love you."

Now it all made sense. The moodiness, the teasing, the almost angry look when she accused him of subdrop. "You've never been in love be-fore either, have you, Elwess?"

He was quiet for so long, she thought he was going to ignore the question. With a sigh, he finally replied, "No. And it scares me just as much as you."

"But you live in a totally different world. Your ideas of love are very different from the norm."

"You make that sound like a bad thing." Elwess rose to his feet and walked toward the bedroom window. As if drawn by some invisible pull, Sydney followed him. They gazed out towards the city lights, the rest-less movement of cars, the throngs of people. London was a giant, ugly animal, prowling in the night.

"Think about this: right now, in this city alone, thousands of people are shagging like rabbits," mused Elwess. "Many of them have just met. Maybe they got drunk and their inhibitions are down. Maybe they're trying to get over a breakup and need a quick fuck to boost their egos. Maybe they just have that old itch for something nicely anonymous and disposable, so they've swiped someone on Tinder.

"They end up in rented hotel rooms, or dark alleys, public toilets. It's dreary and unsatisfying, and over in seconds, and it has all the intimacy of pissing on a bush. And afterward, they couldn't tell you what the other person looked like. Most don't even remember their names, let alone entertain any thoughts of seeing them again.

"You won't find that level of casual in a Dom/sub relationship. You lay down ground rules before you touch one another. You get inside a sub's head long before you get inside her knickers. You memorise every scar and bone and curve of her, and you teach her by finding her break-ing points and her hard limits and leaning on them. Because every time you press her, she's going to fly just that little bit higher, because she knows you're never going to let her fall. And *that* is where *I* live."

He shrugged. "The people you'll meet this weekend aren't so differ-ent from you, Sydney. They abide by their own rules. They show a different face to the everyday world or in their jobs, even to their spouses. But something has called to them that they can't find in a va-nilla relationship. It's the same thing that called to you. It was something you didn't even realise you craved until it was pointed out to you."

Sydney thought of that day on the tube, when Dahlra whispered his intentions and his desires. Before that, the idea of allowing someone to

Dominate her was unthinkable; it had always felt like she would be relinquishing too much of herself. It had never occurred to her that submitting to Dahlra would be the most empowering voyage of self-discovery she would ever take. Every time she thought she had this lifestyle sussed out, she discovered another set of rules and regs nested underneath.

"It's funny. I was approached a couple of times at Ramcat when I first started working with Clara. It just seemed so unlike anything I would want to be a part of. I think I was a little scared of it, like it might turn into something I couldn't control, and I never wanted that."

Sydney half-expected Elwess to retort with something either a bit on the tawdry side or, even worse, pity. Instead, he regarded her with something akin to respect. "I've seen it happen. Especially the uptight, repressed types who were brought up on Sunday School and sin. Once they break the seal, they're all over the place. They're the ones that Doms either end up avoiding or spending all their time on damage limitation."

She could not help but smile. "The 'How're you gonna keep 'em down on the farm after they've seen Paree' syndrome?"

He gave her one of his vintage wolfish smiles. "Exactly." His expression grew thoughtful. "The vanillas of this world don't understand us, kitten, and they never will. They think it's all about rough sex and kinky costumes and porn. They have no idea how beautiful and grounding the Dom-sub dynamic can be for two intelligent, consenting adults. And they *really* don't understand the kind of Daddy-little girl relationship you and Dahlra have."

"I'm not all that sure I understand it myself."

"When they hear 'Daddy, little girl,' they automatically assume it involves degeneracy. They think it's dirty old men enticing women to dress up like school girls. Or worse, they visit their own ideas of pedophilia and incest on it. Because that's the way they think *we* think." Elwess snorted with derision. "And they call *me* a pervert."

Sydney was not about to mention some of the fantasies she and Dahlra had played out. "Are you saying then that I have some unresolved 'daddy issues,' and that I'm working them out with Dahlra?"

He shrugged diffidently. "I can't honestly say yes or no, and in the end it's no one's business but yours if you do. But that's not the relationship you two have; neither do most couples who practice this dynamic, for that matter." He paused, searching for the right words. "'Daddy Dom' is more of a feeling; it's a way of life you two have created. There's a saying: 'a Top is for one night, a Dominant is for as long as she is submissive, a Master is there until she is no longer a slave, but a Daddy is forever.'"

He cocked a dark eye at her. "Dahlra is your protector, your teacher, your anchor. He babies you, and pets you, and will go to any lengths to satisfy you. He doesn't need chains or whips to subjugate you. He can put you on your knees with one word. I've seen it.

"The fact that you've been worthless without him here speaks volumes. And that's how it should be. You know I've never considered you a natural submissive, but you do fit the perfect 'little girl sub' profile; strong, independent, loyal. A one-Daddy sub."

"Yeah, maybe so. But what about you, Elwess? The Chine isn't some boudoir out of a Harlequin Romance. It's a hardcore dungeon. You have a rep for being BDSM all the way. That's the kind of Dom *you* are. Are you a 'Daddy' too?"

He sounded unapologetic. "I'm a sexual Dominant; I'm a Master to those who seek me out, and a Top when needed, but no, I don't have the temperament to be anyone's Daddy. Most women aren't worth the trouble."

"Then why did you train Dahlra that way?"

He laughed. "You don't teach a man like Dahlra Gar how to be a Daddy Dom; it's how he's wired. He could have had dozens of gorgeous women bending over his lap before you came along, but he didn't want to be *the* Daddy; he wanted to be *your* Daddy.

"That's the reason I fought so hard to get him assigned as your Minder. It's why I stayed out of his way until he could imprint himself on you without any distractions. He just had to be patient. I knew he was exactly the type of man you needed."

This conversation was not going in any good direction. "And how *exactly* do you know what type of man I need?"

"Call me a student of human nature."

"Pull the other one."

Before she could react, he wrapped both hands around her neck in a choke hold. His dark eyes burned into hers like a kestrel's, without pity or conscience. "Do you think I could enjoy making you suffer, Sydney Chapin?"

She made herself stay still. To move was to show weakness. "Maybe."

"But you don't know for sure, do you?" The hands around her throat tightened. "You aren't afraid of me. Should you be?"

"I'm not afraid of you, because I could kill you, right here and now."

He gave her a smirk that was fully intended to get right up her nose. "You don't seem all that threatening to me, kitten."

Sydney pushed her arms between his, and caught his thumbs, pulling them back with swift, deliberate pressure. His eyes widened, then narrowed in pain, but he held on, locked with her in a silent dare. She hooked her calf around his, and pushed hard against him, throwing her weight forward as she forced his hands from her throat. Soon he was so off-balanced he had no choice but to concede.

He stepped away, flexing his hands, but his sardonic expression remained. "Okay. I believe you." He sneered with a little too much spite to be strictly playful. "Look at you, the little lioness ready to defend herself against Mr. Bad Guy."

There was a lot of stuff going on in that sentence. Sydney tried to unpack it; there was condescension, no doubt. But underneath she detected longing, envy, even a touch of self-deprecation. And gilding the whole mess was something else, something covetous and possessive. Coupled with her own fading adrenaline, it left a bad taste in her mouth.

"Well, that's what happens when you don't leave me any choice."

"You will always have a choice, kitten." Softly, almost sadly, he added, "You realise you don't know everything about me, Sydney. Not yet."

After that little stunt, boyo, I'm not sure I want to.

For a moment, they silently fronted one another out. Then Elwess gestured toward the two mysterious packages he had purchased the day before. They were where she had left them, propped up against the wall. "Let's do this, shall we?" He untied the string on the first box. "Now, undress completely."

Still feeling wary and wrong-footed, Sydney complied. Elwess nodded toward a nearby chair. "Sit here. It's easier to do this if you're not on the bed."

He knelt, and took her bare foot in his hands. At the sight of her mangled toes, he grew still. Sydney sighed inwardly. There were things she did not give a great deal of thought to, and the state of her toenails was one of them. During her time in the Cell, being repeatedly tortured by guards using hammers, nails and pliers, her toes were marked early on as a particularly vulnerable spot. Some nails were missing, others ridged and misshapen.

Still smarting from his little physical mind fuck, Sydney quipped, "Part of the cost of walking in that shadow, you might say. This is a classic interrogation technique. Your enemy removes the nail with pliers. They don't grow back. Or he takes a small tack, and hammers it beneath the nail, then replaces it with a larger one, then—"

"Jesus!" he gasped. He looked up at her, and the dismay reflected in his expression wiped away every ounce of his arrogant Dominance. There were still days when Dahlra carried that same, haunted look.

"What? You get off from the scars on my back, but a few messed up toes squick you out?"

"Why didn't I notice this before? I took off your boots that night—"

"Maybe you had your mind on other things."

"Fuck." The grip on her foot changed, became at once more tender and encompassing. Mr. Bad Guy had left the building. "I'm sorry, Sydney. About pulling that crap a minute ago. That was... that was childish." Suddenly he bent and kissed each foot.

Taken aback, Sydney replied, "It's alright, really. It's not something that bothers me all that much anymore. Hell, I was lucky. They threatened me with bolt cutters more than once."

He flinched, and turned his head away. To try to salvage the mood-kill, she added, "Of course, I don't wear open-toed shoes or backless dresses anymore, but that's more for the benefit of everyone else. Just because I can live with them doesn't mean others have to see them."

His gaze returned to her mangled feet. "Hey, kiddo." Sydney tugged on his hair until he looked up at her. "Don't cry for me, Argentina. I'm good. It's all good." When he did not reply, she tapped her free foot on the box. "Come on. Jolly up. I wanna see what's behind Door Number One."

She could actually see him pulling his Dom masque back into place. "Yeah. Alright then." He pulled the box closer, and lifted the lid.

"Whoa."

Inside the box was a pair of thigh-high leather boots. They were a pearlescent navy colour, beautifully made, with five-inch heels that looked capable of firing 38-calibre bullets. Sydney's grudging respect for Low Change reluctantly rose a notch.

Elwess slipped each boot on her feet and deftly laced them up her thighs. The leather was so soft and fine she could see the outline of her toes, and when he caressed the instep, she could feel his fingers as clearly as if he were touching her naked flesh.

"Right. Next piece." He opened the larger of the two boxes on the floor, and produced a thong in the same buttery leather as the boots. It fastened with sterling silver clasps on each hip. A quick push together and the clasp released easily. He made her stand while he pulled the back tightly between her bum cheeks. Sydney shifted uneasily; she had never truly got on with thongs. This one was so tiny she could hardly feel it.

Then, with a flourish, he unwrapped the next item in the box. It was a leather corset in a matching shade of navy blue. "Holy shit," she muttered.

"Oh, yes. That just about sums it up." He placed a small wooden box on the bed; it contained a fine, shimmery powder. "Never try to put on leather over damp skin." He dusted the fragrant powder over her breasts, back and abdomen, then dropped the corset over her head, and tugged it into place.

"Now, come here." He patted the tall bedpost. "Hold on to this, and take a deep breath. It's going to be the last one for a while." He took the laces in hand, and started pulling with slow, even deliberation, like a fisherman reeling in a marlin. "Wearing a corset can be a bit uncomfortable at first, not to mention dangerous. We don't have as much time as I'd like for you to adjust, but I think you'll be alright. This is a fashion corset, so it's not used for actual body training. That's a different fetish altogether, and one I don't have the patience for."

As he pulled, the boning tightened into place and hugged her figure. Her breasts swelled into the bustier, leaving her breathless yet amazingly supported, as if housed in a protective cage. "You'll learn to take shallow breaths wearing this. That first deep breath when the corset is removed will be like a hit of speed. All that oxygen will make you high."

"Does that mean when we, um, when I—"

"Don't let go of the bedpost; I'm almost done. And the answer is yes.

It's like autoerotic asphyxiation, and yes, you will enjoy it very, very much." He tied off the laces and turned her to face a full-length mirror. With almost proprietary fondness, he drawled, "What did I tell you? The perfect female silhouette."

Sydney gaped at her reflection. *Holy hell. I look good. I look* damn *good.*

She turned to the side, admiring her profile. She had never been so scantily dressed while covered so completely. Her round bottom peaked beneath the lower edge of the corset. In the boots she stood almost as tall as Elwess.

He was standing so close she could feel his heat, smell the sharp tang of testosterone beneath his cologne. "I know black is *de rigueur*, but it would have been too severe. Ever since I saw you in blue at the New Year's party, I knew this would be perfect for you. It complements your colouring and hair."

In the mirror, Sydney watched his strong hands creep down the sides of her torso. They slid around her waist with slow, intimate sensuality. "Now tell me you don't like what you see." Their eyes locked in the mirror. His were black and luminous with undisguised lust. "Tell me you couldn't bring a man to his knees with one look."

He quickly spun her around until she was facing him. He pressed against her, his erection nudging sinuously at her belly. Her adrenaline kicked in again, sending her heart skittering in her chest and making it even harder to breathe.

His breath was hot and heavy against her cheek. "I could fuck you right now, kitten. I want you more than any woman I've ever had. And I've never had one tell me no."

She placed her hands against his unyielding chest. "We're covering old ground, Elwess. Choices? Remember—"

"Do you *want* me on my knees?" Without warning, he knelt down before her, his hands slipping down her body to rest on her thighs. He looked up at her with all the humility of a Spartan. "You'd be amazed what I'm willing to beg for when properly motivated. Dahlra thinks about it, too. He knows I want him as much as I want you."

"You mean you actually want him? Like—"

"No. But if *you* told me to, I'd stay here on my knees and suck him off with every bit of skill I could lay claim to, and I'd fucking well make sure he was satisfied— if that's what you wanted from me."

Something indefinable fluttered uneasily in her stomach. "What exactly do you *want* from me, Elwess?"

He rose quickly, his hands tightening around her waist like iron bands. "Don't be dense, girl. I want you in my bed. I don't ever want you out of it."

"Elwess, Dahlra is my lover."

"*I* have been your lover. I fucked you blind in my dungeon, and I'd do it again right now, if you'd let me. And you want to let me. Don't insult me by denying it."

She was trapped between the cool surface of the mirror and the furnace heat of his body. The gruff rasp of his voice flayed her, and his face was full of such intense desire she could barely maintain eye contact. His hands slid downward to cup the globes of her bottom, and he pulled her off her feet, until she was forced to hold onto him. He rocked against her, hot and hard and deeply, destructively male.

A barb of unexpected arousal clenched deep within, and her hips surged against him of their own accord. Sydney turned her face away. If she gave in, it would be impossible to snatch back enough self-control to stop him.

Sensing her imminent surrender, Elwess lowered his lips to her throat and nuzzled her. "I won't tell if you won't." She heard the conquest in his voice as he closed in for the kill. "Oh, kitten, I'm gonna take you places Dahlra has *never* been..."

Her lover's name was a blast of arctic-cold reality, and her entire body froze with it. Elwess had been testing her, teasing her, and as sure as grits were groceries, he would gleefully spill all the juicy details, because Dahlra was now *his* Dominant as well...

Sydney pushed him away, clumsily landing on her feet. Elwess released her with no surprise whatsoever; just a treacherous, triumphant look on his angular face.

She felt bewildered and queasy, struggling to divorce herself from the rapid-fire, conflicting emotions he had alchemised out of her. Quickly following on the heels of her anger was a cold guilt much easier to analyse. Her obvious and pathetic attempts to claw back some self-respect had fooled neither of them. "Your act's pretty good, but you really need to work on that sincerity thing. Not to mention respect. Did you honestly expect me to believe you think so little of Dahlra you'd try to get your leg over behind his back?"

They stared at one another for several moments. Suddenly Elwess burst out laughing.

"'Leg over behind his back'? Even *I'm* not that flexible."

Sydney glared at him, refusing to be placated. She had always understood how compelling and exciting Elwess could be. He presented a thousand different facets of himself and they would all be as real and legal as his whim dictated. Every moment spent with him was minted and stored away in a tightly locked vault. If she allowed it, he would rearrange her personal geography, her internal economy—hell, her *DNA* would be altered and reshaped to see and feel and taste nothing but him.

And when he had stirred her up to the point where she had to have him or know him or be with him or she would die from lack of oxygen, that gold-lined vault would become a prison. And even though she cared for him more than she wanted to admit even to herself, Sydney would not allow that to happen to her, Dahlra or no Dahlra.

As she examined her thoughts, the weird Nine and Half Weeks shit thankfully bled away. Elwess no longer looked jacked up and spoiling for a fuck; he looked tense, and not in a good way. Sydney wondered if he, too, thought things had gotten way out of hand. Fine; he could diffuse his own bomb.

When he finally spoke, his voice was aloof and a tad brittle. "Well done, kitten. Don't *ever* allow another man to manipulate you. And never play, without the permission of the Dominant who collars you."

Little toerag. "So I was right; all of this was some twisted sort of test?"

He snorted. "You muppet. Of course not! I'd have fucked you senseless where you stand." He spoke to her as if he were addressing a dimwitted child. "I'm a heartless bastard, remember? I'm also in love with you. But that doesn't mean you shouldn't be careful."

Trust Elwess to try and deceive with the truth. His Dominance was back in place, screwed down tight, no cracks showing. Sydney told her jangling nerves to stand down. "You're not heartless, Elwess. Shameless, maybe, but heartless? Nah. I don't buy that."

He sighed, then tugged his ear. "One thing *is* certain, you bleedin' well need to be disciplined, and soon. You're far too bolshy." He smiled. "But Christ, you're a fucking goddess when you want to be."

His stance relaxed. "I'm sorry. I was an arse. Again." He held out his arms. "Friends?"

She stepped into his embrace and he pulled her close. "Yes. We are. I could give you a slap right now, but yes, Elwess, we are friends."

There was nothing sexual about his hold this time; instead, it felt like a promise, a plea, something honest. Something she *could* take to the bank.

CHAPTER TWO

The Library

On Valentine's evening, Sydney and Elwess donned their heaviest coats and took a cab into the heart of Soho. By unspoken agreement, they chose not to discuss the previous night's bad comedy, and Sydney was grateful. She was fond of Elwess, but he was nervy and high maintenance enough when all three of them were together. Spending time alone with him was the equivalent of hopping on one leg through an uncharted minefield during a tornado.

He had been on his best behaviour all day, so she was prepared to give him the benefit of the doubt. Add to that the fact that the cheeky git could be perfectly charming when the mood took him. He had been funny and entertaining and at times very sweet. She had even enjoyed his elaborate preparations for the evening, so much so that by the time they were dressed and headed out the door, Sydney realised she had not called Dahlra all afternoon.

As they drove through the damp streets of London, Sydney almost but not-quite flirted with the cabbie. He was a Compleat East London chancer who clearly drove them the long way into Soho to bump up his fare. "'Ere, where're you two going this fine Valentine's evening? I'll bet you lovebirds are doing the Full Monty tonight: dinner, dancing, romancing. Go on, tell me I'm right."

With good humour, Elwess replied, "Should I tell him where I'm taking you, Sydney?"

She caught the cabbie's eye in the rearview mirror and gave him a wink. "Best not."

"Ah, mystery couple. Those are the best kind. I'll be making up stories in me 'ead about you two all night."

Elwess took her hand as they pulled up to the kerb of an innocuous-looking two-story brick building with black, shuttered windows. The door was flanked with elegant Victorian-style gas lamps. A small brass plaque on the door was engraved with the words, "The Library" in a florid script. The understated simplicity of the club's facade was at jarring odds with the long line of kinkster wannabes queued up by the entrance. Two gargantuan doormen, their black suits stretched tight over their massive shoulders, kept the clubbers at bay.

As Elwess sauntered toward them, the bouncers sprang to attention as if they had been pinched upright by their shaven, bullet heads. "Good evening, sir," the larger of the two rumbled, sketching a grave little bow. He spoke quietly into his wrist mic. "Master Elwess and guest."

One of the waiting hopefuls vying for entrance into the club took offense. "Oi, I've been waiting here for thirty minutes!" He drew himself up to a respectful height; he wore five-inch platforms, and looked like a cross between a vampire and a steampunk engineer. "You can't just let them—"

"I can and I will, tit. Keep whinging, and the price'll double." The bouncer and his partner gave Sydney matching jack-o-lantern smiles. "Enjoy your evening, sir. Miss."

"I think you need to feed your boys," whispered Sydney, as Elwess ushered her inside. "That big one was eying me up like a cheeseburger."

He looked smugly complacent. "Get used to it, kitten. He won't be the last man to look at you that way tonight. I feel a bit like Dandini, bringing Cinderella to the ball."

"The last time I saw Cinderella, Dandini was played by Julian Clary, and Prince Charming was—"

"Fanny the Wonder Dog?"

"I think it was Leslie Grantham, but don't quote me."

Elwess laughed. "I've got a better Prince Charming for you tonight. Besides, this isn't exactly Cinderella's neck of the woods." His smile was positively feral. "We're going to Wonderland."

They made their way to the anteroom, where a pretty but overly-made up blonde was taking money and checking coats. She eyed Sydney appraisingly, but dropped her gaze as Elwess approached. "Good evening sir."

"Evening. Do you have something for me?"

The girl's eyes widened. "Oh, yes, sir..." She reached behind her counter and presented Elwess with a small envelope. "Are you here for the special event?"

"You already know we are *not*." Elwess possessively smoothed Sydney's hair. "We've got a bit of an event of our own to attend, don't we, kitten?"

The blonde's stare was two parts envy and one part loathing. It was not a look Sydney enjoyed receiving. "Have we met?" she asked pointedly.

When the blonde remained silent, Elwess commanded, "Answer her."

She dropped her eyes sullenly. "No, Mistress."

Elwess turned on the Dominance. "That's better. Remember your manners, Kofry."

Chagrined, the girl snatched an iPad from the counter, tapping rapidly on the screen with her three inch nails. Elwess produced a card, which she swiped on the card reader. His name and photo appeared on screen, along with a flashing box. He placed his thumb inside the box, and the screen read, *"Identity verified. Access all areas."*

It seemed pretty high-tech for a nightclub. Then again, Sydney had grown up in a place where you could get into the local clubs free if your friend could draw a convincing facsimile of their logo stamp on your wrist. "I'm impressed. Very state of the art."

"Keeps the riffraff out."

"Why do they let you in, then?"

Elwess sucked on his teeth, and cut his eyes at her. "Careful, kitten."

After watching their little exchange intently, the girl tapped a few more commands on the iPad, then turned toward Sydney. "Name?"

"She's with me."

"Everyone who walks through the front door is photographed and fingerprinted." She gave Sydney a patronising smirk. "House rules. No exceptions. Soz."

Elwess leaned in close, and whispered something in the girl's ear. Her face fell, and with it her supercilious expression. Confident that he had made his point, Elwess stepped away, and pulled Sydney into a possessive embrace. This dumbshow was strictly for Blondie's benefit; for a moment, she looked as if she were about to cry. Whatever history these two shared, Sydney had no desire to get caught in the crossfire.

He helped Sydney out of her coat before taking off his own and handing them both over. Blondie's eyes widened as she took in the blue corset and boots, missing no detail. Sydney had a vague uneasy feeling she might find her best coat in shreds when she retrieved it at the end of the evening.

Elwess tucked the envelope in his breast pocket, and placed his warm hand on her back. "Ready?"

"As ready as I'll ever be."

"Good." He led her a few steps into the dim room, until they reached a metal door. Over the entrance, a cone of glaring, yellow light spilled from a tin lampshade straight from the props department of a 1950's film noir. Music from the interior of the club battered against the wall like an invading army.

"Welcome to The Library."

He pushed open the door, and Sydney was nearly knocked off her five-inch heels. *Rough Sex* by Lords of Acid was blasting from the overhead speakers. The bass bins, thumping in an erotic, driving rhythm, all but braided her hair with physical volume.

As she waited for her ears to adjust to the onslaught, she took a good look around. She had heard of The Library, but this was her first reccie.

For an exclusive club, it was surprisingly crowded. It consisted of one large, square room. The bar ran the entire length of the nearest wall, and the remaining sides were lined with sofas, armchairs, tables and benches. Covering the opposite wall on the far side was a floor-to-ceiling mural of Hieronymus Bosch's 'Garden of Earthly Delights.' It was the tamest thing in the room.

A dance floor made up most of the centre. A waist-high wall separated it from the other furniture, like an old-fashioned skating rink. Flashing strobes in shades of hellish red, freezer blue and underwater green lit the blank faces of the gyrating dancers. They ground and churned their bodies together in a trippy, rhythmic parody of sex.

In the seating area lining the perimeter, others were doing a different kind of dance. In one corner, a beautiful black submissive was tied to a St Andrews Cross, being whipped into an orgasmic frenzy by a tall Dom wearing a tuxedo and a carnivale masque. Kneeling at the feet of a woman in a black leather corset, decorated in beautifully vivid tattoos, was a stunning man with long blond hair and a body straight out of gladiator training. He was wearing nothing but a collar. His toned, oiled body gleamed in the lights like sculpture, and he was reverently licking his Mistress' DMs while she casually chatted away to friends and checked her mobile. He glanced up at Sydney, and his eyes grew wide. His chiseled jaw slackened with lust; his mistress gave him a smart rap on the back with a riding crop, and he returned to his task.

Around the room, submissives were being disciplined with floggers, or servicing their Dominants in a myriad of positions and activities. Some merely sat on laps or at their Doms' feet, preening as they watched the collective animal writhing on the dance floor. Long-legged women in fetish boots and black PVC catsuits stalked among them, carrying refreshments.

For their night out, Elwess had dressed in his customary black on black. His long hair lay against his shoulders like oil, iron straight and iridescent in the lights. Sydney was bemused at the amount of attention he commanded. Women swarmed around him like semi-clad butterflies, but he waved them off dismissively, focusing his concentration on Sydney. As she watched, unsure if there was some sort of kink protocol she was supposed to be following, he placed his fingertips beneath her chin and tipped her head upward. His black eyes glowed red in the lurid lighting.

"Hold your head up. Be proud, girl." He leaned in close to be heard in the din. "You said you wanted to be Dahlra's sub. Now claim it."

"Where is he?" She had to shout to be heard.

"Oh, he's here, kitten." He took her hand. "Let's show off a little. Come on. It's time to stun the room."

He led her to the dance floor as the music changed to a slow, sultry beat. The crowd parted like the Red Sea before him. Men watched them pass with hot, hungry eyes; women whispered Elwess' name. Sydney wondered if Dahlra was watching her from some hidden vantage point in the club, and suddenly she experienced a whole new appreciation for exhibitionism. As Elwess drew her into his arms, a thrilling thought zoomed into her consciousness: *He's waiting for me. He wants to see me like this, dressed like sin on the hoof.* She slid her arms around Elwess' neck, and he pulled her close, his eyes gleaming with power and desire. This was supposed to be fun—why not enjoy herself?

As they began to move with the seductive, hypnotic music, his fingers drew slow, delicious circles on her bare skin, making her shiver against him. His long leg parted hers and ground lewdly against the junction of her thighs; their hips locked together in a slow ride to the music.

The changing lights threw the harsh planes of his face into relief, his cheekbones carving shadows into the darkness. His finely sculpted mouth was slightly parted, and it was not until he licked his lips and twisted them into a smirk that she realised she had been staring at them.

The song's beat pulsed in time with her own heart. The lyrics, sung in a husky voice she did not recognise, seemed to mirror her thoughts:

He was mysterious, like an altar boy,
He was a sorcerer, he was Sigmund Freud,
He was evil, a beautiful devil.
I always wanted to be swept away,
Love is an ocean and desire's a wave.
When it found me, I let it drown me.

Elwess' lips brushed against her ear. "Every man in this room is watching us and wishing they were me. They're asking themselves, 'Is she a Domme or a sub? Is she available to play?' They're all wishing they could have you, if just for one night. They want you almost as much as I do. I'd fuck you right here on the dance floor, just see the envy in their eyes."

"Elwess—"

He pulled away from her, unsmiling. "Come on. If we stay here much longer, I'll keep you for myself." He turned away impatiently, almost angrily, leaving Sydney no choice but to follow.

They walked to the far end of the main room. At the back wall, they stopped at an innocuous-looking numeric keypad. A tiny red light showed it activated and locked. Elwess reached into his coat, and retrieved the envelope the coat check girl had given him. Solemnly he placed it into Sydney's hands.

Inside was another keycard, along with a note in Dahlra's handwriting:

My love, remember our first night at Maidenvine, how we played our dirty little game of hide and seek? Now, it is your turn to find me. I am somewhere on the other side of this door. Elwess will not unlock it for you, and he will not let you in. You must open it yourself, and enter of your own free will. If you are prepared to accept this and all that will happen beyond, the passcode is 2376.

I am waiting for you.

Dahlra

She read the note a second time. *I am waiting for you.* The time to turn back was long past.

Her heart was pounding as she handed the note back to Elwess. She swiped the card, and when the red light changed to green, she punched in the code. There was a metallic click, and an anonymous black door seemed to magically appear. Now that she could see its outline, Sydney noted how perfectly camouflaged it was. No hinges, no moulding, no latch, no sign, no hint of what lay beyond. Wonderland, indeed.

Through the doorway, a narrow hall gently curved to the right. The gunmetal-gray walls were completely unadorned; no pictures or ornaments, no moulding or trim. Recessed doors stood sentinel every ten feet.

"The front club itself requires private membership, but it's not all that hard to attain," Elwess explained. "From here on out, you need a bit more *carte blanche* to gain access."

"Are you coming too?"

His expression turned predatory. "Oh, I'll be right behind you, kitten."

With a final glance back at The Library's main room, Sydney stepped over the threshold. The door swung closed behind them, cutting off all sound from the dancefloor so abruptly, her ears popped.

Once inside, Elwess strode ahead; Sydney followed two steps behind him, her heels clicking loudly in the thick, padded silence. At the end of the hall, Elwess stopped at the door marked *Private – Room Eleven*. This time, Elwess keyed in the number himself.

The windowless room was pitch-black, except for an overhead spotlight. It shone down on a round dais, which stood in the centre like a platform for a slave auction.

Dahlra Gar had been waiting in the shadows for almost an hour now. An anonymous girl in bondage wear had presented him with a double Jamesons, then left as silently as she had entered. He sipped it sparingly, afraid if he did not discipline himself he would drink too much out of sheer nerves. It was up to him to maintain control of the evening.

He see-sawed between the excitement of pulling off this surprise and that feeling all men have when they are afraid of being made to look foolish. He had looked foolish before; the world had not ended. True, it had been a smaller and less colourful world then, and he had had a lot less to lose. Now he was on the brink of having everything he had ever wanted, and he was damned if Elwess, or Inigo Lightoller and the bloody Agency, were going to stand in his way.

The door finally opened, and in strode Elwess, with Sydney a few steps behind. Nothing had truly prepared Dahlra for the sight of this lush, divine creature walking into the room, her head held high, her erect carriage taut and perfect, her body encased in a leather corset that looked positively lethal.

Her hair was pulled up in an elaborate braid which hung like a rope down her back, emphasising the lovely planes of her face. Dahlra could see Elwess' touch in her makeup as well; her protean eyes were painted in smoky greys, giving them the jeweled look of topazes. Her beguiling mouth was a deep, velvety shade of burgundy. She looked darkly powerful, like a huntress; dangerous and ruthless, and only a little tamed. A prize any man would covet; a gift given only on her terms.

Elwess assisted her up onto the dais. "Look straight ahead." His voice sounded cold and flat in the dark room. "It's almost time for you to greet your Daddy. Get on your knees, girl."

Obediently, Sydney sank to her knees and rested her arms against her thighs, turning her palms upward. She stared straight in Dahlra's direction, breathing hard, but the bright spotlight and the darkness beyond kept him well hidden. As lovely as she looked, Dahlra knew her well enough to see the tension and impatience in her eyes. He had to hold himself in check, force himself to stay quiet, out of sight.

Elwess stepped up onto the dais and placed his booted feet between her knees, forcing her thighs apart. "Knees out, toes together. This is for your Master's pleasure, not your personal comfort." Sydney widened her stance, and Elwess glanced Dahlra's way, a wicked smile on his angular face. He took a final walk around the dais. Once he completed his inspection, he positioned himself behind her, presenting her like the gypsy slave peddler whose blood no doubt still flowed in his veins.

"And this will be a very nice little surprise for you both." With a gleam of power in his snapping eyes, Elwess leaned over her and slid his fingers down the bra of the corset. Sydney's eyes widened as his long fingers pushed apart the seams bisecting the cups. With a pinching tug that made Sydney wince and arch her back, Elwess pulled her nipples proud of the slits. They had been painted a dark rose, and peeked lewdly between the seams like ripe cherries.

Hot, almost livid desire flashed over Dahlra. His sudden impulse was to rush up onto the platform and pull her into his arms. Two lonely days of spinning fantasies had left him even more anxious than before they had become lovers. Now that he *knew* what he was missing, some primitive part of his brain was sending caveman signals of *mine, mine, mine.*

Elwess stepped off the dais. "I wouldn't get too comfortable, kitten." As he exited the room, his shadow, captured in the lights of the hall beyond, passed over her like a hawk. The door closed softly behind him, leaving Sydney alone at last, still as a statue, her eyes downcast and unfocused. In the tense silence, Dahlra noted her fingers were trembling.

Alright, my love, enough. There is anticipation, and there is torment. I'm not playing Elwess' games anymore. Not with you.

"Sydney."

Her head shot up, as if she could scent her name in the air.

I wouldn't get too comfortable. That should be the tagline on your business card, Talbert.

Kneeling on the dais brought to mind those stolen moments in the Cell, when Dahlra released her from her bonds and allowed her to be herself. During those horrible nights, she had run laps around her narrow, hard bed, sang at the top of her lungs, touched herself to both seduce and overpower him. He had ensured the cameras were off, the guards were asleep, and no one would see her. Except for him.

Now, she was on display for him in a way that was both erotically thrilling and liberating. *Strange,* she thought, *how our lives keep running around and tapping us on the shoulder.*

This was what a submissive was *supposed* to feel; the wild joy of being on show for her Dominant. Gradually she calmed enough to release some of the tension in her shoulders and chest, and was able to covertly take in some of her surroundings.

The spotlight above was a blank, white glow, throwing her shadow across the dais. Beyond was a sea of black; she could not detect how large the room was, or if anyone else was in it. The soft, white-noise hiss of the central air system muffled any sounds. The surface beneath her knees was hard, but the soft leather of her boots provided some padding.

For the smallest eternity, Sydney remained as still as she could, her heart beating slow and heavy in her chest, measuring time by the number of breaths taken as her lungs shallowly filled and emptied. Adrenaline pulsed through her body and a trickle of sweat rolled down her back. The lack of breathing space in the corset left her lightheaded. It was all an incredible head-rush. The only thing that came close to it were those silent, fuel-injecting moments before engaging in a firefight.

The hairs on her arms rose, and her flesh goosebumped. Endorphins were singing in her blood. Hell, this was *better* than a firefight. *He's here, in this club, somewhere, waiting for me. He'll walk in and find me here. He'll see me on my knees oh my God he'll see me like this maybe he'll stand right here and unbuckle his belt and lower his zip and I'll—*

"Sydney."

The breath left her lungs, as the voice rolled through the room like incense, and Sydney felt a sweet coiling in her gut.

"Yes, sir?" Her eyes quickly darted around, peering into the darkness, trying to pinpoint the origin of his voice. Gradually, the lights rose, revealing a black leather sofa, curved to follow the line of the dais. Dahlra sat directly in front of her, one arm draped carelessly against the back of the sofa. His other elbow was crooked as he rested his chin on his hand. He was wearing an elegant black double-breasted suit, a snowy-white shirt, and black Hermes boots. He looked every inch the Daddy.

Silently, he rose from his seat and walked to her, and her breathing increased until she was almost hyperventilating. He stepped up onto the dais. "Stand."

She took his proffered hands and shakily rose to her feet. A wave of dizziness caused her vision to swim, and he caught her easily, pulling her completely to him, until they were pressed shoulder to ankle. Her emotions were flying in so many different directions she could not catch them, and she tried to ground herself by saying his name. It came out as a strangled cry. She swallowed, trying to clear the lump from her throat.

"Jesus. I feel like I'm having another panic attack."

"Shh." He soothingly pressed her head against his shoulder. His warm, solid body felt like a home she never wanted to leave again. *Home... I'm home—*

"I'm here now. Everything's alright." Something in his voice tripped some sort of trigger within, and the panic broke open into wild elation, and she threw her arms around him with such manic force she almost knocked them both over. She kissed him feverishly, nipping against his throat; biting, stinging kisses she knew would make him lose that cool, calm demeanour. He laughed in delight, but stayed implacably in control.

"I missed you too. It's alright. I'm not leaving without you."

"I know." She wanted to laugh with relief, but her stupid eyes were filling with tears. She blinked them away impatiently and tried to smile. "I'm sorry I'm acting so ridiculous. I've just been so-"

Her words were pushed back into her mouth as he caught her in a deep, triumphant kiss that burst her open like a treasure chest. He tasted of good whisky, warm and sharp and sweet. He wrapped his hand around her neck, opening her, pushing his need and his ownership into her. Her tension blessedly unrolled into something more convenient.

Gradually, his possessive kisses eased, until he was gently teasing her lips, suckling against them with languid, decadent sips that sent little ripples of pleasure over her body. Finally, he pulled away, and she laid her head on his shoulder, grateful for the arms caging her. "Let's not do this again anytime soon. I don't think the separation thing works too well for us."

There was a time when she would have run screaming from the room at such a declaration. Now, the truth of his words hit her like a ton of bricks. She whispered in his ear, "Are you pleased with me?"

He answered by capturing her exposed nipples between his knuckles, brushing them lightly with his thumbs. One hand left her breast, and slipped between her thighs. His eyes fluttered as he found her slick and wet. His knowing, talented fingers teased her until she was holding onto his shoulders to keep upright. She moaned and canted her hips forward, trying to find that one, sweet spot, but his touch remained maddeningly elusive.

He laughed at her petulant distress; it was a soft dirty sound that made her head light up with frustration and lust. "Poor baby. So beautiful, and so needy." His tone changed, became at once more playful and more sinister. "You look like every fantasy I ever had about you."

"Have you had many fantasies about me, sir?"

"I fantasised about you before you even knew me." His kiss was feral and wild and almost split her in two, and she grabbed his hair and pulled him closer, willing him to test her mettle, and find her worthy. They fused together, their heavy breaths mingling, echoing in the room, until Sydney's head was swimming with desire and surrender. Dahlra released her, and she bit back a demand for more. Tonight, it was not her place to demand anything.

He left her standing there, fizzing and trembling, while he stepped down and resumed his seat on the sofa. Patting his knee, he drawled, "Sit on my lap, little girl." He gave her a look that would melt a glacier. "We have a nice, long evening before us, and I have many plans."

Suddenly her heels seemed too high, her legs too unsteady, and before she made a fool of herself careening into his arms, she sank to her knees again, and crawled to him. Dahlra's eyes widened, first in surprise, then in mounting lust. It was the most incredible sensation, watching his expression grow dark and intense, knowing she alone was the catalyst for this desire. She could see it in his tense posture, sense it in his crumbling self-discipline, hear it in the heavy breaths that tumbled from his lips.

With all the gratitude and love her heart could display, she lowered her head, and touched her lips to his booted feet. It was difficult; the corset restricted her movements. She was breathing hard by the time she sat back on her thighs. He was watching her with a look of absolute wonder, and Sydney smiled as she reached for his belt. She was going to make him feel like a king.

His hands closed around hers, stilling her movements. "No."

"No? Not even a little lick?"

His lips curved into a slow smile full of little-boy-pleased wonder. "You're a very bad, bad girl."

The entire night had just paid for itself, as far as Sydney was concerned. "Then punish me, sir." She let the last word spin between them.

He studied her so intently for a moment, she felt self-conscious. "If you sit on my lap, you delicious thing, you just might get what you want."

Sydney felt the balance of power between them, a pendulum rocking on a knife edge of desire and control. She knew she could take over, and he would submit with breathtaking generosity. And even though he would switch without so much as a ripple of dissent, in the end, she understood that pleasure was only a part of what tonight was all about. *Remember who's in charge.* Right now, her best, her *only* gift for him, was her submission.

She closed her eyes, and surrendered to it. "But I want to show you what you mean to me. Surely my... my first priority is your pleasure."

He was looking at her in a way she could not quite wrap her head around. With indulgent reproach, he replied, "Don't you think it's up to me to decide what my pleasure should be?"

"But I- Wouldn't you like to get off, too?"

"You misunderstand me, love. I am getting off on *you*." She tried to speak, but he silenced her with a shake of his head. "Trust me, Sydney, you're giving me pleasure. All that I want, and more."

He reached for the clasps on either side of her hips. "Ah, I see how they work." They separated with a soft, metallic click, and the thong came apart. "Now, this is just in the way."

Well, there's something we can agree on.

The thong slipped from her body and fell to the floor. Dahlra picked it up, and studied it, smirking at the damp patch that darkened the crotch of the garment. He brought the leather to his nose and inhaled deeply, closing his eyes. "Hmm. Like candy. And so very wet, my dear." He raised a cool eyebrow. "Something has left you all wet and wanting. Has Elwess been selfishly playing with my little girl like a toy, fingering her cunt in the dark?"

Just the sound of the word *cunt* coming from that mouth made her heart trip along in double time. The tops of her boots would soon be wet, at this rate. Nodding and breathing; that was the extent of her thought processes.

Dahlra pushed the cups of the bustier further apart. His skillful fingers rolled and pursed and plucked her nipples, and she moaned in a delirium of smoky, thick lust.

He hummed appreciatively. "Such sweet little cherries. So hard and red. Just begging for a suck."

"Jesus, Dahlra." Sydney swayed on her feet. Bracing her arms against the back of the sofa, she leaned in closer, offering herself to him.

He flicked his incredible eyes up to hers. "Would you like that, my girl?" His words were as smooth and soft as sin itself. "Would you like me to suck those sweet little tits until you can't even remember how to beg? I will, you know."

"Please..."

Dahlra roughly pulled her to him, sucking a nipple into his mouth with greedy, growling ferocity. His tongue flicked hard over the aching peak, and a shiver of pleasure carved into her belly. Her hands clenched the leather of the sofa. "Bite it a little," she whispered.

He took a swift intake of breath, then devoured her with a moan of his own desperation. His teeth, his tongue, his wet mouth worried at the ruched flesh, setting off a chain reaction of torment so intense it made Elwess' earlier clumsy attempt at seduction seem laughable.

Sydney was only dimly aware of her whining, litany of filth, but with each word, Dahlra pulled her closer, teased her harder, pushed her further. Then, with a biting, sucking pull, he released her, holding on to her to keep her upright.

He made a twirling motion with his finger. "Turn around." Shakily, she turned her back to him, and he drew her down on his lap, pulling her close, until her back was pressed against his chest. He hooked her thighs over his and she dropped her head against his shoulder. His large hands slid over her inner thighs, moving inward, and she raised her hips to meet his touch.

His fingers eased unerringly over the tiny bud, and she almost fishtailed off his lap. He nipped at her shoulder, a sharp, sweetly painful bite that brought her back to herself. "Hold on. Let it burn, until you truly can't bear it anymore."

She tried to obey his command, to drag herself away from the edge of this impossible high, but she was losing ground-mainly because he wanted her to. His fingers cast their teasing, curling magic against her distended clitoris, rocketing her toward a peak that extended higher with every gentle circle he drew on her flesh. His warm body against hers, the mouth-watering scent of his cologne, the very knowledge that it was *him*... He forced her to rethink the words bliss and torment, until they melded into one powerful addiction, with him as her pusher, her needle and her withdrawal.

The corset was tightening around her ribcage, and the tremours within rushed suddenly together, dragging her into its undertow, her pelvis twisting to meet his relentless, insistent touch.

He widened his stance, and she hooked her ankles around his calves until she was obscenely, wantonly open to him. "Do you know how beautiful you are right now? You look so decadent and debauched and dirty. I could come just watching you like this." His fingers plucked her like a string, and her body locked in a rictus of ecstasy. "Let. Go."

Heat and pleasure washed over her like cresting waves, and her orgasm burst from her like the pounding surf, each surge more powerful than the last. Her keening voice rebounded through the room, and in it seemed every cry of release and relief she had ever felt or would ever feel again.

CHAPTER THREE

Bait and Switch

Her first thought as her brain came back online was that she must look like a limp, boneless squid sprawled in his lap, gasping for air, thighs twitching against his gentle hands. She wanted to thank him for... what, exactly? For the safety and sanity of herself and those around her, probably; that mind-bending orgasm really had been a public service.

She would have been more than happy to lie there, groggy and stoned on endorphins, as Dahlra waited patiently for her to return to the land of the coherent. "Are you with me, love?" She could hear the smile in his voice.

"Hmm."

"That's not an answer."

She stretched as luxuriously as the confines of the corset would allow. "Who are you gonna believe?"

Dahlra casually glanced at his watch. "Come, my dear. Up you get." He put his hands on her waist, and pushed her upright, rising with her. "As much as I'm enjoying our reunion, we have a small matter to attend."

While Dahlra retrieved the discarded thong, Sydney managed to get vertical, but a wave of giddiness made her grab his coat.

He caught her easily. "Are you alright?"

She tried to answer, but here, at eye level, she became too distracted to form any reply. God, the way he was looking at her, all smoky-eyed and kiss-bruised lips and mussed hair—she was sweaty and buzzing and still turned on, and this was the man who had made her that way, simply through the medium of his absence. Past the Dom/sub stuff, he *belonged* to her, and he knew it. All Sydney wanted to do was wrap herself around him and reassure him she was more than fine. She tugged his hand. He waited for her answer, one eyebrow raised imperiously.

She pulled him closer, and he melted in her arms as pliant as a slave. "I love you so damn much."

He gave her one of those smiles that stopped nuns in their tracks and made songbirds rush for the recording studio. Then, he tipped the balance back by switching her grip, and ensnaring her wrists in his large hands. "You are my heart and soul, and you're *mine*." He placed a quick kiss on each hand. "Now, there really *is* somewhere we need to be."

"Oh?"

"Let's get you properly dressed again. I want to show off my girl to every hard-case Dom in London, just to see the envy in their eyes."

"You sound like Elwess."

"I'd heed his advice if I were you. Just because I haven't spanked your gorgeous arse doesn't mean I'm not planning to." He stepped away, gesturing for her to follow.

They walked out of their room and back down the corridor, until they reached a door labeled, *One*. Underneath the number was a brass plate which ominously read, "Viewing Room." With his eyes locked to hers, Dahlra rapped several times on the door. "Word of warning: a sub was debuting this evening, and Elwess was presenting her. They should be through entertaining the others."

A frisson of excitement raced through Sydney. "And if they aren't?"

"What do you think?" His eyes smouldered. "He hasn't exactly been teaching her how to curtsey and use her forks."

The door was opened by a woman holding a tray of drinks. She had the kind of face that made men jump through hoops; creamy, poreless skin, high cheekbones, large brown eyes and a finely sculptured mouth. Dark, curly hair framed her face, and through her gauzy, sheer peasant blouse her bare breasts were a wonder to behold. In addition, she was ridiculously pregnant. Sydney wondered if they had been invited solely to assist with the birth.

A radiant smile lit up her face as she recognised Dahlra. "Hello, sir! It's so nice to see you again! Come in and join the fun!"

Dahlra kissed her cheek and nodded approvingly to her large belly. "I see you've been busy since the last time we met."

"Goodness, is it that obvious?" She turned to Sydney with a warm, open smile. "Hello. I'm Kay. Your corset is gorgeous, by the way. I'm positively envious." She gave a sigh. "And to think, it'll be *ages* before I'm back in one of those again."

She nodded toward the tray, which held a variety of cocktails, mostly of the exotic, poncy-glass variety. "Would you like a drink? I think it's a bit close in here this evening, but then again, my thermostat's permanently stuck on high."

With a nod of thanks, Sydney selected a small green shot glass, the least frilly of the drinks on offer, and took a quick look around. Like Room Eleven, there was a spot lit dais, but it was at the end of the room. The light dimmed outward, disappearing around the dark edges. Scattered randomly about were several sofas and benches, giving the room the look of a home theatre.

Peering into the shadows, Sydney counted at least nine other couples. They were milling around, chatting, laughing at jokes. The room smelled of expensive perfume, sex, leather, testosterone and power. There was the soft jingle of chains, and the more elusive whisper of pleasure, as masculine voices spoke quietly, and were answered with the sighs and husky replies of their submissives. It was like being at the world's kinkiest cocktail party.

Each of the couples in their turn casually observed the new Dominant and his leather-clad sub, then returned their focus on one another. Far from the clichéd picture of the Master beating his slave into submission, these couples treated one another with indulgent affection. Certainly no one looked afraid or cowed or cruel. These were not the kind of men who had bad days at the office and took it out on their girlfriends with their alcohol-fueled fists and their belts. That was not the sort of man who constituted a true Dom.

They were not the type to take just any shit from a man. These were the elite, the big leagues, the men who had power and money and time enough to play, and their partners were intelligent enough to know what they needed and strong enough to find the right person to give it to them. All the women looked relaxed, intelligent, and comfortable in their own skin.

Just as this was the ideal of the sensual world of Dominance and submission, Sydney knew it was but one arm of a very large, multi-faceted entity. Even in an exclusive club like The Library, or in the rarefied elegance of Ramcat, there was an addictive temptation toward the forbidden, the unspeakable, the unconscionable seedy underbelly. Silverbirch had recruited and performed their dirty deals from the dark corners of private rooms, in legal establishments like The Library. The kinkster world was one of control, of choices, but it also attracted a criminal element with the lure of easy flesh and indulgence to twisted proclivities.

And while being there was fun, and scintillating, and carried with it a tangy, slick taste of the forbidden, she and Dahlra did not belong there any more than the pale-faced wannabes jockeying for admission at the door. This was Elwess' playground, but Sydney and her Minder were a mile outside their wheelhouse.

"You're mentally working, aren't you?" Dahlra whispered in her ear. She nodded. He caressed her shoulders, coaxing her away from her thoughts. "There'll be plenty of time to case the joint later. For now, just relax."

From behind them they heard a voice call out. It was deep and measured, with the slightest hint of cultured, Northern inflection. "Now here's a face I haven't seen for yonks. Where have you been keeping yourself, Dahlra Gar?"

Sydney turned toward the source of the voice, and saw a man in his late fifties, a smile on his severe, handsome face. His silver hair was thick and immaculately barbered; a crescent-shaped scar teased a dimple in his cheek. As he shook Dahlra's hand, Sydney noted an obvious mutual respect and friendship between them.

There was something familiar about him beyond the archetypal Dom identi-kit profile. His grey eyes pinned Sydney down with their steely, take-no-prisoners intensity, and it was at that exact moment she clocked him. His expression told her he knew it, too.

Inwardly she cursed. *Sloppy. You're getting slow and sloppy, girl.* Later, she would tell herself that it was not that at all; he had wanted, even expected her to recognise him. He would have probably been strangely hurt if she had not.

"And this is the lovely creature I've been dying to meet." He kissed her hand. "Brian Collins. It's a pleasure to meet you at last."

Since he seemed content to continue the strangers in the night routine, she was not going to rumble him in a room full of people she had never met. *Okay, I'll play along, M'Lud.* "Please call me Sydney, sir. I'm sorry. I'm new to all this. I hope I'm not doing or saying something wrong."

Collins beamed at her, perfectly at home playing the role of elder statesman. "Not at all, Sydney. We're all friends here. We don't stand on ceremony." His gaze was frank and openly appraising. "At least, not too much."

"Oh, good. I'm never sure if I'm supposed to kneel or bow or strew rose petals in your path or some such shit."

His face fell in disappointment. "You mean you didn't bring the rose petals? Oh, dear. And you were doing so well."

She held out her empty hands. "I must have left them in my other corset."

He threw back his head and laughed. "Oh, Sydney, you are a breath of fresh air! So many newbies are so afraid of saying or doing the wrong thing they absolutely kill the buzz with their anxiety. Something tells me that's not something we have to worry about with you." He looked at Dahlra approvingly. "I can see why your Daddy is looking so happy."

Dahlra's arm encircled her waist. "I have a lot to be happy about."

"Quite right, too." Collins saluted them both with his drink. "Well, my dear, I'll let you off the hook. You may bring your rose petals next time. I shall be expecting them." His expression darkened; he was really sizing her up. "I understand a little more why Elwess is so enthused about you both. Oh, he doesn't say much, but I've known him a long time. And I hope we will be seeing more of you in future, now that you've seen we're none too scary."

Kay, who had watched the entire exchange in respectful silence, leaned closer confidentially. "You've missed the first event. Elwess debuted a spectacularly beautiful young sub tonight. There were two Doms practically fighting over her." Her eyes sparkled. "Although, I think if *you* had been here, you would have given her a run for her money. I'm sure everyone has told you, but you look absolutely stunning."

There was a hint of movement, and Collins glanced around. "Perhaps we can catch up another time. I gather we're about to start." With that cryptic remark, he gave them a quick nod of dismissal, and led Kay to a nearby loveseat.

Sydney turned to Dahlra. "Start what? I thought the debut was over."

He tucked her hand in the crook of his arm. "Oh, you never know what sort of entertainment they have planned."

Sydney quickly glanced around to make sure they were out of earshot. "Do you know who that was?"

"Brian Collins? Of course. I've known him for years."

"He's a bona fide-o silk, you know."

"I'm well aware."

"So, what the hell is a member of Her Majesty's Counsel, Learned at the Law doing slumming it down here at The Library?"

Dahlra chuckled. "He might be asking the same about Special Agent Sydney Chapin."

Well, he had her there.

In the early incarnation of Operation Silverbirch, there had been a lot of very influential persons in the judiciary and executive systems involved, and many of them had not been on the right side of the fence. One of the good guys, Q C Brian Collins, was one of Lightoller's cronies, and an aggressive prosecutor in his own right. His name had often cropped up in confidential Eyes Only briefs and statements. And like Elwess', his was a name Sydney had never bothered putting with a face after Silverbirch got chloroformed.

But that had been years ago, and this was a far cry from the Old Bailey. It had never occurred to her that Collins might be involved in the kinkster world at all, though knowing Inigo's propensity for sourcing local, she probably should have anticipated any eventuality.

Dahlra plucked the untouched shot glass from her hands and held it up toward the light. Its green glow was eerily hypnotic. "This is absinthe. When Elwess first brought me here, he plied me with absinthe to loosen my inhibitions. It didn't work." His eyes gleamed. "I only had one person I wanted to lose my inhibitions with, and now I have. Several times over, in fact." He held the glass to her lips. "But I still associate absinthe with decadence and surrender. And after tonight, so will you."

He lightly grasped the back of her neck, and carefully tilted the glass until the liquor flowed into her mouth, like a potion being administered by a dark, seductive sorcerer. His eyes never left hers as she drank the fiery liquid. The first swallow sent the liquor's seductive heat to every pulse point in her body, and her head buzzed pleasantly. He smiled at her reaction.

"Very good. Your obedience is very erotic. All I ask of you tonight is that you trust and obey me. Will you?"

"Of course."

"Gentlemen, would you and your ladies like to take your seats?" Elwess was standing in the spotlight, a decadent master of ceremonies. *All he needs is the top hat and and jodhpurs.* As the last of the couples settled onto their sofas and chaise lounges, Elwess turned toward Sydney. "Master Dahlra, I believe you requested an audience with us." He moved back into the shadows, granting her and Dahlra the room's full attention.

"I did. Thank you, Elwess." Dahlra stepped onto the dais and held out his hand. "Sydney, will you join me?"

She could actually *feel* all eyes on her as she took Dahlra's hand and stepped up onto the platform as gracefully as her corset would allow. In the bright, unforgiving spotlight, Dahlra looked pale, and a little severe. To her surprise, he was also sweating.

His voice, however, gave away none of his nerves. "How long have I known you, Sydney?"

"We, um, we met almost two years ago—"

"No, love," he interrupted. "How long have *I* known you?"

Oh. "You've known me for almost seven years."

"And during that time, I want it stated in front of these witnesses that I have never so much as looked at another woman."

From over his shoulder, Elwess chimed in. "No, he fucking didn't, and believe me, I threw every woman I could get my hands on in front of him."

Sydney could hear laughter coming from their audience. "Right." She honestly had no idea how to she was supposed to react. "Well, I believe you."

"And I want it known, right here, right now, that from the moment I met you, there was no other person for me. You are my partner. You are my submissive. You are mine in every sense of the word."

"Again, I'm with you."

"Good. I believe *you*." The crowd laughed again, even the subs. Dahlra took a deep breath, then let it out slowly. "My only other question to you is this: Are you ready, are you willing, to wear my collar? Are you ready to wear my chains?"

Sydney felt a silly grin dancing on her lips, and nodded. "Yes, sir. Yes, I am." She leaned in closer. "Tell me what to do."

He kissed her hand; he was wearing that same look he had on Christmas morning, when she had told him he was everything she wanted. "Then turn around, my love, and get on your knees."

Sydney's heart was doing the amphetamine junkie polka as she knelt before him. The room was quiet; the time for levity had passed. She heard Elwess' measured footfall as he approached, and from the corner of her eye she saw the collar in his hands. It was made from the same buttery leather as her corset and boots. On the front side, there was a sterling silver oval disk in the center. In an elegant, cursive script was engraved:

His Precious Girl

The fastenings were made of silver filigree, and the heart-shaped lock was delicately engraved, like a locket. It looked strong and at the same time delicate; more like jewelry than a symbol of ownership.

From behind, Elwess clutched her braid, lifting it by the nape, forcing her head down. "There's nothing more beautiful than a woman who's strong enough and scared enough and brave enough to wear a Dominant's collar." He watched intently as Dahlra fastened it around her neck. "Especially a woman like you."

The width of leather forced her shoulders down, and when she tried to raise her head, Elwess pulled her braid again.

"Easy." At Dahlra's quiet comment, Elwess relented infinitesimally, allowing her to at least swallow. As Dahlra fastened the heart-shaped lock in place, Elwess attached a thin, silver lead to a small ring on the collar. He ceremoniously passed it to Dahlra.

"Thank you, Elwess."

"A pleasure, sir." Elwess' long legs stepped out of view, to be replaced by Dahlra's.

"Look up." Sydney obediently glanced upward; Dahlra looked about ten feet tall. "This is more than a sign of obedience, my love. It is a sign of ownership. You are mine, but always remember, I belonged to you first."

It was hard to swallow; the collar was stiff and wide, and Sydney could feel tears threatening again. Yes, she was on her knees, but the beautiful man who stood before her was hers and hers alone, and she would never know a more powerful certainty than this.

"And do you consent to wear my chains?"

She nodded as much as the collar would allow. "Yes, sir."

"Then behold my chains." He held out a stunning platinum bracelet. Countless, intricate loops and knitted strands coiled and writhed around one another, gleaming whitely silver in the spotlights. Another little heart-shaped locket, a smaller mate to the one on her collar, dangled from one end.

"It's beautiful," she marveled.

"Then it definitely belongs on your wrist. But be warned; once I place it there, only I will take it off."

"Deal," she added quickly. Masculine laughter met her ears. Even Elwess joined in. The sound carried a note of indulgence, and Sydney relaxed. She knew she was playing with the big dogs now; it felt important that she do everything in the correct manner. She certainly did not want to make either Dahlra or Elwess look bad. "I'm sorry. Sir."

Dahlra smiled down at her. "I wouldn't have you any other way, my love. Give me your right hand."

The bracelet was cool to the touch, and fit as if it had been molded for her wrist alone. Dahlra fastened the tiny lock, and snapped it closed. It dangled just beneath her pulse point, a heavy, gentle weight. "Thank you. I wish I had—well, I didn't bring you anything."

"I'd say you were gift enough, my dear," Brian Collins replied.

Oblivious to the others in the room, Dahlra grasped the lead and drew her to her feet, pulling her close until their noses were almost touching. His words were a soft susurration against her lips. "The point of our lives is balance. Minder and Agent. Dominant and submissive. Daddy and little girl. One must balance the other." He stroked her cheek and gave her a quick kiss on the nose. His voice rose, more for the benefit of the audience than her. "I certainly can't adorn your right hand and neglect the left, now, can I?"

Sydney's face went numb, and her breath left her lungs in an audible huff as Dahlra got down on one knee, and took her hand. He produced a platinum ring, a monstrous pillow-cut diamond, surrounded by sapphire baguettes. Looking up at her with so much love and hope Sydney nearly swooned, Dahlra placed the ring on her finger. "Sydney Rachel Chapin, will you marry me?"

The room erupted into surprised laughter and applause. She stared at the enormous rock sitting on her finger. "Dahlra. Oh, God—"

Clap... clap... clap...

The cheering voices faded at the slow hand clap, breaking the sweet spell of romance. Every head turned toward the source of the dry, mocking claps, clanging like pig iron through the room.

"Oh, well done, *Master* Dahlra. Well done!" The scornful voice was dripping with contempt. "And what will you do for an encore?"

The bright overhead lights caught a flash of blond hair as the unwelcome guest sauntered into view, his malicious face twisted into a jolly sneer.

Silas Markham had just gate-crashed Dahlra's proposal.

CHAPTER FOUR

The Takedown

He was wearing a black double-breasted suit with black leather gloves. A white silk shirt and eldritch-knotted pink tie completed the old-school Krays look. It was the same overstated elegance Sydney remembered from their first unpleasant meeting at Ramcat, when she had filed Silas Markham away in her memory under the 'Bellend with a chip on his shoulder' heading. That day, he had been condescending and patronising to both her and Dahlra, and her friend Clara Liggon, Ramcat's owner, had marked him as trouble.

Elwess had his own run-in with him at Christmas, when Silas was house-sitting. At the time, Elwess had been unusually chary about the incident, and Sydney had always suspected there was more going on between the two men than Elwess would admit. In any case, Sydney had a feeling the trouble Clara had warned them about just might be coming home to roost.

As he made his way through the maze of sofas and chairs, there was the slightest waver in his stance. Either he was very high, or heading toward very drunk. "What a *moving* declaration. I'm touched. So very twee, Doctor."

His diction was slurry. *So... drunk, probably.* Sydney's vision clouded with red mist; between the tightly-laced corset, the absinthe, and her pounding heart, she was at too much of a physical disadvantage to rake him over the coals without running the risk of dragging herself behind him. Impotently, she watched as he strutted toward the dais.

Brian Collins intercepted him as he was about to mount the platform. "Silas, good to see you. I'm afraid there's been some misunderstanding. This is a private party, you see. Invitation only." He genially took the younger man's arm. "Why don't you and I go and get bit of fresh air? This really isn't—"

"No, it fucking *isn't*, is it, Master Brian?" Silas shook himself free and wavered unsteadily. He cast another sly glance at Sydney. "Clearly, Ms Chapin only issues her invitations to her very closest friends. I'm afraid you'll all just have to get in the queue behind Elwess and wait your turn."

"What do you want, Silas?" Dahlra's voice was tight with the wafer-thin veneer of distaste.

Silas gave him a look of mock surprise. "I've merely come to congratulate the happy couple. Or trio, as it were. Have you already proposed to Elwess? Or is he flagging as a top this time?" He gave Elwess a look of leering contempt. His flushed face and twisted smile made him look grotesque. "He *has* been known to get on his knees for the right man."

Sydney's anger torqued up to a deadly whine. She stepped toward him, but Dahlra caught her arm. "No, Sydney. Not here."

Silas could not have looked more pleased at her reaction. "Oh, I see you've yet to find your balls since last we met, Doctor Gar. They must be dangling from that trinket you so magnanimously placed on your slag's wrist." He stepped up onto the dais, his unsteady stance causing him to stagger. "Watch and learn, Gar. If you were a *real* Dom you'd *never* get on your knees for anyone, even if she does go like a train."

His voice took on a commiserating tone. "But don't feel bad. Not every man is cut out for this lifestyle. If I were you, though, I'd ask Talbert for my money back. Clearly his training is subpar, as usual. Pun fully intended." His tittering laugh set Sydney's teeth on edge.

The room was sickly dense with silence. Several women looked around uneasily; others watched raptly, their expression smeared with a strange look of battle lust. To a man, the Doms stood back, unwilling to give either Dahlra any unasked-for support, or Silas the oxygen of acknowledgement. Sydney could feel fury radiating from Elwess in waves, but she ignored him. She was too busy clocking the distance between the dais and the exit, wondering if she could produce enough lung power to kick the blond bastard's arse out the door.

Silas caught Sydney's flat, even gaze. "Now, slut, if you want to know how a slave really should be treated, do feel free to get on *your* knees." He made to unbutton his trousers. "I'll be happy to demonstrate to these dilettantes how to please a true Master—"

Dahlra stepped up to Silas, his face dark with anger. "That's enough. Out, now. You're about three seconds away from—"

"From what, *mate*?" Silas spat the word, as his face contorted with disgust. "Tell me, Dr Gar, is it just me you object to sharing your little whore with? From what I recall, you were more than willing to allow

Elwess to do anything he wanted with her. You certainly weren't protesting when he fucked her in the arse." He cast Sydney a cool, appraising look. "Come to think on it, neither were you, *kitten*."

Sydney's anger bled away to shock. She looked past Dahlra to Elwess, and behind the rage in his dark eyes was something completely foreign. It looked suspiciously like panic.

Silas was playing to the room now. "And so I ask you again, Dr Gar, does your ever-so-romantic proposal include Elwess as well?" He gave an exaggerated shrug. "You never struck me as liking a bit of cock, but I'm sure Elwess would be more than willing to oblige—"

With a growl of fury, Elwess lunged for Silas, but Dahlra caught him before he could connect. Silas roared with laughter. "Still letting your pets fight your battles for you, Doctor? Do you let them take turns? I seem to recall you both giving *her* a damn good seeing-to. I'm surprised that lovely little recording wasn't on the schedule for tonight's festivities! We all love to watch a bit of homemade porn, don't we, lads? Even if it is a tad vanilla."

Dahlra released Elwess with slow, deliberate movements; he even straightened Elwess' tie. Sydney's anger morphed into a sudden, hot headache. Her palms were sweating; the leather was tight and chafing. If she had been a betting woman, Sydney would have laid money Dahlra felt just as exposed and vulnerable as she, but he was handling it a lot better. She was an untidy, seething mess, compared to Dahlra's unflappable, upper-class calm.

With more Jesus-of-cool savoir faire than Mister Spock, he said, "I think I would prefer to discuss this in private, if you please."

Brian Collins quietly interjected, "I could ask everyone to leave—"

"No, Master Brian," replied Elwess. His voice was also calm, but his eyes still held their murderous glint. "I wouldn't hear of it. I'm so sorry, everyone. It seems Master Silas has played a little prank in rather questionable taste. I cannot apologise enough for interrupting your evening with it." He nodded toward the door. "Come on."

Silas laughed. "Oh, *do* lead on, Master Elwess."

Wordlessly, the four of them left the room and headed back down the long hall toward Room Eleven. Elwess led the way in fuming silence, and Silas followed, his manner and bearing decoupaged in arrogance. Dahlra and Sydney lagged behind, their hands clasped. She glanced up at her Minder, and he squeezed her hand reassuringly.

Suddenly, Elwess spun around and grabbed Silas by his lapels. His angular face was flushed with fury. "I told you what I'd do, didn't I? Didn't I?"

He slammed Silas hard against the wall. The breath left Silas' lungs in a startled *woof*, and before he could recover, Elwess right-crossed him, catching his left cheek with a solid clout.

Silas raised his arms to protect his face, and Elwess punched him squarely in the solar plexus. Silas dropped like a stone to the floor, holding his stomach. As he lay helpless, gagging and coughing, unable to catch his breath, Elwess viciously kicked him in the ribs. Silas screamed and rolled around on the floor, sucking wind and retching. He tried to escape, but there was nowhere to go in the narrow hallway.

Breathing hard, Elwess took out his phone, speed-dialed a number and said, "Security. I have a situation in the hall near Room Eleven."

Silas tried to rise, and Elwess kicked him again. "You couldn't keep your mouth shut, couldja? Had to be the big man! What did I tell you, eh? What did I say?" Elwess drew back to kick him a third time, but Dahlra held him back.

"That's enough, Elwess! I said *enough*!"

"It'll never be enough!" He spun out of Dahlra's grip, unbalanced, panting with exertion. "I want to kill the fucker!"

"Nevertheless, you will stand down!" Dahlra commanded.

The door on the far end banged opened, and a cresting wave of deafening music roared down the hall. In its wake, a giant of a man charged through and thundered toward them, his breath snorting through his nostrils like an angry bull. An enormous suede head sat directly on top of his thick neck. Two beady, Baltic blue eyes peered at them above a nose that had been broken more times than it had been set. He wore a discreet name tag that read *Barry Stone: Head of Security*.

"Is everything alright, boss?" His voice rolled down the hall like a bowling ball. He nodded curtly toward Dahlra and Sydney, then glanced down at the man heaving on the floor. His lip curled in derisive recognition. "Want me to get rid of this for ya?"

"As a matter of fact, I do, Baz." Elwess straightened his jacket with a hard jerking motion. "Get *that*-" he pointed to Silas, "out of this club. Destroy his keycard and mark his file as barred for life. If he ever tries to set foot in here again, throw him out so far he lands in Chinatown.

And tell everybody from the door girl to the oik scrubbing toilets if he tries to buy his way back in, it's immediate dismissal for anyone taking his money. I don't want to see this filth again."

Baz nodded, his rubbery lips stretching into something resembling a smile. "Don't worry, boss. When we get rid, they stay gone."

"Use caution, Chief," warned Sydney. "He's drunk, and he came here spoiling for a fight. He may be armed."

"Duly noted, miss. Now, up you get, mate." He yanked Silas up by the back of his collar and frog-marched him down the hall, barely allowing the shorter man's feet to touch the floor.

Even as he was being dragged along the corridor, Silas was snarling like a fox. "You think you're so fucking hard, Talbert," he rasped, craning to look back, "but this is not the end of this! You and your fuck toys think you can push everyone around, but when I let—"

There was a horrid clang as Silas' face met the door jam. "Oh dear. You seemed to have misjudged the wall." Stone's voice rumbled with cheerful commiseration. He dragged Silas into the melee of the main room, and the door closed behind him with a thump. In the stark silence that followed, the smear of blood on the wall screamed its epitaph; Silas Markham would leave The Library a little less handsome than he had arrived.

For a moment, the three of them stood in the deafening quiet. Dahlra fixed Elwess with a solemn, unreadable look. "Is your hand alright?"

"What?" Elwess looked at him blankly, then glanced down at his bruised knuckles. "Oh, yeah, it's fine." He laughed shakily. He took a deep breath, then puffed it out. "Look, why don't we take a breather. I'll ring the bar to have drinks brought round—"

"No." Dahlra's voice was cold; of the three of them, he was the only one truly angry now. He nodded toward Room Eleven. "We're going in there, and you're going to explain what that little scene was all about."

Elwess opened his mouth to protest, but Dahlra calmly fronted him out until he gave in with an uncharacteristic lack of grace.

Inside, Elwess flicked a few switches on the wall, killing the hard, overhead spot, and dialing up the ambient lighting. Without the interrogation-style cones of light sterilising the room, it looked less like a movie set and more like a typical corporate conference area. That is, if typical corporate conference rooms had St Andrews crosses and whipping benches tucked away in the corners.

Sydney collapsed on the sofa with a heavy sigh. The fight-or-flight juice was rapidly drizzling out of her system, leaving her tired and parched. "I know corsets are supposed to be this tight, but I really could do with some breathing room."

Dahlra sat down beside her, loosened the laces of her corset and gently pulled them slack. She took the first deep breath in what felt like days, and the oxygen rush was like a hit of cocaine. He watched her carefully as the dizziness passed. "Better?"

"Yes, thanks." They both turned their attention to Elwess. He was staring moodily into the dark corner of the room, unwilling to meet their eyes.

It seemed a long time before Dahlra spoke. "Elwess, an explanation right now would be appreciated."

Elwess took an equally long time to reply. He seemed to be considering his words very carefully. "When I had the Chine built, I had CCTV monitors placed throughout so I could record my sessions."

"A little CYA?" asked Sydney.

"A *lot* of arse covering. I have," he coughed self-consciously, "some rather well-known clients. I don't touch anyone without a signed contract. I take no chances. None of us need that sort of unwelcome publicity. And to show it's not all about liability, I sign one as well."

"Because you're all about the trust, right, Elwess?" Dahlra's voice was viper-sharp. Elwess shot him a look that was equal parts shame and defiance, but did not rise to the bait.

To get him talking again, Sydney asked, "What sort of setup do you have?"

"Four cameras are activated by motion detection. They film simultaneously in a multi-screen format onto a single MKV file, which is saved onto a stand-alone PC. It's got no external access, no internet, nothing. It doesn't even have a modem." He warmed to his subject. "I've been looking into a direct access link-up for my phone using the Agency's scramble technology, so I can monitor the room when I'm away. The lads in surveillance assure me it would provide the same level of security I already have.

"After a session, I usually burn the recording onto a DVD, and hand-carry the disks to my bank vault. After three years, the disks are destroyed. I use the Agency incinerator to ensure total confidentiality."

Dahlra leaned forward, resting his elbows on his thighs. He absently ran a thumb over his chin. "I vividly recall a discussion in which we agreed the cameras would be turned *off* that night."

Elwess studied a point over Dahlra's shoulder, his eyes shuttered. Dahlra huffed, then sat back against the sofa. "You just couldn't help yourself, could you? The master voyeur just couldn't resist recording the event for posterity, eh? And should we surmise that you did *not* store this particular recording in your bank vault?"

"No." Elwess' shoulders were hunched, his posture defensive. Sydney had an eerie sense of déjà vu; he looked very much like Dahlra the day he had walked into her hospital room to offer himself as her Minder—a man expecting the fallout to be more than he could bear.

It all made sense now; the tension when he arrived at DeVere Gardens on Christmas Eve, presenting the key to his flat like the deed to Buck House. "At Christmas, you mentioned Silas had been house-sitting while you were out of town. I recall you were pissed off about something. You came home early, and caught him watching our recording, didn't you?"

"Yes." Elwess' eyes narrowed. "Ever since that night I've been trying to figure it out how he found it. I was running late for my flight, and I left the flat in a hurry. But I distinctly remember locking the disk away. I kept it with... I keep it with the pair of knickers you were wearing that night, Sydney. The ones I took from you." He shook his head. "I *know* I locked the fucking thing away. It was not for anyone's eyes but mine.

"When I arrived home and let myself in, he was watching it." His voice was bitter and embarrassed. "The berk was so into it he didn't even hear me walk in."

"I don't suppose you took the opportunity to destroy it then, did you?" When Elwess did not reply, Dahlra's expression darkened. "I didn't think so. You're still watching it."

"Daily. It's like I'm addicted to it. I don't even watch regular porn anymore." The words came out in a monotoned, automatic rush, and Elwess grimaced. "Sorry. That wasn't funny."

"So that's why you sent him packing, and invited us to be your house sitters instead."

"No!" Elwess vehemently shook his head. "No, that wasn't it at all. You know that wasn't why I gave you—"

"I know no such thing, now." Dahlra's voice was cold. "And you were planning on telling us about this, when?"

Elwess sprang to his feet and began pacing the room. "I never thought it would be necessary. You don't run in the same circles. He wasn't invited this evening." He glanced at Sydney. "It was just something I made for me. I would never have shared it with anyone. That's not why I kept it."

He looked at them entreatingly. "I know you don't believe me right now, but I am so sorry."

Dahlra also rose to his feet, his expression sombre. He faced the younger man, like a disappointed parent addressing a recalcitrant child. "Elwess, you're not sorry you lied to me; you're not even all that sorry Silas found it. You're sorry you got caught out. If Silas hadn't come tonight, were you ever going to tell us about the recording?"

For a moment, the room was so quiet Sydney could actually hear the creak of her leather corset as she breathed. Elwess looked about as miserable as a man could look. Dahlra shook his head. "If you want a real relationship with us, do you think this is an auspicious start? You lied to us by omission. You've compromised your credibility with Brian Collins and his entire group, and now you've made an open enemy. You've damaged our trust in you. And more than all that, you've potentially compromised the Agency."

"I know, I know!" Elwess raked a hand through his long hair. "I truly thought I'd put the frighteners on him at Christmas when I sent him packing."

"You haven't answered my question, Elwess. But I'll do it for you." Dahlra sat down again and took Sydney's hand. "I think you told yourself that as long as we didn't find out, it was okay. Responsible, even; after all, you record every session as a precaution. But I also think you've been looking over your shoulder ever since you caught Silas watching it, waiting for the hammer to fall."

He smiled indulgently. "Come on, Elwess! Did you honestly think that a wanker like him would miss an opportunity to throw something like that in your face? He's not stupid. Whatever you said or did that night was enough for him to confer how important it was that no one find out about it, and so it became something he could use against you."

"Maybe he thought it was enough to cost you our friendship." Sydney added thoughtfully. "He's not stupid, but he's plenty petty and spiteful."

"Do you know what I think? I think deep down you're relieved; I think you *wanted* to get caught."

Elwess scoffed, but there was no real conviction. "That's bollocks, Dahlra—"

"You thought about confessing that night, didn't you? But, as usual, you were able to talk yourself out of it. You're good at avoiding things you don't want to deal with, aren't you?"

With almost fatherly tenderness, Dahlra added, "You have to come clean, Elwess. That's what you wanted."

"What I *wanted* was to keep you from finding out," Elwess replied, through clenched teeth.

"Ah, so there's my answer."

There was a dangerous tension building between the two men. Sydney could see it in Dahlra's posture. Elwess looked like a cornered animal, ready to strike out in fear.

She squeezed Dahlra's hand. "Okaaaay Elwess, maybe I can understand why you recorded it, but why—"

"Because it was all I had of you!" snapped Elwess. "I was afraid that was all I would *ever* have of you!" He turned his back on them, and in a defeated, stunned voice, he added, "And I couldn't stop... *wanting* you."

The three of them were silent as this declaration pinged around the room. Sydney caught Dahlra's eye, and she knew exactly what he was thinking. *What are we going to do with this?*

"Do you know if Silas made a copy?"

"No. Not for sure."

Sydney huffed and rose from the sofa, wincing as the leather bit into her waist. "I'm going to have to tell Inigo about this. It's not exactly scandal material, but you know he's not going to be thrilled at anything that has the potential to compromise the integrity of one of his precious agents."

Elwess' expression was desolate, full of naked regret. He caught her eye and quickly looked away, as if he could not bear to be seen like this. Sydney marveled how the evening had gone from fairy-tale perfect to pear-shaped in a matter of minutes.

"Elwess, look—"

"Sydney, please. Just don't." He held up his bruised hand. "I'll get a hotel room, or something. You two can stay the night in the flat. I won't bother you again." He pulled the tattered remains of his pride around him, picked up his coat, and headed for the door.

"I haven't given you permission to leave."

The words, though spoken in the softest of tones, hung in the air like a chiming bell. Elwess froze in his tracks. He turned slowly and faced Dahlra. There was the faintest trace of defiance in his voice. "No, sir, you haven't."

Karma-calm, Dahlra stepped up close. "Do you think what you have done is beyond forgiveness, Elwess?"

He looked searchingly into Dahlra's face. "I think you're the only one who can answer that question."

"And what about Sydney and me? Are we so weak and fickle, that you believe us incapable of forgiving you? Of leaving you to face the music on your own?"

Sydney could see stunned hope elevating Elwess' posture. Dahlra continued, "I suppose the next question is what to do about this. You will have to accept punishment."

"Yes, absolutely." Elwess looked like he had just been told to step down from the gallows and go home. "I'll do that. Gladly. Look, I'll give you the disk—"

"And any copies you've made in any format. I want every trace of it. And I don't want you spending your ride home thinking up a loophole of how to keep one."

"Ride home? You said I had to—"

"You will leave now, and go home. We will join you at the Chine shortly. It will be done there. Scene of the crime, and all that. And this session *won't* be recorded. You will be naked, Elwess, on your knees. And it will hurt. If you endure your punishment to my satisfaction, we will discuss the way forward. Do you accept that?"

Elwess looked from one to the other. For the briefest moment, Sydney was sure Dahlra had pushed him too far. Finally, he took a deep breath. "Yes, sir. I accept. Thank you for the chance to make things right."

"It will be your only chance." Dahlra nodded toward the door. "*Now*, you may leave."

Elwess all but slunk out of the room. Sydney stared at Dahlra, dumbstruck, but he looked straight ahead, his bearing regal and aloof. In the few moments since Silas' ill-timed revelation about the recording, everything between the three of them had done a one-eighty.

And it was Dahlra Gar, the mild, patient doctor, the quiet one, who had taken over.

Elwess quietly let himself into the flat and laid his keys on the hall table. He walked up the stairs to his study, and crossed to the small closet next to his desk. From there, he retrieved a lockbox from the top shelf; it was made of stainless steel, the kind used to store important documents. Placing it on his desk, he dialed the three numbers of the combination, 7-2-6, and opened it.

Lying on top were the peach-coloured silk knickers Sydney had worn the first night she and Dahlra came to the Chine. Out of habit, he picked them up and brushed them against his cheek. If he closed his eyes and inhaled, he could almost believe he could smell her perfume.

In spite of everything, he felt the grim satisfaction of giving Markham a good hiding, the smug dick. His only regret was that he had not knocked seven shades of shit out of Silas the night he had actually caught him in the act. Instead he had just thrown Silas and his half-packed suitcase out onto the street with a lot of big talk and hurried threats.

He studied the buttery fabric of Sydney's underwear. They had been lying on the floor forgotten when Elwess walked in and caught Silas red-handed. He had been as angry about those discarded knickers as he had about Silas watching the recording. They were hers; they were the physical proof that she had given herself to him. Silas had defiled them. He had defiled everything. And he wasn't the only one, was he?

Elwess had fully intended to come clean during the Christmas holidays, while they were sitting around, eating Dahlra's pukka cooking and drinking good rum. They had been full of the ol' booze and bonhomie ... He had told himself there was no point in upsetting his hosts, much less spoiling the holiday confessing to something they would never really need to know about anyway.

As usual, you were able to talk yourself out of it. You're good at avoiding things you don't want to deal with, aren't you? When he was still a green Dom, Clara Liggon had warned Elwess this was a character flaw he should try and amend. Confession being good for the soul, and all that shite. He was just as rubbish at it now as he was then.

For the first time in my life, I'm actually atoning for something I've done. If I do it right, I'll get what I want. Is this what you really want, Talbert? It's an all-or-nothing deal; they play for keeps.

Elwess placed the knickers back in the box, on top of the damned disk. As he rose to leave, he saw a jump drive slotted into the side of his PC. Cursing under his breath, he pulled the stick from its port and added it to the box's contents. Finally, he disabled the Chine's automatic recording program. He closed the box, spun the combination dial and tucked it under his arm.

He decided to take the stairs instead of the lift, unbuttoning his shirt as he descended. The long walk down would give him time to get his head on straight. He winced as he flexed his bruised knuckles; they were going to hurt like a bitch tomorrow, but then again, so would the rest of him. He paused on the steps, halfway between the sanctuary of his flat and the retribution that awaited him below, and wasn't that just a metaphor for his life right now?

They wouldn't punish me if they weren't planning on staying with me. This is what tonight is all about. Well, that was his agenda, anyway. It was full-on pretzel logic, but hell, he had to be able to live with himself.

At the bottom of the stairs, Elwess finished undressing and placed the lockbox beside his neatly folded clothes on the side table. Shivering in the cold room, he thought about how he had gotten himself into this situation. He wanted Sydney. Even as Dahlra got down on his knees to propose, Elwess had wanted her so badly he could barely breathe. His head had been spinning with fantasies of what he would do with them after Sydney said yes and the room erupted in applause.

Except that, of course, she had not, and they had not. His agenda might have been to get them back in his bed tonight, but Dahlra had meticulously planned this proposal three years ago, before Sydney Chapin had even heard of him. "You're like a twelve year-old girl, planning her wedding," Elwess had jeered. Yeah, too jaded and worldly to believe that a romantic's dream might possibly come true.

But it had. All of Dahlra's dreams had come true. And it had gone swimmingly, until—

The most beautiful fucking romantic moment The Library would probably ever see, and he had stood there like a lemon while Silas ruined it. *Sure, blame Markham all you want. Then convince yourself he put a gun to your head and made you press the 'Record' button.*

When Sydney and Dahlra exited the lurid confines of The Library and stepped out into the frigid February evening, the elegant old Bentley was parked at the kerb, like a magic carriage come to whisk them home. Terry, looking smart in his chauffeur's cap and long black driving coat, smiled and tipped his hat.

"Good evening, miss. A pleasure to see you again. Happy Valentine's Day."

"Oh, it's great to see you too, Terry. How are things?"

"Very good, thank you." He opened the door with his usual flourish. "Kim and I are moving to Madrid next summer. I can't wait to get somewhere warm." He gave a pretend shiver and rubbed his hands together. "I've been practicing me Spanish and all."

"We shall have to start calling you 'El Tel,' then." Dahlra helped Sydney into the back seat. "But who's going to squire us around after you quit for sunny Spain?"

"My oldest boy, Rick. He's taking over the business. But don't you worry." Terry tapped the side of his nose with a pudgy finger. "I've already told him to take special care of you."

The Bentley smelled of good leather and tender loving care. On impulse, Sydney said, "Hey, 'El Tel,' how about driving us around the capital for a bit before we head back to Kensington, *por favor*?"

"*Si si, Senorita*! Sure thing. Just buzz the intercom if you need anything." He raised the window between the front and back seats, enveloping them in the warm, cozy darkness. For several moments, they silently watched London through the Bentley's tinted windows.

"Dahlra, how do you really feel about all this?"

"How do I feel about him lying to me, or watching the recording on a daily basis?"

"Both."

"Honestly? I'm not one whit surprised at either."

Sydney laughed ruefully. "Neither am I."

"I can't stay angry for something I should have known he couldn't resist doing. I know he's a voyeur—and an exhibitionist. Why should I be shocked that he'd record us?" He took her hand. "And what about you, Sydney? You're the focus of attention there. Is this something the Agency truly might carp about?"

She considered it. "Well, it's not like some MP with three kids and a loving wife is involved. A single agent having sex with two men might make good water cooler gossip, but beyond that? Okay, I could see where it might irritate Inigo a bit—if I squint."

"But how do *you* feel? I knew about the recording equipment; you didn't. Are you upset?"

Suddenly, it all seemed a bit ludicrous. "I guess it all depends. You know, did my bum look big in it; that sort of thing."

He was startled into laughter. "I'm sure you looked like candy." He put his arm around her, and she snuggled against his shoulder.

"You know, for a minute there, I was genuinely afraid Elwess was going to seriously injure the little blond shit. Not like he didn't deserve it. I wanted to have a go at him myself. But in all honesty, it was a little OTT, didn't you think?"

Dahlra nodded. "I thought as much. More about them than us."

"Yes. There's more going on here."

"True. In a way, though, it couldn't have played out better as far as our own agenda goes."

Sydney gazed up at his handsome profile. "It's not quite how we planned it, but it is what we want." When he did not immediately reply, she nudged him. "Hey. It *is* what you want as well, isn't it?"

He nodded. "Yes. It's time to become his Dominant. For real." He sighed. "And I've got to make it hurt."

"With great gifts..."

"Come great responsibilities. And although I'm not afraid of him, I'm a little nervous."

She patted his hand reassuringly, and the bracelet's lock clinked like a little bell. Sydney stared at the intricate platinum knots. "Oh, God."

"What?"

She held up her left hand, and the diamond engagement ring flashed in the low light. "I'm so stupid! Ah, Dahlra, dammit, I'm sorry. No wonder you were so pissed off! I was so busy wanting to punch the bastard's face in—"

He caught her hand in his, and kissed it. "I will admit, I felt like a fool, kneeling there while he—"

"Oh, dear heart, no." Sydney's gut clenched with remorse. "I feel so... Oh, God, I'm so insensitive sometimes."

"Nonsense. So my big moment was spoiled." He shrugged. "To tell the truth, this whole recording business didn't piss me off half as much as being interrupted in the middle of my big, dramatic proposal."

"I'll admit, I didn't see it coming."

"That was the idea. I've been working on the particulars since Christmas."

Sydney had known he was up to something, but she had been focused on the Great Sub Mission thing as merely an exercise in kinky play dating. She should have been more observant; all the secret squirrel conversations with Elwess, his nervousness in The Library. It was all there, if she had only paid more attention. Amateur, that's what it was. Man, she *had* gotten soft.

He had looked so beautiful, down on his knees, looking up at her with those huge green eyes, glowing with love. He deserved better than to have his special plans ruined, to be humiliated and upstaged by an arrogant prick like Silas Markham. Sydney almost wished he was there right now; she would love to kick his smug teeth in and... Dammit, it was unfair, after all they had been through. She felt entitled to be hurt and angry on Dahlra's behalf.

Yeah, they had been cheated of a really romantic moment, but it did not mean she could not make up for a less-than-momentous proposal with a fantastic marriage. Sydney felt an overwhelming desire to tell Terry to just keep driving, all the way to Spain—someplace warm where she could wrap Dahlra in her arms and never let him go. He deserved that. Come to think on it, so did she.

"You know, we were in this very car the night we became lovers."

He purred like a large cat. "Funnily enough, I remember it quite well."

"It was also the night I realised just how much you meant to me."

He took her hands in his. His face was close to hers, and she could see the emotion in his eyes. "I was asleep before I met you. You woke me up. You say I've conditioned *you*? My girl, I don't think my heart knows how to beat without yours to set the pace. I can't breathe if we're not sharing the same air. You're in my blood and my bones, Sydney Chapin, and you should never have to question why or how much I love you. God knows I don't. It's the easiest thing I've ever done."

His hands tightened. "But it's not enough, Sydney. If you don't feel those same things for me, then all we are is great sex and Scrabble and good cooking. That might be enough for some, but not for me."

A feeling of unabashed joy bloomed in her, making the corset feel even more restricting. Thousands of butterflies were flexing their wings inside her chest, ready for liftoff. She leaned in until they were nose to nose.

"Now you listen to me, Scrabble Boy. I've spent the past few days moping around like a lost puppy without you. And it made me realise one important thing." She took a deep breath, but her voice still shook with emotion. "I never trusted love. It was dangerous, because it didn't follow any rules. I was always better at things I could see or touch and put a label on."

Sydney maneuvered until was she was straddling him. She stroked his cheek, and he closed his eyes. "Then *you* came into my life, and suddenly all the rules I associated with love changed. You changed *me*. I thought loving would make me weak, or put me in some kind of trance. But it woke me up, too. It's turned me into one mean, protective bitch. I'd kill for you, I would. I'd kill anyone who tried to hurt you."

He stared at her, speechless, a tiny smile touching his lips. She laughed shakily. "Okay, maybe I *am* a bit crap at expressing myself, but let me be perfectly clear on this one thing, Dahlra Gar: tonight, when you called my name, and the lights went up and I saw you sitting there, I knew you were every fucking thing in this world to me. And I'm not going to be satisfied with anything less than that."

She removed the ring, and held it out to him. "Now, ask me again." When his eyes shot up to hers, she smiled. "You won't be sorry."

His hand trembled slightly as he placed the ring on her finger again. "Sydney, will you marry me?"

"Yes, Dahlra Benjamin Peter Gar. Yes, I will most certainly marry you." She nuzzled against his warm neck. "Because when the sex is over and Scrabble is won and the food is eaten, you will still be every fucking thing in this world to me."

He whispered her name, a soft, crooning caress that melted into a kiss. He pulled her close, and they held one another until the Bentley glided to a halt on Pelham Street.

CHAPTER FIVE

Punishment and Reward

Years before, Elwess brokered a deal with London Underground to permanently lease a shallowly-built ghost station on the District Line between South Kensington and Sloane Square. Ostensibly, it had been requisitioned by the Agency for 'surveillance purposes.' He just fudged on the blueprints and massaged the paperwork a bit.

The platform and the stairs leading topside had never interested him; the Underground engineers sealed them off, leaving only a former maintenance tunnel, which ran perpendicular to the Old Brompton Road pedestrian walkway.

The tunnel led to a large room, its walls rounded at shallow angles his builder had called 'chine hulls.' Forty-five degrees to the left, a narrow, winding staircase connected the room to his Pelham Street flat upstairs. Later, Elwess added a cage lift. It had cost a small fortune, but saved his knees. Two other short tunnels radiated from the opposite side; they eventually became a bedroom and the bath.

Elwess had wanted to give the space a name like no other in the world, one that would be remembered and talked about. It had to be a strong name, with as many connotations as his imagination decreed. A dungeon that would be as well-known and notorious as its Master; a name worthy of the dark, secret ravine carved out of London's cold bedrock.

And so he had taken a leaf from his builder's book, and christened it The Chine. The dark cleft, the backbone, the hull, the secret heart of a Dominant, born in the hidden, rumbling arteries of the city. Kinksters, being who and what they were, had immediately pronounced the name 'twee' and 'obvious.' He had ignored all the jokes; by the end of the year, the Chine was the envy of every Dom in Europe.

In his moody underground lair, Elwess reigned supreme, and honed Dominance to an art form. Through the mediums of tears and blood and sweat, passion and pain and ecstasy, the Chine became his canvas. He controlled every physical, mental and emotional thermostat to his exact specifications.

A submissive, he had often lectured, here in this very room, *is the true Master in a Dom/sub relationship. Nothing happens that the submissive doesn't allow. Only when you submit, will I Dominate.* Was not that his mantra, that a sub held the true power? That without submission, Dominance was an empty, impotent fist?

Oh, he had preached it, but truth be told, he had never really subscribed to it. Nothing was more powerful, no drug more potent, no sex more pleasurable than enticing a submissive to his will, watching her give up herself, surrendering voluntarily to the pain or the fear, then begging for more. Nothing was more intoxicating than seeing her shudder when he whispered, "Very good. Just one more, then, for tonight." The lingering, promise-threat for the next time was every bit as sweet as the reward. Sex was not the destination; it was just part of the scenery on the journey. Surrender was the ultimate orgasm.

On that fateful night, when he had turned off the cameras, then gave into temptation and switched them back on again, he had forgotten who he was dealing with. Sydney Chapin was not some kinky bird he had hooked up with at The Library; Dahlra Gar was not some jaded denizen of Ramcat showing off his new toy. Elwess had betrayed their trust with no more regard for the consequences than if he had downloaded porn through Pirate Bay. What had he said to Sydney, not twenty-four hours ago? *You won't find that level of casual in a BDSM relationship.* Christ, he was such a hypocrite.

There was a rough, uneven patch on the floor; he made his subs kneel there for punishments. He knelt on it now, wincing as its sharp edges bit into his knees. He always encouraged a sub to contemplate why she was being punished, to accept it as an act of contrition, not cruelty. "You should be ruminating on what you've done to displease me," he would purr into their shell-pink ears, using his voice like a lash. "You've disappointed me. You have a chance to make amends."

While he never said it aloud, the inference was always there: dread, anticipation, remorse, fear—as much a part of the punishment as the pain itself. As tears welled in their eyes and they trembled in readiness for his singular brand of justice, the power he held over them went to his head like a noseful of high-grade coke.

How many times had a sub kissed his hand afterward, her face alight with the joy of enduring his pain, knowing that pleasure would await?

Forgiveness brought reward, and was not that the entire point? Penitence was sexy as fuck.

What sort of pleasure would await him, when Dahlra was finished with him?

His heart was kicking along in his chest. One thing was for certain; everything would change. He would belong to Dahlra, just as Sydney did. This time, he would be the one on bended knee, issuing his own kind of proposal—proposal by submission. He had told himself he only pretended to submit to Dahlra in order to get to Sydney, and that was the biggest lie of all. It had been hard enough to admit that he had fallen in love with Sydney Chapin; it had been almost impossible to accept and explain his need to submit to Dahlra Gar.

He would kneel here all night if he had to, until his knees bled and his body failed, before he would accept their rejection. He would empty his mind and heart of himself, purging his pride and his defiant arrogance until he was shriven—some kind of pure that he had never been before. He would be cleaned out, a vessel suited for their purpose.

When they came—*if* they came— it might just mean that he still held power over them—the power to make them love him. If they did not come, he had a sudden fear that his heart would escape the skin it stood in and chase after them, leaving nothing behind but an echo of everything he might have become.

His pale body goose-fleshed in the cool dungeon. It seemed that while he was busy rolling this information around in his mind, his body was quite confident about its opinion on the subject. While the idea of receiving some form of punishment from Dahlra was not exactly a turn on, it wasn't exactly... not.

The upstairs door opened with a long, slow grinding noise, and relief swept over his body. The clank and hum of the lift was both comforting and foreboding. Elwess had deliberately designed the long descent from his flat to the Chine, in order to create tension in the mind and body of a waiting sub. Now that it was his turn to wait, his heart beat heavily with equal parts relief and trepidation. He flexed his cold-numbed fingers, and took several deep, steadying breaths. It was enough for now; they had come to him—

The lift stopped, and Dahlra pushed the door open and stepped out. He held out his hand, and Sydney joined him. They were both still bundled in their winter coats, and Elwess' eyes crawled over them hungrily.

They ignored him, talking softly to one another as Dahlra helped Sydney remove her coat. Elwess could just make out her scars through the laces of the corset. She turned around, and that was when he spied the diamond on her finger. He swore under his breath.

"Do you have something to say, Elwess?" asked Dahlra.

"No, sir, I—" Elwess sighed. "I'm sorry your evening was spoiled."

"I wouldn't say it was spoiled entirely."

"Perhaps Silas tried, but he failed." Sydney favoured Dahlra with a dazzling smile as he grasped her hand and placed a kiss directly onto the ring. "No proposal is spoiled when the answer is yes."

Some of the tension left Elwess' shoulders. All of Dahlra's planning had not gone to waste, then. "That's—that's great news. I'm dead chuffed for you. I mean it."

For the first time since they had entered, Dahlra leveled his gaze toward him. "I know you do."

Elwess lowered his eyes to the floor tiles. "And you don't have to avert your gaze," Dahlra added affably. "We aren't going to turn you into a pillar of salt. You have my permission to look at us. In fact, I think you should." His tone took on a more reproachful note. "After all, looking is what brought us to this pass. And I want you to remember exactly why we're here."

Dahlra tugged on the silver lead attached to Sydney's collar. He pulled her into his embrace, and caught her lips with his for a slow, deep, sensual kiss. She whimpered softly and melted against her lover. He finally broke from the kiss, leaving Sydney panting, her eyes heavy-lidded. "Isn't this what you wanted, Elwess?" He stroked Sydney's luxurious hair. "To watch?"

Elwess' eyes burned. Against the backdrop of Dahlra's immaculate black suit, Sydney's skin was creamy and luminous. Dahlra's large, graceful hand caressed her waist possessively, and she nuzzled against him like a cat. It was hard to be with them like this, yet separate, excluded, with the possibility they might deny him forever. Desire and tension and something he was much more reluctant to define warred within Elwess' breast.

A dozen different replies came to mind, but he settled for the simple truth. "You're both beautiful. Yes. I like watching you."

Sydney caught Elwess' gaze and held it as Dahlra approached him.

"Now, you were given a set of instructions to follow."

"There." Elwess nodded toward the lockbox on the table. "It's all there, including a copy I made. The combination's seven-two-six."

With a glance at Elwess, Dahlra opened the box, and removed Sydney's knickers from the top. "I can only imagine you kept these for inspiration." He turned them this way and that in the light, then brought them to his nose, and sniffed delicately. "So clean. Look, my girl—freshly laundered. It almost begs the question of what you've been doing with them."

Dahlra emptied the box and deposited its contents in his coat pocket. "Well done. I'm pleased with your obedience."

Elwess swallowed. His mouth felt like dust. "I'm sorry, Dahlra. I never meant for this to happen."

"I know. I forgive you."

Elwess glanced toward Sydney, and she nodded. "So do I."

He slumped tiredly, relief battling with exhaustion. "Thank you. Really, I'm grateful. Look, I know we—"

"However, there is still the matter of your punishment."

Shit. "Yes, sir," he bit out. "I haven't forgotten."

"No, I'm sure you haven't," Dahlra replied dryly. "Lean forward. Hands and knees."

Looking up into Dahlra's steely eyes, Elwess did as he was told. He heard the soft tread of the other man's boots on the tiles as he walked behind him. Sydney was looking down on him, her large eyes alert and watchful.

He caught an acrid whiff of latex, and heard the snapping, rustling sound of gloves being drawn onto experienced, practiced hands. Dahlra knelt behind him, and placed his large hands on Elwess' back. They slid down past his hips, and perfunctorily parted his arsecheeks. "What the f—"

"Breathe through your mouth," Dahlra intoned.

"What are you—"

Dahlra removed his gloved hands. "Are you questioning me?"

"No sir! I just was so—"

"Oh. It's just a matter of trust, then? You know, given the circumstances, I'd say that's a bit rich."

Almost panicking, Elwess blurted, "I do trust you!" When Dahlra did not reply, Elwess bit back his frustration. "Whatever you want. I accept it. Truly. Fuck's sake, Dahlra—"

"Alright. Calm down." Dahlra's voice was like feathers floating over his skin, and Elwess shuddered as the warm hands touched him again. Cold, slick lube rimmed his arsehole, while dexterous fingers opened and stretched him with deliberate, clinical precision. He hissed as a large plug was firmly inserted into his rectum. He felt it push past his sphincter and enter his body in one long, slow burn.

He bore down, doing all the things he had ever ordered a sub to do. It nestled inside, and the muscles closed around it, and when he allowed himself a moment of relief, Dahlra smacked the plug, tapping it against his prostate. Adrenaline flooded his system, making his heartbeat swoosh in his ears.

Dahlra stood. "There. You may stand up now."

Feeling sick and stirred, Elwess rose shakily to his feet, wincing as his knees protested the long vigil on the hard floor. Again, he looked to Sydney, hoping for some sort of reassurance, but her face was now a perfect, unreadable oval.

Dahlra appeared by her side, casually removing the gloves and tossing them into the rubbish bin. "Now, it occurs to me there are several implements I could use here." He glanced around, as if considering his options. "The Chine is nothing if not well-equipped." He turned back to Elwess with a look of chilling calm. "But then, you always stressed the importance of making punishment... personal."

He reached for his belt. Elwess watched with a pounding heart. He knew this belt, knew its history. Dahlra released the buckle, and it slipped free with a soft clink. "Sydney gave me this belt the night she disciplined me. And now, I'm going to use it to discipline you."

Dahlra pulled the belt from around his waist with slow deliberation. The sound of leather sliding through belt loops was disturbingly visceral, like a knife slicing through muscle. Elwess felt his face grow hot, and his body instantly responded. Once the belt was free, Dahlra doubled it into a short strap. It looked lethal in his large hands.

Elwess understood; there would be no reprieve, no bargaining. This was something he could not escape through reasoning or guile or charm. He must either accept and be broken, or refuse, forever unredeemed. At that sweet, bitter moment, he let go of any residual resentment, and he surrendered. All that was left was edgy, skittish anticipation, and incredibly, his cock twitched. He stared straight ahead, unable to look either of them in the eye while his treacherous body flushed and strained and hardened.

Dahlra placed a hand on the back of his head, and thrust the strap toward his face. Elwess pressed his lips to it. It was still warm, and the faintest scent of Dahlra's cologne danced with the lush aroma of leather.

His voice was as hard and smooth as polished marble. "I cherish this belt, Elwess. Don't dishonour it."

A feeling of delicious terror overcame him. *I'm going to be beaten by my Dominant, and it's going to hurt, and God I want it...*

"Do you accept my discipline, Elwess?"

"Yes, sir."

"Safe word?"

Christ, when was the last time he had needed one of those? Elwess muttered the first word that came to mind. "Silas."

Dahlra moved to stand behind him again. "Very well. Twenty lashes. You will count them. If you lose count, we'll start over. Do you accept this?"

Sydney finally moved, stepping in close, almost touching him. Some signal passed between the lovers, and she sank to her knees before Elwess, her mesmerising eyes locked with his. He stared down at her stupidly, his cock swelling so rapidly it left him lightheaded.

Dahlra grasped the back of Elwess' head, and unceremoniously yanked his hair. "Do. You. Accept, Elwess?" His voice was like the stone beneath their feet. "I won't ask again."

"I accept!" Elwess took two deep breaths in quick succession. "I accept, sir."

"Hands behind your head." As Elwess laced his fingers together and cupped the back of his head, Sydney leaned closer, her perfect mouth so tantalisingly close he could feel her warm breath misting the head of his cock. "Oh, shit..." He shivered as her tongue darted out and flicked teasingly over the head, and even as he whimpered in anticipation, the leather lashed across his arse like a brand, sending a hot spark of pain across his skin, through the plug and straight into his anus.

His breath left his body in an explosion of shock, and the burning pain quickly followed. "Thank you, sir, that is one." He took a deep breath to prepare for the next blow, but the belt landed in a searing blaze across his skin and fuck, it *hurt*—"*Th*—Thank you, sir, that is two..."

Sydney surged forward, and his cock parted her beautifully-shaped mouth—that same mouth he had fantasised about since the first time he laid eyes on her—warm, wet, rough and silky. She sucked him expertly, greedily, painting his cock with her velvety tongue and soft lips. She teased him with her teeth, delicately scraping against the underside of the head, nibbling, opening the slit and fucking it with the tip of her tongue.

As Sydney took him down her throat, the belt striped a trail of white-washed agony across his flesh, driving the plug deeper inside him, tapping his prostate with each blow. The twin sensations of pleasure and pain overloaded his senses, trapping him between his beautiful tormentors as they punished him with the exquisite heat of her mouth, the burning sting of the belt and the violation of the plug.

By ten lashes, Elwess was on tiptoe, his eyes locked on Sydney, who watched him with wide-eyed lust. He babbled a number, no longer certain, and Dahlra laughed roughly. "I think you're enjoying my little kitten too much to pay attention."

He smacked the buttplug with the flat of his hand, and Elwess snarled. "Ow, fuck! That hurt!" Tears of pain sprang into his eyes. "God-dammit—"

"Of course it does. You knew it would; you've punished others enough to know." Did that hard, pitiless voice really belong to Dahlra Gar? "I'm hearing more defiance than true remorse. You accepted this, Elwess. Perhaps you're not taking this as seriously as you pretend?"

"I am, sir." Elwess moaned deliriously, blinded against the delicious assault of his cock, punctuated by the roaring counterpoint of his tortured arse. *Oh, fuck, it feels so good, don't stop.*

Perversely, Sydney drew back from him, leaving his cock to bob wildly on its own. She grasped his balls and pulled them firmly away from his body. "Who do you belong to, Elwess?"

"You. I belong to you." The words fell from his lips with no thought other than they were the absolute truth. "I belong to you both. I'm yours. Do anything you want. I don't care."

Dahlra's laughter sounded drenched with power. "Right answer. Now, we're going to start over." He leaned closer. "If you lose count again, that pretty mouth is going to stop sucking you. I don't think you want that, do you?"

The belt sang out, again and again until it felt like boiling water sluicing over his arse. His thighs were on fire, even as his cock was bathed in that sweet, wet, unrelenting heaven. Dahlra was panting with exertion, hitting him with dead-solid, ferocious accuracy.

Elwess was howling by fifteen, and by the time he reached twenty, he was floating somewhere outside himself, suspended in a strange delirium of exquisite suffering. Stripped of self-awareness, dignity and pride, he could not tell torture from tenderness, the belt that struck him or the mouth that sucked him. His only lucid thought was blanketed in the muffled triumph that he had obeyed, that he had been tested, that he had endured and been found equal to the task.

The blows stopped. It hardly mattered. He would have gladly taken twenty more, as long as it was *this* man beating him, *this* woman sucking him. He would not have cared if blood was running down his thighs; he would have died at that moment and thought it a fair trade. He knew he was nearly demented and his body was on the verge of collapse and he was thanking them, he was fucking *thanking* Dahlra for whipping him, thanking Sydney for the slick, pink tongue that rolled over the head of his cock until he was a raw, shuddering thing begging to come in her mouth.

Even as he tried to catch his breath, Sydney grew more urgent. She stroked his cock, taking him so deep he could feel the back of her throat as she swallowed him down. "Oh fuck, I'm so..."

Dahlra pressed close against his back. His body was hot, his breath warm and panting, his voice low and throbbing in his ear.

"You're so close, aren't you, Elwess? Aching and wanting to fuck that mouth hard enough to hurt." His gave a low, feral laugh. "I know. And I know how sweet she is." His mesmerising voice was demonically low. "Make him suffer, pet. Make him understand just what he has to lose."

She moaned rapturously around his cock, and bright sparks exploded behind Elwess' eyes. His chest felt stretched impossibly tight over his ribs. He could not catch his breath. "I'm going to pass out..."

Dahlra shook him, hard. "No, you're going to come. From now on, you belong to me. Your cock belongs to me. Say it!"

"I belong to you, Dahlra. My cock belongs—" Suddenly Dahlra grasped the plug and gave it a vicious, pushing, pumping twist that hit *something—*

Hot, liquid pleasure melted his entire pelvis like wax, rushing into his balls and swelling his cock to the point of bursting. His orgasm boiled through him like an atomic explosion. He rode it, and was ridden by it, controlled by the mouth fucking his cock and the plug fucking his arse. He jerked and juddered as agony and ecstasy fought for dominance, and he hunched forward, gripping Sydney's head while his cock sprayed into her waiting mouth with deep, shuddering, endless pulses.

Sydney gently released him, and his spent prick slipped from her mouth to cool in the damp air. Only Dahlra's iron grip around his waist prevented him from collapsing. He sank to his knees, and Dahlra followed him down, easing him onto the floor. He felt torn open, as if this screaming orgasm had flayed him alive in its violent haste to leave his body.

Elwess fell back against Dahlra's broad, steady chest, the only solid warmth in the spinning room. He gulped in air; spots danced in his vision and he shook his head to clear it. He tried to pull his brain back into his head, but it was gone. The wool of Dahlra's trousers rasped against the tender skin of his arse, and he hissed as the fabric scratched and abraded the angry welts.

As his mind slowly came back online, the blistering pain of his sensitive rectum pulsed around the plug with every heartbeat. He was sweating in spite of the temperature, but his teeth were chattering.

A large, warm hand stroked his damp hair. "It's alright." Dahlra's voice, so close to Elwess' ear, was as soft and palliative as cashmere. "It's done now. It's over."

"Is it? Are you leaving now?" He coughed, and coughed again, and when he found himself unable to stop he realised he was crying, great gasping sobs that made his throat feel as if it were bleeding.

Soft but strong arms encircled him, and drew him forward. "No one is going anywhere, Elwess." His name sounded beautiful in Sydney's mouth. "Why would we put you through this if we were planning to walk?" She kissed him, heedless of his tears and running nose and clammy skin. He looked back at Dahlra, and saw affection and care in his eyes.

Together they helped him to his feet and led him to the sofa. They wrapped him in a bathrobe, and Dahlra made him blow his nose and dry his eyes. Elwess curled up against Sydney, burying his face against her warm neck. She put her arms around him and held him as Dahlra cleaned the embedded grit from his knees and warmed his bare feet.

As they fussed and petted and soothed him, Elwess realised they were not leaving. If anything, they were staying close, enveloping him between them. He shifted, and the plug made him wince. "And you call *me* a kinky fucker."

They both laughed. "Now you're starting to sound like the Elwess we know and love," said Dahlra.

The Elwess we know and love. They gave him almost identical indulgent smiles. Dahlra gently stroked the soft column of Sydney's neck, and she glanced up at him with proud, passionate love. In that moment, Elwess knew he was part of them; not the part they saved for one another, but something that fit, and made sense.

He leaned forward and captured Sydney's mouth with his. He could taste himself on her lips. "I love you." The words were rusty from lack of use, but they felt right in his mouth.

He lay against her breast, pushing the corset seams aside, finding a red nipple and nuzzling his lips against it. When it drew up hard and tight, he closed his mouth around it, aching for her succor as much as her sensuality. He felt her breath hitch, and his tongue flickered against the areola, needing to pleasure her as well, and she made a soft sound of delight as Dahlra's fingers parted the opposite cup, and his mouth found that nipple hard and ready for him.

For a long moment they sucked and licked and teased her succulent tits until she was writhing. Elwess slipped his hand between her thighs, brushing his palm against the soft leather thong, and found it hot and damp. He pushed it aside and felt the slippery flesh glide against his fingers. She whimpered his name beseechingly. The gratitude that had flooded his heart in the mind-bending moments after the beating warped and twisted into molten, aching desire, and his cock had never recovered so quickly on the heels of such an intense orgasm.

Together he and Dahlra undressed Sydney. They quickly extricated her from the corset, soothing her tender flesh where the leather had begun to chafe. Next they removed the boots, peeling them down her calves with eager, anticipatory pleasure. Elwess kissed her deeply, reveling in her taste and her impatient desire. Her eyes fluttered open and met his. "Stop playing around. You've had your fun; it's our turn."

He laughed. "Fun? Your fiancé might have something to say about that. My arse would, in any case."

"Don't sulk." Her lips curved into a wicked smile that begged to be wiped off her face with a hard fucking. "It looked fun from my vantage point."

"Then I suggest you to go the bed, and present that gorgeous arse for *my* pleasure. I've always liked the idea of giving you a good spanking."

He unbuckled the tiny thong and tossed it aside. Drawing her into his arms, he cupped the soft globes of her bottom, and pulled her snugly against his groin. "You're so beautiful. Especially on your knees."

Dahlra pressed up close behind Sydney, looking every smug inch The Daddy. He fondled one erect, cherry nipple, flicking and teasing it until she squirmed. As his hand slid downward to cup her mound, he purred playfully into her ear, "Well, what do you think, kitten? Has Elwess earned our forgiveness?" He looked directly into Elwess' eyes. "Does my little girl want to fuck him?"

Sydney's expression went from relaxed to very alert. It reminded Elwess of their conversation about dark needing dark. "If you're done with him, love, then yeah." She licked her lips. "I wanna fuck him."

Dahlra laughed softly. "Greedy girl. You'll wear him out."

Elwess felt his lips curl into a sneer. "She can try. Get on the bed." He nodded toward the bedroom, and in a voice he barely recognised, he added, "On second thought, I don't want you on your knees. Get on your back. And spread those legs nice and wide, kitten. I want to taste some of that honey."

Dahlra gave Sydney a smile of rich anticipation. "I wouldn't mind some of that myself." He gave her arse a gentle, fond pat. "Go on, my love. Get in bed, all tucked in and ready to play." He gazed at her for a beat, in that uncanny, silent communion they often shared. His expression softened, and he whispered, "We'll be there in a moment."

Together, they watched her walk into the dimly-lit alcove, her lithe body moving with grace and confidence.

As Elwess made to follow her, Dahlra suddenly caught his arm in a tight grip, locking it behind his back. Elwess tried to turn to face his friend, but Dahlra did not budge. "What the—"

"Tell me something, Elwess." The dark voice whispered close to his ear. "Do you remember the day we met?"

"What are you talking about—"

"Keep your voice down! I asked you a question: do you remember?"

"You know I do."

"Do you know what *I* remember most? You laughed at me, and called me a fool." Dahlra's voice had a growling, dangerous undertone. He tightened his grip, nearly propelling Elwess up on tiptoe.

"I was wrong. You proved me wrong over and over—"

"Do you remember telling me the first rule of Dominance?"

Well and truly baffled, Elwess tried to break Dahlra's grip, but it was like trying to shift a concrete pillar. "Dahlra, what are you talking about?"

"Oh, come on. Surely you recall *that*. You've said it to me enough times." His free hand stroked Elwess' hip with warm, languid possessiveness. "You have it tattooed right here. Tell me what it says."

Elwess answered hesitantly. "'Desire shall not preclude Dominance'."

Dahlra's fingers were shockingly intimate against his sensitive skin. "I watched as you made every sub recite that on their knees, right before they sucked your cock. To remind them that you would never want any woman as much as you wanted to Dominate her.

"You said a true Master would never put a woman like Sydney above his own Dominance. You said it was my biggest failing, and my greatest weakness." His breath was hot and intense against Elwess' neck. "But I'm not the only one guilty of that, am I?"

The hand slid past his hip, and Elwess grunted in surprise as it curled tightly around his cock. Dahlra gave him a deep, seductive stroke, and Elwess' knees trembled. "The moment you called me yesterday to confess that little stunt you pulled with Sydney, I knew it was all a lie. Because all that 'Dominance before desire' shite is bollocks where she's concerned. You didn't give a damn about Dominance or submission; you just wanted her badly enough to try and seduce her behind my back. That's why you recorded us. If Silas hadn't rumbled you, you would have never told me about it."

Elwess shook his head, but they both recognised it for the pitiful denial it was. Dahlra had opened him up, dispassionately ripping the gauze off the lens and baring his soul to the light, and he had to face its blinding reality.

"The first night I brought her here to play, I didn't worry, because sex was just sex to you. You were just another toy I could let her use.

But the moment you met her, your most sacrosanct rule went out the window, didn't it? Do you think I would have brought her here if I had known?"

The hand on his cock was hot and skilled, and began to stroke him hard. It felt like another punishment. He leaned back into Dahlra's arms, wanting to surrender, wanting... "It's not just—"

"Oh, I don't blame you. I don't blame you at all. I *know* her. She's beautiful and strong and powerful. She melts around you and your prick fits inside her like a stone in a cherry."

Elwess curled his hips against Dahlra's insistent, sure hand, moaning helplessly. "Dahlra, please, I—" The stroking stopped, and he nearly collapsed in frustration. "What do you want?" Anger and lust warred for centre stage. "If this is some kind of mind-fucking shit—"

"That's your department, not mine." Dahlra's voice was like ice. "This is just a reminder, Elwess Talbert: she was mine first. You were the one who changed the rules. So we're playing my game now, my rules. You accepted those T's and C's the minute you let me shove this plug up your arse and beat you to orgasm. Tonight happened because I allowed it, not because you manipulated it."

Elwess made one last half-hearted attempt to break Dahlra's hold, but too much of him wanted Dahlra to take over, to accept and control him again. "Then why are you letting me anywhere near her now?"

"Because this is mine to give, not yours to take. But if you ever try to come between us again, there won't be a next time. You're forgiven, Elwess. But this is not forgotten."

Dahlra relaxed suddenly, and his hand slid from Elwess' cock. "Are we clear on this?"

Elwess felt repentance, like a chastity belt, zapping his libido down to zero. "Crystal."

Dahlra released his rock-hard grip at last, and in his mind's eye Elwess could *see* him fastidiously tucking in his shirt, trying to claw back some kind of dignity. He turned around. Dahlra was watching him closely, his entire body tense, as if he expected a fight. In that exact moment, Elwess could not say he was not prepared to give him one.

Finally, Dahlra's posture relaxed, and his countenance was calm and open again. "Alright. I've said what I've said. I won't spoil her evening by repeating it." He held out his hand, and met Elwess' eyes with that clear, earnest gaze of his. "Still mates?"

He sounded more vulnerable than he had a right to be, and Elwess felt a huge gulf of conflict. There were so many things he needed to say and do, and none of them on their own would ease Dahlra's mind. Somehow, he had to convince Dahlra that he wanted the same thing from them—that one day they might *want* him more than they wanted to *fuck* him.

He took Dahlra's hand. "We'll always be mates, Dahlra. Always. But you *are* wrong about one thing. It's not just about wanting *her*." Still holding his hand, he yanked Dahlra into his arms and kissed him. It was a hard, violent kiss, tinged with angry passion, and their teeth and lips crashed together with such clumsy force he tasted blood. Dahlra grabbed his wrists and tried to push him away. Elwess stubbornly refused to release him.

Dahlra's mouth was tight against his own, but his lips were as warm and soft as Sydney's. Elwess' heart thundered in his chest, and his cock pushed against Dahlra's crotch; instead of shaming him, it excited him. Dahlra was shaking, as if straining to break free, but Elwess held on, plundering him with every skill he possessed, stroking his warm face until he forced Dahlra to relent. Only then did Elwess' lips gentle against his, and they shared a true kiss.

He eased back, releasing Dahlra's mouth, smirking at his flushed face, his startled eyes. He pulled Dahlra into an embrace that held no passion, only affection and respect, and he kissed him again, because his heart demanded it. That kiss held all the tenderness of an apology, and thankfully Dahlra's lips tentatively moved against his at last.

And to show that he meant business, Elwess ended the kiss by dropping to his knees, and pressing his lips against the tops of Dahlra's boots.

From above, he heard Dahlra's unwilling laugh. "Get up, you dozy prat. I'm not the sodding Pope."

That broke the tension, as he knew it would. Elwess rose to his feet, wincing again at that damned plug. "And I'm no choirboy, but I suspect that's no surprise, either."

Dahlra ran his hand through his ruffled hair, and this time he actually *did* tuck in his shirt. Dahlra was Dahlra again; all was right with the world.

Elwess took his arm. "Come with me. Sydney's waiting for us. Let me show you both what I'm prepared to do to win back your trust."

Dahlra had been correct: the first night he brought Sydney to the Chine, it had been all about the sex. When it came to the power of pleasure and how to wield it, Elwess was one of its masters, plying it with equal proficiency as both drug and whip. He had been only too happy to play his role in the three-way. It was one he had done many times with other Doms and their subs.

But something had changed for him that night. It had not been all Business As Usual. For one thing, Dahlra had been very strict with what Elwess could and could not do with Sydney. The unspoken message was that Dahlra was keeping the best for himself, leaving Elwess to speculate about what he had not shared.

Maybe that had been the trigger. Or perhaps it had been the recognition of Dahlra's long obsession, now made flesh. And maybe it was the flesh itself; those stunning, pitiless eyes, that irresistible mouth. The deep, humiliating scars, healed only with Dahlra's devotion and Sydney's stubbornness.

Did it matter?

Sydney was truly unlike any woman Elwess had ever known—intelligent, dangerous, strong and lethal, all tied up in a butter-soft, handsome package. And she was his now. Tonight, Elwess was going to make sure she never looked at a bed without wanting him in it.

He approached her like a meal about to be consumed, all piss and swagger, his cock stiff from Dahlra's clumsy but effective power play. Sydney was on the bed, her back against the headboard, her large, protean eyes burning with desire and arousal. Perhaps it was due to sucking him off as Dahlra beat him, or perhaps she had enjoyed watching her lover jacking him up. That it might be both excited Elwess all the more.

Pressing into her smooth body, he kissed her slowly, warming up to his subject. "Such a sweet, pretty little mouth," he whispered, savouring those baby-plump lips. "It looked so good with my cock in it." He dove in, tasting his spunk on her tongue, drinking down her scorching moan of desire. When he finally broke away from the kiss, she made a delicious little sound of disappointment that lit his head up with a million fantasies. He rocked back, ignoring his still-searing arse, and quickly pulled her into his lap, wrapping her thighs around his waist.

Elwess watched with approval as Dahlra settled into the comfortable armchair beside the bed. He leaned back, legs crossed, seemingly relaxed and casual, but there was no mistaking the hard glint of arousal in his eyes as he watched them. Elwess knew beyond a doubt that the good doctor was going to enjoy this.

He turned his attention back to the woman in his arms. "Now, kitten, I'm going to do whatever I want, and you're going to do whatever I say. I will require some quality feedback, so I want to hear every filthy sound I can drag out of you." He leaned forward, placing soft, butterfly kisses on the tips of her rock-hard nipples.

"Still, you might want to rehearse your safe word. You'll have plenty of chances to use it."

He had never spent so much time preparing a woman for pleasure; kindling a slow fire inside her, building it degree by degree, cataloguing each and every reaction. Though he pushed and pulled with expertise, her powers of discipline were equally formidable. Each time he eased back on the throttle, her body responded, instantly cooling the engine.

She whispered his name when he was gentle, and screamed it when he got rough— and oh, he got damn rough. He growled dirty promises and then performed them. He made her play with herself, and say filthy, nasty things to him ("*Please suck my little titties, Daddy... please lick my wet cunt... please finger my hole, Daddy...*").

He taught her everything there was to know about denial and favour, using the same stylish pedagogy that Joshua taught Jericho. And one by one, he found her negotiable limits and crashed through them, until the foundations of her self-control trembled, then crumbled beneath her.

It was thrillingly erotic, holding her back until she was in complete, abandoned submission. Fuck, what man would not feel powerful to have a woman like her in his arms, coming undone beneath him? Now she was at his mercy, and his own limits of patience and self-discipline were hanging by a thin, unraveling thread. As he basted his cock with the moisture welling from her sex, he teased, "Do you want me to fuck you, kitten?"

She looked feverish. "Elwess, do it—"

"Oh, I'm gonna do it." She arched her back in delirious anticipation. "But you have to ask me nicely. Say, 'fuck me, Daddy'."

As he spoke, her hand closed around his cock. She ran a finger under the foreskin, then eased her nail into the slit, tuning it up to a sizzling-sensitive pitch. Lust spiked in his blood like venom, burning him right up to the tip of his prick.

Those incredible eyes of hers met his, angry and defiant. "Make me."

In one swift movement, she threw him off balance and rolled him over onto his back. They grappled until they were wrestling on the bed. She was strong; he finally had to use his entire body weight to physically overpower her. As he pinned her arms over her head, he marveled, "You wicked little bitch. Just for that, I ought to leave you here to boil in your own juice."

There was wild elation in her eyes; her hair was a long tangle beneath her, and her lips were wet and as dark as her stained nipples. Her helplessness only served to ramp up her arousal. She laughed softly, and slid her long legs around his waist. "Fuck me, Daddy."

"Louder."

"Fuck me, Daddy," she repeated, her voice tight.

Power slid into his veins like the most delicious poison. His fingers slipped inside her, as teasing and tantalising as a kiss, and her eyes rolled back. "Does it make you feel like a bad girl, begging Daddy to fuck you like a bitch in heat?"

Her eyes met his, full of stark shame and lust and naked openness. "Yes."

Now that she ready for whatever he chose to give her, he would reward her. His mouth lowered to hers, teasing her with a slow flick of his tongue. "Good. Because I'm going to fuck the bad right out of you." He dipped his head to her ear, so only she would hear his words. "Come into the dark with me, Sydney."

He hooked her knees over his forearms and plunged straight into her.

She was *fuckinghell!* tight, and so hot and wet she melted around him. like she had been custom built for him. His breath left his body, and he had to close his eyes and fight against coming right then and there. "Jesus," he breathed. His Mr Bad Guy persona disappeared somewhere between his heart and the woman impaled on the other end of his cock, and he knew he would never truly be content anywhere else.

He fucked her, growling with each relentless thrust, her blistering heat incinerating him. He shifted until he hit that sweet spot inside, and she roared like a lioness, filling his head with crippling, fuel-injected pleasure. The tight sheath of her sex rippled around him, and he thrust and thrust and *thrust* in her, to the tune of his name searing from her throat, wanting to crawl inside her head and claim ownership, to mark her, *piss* on her if he had to. Anything to keep her, to make her as much a slave to him as he was to her...

Intense pleasure bloomed deep in his groin and raced down to the tip of his cock, drawing his balls up tight. His orgasm blasted out of his body, and he howled as he poured out his need and his relief into her. She greedily took it, clenching around him, sucking him dry, and it was so mind-shatteringly good he was already mourning it before it was actually over.

"Jesus H." He collapsed in exhaustion against her. "Jesus H. Christ on a sidecar."

It took several moments to catch his breath. With a final slow inhale, Elwess rose onto his knees and knelt between her thighs. Her sex, so small and neat, was bright red, glazed with his pearly seed, and her clitoris was hard and distended, pushed proud of its little succulent velvet bed. He ghosted his breath over the rigid bud, and her thighs trembled. Then he gave her a long, slow swipe with the flat of his tongue. She quivered and braided her fingers through his hair.

He tasted himself, mingled with her own juices, and she moaned and shuddered as he cleaned her, his tongue flickering over her hypersensitive flesh. He finally backed off and swiped the back of his hand across his sticky face. Tangled, oily hair fell in his eyes, but he was too tanked to push it aside. A bone-deep exhaustion washed over him, borne of adrenaline burn out, followed by a shitload of carbon dioxide being dumped back into his bloodstream. Christ, he had ejaculated his brains out.

Before he could settle, Dahlra was behind him, grasping the buttplug. "Bear down." He eased it out with slow, methodical care. Elwess winced during the eternity it took to scrape its way past his rim. Once freed, he collapsed back onto the bed; he even managed to roll to the side to keep from crushing Sydney beneath him. His body was drenched in sweat, his cock still twitching. He was surprised it was not steaming.

Sydney was sprawled on the bed like a crime victim. Her makeup was smeared, her hair a mad mess. She looked glutted and limp and sexy as sin. He gave her a lingering kiss of pure gratitude. "You look very pleased with yourself." She smiled lazily in reply. "Now, what would *you* like to do, kitten?"

She looked from him to Dahlra. "I want to get my fiancé naked."

Dahlra held out his arms invitingly. "All yours."

Elwess lay back on the far side of the bed, and watched as Sydney removed each article of Dahlra's clothing as if it were precious. Dahlra stood still, allowing her access to his body, his breathing slow and heavy, his gaze heated and intense. She reached up on tiptoe and kissed him, and he melted against her, pliant and submissive.

Dahlra took hold of her hand and drew her down to the bed with him. His breath stuttered from his chest as Sydney carefully lowered herself onto him. There was no resistance, only the slow drag of flesh against slippery flesh, and she trembled from head to toe as her body accepted his length and girth. His hips twisted and locked against hers, and they moaned in unison as she settled all the way, taking him stem to root. She sighed, "So deep, I can almost taste it."

He laughed breathlessly. "And what does it taste like, love?"

She rocked a figure-eight on his crotch. "It tastes like this." She rose like Venus from the waves, until the head of his cock just kissed the entrance. Then she plunged back down with such force the bed shook, and even Elwess felt it in his stones. *God, what a woman.*

Dahlra let Sydney take him on a slow ride, her hips rising then dropping down on him like a warhammer. She leaned forward, bracing herself on his shoulders, and fucked him like everything up to that point had been Amateur Hour.

Dahlra's hands were everywhere; her breasts, her rolling, undulating belly, her long neck. He reached down between their joined bodies and Sydney made a low, growling noise in her throat. Incredibly Elwess felt his cock stir, as if called to life by this enticing siren.

Dahlra's strong thighs nearly lifted Sydney off the bed, and her gorgeous breasts swayed as she received her lover's powerful thrusts. He sat upright, dragging her into his arms, and he rocked her, whispering something low and urgent in her ear. She whimpered, completely abandoned, her eyes locked with his as if he held the answer to every mystery and the key to every door.

At that sweet moment, the orgasm rose up from her body and out of her mouth in a long, wrenching cry, head flung back, body shaking with pleasure. Dahlra rocked her through her climax, holding her tightly as she sobbed and trembled with each thrust. He slowed as she fell limply against him, quaking. "Are you alright?"

"I'm fine." She hiccoughed. Her face was glowing. "I'm so fine." She covered his face with quick, tiny kisses; they fell on his skin like rain, until she traveled down to his neck. Dahlra's eyes fluttered closed, and for a moment, his face tensed, as if the sensations were more than he could bear. Elwess had never seen such naked ecstasy on a man's face.

In one graceful movement, Dahlra rolled her over, covering her with his body, and began his urgent climb toward his own release. Their bodies moved in that perfect dance of desire and lust, faster, harder, until Dahlra's head kicked back and his expression dissolved into absolute abandon. Through his arcing, sublime orgasm, Sydney held him, supported him, whispered her words of love to him. Gazing into one another's eyes, they kissed, a long, soothing embrace of complete devotion and adoration.

When they both exhaled an endless, sated sigh at the same time, Elwess laughed. "Harold and Hilda. I'll bet you two fart in harmony."

Sydney turned and feigned surprise. "Oh, look honey, Elwess is here."

"I thought I heard heavy breathing." Dahlra absently stroked his lover's back, his blissful smile slightly out of focus.

Elwess scoffed. "I'm surprised you two even noticed."

Sydney made a little moue of sympathy and reached for his hand. "Poor baby. Feeling left out?"

Perhaps it was the wistfulness in her voice that sealed the deal. Perhaps it was just that he was in love. In any case, he found he did not have to lie.

He brought her hand to his lips, and looked straight into Dahlra's eyes. "Not at all."

Sydney twitched in her sleep, jostling Elwess awake. He rolled onto his back, grimacing as his arse made contact with the mattress. With a sigh, he rose and padded to the toilet for a much-needed piss. From his aching hand to his bruised arse, he felt as battered as a cod, and he knew it would get worse before it got better.

He ran several large flannels beneath the hot tap, and returned to the bed. Sydney and Dahlra were fast asleep. He gently rolled Sydney onto her back and parted her thighs, cleansing her, then drying her with a soft towel. When he had finished to his satisfaction, he glanced over at Dahlra, who was regarding him with sleepy, solemn eyes.

"Alright, Elwess?"

"Yeah. Yes, sir. Sore, but good."

"I'm sure. Take it easy for a few days."

"I don't have a choice. I'm not as young as I used to be. Takes longer to recover from this sort of thing now." Elwess placed the remaining flannel in Dahlra's outstretched hand. "All yours, mate."

Dahlra regarded the cloth, then looked back at him. "Are you talking about this, or you?"

It took the space of a heartbeat for Elwess to answer. "Both. On your terms."

"You accept them?"

"I do. Willingly."

"Then so do I." Dahlra yawned as he swiped perfunctorily in the general vicinity of his genitals, then dropped the flannel to the floor. "Back in bed then. Get some sleep."

Elwess climbed beneath the warm sheets and urged Sydney back into her Minder's arms. He spooned against her and put his arm around them both. Dahlra gave Elwess' hand a reassuring squeeze, then pulled Sydney into his arms. "Goodnight, Elwess."

Sydney twitched again, and made a soft sound of distress. Elwess gentled her, and when she did not stir again, he felt absurdly pleased with himself. He fell asleep, already looking forward to waking them up in the morning.

"I'm disappointed in you, Silas. It's not like you to make such an embarrassing scene in public. Had you been drinking?"

Silas forced himself to take slow, deep breaths. He had not been home from the A&E ten minutes when he got the call. How did the gruesome son of a bitch find out so quickly?

"So what if I was?" He snatched an ice bag from his slave's trembling hand. "Get me a towel to wrap this in, you idiot!" Silas rewarded the sorry piece of shit with the back of his hand. Breathing hard, he turned back to his phone. "It's a free country. I have the right to go to a dive like The Library and have a drink if I want. Nothing gives *him* the right to do this!"

"Life is unfair." There was the unmistakable sound of tutting. "I can imagine the entire sordid little scene was quite distressing."

"The bastard broke my nose, and two of my ribs! *And* he cut my face. I'm going to have a scar!" He hated the clogged, nasal whine in his voice, but it could not be helped. The A&E doctor told him the swelling would go down in a couple of days.

"Oh, I shouldn't fret over that, if I were you." Silas could hear the laughter in Lorcan's voice. "Perhaps it will make you look windswept and interesting."

"I don't want to look windswept. I want to cut Talbert's balls off and stuff them down Dahlra Gar's throat while that bitch of his watches. I want to slit her throat while I fuck Gar up the arse with a hunting knife! I want—"

"Silas, enough. I'm not Father Christmas. Your wants don't concern me. A true Master takes what he wants."

"I thought that's what you were there for."

"If it's vengeance you seek, do it on your own time. Whatever happens to the agent and her Minder is judiciously deserved. You can slit both their throats for all I care." There was a slight hesitation. "But you don't touch Talbert."

For a moment, Silas thought he would burst a blood vessel. "This is between him and me, and if I want—"

"If you want to remain under this organisation's protection, you will do as I say. Or else you may find your own cock and balls nestled in some unsuitable repository. Do you understand?"

Silas swallowed, and some of his anger bled into fear. "Yes."

"Yes?"

"Yes, sir."

"Good. Very good." Lorcan's tone grew genial. "Now, I want you to put this unpleasantness behind you. You have other matters to attend. And in the meantime, perhaps I can provide an enjoyable distraction from London and this little episode."

His voice darkened. "I think I may have just what you're looking for."

CHAPTER SIX

Clod and Pebble

They spent the following week in London, where they learned just what a force of nature Elwess Talbert could be when fully engaged. As Sydney had predicted, Dahlra loved the drawing hanging over the mantle, so Elwess promptly gave it to him. But like his other gifts, it came with a price.

He sketched the couple at strange and random times. If they were asleep, he usually ended up waking them, or joining them; if they were cooking, he might toy with Sydney while she was wrist-deep in the soufflé. He had a way of luring them into bed and keeping them there until they were nothing but dry husks under the duvet, all while making it seem like it had been their idea in the first place. He orchestrated sessions with other subs in the Chine and magnanimously (and somewhat hypocritically, given his past transgression) encouraged them to watch on the CCTVs.

"The problem with Elwess," Dahlra explained one evening, as he brushed the knots from Sydney's hopelessly bed-tangled hair, "is that he assumes everyone is as highly sexed as himself."

"Highly sexed?" She scoffed. "Rabbits on Viagra have lazier libidos."

To Elwess, sex was both cure and disease, both weapon and entertainment. Good news should be celebrated with it, bad news softened by it. He was a practitioner of this obscene gospel, a charismatic High Priest of the profane. At times, he treated Dahlra like a brother, as they slobbed around watching Match of the Day. Other times, he treated him like a lover, as together they conspired to rearrange Sydney's head with mind-scrambling sex.

The way in which the two men approached this could not have been more different. Making love to Dahlra was the ultimate fantasy of being mastered and adored inch by inch in the arms of a handsome, skilled lover. He was the gentle master; the trademark of his power the sweet contrast of her naked flesh against his long, black coat, the whisper of his stunning voice a purr in her ear. There was a touch of freshness, of newness about him reserved especially for her; she would never be one of hundreds whose conquests were notched on his bedpost. He was not about breaking the sound barrier just to impress her with fancy tricks, and he did not make her feel like she was being graded on her performance, either.

If Dahlra was Debussy, then Elwess was Bach's *Toccata and Fugue in D Minor*, all drama and fire, tension and complexity, exhilarating and exhaustive in his endless variations. And yet, the more time they spent with him, taking him out of himself, watching him let his guard down, Sydney could see his controlled exterior dissolve, revealing an intense yet vulnerable man underneath. That brand of openness was kryptonite to most women, and Sydney was no exception. Getting him there was like pushing a massive stone up a steep hill, only to have it roll back down just as she got to the top. Thrilling, but exhausting.

As the week progressed, sex between the three of them became a form of mental as well as physical therapy. Elwess ruthlessly delved into her head and her knickers with the same single-minded concentration, and his discussions with Dahlra often ended with cathartic sessions bordering on Freudian. He taught Sydney new respect for the cane, the flogger, and her fiancé's right hand. He also taught her to appreciate the beauty of Dahlra's strong, pale wrists tied to a headboard with red silk scarves.

At times, he was edgy and manipulative. He could also be charming and selfish, and a cunning little tick. He left her so knackered and over-stimulated she could only growl and curl up into a ball, leaving Dahlra to back him down like a lion tamer. He quickly uncovered Sydney's prideful reluctance to use her safe word, and gleefully danced her right up to that ragged precipice as much as possible, just to see how long she would allow him to dangle her over. They dubbed him The Edge, and joked that the words "Not Yet" would be carved on his gravestone. Anticipation was his favourite form of foreplay.

The end of their visit was both a relief and a burden. While Dahlra packed the car, Elwess slouched against the doorway of their bedroom, shoulders low, hands stuffed in his pockets. In silence, he watched as Sydney folded and packed her few remaining items. "This place will feel like a tomb without you here."

"Heavens, melodrama much?" She pushed the bedclothes aside, then gave a relieved huff. "Oh, here it is. We turned the room upside down looking for this." Sydney carelessly stuffed Dahlra's shaving kit in her bag.

She turned her attention back to the problem at hand. "You don't fool me, Elwess Talbert. You'll be up to your nipple clamps in beautiful subs before the weekend's out."

"I'm serious."

Sydney caught the edge of fear in his voice. She stroked his arm entreatingly. "Hey, kiddo, it's not like you'll never see us again. You know Maidenvine is always your home. Come and stay for as long as it takes to grow sick of the sight of us. Hell, I'm surprised you're not throwing us out—"

"Stop talking rubbish, Sydney. Don't you get it?" He impatiently pushed off from the door jamb. "Oh, fuck it. Don't mind me. I'll be fine. Just got used to you being here, that's all." He smiled, but it was a poor substitute for the real thing. "Now, go on, bugger off. I have stuff to do before tonight."

Sydney zipped her case and turned to hug him, but he sharply pulled her into his arms, nearly robbing her of breath. His morning stubble was rough against her cheek. "Don't make the mistake of thinking I'm done with you."

His grip lessened, and suddenly he was caressing her instead of holding her. "And I know you feel the same, in that little part of you that doesn't belong to him. You can lock yourselves away up in Windsor and shut the world out all you want. But remember: when you're in London, when you're in this flat, you belong to me. Both of you."

He released her slowly, and favoured her with a smile as wicked and crooked as he was. "You may not believe it, kitten, but you're gonna miss me."

Before she could reply, Dahlra returned to the room. Elwess gave him a brotherly hug, then kissed Sydney goodbye. He even asked permission first.

On the drive home they spoke of little else but the previous week. "I don't know if I'm happy or sorry the week's over, but I am glad to be going home. I feel like I need a long bath."

Dahlra smiled and kissed her hand. "I'm glad to have you all to myself again."

There was a light feeling in her chest, as if she had been holding her breath and could let it go at last. "You know I love you, don't you? I mean, really, seriously love you?"

He kept his eyes on the road, and laid her hand on his thigh. "Oh, yes." As her fingers drifted toward his crotch, he smirked. "I've had a thought. You know that large armchair in the bedroom? Well, I think if you sat on my lap, your thighs would fit very comfortably over each arm..."

They had barely shut the massive front door behind them before they were tearing at one another's clothing. Dahlra pressed her against the door, kicking her feet apart with a combination of Dominant badass and uncontrollable urgency that had her knickers soaked in seconds. He dragged his nails over her ribs. "Shake a little for me, baby."

She moaned, grinding shamelessly against him. "Good girl." His first thrust drove her against the door so hard she saw stars. Their coupling was wild, dirty and completely decadent. He took her fast, pulling her back onto his hips, twisting and rolling her nipples in his skilled fingers. As he pistoned and panted and whispered his foul-mouthed promises in her ear, she was reduced to a moaning, shaking mess, rocking against him until she was... Oh fuck yes, she was gonna come—

She climaxed twice before he arched his back and growled his orgasm into the room. When it was over and their heads cleared, they lounged on the floor, their cooling bodies tangled and limp. She snuggled close. "I think you've just taken the concept of 'homecoming' to a whole new level."

He rewarded her with a closed-eyed, beatific smile. Sydney sighed contentedly. "Now, what's this about that armchair upstairs?"

That night, lying in their massive bed, the flames of the fireplace providing the ambient soundtrack to Dahlra's aftercare, their conversation inevitably returned to the enigma-stroke-hot-mess that was Elwess Talbert. "He and I are like that Blake poem, 'The Clod and The Pebble'." Dahlra stared pensively into the flickering flames. "I'll give you two guesses as to which is which."

"I can see where he might be the pebble, but I think it's unfair to call yourself a clod."

"Like it or not, I am the clod. And the clods of this world are soft and mushy, and the pebbles end up pulverising us." A glum timbre crept into his voice.

It was not in Dahlra's nature to brood; some reassurance was in order. "Clods cushion the blow and make life easier for others. They're fertile, and make things grow. They smell good. You can get dirty with them."

He seemed disinclined to be humoured. A powerful wave of protectiveness washed over Sydney. She rose onto her elbow and looked down at him. "Are you feeling insecure about Elwess? Because if he's done or said anything, or heaven forbid, *I've* done or said anything that made you—"

"Oh, no." He looked troubled, nonetheless. "But I allowed him to manipulate me. We set out to ensure his loyalty to us, but I'm not so sure that the exact opposite didn't happen." He sighed. "I suppose this week has made me realise just how ordinary I must seem, next to a man like Elwess."

"Is that what that little homecoming downstairs was about? Trying to prove you're not ordinary?"

"No. That was about being unable to keep my hands off my beautiful fiancée."

"Flattery is a good defense. Well played." A little pang of something took root in her heart. She was not sure if it was sadness, or regret, or guilt, but whatever it was, she was not going to sleep on it.

"Come on, budge up." She rolled him over, until they were face to face. "Let's get this straight Dahlra Gar: you are many, many things, but ordinary isn't one of them. You might be a clod, but you're *my* clod. And I don't want any other clod, or pebble, or twig or rock. Last week was fun, but it's not my fetish. *You* are."

"Last night while you were asleep, Elwess told me he wouldn't mind if we moved in."

"Elwess doesn't call the shots, no matter what he thinks. You belong to me, and *this* is our home, and I missed it. I missed being able to play the piano while you make dinner, and working out uninterrupted. Mainly I missed putting on some Marvin Gaye and chasing you around this room trying to get you naked. Without an audience." That made him laugh, and he looked shyly pleased.

Sydney idly ran her fingers over his taut brown nipple, and he hummed pleasurably. "Sure, Elwess is a lot of fun. And I honestly believe he cares for us as much as he's capable of caring for anyone. But I can't take him in massive doses."

"That's the problem. He only seems to come in one dosage."

They were silent for a long time. "One more thing. You have *never* fallen apart under pressure, Dahlra. If you had, I wouldn't be alive. You may have a tender heart, but you're nobody's pushover. Clod you may be, but if anyone tries to pulverise *you*, they're gonna find themselves at the business end of this very pissed-off rock crusher."

That seemed to restore his good humour at last, and as Sydney snuggled against him, she thought, *nobody messes with my land, especially not Elwess Talbert.*

During the next few months, the British adage, 'If you don't like the weather, wait five minutes,' seemed to be constantly in effect. They had incessant rain, then snow kept them housebound for several days. The daffodils bloomed early, only to be wiped out by an ice storm. A week went by without rain, and the council declared a hosepipe ban. Then a torrential thunderstorm blew in, knocking out the power and sending them into darkness. "Four seasons in one hour," quipped Dahlra, as they struggled to fire up the house's obstinate generator.

Elwess took up their offer and spent several weekends with them throughout the unpredictable and capricious spring, but gardening and great sex notwithstanding, country life simply did not appeal to him. He missed the relentless rhythm of the city pounding beneath his feet. Dahlra was British, but Elwess was London.

He was too polite to come right out and admit he was bored, but each time he left, he did not look all that sad to go. "When are you coming back to the city?" he demanded, as he threw his bag into the car.

"July. I'll be starting light duties again, on an *ad hoc* basis. I've got to get my brain back in shape. God knows I haven't been using it for much besides sex lately."

"You make that sound like a bad thing. Make that Daddy of yours bring you back to the land of sin sooner than that." His black, salacious eyes raked over her body like a pirate's in a penny dreadful. "You're getting as lazy as a cat in the sun, fannying about up here in the country."

She laughed, in spite of wanting to tell him to stick it. He was right. After two years of garden leave, she *was* lazy. She had always prided herself on staying in top physical condition, thanks to good genes and a better than average metabolism, but mentally she had grown indolent.

And while Dahlra was the very model of a good Minder, it concerned Sydney that she had grown too complacent with him taking care of everything. The best way to swing the pendulum back into place was to return to work, but every time she tried to broach the subject of getting back in the saddle, he smoothly changed the subject.

Sydney knew him enough by now to let him; she was in no hurry to put any undue pressure on him. She thought some team training might allay his apprehension; one of the Minder's roles was to provide field support, after all. Perhaps that would be the final convincer that a field agent's assignments were typically two percent kick ass and ninety-eight percent paperwork.

Two months before Sydney's planned return to London, she received a text message from Garnet Pinkerton, and the decision was made for her.

"Something's up, Syd. Time to dust off your brain box and come back to work."

"Sydney. Good of you to come on such short notice, old thing." Inigo Lightoller escorted them into the conference room adjacent to his office. "Sorry to be so cryptic over the phone, but this is a discussion best held in person. Do sit down." He gestured toward the plushly upholstered chairs surrounding the table. No cheap plastic, arse-numbing seats in one of Lightoller's meeting rooms.

As Dahlra helped Sydney to her chair, the door swung open, and Garnet sauntered in, carrying a number of slim, black portfolios. His homely face lit up with pleasure when he spotted her, and he gave her a swift kiss on the cheek. "Glad you could make it, Syd. Good to see you, Doc." He clapped Dahlra on the shoulder good-naturedly. "Wish it were happier circumstances, of course, but..."

"What exactly *are* the circumstances, Pink?"

He passed around the portfolios. "We were contacted by Hampshire Constabulary day before yesterday. Female, discovered about ten miles off the coast of the Isle of Wight, in the Channel."

Sydney glanced at the cover: it was embossed with the words, '*Unidentified Female, 05/12/2018, English Channel, E.B. Morgan, Photog, Hampshire Constab.*' The portfolio contained a bound series of A4 photos. "A small pleasure craft alerted the Coast Guard, and the local Old Bill was contacted immediately. Normally Payne Shaw's Special Crimes Unit handles investigations of this sort, but he thought we ought to give it a look.

"She's still being identified. No matches in any of our missing person's files. She may be a vagrant or European; in either case it takes a bit longer to trace."

Sydney kept her expression neutral as she leafed through the photos. The girl appeared to be in her late twenties, and she had been horribly mutilated. Both legs were missing from mid-thigh down; her arms were gone from the elbows; all the limbs had been removed by what appeared to be a saw. Her hair had been removed in an Indian-style scalping; in places her skull showed whitely where skin had come away with the hair.

Inigo continued. "Forensics concluded her body hasn't been in the water very long. It was still partially frozen. We're waiting on the final test results of the autopsy, but they ought to be here within the hour."

"Poor girl." Dahlra's voice was suffused with compassion and horror. He was staring at the close up of the victim's pain-ravaged face. She looked like a broken doll, pale, bloodless and innocent. Her eyes were dull marbles, the lids stuck forever at half-mast, looking pleadingly at them from the camera's lens. Her death had marked the end of a terrible ordeal. "How long has she been dead?"

"It's a little hard to tell; the best guess is between two-and-a-half to three months."

Sydney studied the photos intently. "You know, I've got this feeling I've seen her somewhere before." She sifted through her memories in growing frustration. "What's worse is that I don't think it's been that long ago." She pointed to the strange markings all over the body. "What are these? They almost look like runes."

"They're some sort of tags, we think," replied Garnet. "They've been carved into the skin with what appears to be a craft knife."

"Yeah, I see what you mean. Do they match anything—"

"Was she still alive?" Dahlra interrupted. "Did the carvings and amputations happen before or after death?"

"Forensics indicate the wounds were inflicted before death. She eventually succumbed to shock and blood loss." Lightoller's aristocratic face was pinched with disgust. "These savages chopped her to pieces and let her die."

"Well hell." Sydney felt bile rising in her throat. She met Dahlra's eyes, and his bleak expression of pity changed to concern. He rested his hand on her shoulder, his touch warm and bracing.

"Alright, Sydney?" he asked quietly.

"Yeah." She was not in the habit of flashing back to the Cell, but this was about as close as she ever wanted to be. She tried to turn her mind off, but the sick, twisting feeling kept coming back. Those last moments in the Cell, rushing over her in a miasma of sensation and muscle memory...

They came in the early hours, four of them, and roughly yanked her out of bed they roped her hands and looped it over a hook hanging from the ceiling they were laughing as they stripped her and the first slash of the rod the first slash was like fire and they kept coming and it was like agony the pain the pain the last minutes of her life felt like hours and she knew she was going to die and she wanted it to be over and she wanted her mom and she wanted someone to rescue her and it hurt oh fuck it hurt please make it stop oh jesus somebody HELP ME—

"Sydney."

Dahlra quickly moved his chair next to hers and placed his arm around her, pulling her out of her mental bloodbath. She looked up into his haunted eyes and saw the same cramping fear that was roiling in *her* gut. She was not taking this little stroll down memory lane alone.

In the queasy silence, Inigo cleared his throat delicately. "Do you need to step out for a moment, old girl?"

"No, I'm fine." Her voice sounded terse to her own ears. Dahlra's grip on her loosened, but it was all she could do not to crawl into his lap and curl up into a ball until the world went away. Instead, she took a deep breath and let it go. "Really. Hell, I was lucky. Someone cared enough whether I lived or died, which is more than I can say for this poor girl." She touched the photograph. "I'm alright. Well, not great, but good enough."

Dahlra searched her eyes, unconvinced. "I have to trust that you're telling me the truth."

She could not help but smile. It was quite reassuring to watch him move effortlessly from Minder to Dominant and back again. She nodded with as much confidence as she could fake, and returned to the portfolio. "Okay. Um, right. I was going to ask: do the tags match any known graffiti? Gangs? Tribal marks?"

"Still checking," Garnet replied.

"Why did Shaw bring this to you, Inigo? Did he know Silverbirch was back on?"

Lightoller looked cagey. "He called it a hunch." He pursed his lips, an indication he was about to launch into full Basil Exposition mode. "I suppose you've heard of Red Rooms?"

The air seemed to grow colder. With great deliberation, and because she did not *want* them to be real, Sydney answered, "I thought it was common knowledge that they couldn't exist. Tor is just too slow to stream live video in the Deep web, and there's no way somebody could get away with it on the surface."

Lightoller shook his head. "That is the accepted wisdom. But Tor is simply a way to *browse* the Deep web. Sadly, the truth is that Red Rooms very much exist. They're difficult to set up, but if you have a sophisticated enough distribution mechanism, or your access is restricted and secure enough, you could stream anything you want live in either the Deep or surface web.

"They are very difficult to trace as well. You need a bit of technical savvy, good underground connections and a secure location. Equipment can be purchased anonymously, and a blind Bitcoin account can be set up in minutes. If you know how."

Dahlra looked confused. "I'm a little light on the lingo. What exactly *is* a Red Room?"

"It's a site where people can watch someone being tortured or murdered in real time. Members of the 'audience' participate by requesting certain acts or making suggestions. They exchange Bitcoins to enter the site and order up their requests like it's some ghastly menu."

"Dear God. Truly?"

Lightoller nodded, his expression glum. "There are some seriously twisted people out there, Dahlra. For instance, a Deep web site called *Cruel Onion* featured the sexualised torture and death of small animals in real time. It had a forum where requests were taken in exchange for Bitcoins. They had a very active client base."

"Had?"

"It might comfort you to know the owners of this site were arrested and are currently spending a very long time in prison.

"Payne Shaw was seconded to the Australian Federal Police when they broke the Peter Gerard Scully case with the Philippine National Force. Scully came to their attention when he uploaded a film called 'Daisy's Destruction' on his own website, *No Limits Fun*. He's currently on trial for child pornography, along with the kidnapping, human trafficking, rape, and murder of a 12-year-old girl whose remains were discovered at one of his former residences."

"Was she the 'Daisy' in 'Daisy's Destruction?" asked Dahlra.

"I'm not sure. I haven't seen it. But Payne said it was so abominable the Filipino government are actually considering reinstating the death penalty just for Scully's benefit."

Sydney was still skeptical. "So you think this *No Limits Fun* could be a Red Room? I don't know, Inigo. I mean, it's one thing to upload a snuff film or a vendetta killing; it's another thing entirely to turn it into a full-fledged business."

Garnet replied, "Yeah, but Silverbirch is tailor-made to organise a Red Room operation, innit?"

For a long time, no one spoke. Yeah, this was exactly the kind of thing Silverbirch had the proclivities and the resources to bankroll. With the right balance of supply and demand and price-point that such a site would require, it could become a right little moneyspinner. Everyone knew the minute technology went mainstream people exploited it for every vice known to man. The anonymity of the internet made it a perfect vehicle for this brand of exploitation.

Sydney turned her attention back to the photo, willing herself to detach her thoughts from what Silverbirch *might* have done before a live studio audience. Better to focus on the evidence before her and leave Lightoller and Shaw to chase the shadows.

Still, if this *had* been viewed live, if some sick fucker was depraved enough to pay to watch this from the safety of their laptop... if it was *that* easy...

"The missing limbs look like part of some sort of honour or ritual killing. Perhaps the symbols are as well. They must mean something."

Dahlra pointed at a mark near the body's right hip. "Do you think we could acquire a really good close up of this? Maybe check if there are any other prints that give us a clearer view of the image?"

"Garnet, see what Hampshire Constabulary can do for us," Lightoller replied. Pink nodded and slipped from the room.

Sydney frowned. "If you're right, and Silverbirch is involved, someone has made a horrible mistake in allowing this body to be found. First, the human hunts, now this Red Room business. I mean, drugs and trafficking aren't exactly noble pursuits, but..."

Inigo made a conciliatory gesture. "Well, as you know, last year Silverbirch acquired a new man at the helm. It wasn't a promotion of any of the foot soldiers. Perhaps one of the old guard was jealous of this New Broom. Maybe someone had an attack of conscience."

Or someone wanted us to find her and draw a bunch of incorrect conclusions. Sydney gestured toward the photos. "So you're thinking she was kept like some kind of trophy, then they decided to do a little housekeeping?"

"It's a distinct possibility." While Inigo spoke, Pink returned with a manila folder. He passed around a fresh set of prints.

"The autopsy report just arrived as well. I brought it with me."

Inigo took the second folder and quickly skimmed over the documents. "Unsurprisingly, she was sexually assaulted. And most of her teeth are missing; this also happened before death."

"Jesus," Garnet cursed. "Those sadistic bastards."

"There were blood crystals in the inner core of the brain as well as a few of the smaller organs, which confirm the body was stored below freezing before it was disposed of. Blood tests found large traces of several chemical compounds, including alcohol, heroin, cocaine, Dimethyltryptamine, THC, LSD, Rohypnol, Oparim—"

"Oparim?"

"It's a very short-acting benzodiazepine," answered Dahlra.

Garnet frowned. "And what's that when it's at home with its feet up?"

"They're normally used to treat anxiety, panic disorders, insomnia, etcetera. Valium is probably the most well-known. Oparim is popular in the kinkster community. In small doses it's used to reduce anxiety or lower inhibitions. In moderate doses it can induce feelings of euphoria, or enhance sexual pleasure. Since their credo is safe, sane and consensual, it's the drug of choice, because it doesn't cause loss of control or memory."

"I take it there's a cloud in this silver lining."

"In large doses, it has been known to cause depression, unconsciousness, and memory loss."

"So we're really just talking about another type of Rohypnol?"

"Well, Rohypnol is another type of benzodiazepine. But Oparim's nowhere near as strong. Rohypnol's effects are approximately ten times stronger than Valium, which is about that much stronger again than Oparim."

"But could it be used as a date rape drug?" Inigo interjected.

Dahlra shrugged. "I have heard it's sometimes cut with THC or Viagra or even heroin and injected or inserted anally. That's when it gets dangerous. Benzodiazepines become habit-forming when taken in high doses, over a long period of time. The dimethyltryptamine is an extremely powerful hallucinogenic as well. Judging from the cocktail of drugs found in her system, I'd venture she had been with them quite a while before they started cutting her to pieces. She may have even been unconscious, but that would have taken away from their sport, wouldn't it?"

"If this did take place in a Red Room, they could have had quite an audience. A lot of money would have changed hands to watch this." Pink pointed at the severed limbs. "This isn't an impulse attack; this was an execution. Look at the amputations. This was no hack and slash job. Someone knew what they were doing and they took their time. Really played it up for the cameras."

He grimaced; yeah, they all were thinking the same thing. *What kind of sick, twisted animals had eagerly watched this poor girl as she was slowly, methodically mutilated to death?*

And what would they demand to see the next time?

Almost to himself, Garnet mused, "But why would they keep the body hidden that long, then dump it where it could be easily discovered? My guess is that whoever was in charge of disposing of the body seriously screwed up. Makes no sense otherwise."

There was a lot of this that made *too much* sense to Sydney. "So, do we think she was deliberately left to be discovered like some grisly Easter egg, or has Silverbirch given us our first real break?"

"That's the sixty-four thousand pound question," Inigo replied, closing his portfolio.

Sydney barely heard him; she was focusing on the close-up of the girl's right hip.

"Does this look like a tat to you?" She passed the photo over to Pink. He leaned in for a better view, eyes narrowed in focus.

"It looks like it might be, but it's been defaced. See how the edges have separated?" The tattoo had been crossed out with a huge, nullifying 'X' carved into the skin. The compass underneath, however, was unmistakable, and although she could not make out the words that curled around it, Sydney knew what they said.

"Shit." Sydney pushed the photo toward Dahlra. "This is bad. I mean really, really bad."

Desire shall not preclude Dominance. How many times had she looked at this same tattoo on Elwess' hip, stroked it, ran her tongue over it?

Dahlra looked uneasy as understanding dawned. "Damn." He circled the image with his pen. "Elwess Talbert has a tattoo exactly like this one. In the same place on his body."

"Lots of people have tattoos." Sydney's mind clicked into a higher gear. "Logically it follows that an admirer of his might have one done in tribute to him. I mean, at The Library, I saw dozens of beautiful women with all manner of marks and symbols inked on their bodies..."

An image parked itself onto her frontal lobe—a pretty, petulant face, bathed in changing colours of blue, red and green. *Have we met before? Mind your manners!*

She looked at the close up of the dead girl's face, then into Inigo's hooded eyes. "I know who she is."

When his mobile rang, Elwess smiled as Sydney's number flashed on the screen. "Hello, kitten. To what do I owe the pleasure?"

"Hiya, Elwess, I hope I'm not disturbing you, but I have a quick question."

Something in her bright, impersonal tone pinged his antennae, and his internal alert system jumped to amber. "Sure, go ahead."

"Valentine's Day, at The Library. The coat check girl. She got a little shirty with me, and you dressed her down. Remember?"

"Yeah. Well, sort of." When it came to some women, he was an out of sight, out of mind type of bloke.

"I seem to remember you calling her something that sounded like Coffee-"

"Ah, that would be Kofry. Kofryna Urbonienė."

Sydney laughed. "I'm afraid you'll have to spell that one for me. What is that, Latvian?"

"Lithuanian, I think. I'll have to look it up. I can never remember where the accent marks go." He sighed. "What has she done now?"

"What do you mean?"

"Well, there has to be *some* reason you're asking after her."

"I just assumed you knew her. You know, from the way you spoke to her that night."

"I know her, but I don't really associate with her, if that's what you mean."

"Would you have a number for her?"

"Probably, but I can't guarantee it's current. Hang on."

He swiped through his long list of contacts until he reached the U's. "Oh-seven-nine-seven-five, three-oh-one, treble five."

"...oh-one treble-five. Got it. Thanks."

"No worries," he replied. "Look, can you at least edge me into a category?"

"It's nothing to concern yourself over."

"Usually when someone says that, it's definitely something to concern yourself over."

"It's all good. Thanks, Elwess."

Elwess stared at the mobile, and his alert status graduated from amber to red. The voice on the other end had sounded like an agent, not a lover.

After a moment, he speed-dialed a number.

Thirty minutes later, Sydney's phone buzzed and vibrated on the table. She engaged the phone's speaker. "Hey, Stu."

"Syd, baby!" Stu Palermo, the Agency's Coms guru, had addressed her with the same Kojak-style greeting for the past eight years. His voice was deep and raspy, pure Godfather-style Brooklynese. "That number: 07975 301555. It was registered on a Virgin Pay-As-You-Go Sim card. Activated Twenty-four August, 2016. No contract, so no name or address associated with it."

"You said 'was'?"

"Yeah. It lapsed on Thirty-one March of this year and was deactivated. You want I should find out when they re-assign old numbers to new cards?"

"Hold off for now, Stu. Thanks for the help."

"Anytime, kid. Hey, Margot and I would love to see ya sometime. Give us a call and you two come over for dinner. All the homemade cannoli you can eat."

"Will do. See ya, Stu." Sydney ended the call, and almost immediately her mobile rang again. She kept it on speaker phone.

"Hello, Elwess."

His voice sounded scratchy and strained, like the signal of a transistor radio. "I'm assuming by now you know that number I gave you is no good."

"Yeah, I tried it."

"Me too. I thought I'd give her a call and try and talk to her."

She glanced at Dahlra. "Why?"

"Well, at times Kofry can be a little uncooperative, I guess you might say. As you saw, she can be very territorial around other women. I wanted to make sure she didn't forget her manners when you spoke to her." Before Sydney could reply, he continued, "When the number didn't work, I called The Library. I was hoping there was a chance I might catch her there."

"Good idea. Any luck?"

"Well, it's all a bit strange, actually. According to the manager, Kofry quit in mid-February and moved out of the area. No one has heard from her since. They had the same mobile number for her that I do."

Either Elwess was a good actor, or he was as clueless as he sounded. In either case, the phone was not the best place to play True Confessions.

"Did she resign or just walk?"

"She left a text message saying she'd got a better offer in Wales and wasn't coming back. I don't think anyone was very sorry. I know I'm not." Even with the dodgy connection Sydney heard a bitter note to his voice.

"Why not?"

"Well, you know how it is with a place like that. I'm a bit of a name there. They all want to act like I know them. To tell the truth, I'm a bit relieved."

"Why's that?"

"Well, for a start, Kofry's... very high maintenance."

Inigo waved at Sydney to catch her attention, then mouthed, *Bring him in.*

She glanced to the men sitting around the table. "Oka-ay. Tell you what, Elwess. We're here at the Agency. Why don't you swing round and join us?"

"What's going on?" He inhaled. "She hasn't done something idiotic, like threaten you or something?"

"It's kinda hard to explain over the phone. Tell you what, I'll send round a car to pick you up. It'll be there in about thirty minutes, okay?"

"Alright, you're seriously starting to rattle me."

"Everything's fine, I promise. See you in a bit."

Sydney ended the call, then looked at her guv'nor. For the first time since their meeting, Inigo allowed his frustration to show. "Give me a reason not to suspect Elwess Talbert of any involvement."

"He's got an airtight alibi for the week after she disappeared," replied Dahlra.

"Which is?"

"Us."

Lightoller gave him a don't-kid-a-kidder look. "So you can vouch for him the entire week, twenty-four seven? Even where he slept?"

Dahlra looked at Sydney, and she nodded. Might as well throw all the cards on the table now.

"Yes, we can. Because he was sleeping with us. In our bed."

Sydney could feel Pink's stare boring a hole into the side of her head. "The three of us enjoy a... particularly special relationship."

She had to give it to him—Inigo barely blinked. He held her gaze for a fraction too long, then pursed his lips as he smoothed a nonexistent crease in his immaculate trousers. "Well. If you tell me he was with you, then he was... with... you."

By the time Elwess arrived, the photos were safely out of sight. He sauntered in as if he owned the place. "You know, you cloak and dagger types really make me itch sometimes. Alright, here I am." He looked around the table. "Now, what's going on with Kofry that's so important you sent out your second best car to bring me here?"

"Have a seat, Elwess." Inigo gestured toward one of the empty chairs. "We'd just like to ask some questions about your Miss Urbonienė."

Elwess scoffed. "Believe me, she is not *my* Miss Urbonienė."

"Oh? And why is that?"

The two men tried to outstare one another; Elwess lost. He slid into the chair to Sydney's right. "Look, Inigo, I know you're Secret Squirrel and all that, but can you please tell me what this is all about? Has Kofry done something wrong? Is she in trouble?"

The silence was louder than thunder. Sydney opened her portfolio to the photo with the X'd out tattoo. "No, she isn't in trouble. I'm sorry, Elwess."

After a cup of coffee, liberally laced with Lightoller's brandy, Elwess calmed down somewhat. His reaction to Kofryna Urbonienė's photos had been genuine and visceral, and he still looked as if he might be sick.

"You're certain this *is* Kofry, Elwess?" Dahlra asked.

He nodded. "Yes. I'm very certain." His face looked ashen in the fluorescents. "Jesus, how could someone do this to another human being?"

"How long have you known Miss Urbonienė?"

Lightoller had to ask the question twice before Elwess could tear his eyes away from the photographs. It took another moment to gather his thoughts. "I met her about three or four years ago, I suppose. A... a Dom I knew brought her to The Library one night. He asked me to play with them. We had a good time, but right away I could see she was the sort that could be... trouble."

"In what way?" prompted Dahlra.

"You don't get to do a psychological profile on every sub you play with. Some are mentally unstable. They drift into this lifestyle, and sometimes become targets for predators. I felt that this particular Dom might be that sort of predator, so I tried to warn her off. And when I did, she became fixated on me. Hero worship, I guess you might say. She started following me around like a puppy.

"We played a few times, and she asked me to train her. I thought she was alright, if a bit needy. But before she and I could draw up her contract, she started acting very flaky."

"Contract?" asked Pink.

"Before a Dominant embarks on a relationship with a full-time submissive, they agree on how their relationship will proceed," explained Elwess. "They write it all up in a contract, and both of them sign it and pledge to abide by it. A training contract covers the basics—how the Dom wishes to be addressed, hard and soft limits, types of punishments and rewards. Most agree on a short-term contract until they either decide to end their association, or to expand it. That's when a new, more detailed contract is signed. A true Dom-sub training relationship is never entered into without a contract. It would be irresponsible not to."

"What happened with the girl?" asked Lightoller.

Elwess grimaced. "Well, she started pulling a lot of possessive, entitlement crap on me. She got nasty with a couple of my other subs, she started showing up at my house at all hours—you know, the whole stalker routine. That was around the time she got the tattoo," he said, nodding toward the photo. "I suppose she thought it would impress or flatter me. When I told her I wouldn't accept her as a trainee, she really started chucking her toys out of the pram. I had to threaten her with an ASBO to get her to back off." Some of his natural arrogance rose to the fore. "I do *not* do bunny boilers."

He sighed. "Ah, she wasn't a bad kid, just really lonely. She wanted to belong to someone, and I couldn't..." He looked away. "To tell the truth, I thought she'd settled down a bit. I hadn't seen her skulking around for months. She still had a tendency to bristle any time she saw me with anyone, but she hadn't started a cat fight over me in quite a while."

An alarm bell clanged in Sydney's head. "So the last time you saw her was that night? Valentine's?"

"Yeah. I never engaged with her outside the club, and I haven't been back there since. I don't go there much anymore." He shrugged. "It's mostly a go-to when friends visit from out of town."

Under the table, Sydney felt Dahlra's hand close over hers, and she knew, she damn well *knew* what the answer to her next question would be.

"Elwess, who was the Dom she was with? The one you warned her about?"

He took a long time in answering. "Silas Markham." He ran a hand over his face, and the room was so quiet Sydney could hear the rasp of his fingers over his skin. "Silas bloody Markham. He stirred her up every chance he got. Filled her head with all sorts of nonsense about me. "

There was a curt knock on the door. "Come," Inigo commanded.

Melissa Morrin appeared in the doorway. Her lovely face lit up with surprise. "Hello Sydney! I didn't know you and Dr Gar would be here——" She started as she caught sight of Elwess, and she dropped her eyes for a moment. "Hello Mas—Mister Talbert."

"Hello, Melissa," Elwess revealed none of the earlier upset. "It's lovely to see you."

"You two know one another?" Inigo's voice was deceptively innocent.

"We met at your party last winter. We've kept in touch."

Sydney glanced at Dahlra, whose raised eyebrows indicated that it was the first he had heard of it, too.

"Your report, Agent?" Lightoller prompted.

Mel, who had been staring at Elwess, immediately turned her attention back to her Senior. "Yes, sir. I went round to Miss Urbonienė's last known address. She lived with three other girls in Airlie Gardens. According to her flatmates, Kofry told them she had got a new job in Swansea and would have to move there immediately. They said she appeared very excited about it, but she was a little vague about some of the details. She moved out on the twentieth of February. She even paid her share of the rent through the end of the month."

"Have any of them heard from her since?"

Mel shook her head, her curls bobbing. "Kofry promised to forward her new address, but they never heard from her. They didn't follow up on it." She gave them an elegant shrug. "You know how it is. People move on, you get on with your life, and you lose touch."

Inigo nodded. "Thank you, Agent Morrin. That will be all."

"Yes, sir." She glanced again at Elwess as she left the room.

Pink started doodling on a notepad, his SOP for brainstorming. "So let's pretend this Silas bloke contacted her. He promises her something, anything, to entice her to break her ties with London. He takes her to an as-yet-unknown location, and does his Ground Force routine on her, possibly in front of a live audience. It can't be traced online. Unless there's enough DNA for us to match, well, it's all speculation, innit? It sounds like she was instructed not to give too much away.

"I mean, unless we can track her with CCTV, it's going to be hard to retrace her steps. If Markham *is* involved, he made damn sure his connection to her disappearance couldn't be construed as anything more than circumstantial. Someone dumped her, possibly to stitch him up, but who's gonna admit it? His audience isn't going to talk, that's for sure."

"True, but when you take into account that little show on Valentine's evening, it makes for *compelling* circumstantial evidence," Dahlra added.

"I'm sorry, but I seem to be missing a piece of the puzzle." Inigo fixed Sydney with a baleful eye. "What exactly happened on Valentine's Day?"

After Sydney and Dahlra left with their pet Lothario, Lightoller returned to his office. Agent Pinkerton was already seated there, ready for a debriefing from their eye-opening meeting. Lightoller took a seat behind his desk. "Garnet, when do you expect Celia?"

"In a day or two. Her mum's getting bored, so Ceel thinks she's on the mend. Why?"

"Because I don't want anything to leave this room. See if we can pick up this Markham fellow quietly and without a fuss. Given the situation and the circumstances surrounding Valentine's evening, he's a person of interest. Without anything more concrete, I can't hold him, of course, but I can lean on him a little."

"You're thinking of turning him?"

Inigo toyed with the edge of the portfolio, worrying the plastic until it peeled away from the paper. "I trust Sydney to keep Gar and Talbert quiet, but every new person who gets involved is one more potential leak. I'm sorry, but Celia's going to have to stay out of the loop on this one."

"Understood." Garnet's eyes flicked toward the door. "So what do you reckon about those three, then?"

"It's not for me to say, Agent. As long as it doesn't interfere with their duties, it's none of our affair." His mouth turned down. "Of course, I'm none too happy about this little home-made film that was mentioned, but, spilt milk, as they say."

"True." The two men sat in silence for a moment. "Syd handled the photos well. Better than I thought she would."

"I agree." Inigo sat back in his chair. "It's Gar's reaction I'm more concerned about."

"Really? Why?"

"While he was looking at those photos, all he could see was Sydney." He reached for his mobile and punched a number. "Hello, old horse. Word to the wise. Mind your Minder this evening." He smiled into the phone. "Good man. I'll be in touch with any update on the situation. Cheerio."

Lightoller ended the call. "She's already pouring the Jameson's down his throat. Trust Sydney to get a good appraisal of the situation."

Garnet whistled. "Blimey. You never think of the calm ones falling apart."

"They're the ones who usually fall the hardest. And the farthest."

Silas Markham believed in serendipity. He appreciated that a man created his own luck, but he always acknowledged that the best fortunes to be made were simply a matter of being in the right place at the right time.

He had been turning tricks in the gay clubs of Soho to keep from starving when fortune smiled his way for the first time. On a freezing December night, he met Master Robert, a self-made Dominant who instantly saw the potential in the young, pretty lad with a tongue like a lash and a cock like a python. Robert had been a gentleman at heart, classic British middle class. He was cultured and refined, his posh manners and plummy accent at odds with his big, burly shoulders, sausage fingers and thinning hair. He saw Silas as his own personal Galatea, and he set about weeding the younger man's sooty Northumberland roots and polishing the rough diamond with an air of sophistication. He taught Silas how to dress and speak, and use his assets with elegance.

And it was not just about learning his wines and the difference between a half and a full Windsor. Robert taught him the more esoteric lessons of a gentleman Dominant: the subtle parameters that defined the power of pleasure, and the pleasure of power. "It's not about subjugating the weak, it's about breaking the strong," Master Robert explained in his florid, professorial style. "The more defiant, the sweeter the take down. The lower you can make them grovel, boy, the taller you'll stand."

Gradually, he established Silas as the preeminent BDSM Dominant in London, and people travelled from all over Europe just to seek an audience with him. Once he was on top, Silas kicked the increasingly jealous and possessive Robert to the kerb, dismissing him like the liability he had become.

From that time, Silas ruled as the undisputed king—until Elwess Talbert showed up.

Talbert had swaggered into the clubs and dungeons of London like some pikey gyppo fresh from the caravan. Silas had sneered behind his brandy while Elwess held court, watching all those besotted, pathetic subs simpering around him like geishas. The joke soon ceased to be amusing.

Little by little, Elwess Talbert won London over, living up to the reputation he had cultivated in Amsterdam, and fucking anything with a cunt. When cautioned not to push in on Silas' manor, he had merely laughed. "It's not a popularity contest. Silas has his patch and I have mine. I'd say there's plenty enough to go round."

The little shit had even pretended to befriend Silas, sharing his house, his dungeon, even his subs. Everything, in fact, but his bed. And every time Silas saw those sardonic eyes sweep over a trembling supplicant, every time he watched Elwess' black hair glistening in the light of blazing candles as he fucked a kneeling sub, every time he heard that silver voice slide over a woman's eager body, Silas wanted him.

And he would have eventually had him too, if Elwess had not caught him wanking to that pedestrian recording, walking in just as his recorded self was pumping in and out of that bitch's creamy arsehole.

Mentioning that disk at The Library had been a shot in the dark, but it had hit a very satisfying bull's eye. It had also cost Silas his perfect nose and two expensive veneers. Now, every time he beat a slave, every time he choked a dark-haired man on his cock, every time he made someone scream in agony, he pretended it was Elwess. Once he had wanted to fuck him. Now he just wanted to make him suffer.

The phone rang, jangling him from his musings. Silas glanced blearily at the clock on his bedside table. The Caller ID simply said 'It.' A slave being punished was always called 'It,' or so Robert had instructed. It was totally devoted to Silas, but he was still angry at It. When It feared Silas more than Its boss, It might earn the right to be called its name again.

"Why are you calling me at seven-thirty in the fucking morning?" asked Silas, keeping his voice calm. Silas always forced himself to speak calmly to a slave. To the world, Robert had instructed, a Master must be the Sea of Tranquility, in perfect control of everything.

"They found her." Its voice was a hoarse, frightened whisper. "Master, please! I didn't know what to do, but this morning the photos came in from Hampshire, and they'll suspect you! You need to—"

"What are you talking about?" Something in the panic-filled tone was contagious, bringing Silas fully awake.

"I'm sorry, Master. This morning, we received photos of... of *her*. Someone found her body in—"

"Wha—? How? How on earth did they find the body?" His voice rose in volume. "I was told she would never be found. Was the house raided? I thought they said it was impregnable-"

"She was floating in the Channel!"

"The Cha—don't be stupid! It must be someone else."

"I saw the photos. It's her."

For a moment, Silas thought his heart would stop. He leapt to his feet and started pacing the room. "Do you mean to tell me that after all this time she just showed up, bobbing around in the sea like an ice cube? Who in the name of God threw her in the Channel?"

"I don't know! I don't know! But she was found and they've already done the autopsy! And Sydney Chapin and that doctor of hers, they're coming to the Agency this morning! If they recognise her—"

"Oh, for fuck's sake! Shut up and stop panicking." Silas' stomach was tumbling so hard and fast he felt as if he would vomit. "Who else knows about it?"

"Lightoller, of course, and maybe one or two more."

"Listen to me. You will calm down. If you remain calm, you will be rewarded. Leave everything to me. If you blow your cover, I will kill you myself. Do you understand?"

The rapid breathing lessened, and ended in a sob. "Yes, sir."

"Good. I need to make some arrangements, so I will call you this evening."

"Yes, sir. I used the special phone you gave me."

Silas rolled his eyes at the ceiling. At least the little fool was attempting to think like an agent. "Wait for my call, and don't worry. I'll protect you."

"But Sydney saw her that night! She might recognise her-"

"How could she recognise her? By the time we were done with her, *I* barely recognised her. Just have a cup of tea, and act as if nothing is amiss. This is no time for squeamishness. Yes?"

"Yes, sir. Thank you, sir! I'll make it up to you—"

"Yes, you will. Now go. Dry your eyes and do your job."

Silas ended the call, and took a deep, shaking breath. Those stupid cunts! What complete and total idiot had thrown that girl's body into the water like a bag of rubbish? By God, he would have someone's balls on his keychain!

With shaking hands, he swiped through his numbers until he located Lorcan's. It rang several times before a bored voice replied. "What do you want?"

"Walters, I need to speak to him."

"It's very early."

"I need to speak to him now." Silas used his Voice That Must Be Obeyed.

To his fury, Walters tutted. "He'll call you back."

"You don't understand! They've found—" He caught himself. "There's a problem."

Silas quickly explained the situation. When he was done, he was met by heavy silence. "Well, let me speak to him! We've got to do some damage control. I'll need to leave the country before I'm implicated—"

"And what makes you think you'll be implicated, Silas?" Lorcan's voice rolled into his ear like dark thunder.

"Chapin and Gar both saw her that night. They may recognise her. If they do, it's a safe bet they'll tell your precious Elwess Talbert, and he'll point the finger directly at me."

"Your involvement at this point would be considered purely circumstantial."

Silas felt his temper fraying at the edges. "But it isn't, is it? I brought her there for a little play. I didn't plan on killing her. I just thought we were putting on a show. You and your mates got carried away at the sight of blood and bitcoins."

"Are you threatening me, Silas?" Lorcan's voice reminded him of El-wess', all olive oil-smooth and cold as slate.

Silas made his just as glossy. "I would like to think a friend as power-ful as you wouldn't drop his friends in the shit, especially if there was a chance some might splash back on you as well."

To his surprise, Lorcan laughed. "That's what I love so much about you, Silas. Your selfless, thoughtful nature. Of course I'm not going to drop you in the shit. Go to the safe house in London. Tell some people you're going on an extended trip. I have a few friends who can call down the thunder if Lightoller and his merry men start sniffing up your hole. In the meantime, I think I have a plausible alibi you can use. I usually keep one or two lying about for just such occasions."

He's treating this entire thing like a joke! "What about Talbert?"

"What about him?"

"He's the one who'll bring us all down! He'll see this as his golden opportunity. Why won't you let me put a muzzle on him?"

"Silas, this vendetta of yours is growing tedious."

"You don't know what he's capable of! I could frame him for this. My special friend could plant the seed with Lightoller. He had a history with the girl. If I accuse him first, then his accusation about me will be tooth-less. Lorcan, I can finish him here!"

"You will *not*, Silas. I've lost count of the times I've repeated myself. So let me say this one last time, and it *will* be the last time." Lorcan's voice was like black ice. "Elwess Talbert will not be implicated in this girl's death, nor will you harm him in any way. If you do, there will not be a spare inch of mud in this country you won't be dragged through.

"Witnesses will come forward who remember seeing you taunting the victim at The Library, making her jealous of Elwess and his woman. They will say they overheard you offering her another job in a different part of the country, and you told her what to write in her text message so that she would not be missed by her employers.

"I will personally send Inigo Lightoller a very special present, includ-ing names, dates, videos, stills and sperm samples. A recording will be anonymously posted to his attention, showing you brutally beating and raping this innocent, unsuspecting girl while she screamed for mercy."

"You said there was no recording of the—" Silas stopped. Bile filled his throat, and he put his hand over his mouth, swallowing back the bitter taste.

Lorcan's tone was smug. "Ah, so you do appreciate the irony of it all. What is it the Americans say? 'What comes around, goes around?'" When Silas did not reply, he continued. "I can't say it any simpler. There will be nowhere to run or hide. You will be tried and convicted for murder and spend the rest of your unimportant little life in Strangeways at Her Majesty's pleasure. Do we understand one another?"

Silas sat down heavily on the bed; his knees felt like jelly. "Perfectly."

"Excellent. I'm glad we've settled that once and for all. I'll send a car over to take you to your new residence. It's a very cozy little cottage just outside the M25. You'll be very comfortable there. I'll call you this evening. If you need anything—liquor, Sparklers, money, women, men—just call the housekeeper." Lorcan resumed his role as bon viveur. In an exaggerated Geordie accent, he signed off with a cheery, "*Auf wiedersehen*, pet."

Sydney and Dahlra drove Elwess back to Pelham Street. Elwess stared out the window of the car, watching London pass by. "You'll stay with me tonight." It was not a request. They did not contradict him.

"I thought Mel Morrin looked well," Sydney began. It was the only thing she could think of to say, but the silence was seriously doing her head in. "What's the story with you two, anyway?"

It was a long time before Elwess spoke. His voice was listless. "Oh, you know, the usual. We've discussed working up a contract, but..."

When he did not continue, Sydney shifted in her seat so she could properly see him. He was still staring out the window, his face a closed shop. He remained silent for the rest of the journey.

Sydney held onto Dahlra's hand as the three of them sat around the kitchen table, pretending to enjoy their curry from the local takeaway, each locked in their own private little torture chamber. Sydney had not been exaggerating when Inigo called; she had given Dahlra a huge drink and threatened to pour it down his throat herself. He was obviously rattled about the dead girl. His eyes had that far away, seen-too-much look. Pink and Basil might have been surprised to see Dahlra shaken up, but Sydney was not at all. She was only surprised it had taken him this long.

She patted his hand and he gave her a look of such exhausted misery she felt her throat tighten. She glanced over at Elwess pushing his lamb Bhuna around the plate. He did not look much better.

"Tell you what," Sydney said briskly. "Let's take a leisurely drive back to Maidenvine. You too, Elwess," she added when he shot her a panicked look. "We're all going back, and we're going to relax and work through this. Now eat up, and when you're done, go pack an overnight bag."

While Elwess was upstairs, she took Dahlra into the front room and made him sit on the sofa. Straddling him, she took him in her arms and held him. "It's okay. You've always been here for me. This time, I'm here for you."

He held her close and buried his face against her neck. "Pebble, meet clod." He laughed bleakly.

"Stop that." She took his face in her hands. "Yes, that could have so easily have been me. And *you* are the reason it wasn't."

It was nearly midnight before they returned to Windsor, and by then, both men looked dead on their feet. Sydney plied them with drinks like a Kansas City bootlegger, and babbled about everything but their meeting at the Agency. Both men made all the correct responses and pretended everything was normal. Sydney sighed inwardly. Time. That was all they needed. Time and love and tenderness. It had worked for her.

Later that night, nestled against a softly snoring Dahlra (after forcing him to drink a hangover-inducing amount of Jamesons), Sydney felt the bed dip as Elwess slipped in behind her. He moved close, his naked body cool from the night air, his penis flaccid.

"Alright, love?"

His answer was to press against her back and slip his arm around her.

She rolled over, into his embrace. In the dark, she could not see him, but his emotions were vibrating in the air. She searched for the correct words to release him from this self-appointed court martial, before settling on the obvious. "It's not your fault, Elwess. You have to remember that. Hideous, awful stuff happens to people, and it's not their fault and it's not yours."

"I know. Believe me, I know." Nevertheless, his voice was tinged with remorse. "But she needed someone to protect her and care about her. She died because she went looking for that person and what she found was..."

"It doesn't mean you aren't capable of loving and protecting someone."

"But if I had—"

"If you had, you might be the one on the cooling board, not her."

Dahlra stirred, and made a tense, gasping noise in his sleep. Both Sydney and Elwess instinctively reached to soothe and ease him. "Don't beat yourself up because you didn't love her, Elwess. If she were still alive, you wouldn't feel guilty about that."

She felt his sharp intake of breath. "That's... that's rather cold."

"It's a cold world. And the best, the *only* thing we can do is try and make it warmer for the ones we care about. That's what I do. Keep the ones I love safe."

"I would fight for you, Sydney." Each whispered word sounded raw and desperate. "I would fight for both of you. The thought of you lying dead somewhere, and knowing I was the reason..."

"You aren't the reason Kofry's dead. Shh. Come here." She kissed him and enfolded him in her arms. "Blame is hard enough to live with when we *have* to shoulder it. Don't volunteer for any you don't hold the deed for. Hush now."

With a soft moan, he lay his head against her breast. His large body trembled with energy and tension, and she gentled him, stroking the broad muscles of his back. He pressed close, allowing her to take charge. As his hair slipped through her fingers like liquid silver, he relaxed by degrees, until at last his breathing slowed and deepened.

Lying between those two dark sparks of heat, Sydney stared upward toward the black ceiling, and tried to convince herself none of them were truly to blame.

As Silas packed, he wondered if he should just make a run for it; head straight to Heathrow, hop a plane to Hong Kong and hide out until things blew over. If he could have assured himself of a steady supply of something inspirational to while away the dull hours, he would have, but he did not know anyone in the Far East well enough to guarantee he would not have to go without. It was not as if he was addicted, but he liked knowing he could get it when he wanted it.

Coke had always been his drug of choice until Lorcan turned him onto his own special cocktail, a closely guarded formula combining the inhibition-suppressing Oparim, a very precise dosage of LSD, and the minutest amount of DMT. Sparklers, Lorcan called it.

Bastard he may be, but Lorcan was a true visionary, a long game man, content to let Sparklers gain popularity in the kinkster world before introducing it to the global stage. Silas believed Lorcan's prediction that one day Sparklers would take over the drug world. Already in The Library and other similar clubs it was the number one recreational drug. It would, Lorcan insisted, soon replace Ecstasy and Cocaine, enveloping the world in a sweet haze of colour and pleasure. It was cheap to make if you had the lab and the chemicals, and since it was made in small batches, it was hard to trace back to the source.

It was the perfect high for the lifestyle; the hallucinogenic effects of the LSD and DMT, tempered by the Oparim, left a person awash in heightened sexual pleasure. Colours, sounds, even smells pulsed in bright lights. Sex became an overwhelming mélange of light and stimulation; blood looked like blooming roses on a body, semen like phosphorescent paint. It could be ingested by mouth, in either a liquid suspension or vapourised inhalation, or injected directly into a vein. Silas had always hated needles, but that first trip had been enough to overcome his phobia. Safe, sane and consensual, indeed.

Thinking about it, Silas quickly checked his supply. He was a little low; he would have them bring some to the safe house. As he rolled the tiny brown glass bottle of powder between his fingers, he gave in and got his gear. All he wanted was a little skin-pop.

He sat back, slowly pulling the tourniquet from his bicep. Behind his closed eyes burst the first of a million head-swamping, kaleidoscopic brain-chrysanthemums, the trademark hallucinations that gave the cocktail its street name. Within the myriad patterns, scenarios spun in his head, all involving the bitch Chapin and her lapdog Gar suffering exquisitely while Talbert watched, helpless. Perhaps this little holiday was just the ticket. He would have plenty of free time to form a plan.

He addressed his beautiful reflection, swathed in an aura of pulsing light and sound. "Who knows? An opportunity may present itself that's just too good to pass up."

On that sunny June morning, Silas congratulated himself on his patience. He had received the call two days ago. After the debacle with the girl, he had spent the next month laying low, bored out of his skull, his resentment and hatred feeding the vengeance that always simmered away in his mind, until it was almost all he could think about.

"It's a small party," It had explained, desperate to get back into Silas' favour. "I heard Sydney talking to Principal Lightoller. She said it would only be the four of them. They arrived at Talbert's flat this afternoon."

"Which four?"

"Principal Lightoller and his wife, Sir. Pinkerton is up North with his Minder."

"And Talbert won't be there?"

"No, sir! Sydney was grousing about that! She was complaining he had decided to go to Amsterdam and forgot about the party! She was really pissing and moaning about—"

"Shut up and let me think!" Silas hissed.

He stood in the doorway of the flat opposite, waiting. He was not exactly sure what to wait for, only that this might be an opportunity. His instinct paid off; at eleven, the door to Elwess' flat opened, and Sydney Chapin stepped out. She looked up and down Pelham Street, her cold stare taking in her surroundings. Silas quickly ducked back into the shadow of the stoop; if she spotted him, she gave no indication. With a final glance around, she strode down the street like she owned it.

Silas smiled to himself. Gar it is, then. This *was* a treat.

He was a meticulous man by nature, and all the best plans involved detailed preparation. But he also believed in serendipity. Especially when it came to revenge. *A true Master takes what he wants, and takes vengeance on his own time.*

"I can't hurt you, Talbert," he said aloud, a smile edging the corner of his lips. "But I can hurt *them*." His mood brightened. Nothing was more relaxing than the thought of inflicting pain.

CHAPTER SEVEN

Break

Why did I think this was a good idea?

Sydney summoned up every ounce of her patience and strength, wishing it were permissible to pull out her Glock and fire a round into the ceiling of a crowded department store. She must be flippin' insane; there could be no other explanation as to why she was here, risking her vital organs and her sanity at the Harrod's Really Bloody-Stupid-Arse-Why-The-Hell-Bother Big Sale during the hottest June day she could remember. All in the hopes of buying Dahlra a birthday present. *Yep. Definitely mad as a spoon.*

The Bright Idea had come about because they were in London for the weekend to host a little get-together for Dahlra's birthday. He had offered to cook, bless him, and Sydney had moved heaven and earth to get their close friends together in the same place for the occasion. That was slowly going down the tubes. At the very last minute, Pink and Celia had cried off. Elwess, who had turned his house over to them while he attended a play weekend in Holland, hoped to be back in time to toast the birthday boy, but could not make any promises. That left Inigo and Pip, who were used to a fairly high standard of home cooking, and Dahlra's pride would not allow him to create anything but the best.

Up to his parts in spatch-cocked chicken and crème brûlée, Dahlra had smiled at her gratefully when she volunteered to dash over to Fortnum and Mason's to order the wine and nibbles. He absently kissed her cheek as she left, too preoccupied to notice she was practically rubbing her hands in glee.

Without Dahlra riding shotgun, she had contrived to pop over to Harrod's and grab a couple of those lovely silk shirts he liked so much. He would not be expecting it, and she might even model one of them for him—a win-win sitch all round. She figured she had just enough time to run into the men's department, make her purchase, and be back at Elwess' flat before the F&M delivery van arrived. Yes sir, that was the plan—until she got there, along with every other masochist in London cramming through Harrod's doors like pedigree cattle on their way to market.

But hey, again, no biggie. Harrod's Annual Really Big Sale was never for the faint of heart, and this was not her first rodeo. In the past, she had actually enjoyed the mad rush. She would set aside the entire sale day, dress in comfortable clothing and running shoes, and wade in like a commando, reveling in the bargain-hunting, take-no-prisoners lunacy.

Today, though, she was in a hurry. Sydney pushed her way into the men's department, did the grab and go, then fought her way out. By the time she was back on the street, both she *and* the box had been crushed to buggery by the stampede, and she was running late.

Sydney growled under her breath as she looked for a cab. It was the height of tourist season in London; there was no way she was going to get a ride at this time of day. Thinking she might save a few moments, she hopped the Tube back to South Ken station and made a quick sprint toward Pelham Street. There she checked her watch. *Damn.*

Fishing her mobile out of her bag, she speed-dialed Dahlra. He answered on the third ring, sounding a little harried. "Hiya, can I call you right back?"

"Sure. Is everything alright?"

"Just a little rushed. Give me two ticks."

"No need. I just wanted to let you know I ordered some extra wine, so Fortnum & Mason is coming round in a bit to deliver it. Be on the lookout for their van, will you? Love you."

"Will do. Love you too."

The phone went silent in her hand. Trudging up the hill toward Pelham Street, Sydney wondered if things might not be going so well in the kitchen. Dahlra had been known to sink into a funk if the crème brûlée split or his pasta was not al dente. He would be in a right state if he thought his food might be less than perfect for the Lightollers.

"Well, hell," she muttered aloud, much to the consternation of a passing OAP and her equally offended dachshund. Ignoring their disdainful looks, Sydney phoned Dahlra again; the least she could do was tell him she was coming to the rescue. She had a witty riposte planned the moment he answered, only he did not. It rang six times and went to answer phone.

Frowning, she sent him a brief text. *I'm on my way. See you in 20 minutes.*

The phone rang just as Dahlra was lifting the bain-marie out of the oven. After carefully placing it on the hob so the steaming water would not slosh into the custards, he tucked his hand under his arm, tugging one of the oven mitts free, and groped for the phone. He smiled at the readout: *My girl.*

"Hiya, can I call you right back?"

He could hear traffic noises in the background. "Sure. Is everything alright?" She sounded strained and a bit winded.

"Just a little rushed. Give me two ticks."

"No need. I just wanted to let you know I ordered some extra wine, so Fortnum & Mason is coming round in a bit to deliver it. Be on the lookout for their van, will you? Love you."

He smiled. "Will do. Love you too." He ended the call, and turned back to his cooking, when the door buzzed. He removed the second oven mitt and headed toward the door. The buzzer sounded twice in impatient succession. "Hang on. Just because you've delivered on time for once..."

As he opened the door, Dahlra quipped, "That was fast..."

His words died on his lips. Standing in the doorway was Silas Markham. "Hello, *Master* Dahlra."

"Silas—"

The younger man reached for him; there was a hissing, spitting sound, and suddenly Dahlra's eyes and face were on fire. Silas charged him, pushing Dahlra back into the hallway and slamming the door closed behind them. They struggled together in the narrow foyer, but the element of surprise and the blinding effects of the pepper spray tipped the balance in Silas' favour. He threw Dahlra against the wall. Colliding with the hard surface, Dahlra's head snapped back, and white spots danced behind his tightly closed eyes.

A sharp, vinegary pinch, like the sting of an angry bee, flared from the soft tissue just above his collarbone. He cried out at both the pain and the invasion. The drug took effect almost instantly. "What are you..." his legs went numb, and he crashed to his knees.

Silas grabbed his arms, pulling him to his feet. His face was close enough that Dahlra could feel his warm breath. "I was the neighbour-hood, and I said to myself, 'I ought to pop round and have a nice chat

with Dahlra Gar. We got off on the wrong foot. I'm sure we could rem-
edy that if we just get to know one another better'." Silas roughly
propelled Dahlra farther into the flat. "After all, we can't let Elwess have
all the fun, can we?"

Dahlra stumbled clumsily along. Somewhere in the distance, he
heard his phone ring.

"That's..." Even drugged, he knew not to mention Sydney. "That's Elwess. He'll be—"

"Up to his bollocks in slaves and blow in sunny Amsterdam, dear
Doctor. And you will be long gone before the Lightollers show up this
evening." Silas laughed. "Still, there's no reason to miss an opportunity
to teach you a lesson, even if you won't live long enough to put it to use."

Dahlra tried to protest, but his tongue felt like a large and detached
lump of meat, heavy and dead in his mouth. Somehow he stayed upright
as Silas dragged him into the narrow cage of the lift, holding him up with
surprising strength. Dahlra's numbed legs collapsed beneath him, and
through his burning, filmed eyes he saw the floor of the Chine rising up
to meet him. The lift stopped with a loud metallic clank, and Silas
wrenched the accordion-like door open, pushing Dahlra out of the lift.

He fell bonelessly onto the stone floor and sank into unconsciousness.

Silas made sure he had given Gar enough juice to make him pliable,
but not enough to completely knock him out. The fact that he had
fainted was a shame; it just meant Silas would have to do a little more
work. No matter, he thought. All the more reason to punish him.

Gar was pale, his skin clammy, but the temperature of the dungeon
would keep the sedative from sweating out of his system too soon.

Back in the flat, Silas picked up Gar's phone. A message was waiting.
It was Sydney Chapin: *I'm on my way. See you in 20 minutes.* He checked
his watch, and made sure his remaining hypos were ready. He smiled in
anticipation. This could not have worked out more perfectly if he had
ordered it on the menu.

Fifteen minutes later, when Sydney let herself into the flat, she noticed the Fortnum and Mason's delivery basket sitting just inside the door. Strange that Dahlra had signed for it and left it there; maybe he had been in the middle of a delicate step in his cooking and could not be bothered to take it to the kitchen.

She hallooed, but there was no answer. The flat was strangely quiet. She ducked into the kitchen. The desserts were cooling on the counter, and the chickens, splayed flat and skewered, sat in a dish marinating in sauce. Dahlra's mobile lay on the table. Her text message was displayed.

Sydney did a slow one-eighty, chewing her lip. Something was not right. As she headed upstairs, she teetered between two uneasy pillars of suspicion and dismissal. She told herself her paranoia antenna was only twitching because one tiny thing was out of the ordinary, but her head was not buying it. "Dahlra?" No toilet flushing, no running water, no reply. The flat seemed empty. Where the hell was he?

Passing by Elwess' study, she glanced into the room, and the twitch turned to a full-on spike. The Chine's monitors were on. She knew for a fact they were not on when she left, and Dahlra had no reason on earth to switch them on. She walked into the unlit room, peering closely at the screen. A figure was lying prone on the floor of the Chine's main area. "What the—"

There was a rush of movement from behind the door, and it was only then she realised she was already under attack. Even as she turned, she felt the needle jab into her neck, and it was too late to curse herself for being so damn out of practice. Within seconds, all voluntary muscles went into shutdown, and her brain switched into Emergency Auxiliary Power only. Arms, legs, mouth: all stopped working. Her knees buckled and she crumpled to the floor, crashing onto her side like a redwood. Fear and wild panic intertwined, and she knew at that moment she had failed both her Minder and herself.

A pair of black boots appeared in her field of vision, and one of them casually pushed her shoulder, rolling her over onto her back. Her body flopped gracelessly like a rag doll, and her head lolled until she was looking up into the coldly handsome face of Silas Markham. Deep within her sluggish mind she told herself to speak, but to no avail. Nothing, it seemed, was willing to obey her brain.

Silas smirked down at her, his eyes as frosty as ice cubes in gin. He was wearing a sharp grey suit, with close-fitting black leather gloves. With his long, blond hair tied in a ponytail and draped across his shoulder, he looked like a rock star on holiday.

"I was told it would work fast, but even I'm impressed." He sounded pleasant, even friendly. "It's the same kind of paralytic used in tranquilizer guns on safari, you see. Of course, it's not really suitable for humans, so I had to improvise somewhat. Short term, of course, so I believe you'll be able to just about breathe and blink, but all voluntary movement has gone bye-bye."

He leaned in close. "This is for my nose, you snarky little bitch." He delivered a hard, back-handed slap, but Sydney felt no more pain than if he had pinched someone else's cheek. Silas looked at his gloved hand and rubbed his fingers together. His face held an expression of faint disgust. He studied her carefully. "I've never used one of these tranks before. I wonder just how much pain actually registers."

His fist zoomed in, and the hideous smack rocked her head to the side, but all she felt was a heaviness as her cheek split and swelled. "I suppose you can't really tell me, can you? Oh, that *is* disappointing." He straightened again, his pale features pinched with annoyance. "I usually prefer my women to struggle a little. Well, it can't be helped. In any case, I fear that you and I will have ended our association long before the paralysis wears off."

With every fibre in her being, Sydney tried to respond, but her body no more obeyed than if it was a piece of driftwood. Silas knelt down beside her and pulled out a long blade. "Still, I believe in being thorough." He tested the knife's edge by drawing a shallow line across her cheek. Blood trickled from the cut into her mouth, then onto the floor. "I even considered carving Elwess' name on you, but that's a bit cliché, don't you think? No, what I have in mind will be calling card enough to convince Lightoller just who perpetrated this torrid little *crime passionnel*."

A strange sound, like a moan, emitted from the speakers, and Silas glanced up at the monitor, a look of dull anger in his eyes. "Shit. It seems your Dr Gar is a bit more robust than I'd anticipated." He playfully slapped her bleeding cheek, then rose to his feet, placing the knife on the desk. "Don't go anywhere, my dear. I'll be right back." He quickly strode from the room.

Sydney lay motionless, sprawled awkwardly on the floor like a beached dolphin. *C'mon, goddammit, move, you stupid bint!*

Unfortunately, her body was not listening.

Dahlra tried to open his sticky, swollen eyes. He had a bizarre dream, and he thought he might still be in the throes of it. He had been leaning out a window, or perhaps a door, and someone had grabbed his arm and yanked him through. He had gone plummeting down...

He moved, and a sharp pain in his shoulder startled him. He moaned softly, trying to sit up, and the world tilted wildly. Bracing himself, he made a second attempt at vertical, but the task was simply too Herculean.

A clanking, mechanical noise made him look up, and from behind the spiral staircase a man with white hair approached him. Somewhere in the fuzzy dark corner of his dubious consciousness, Dahlra knew that man. He was the enemy, and this time, Dahlra's sheer force of will would not be enough to back him down. He could only look on, stranded and pathetic, as the enemy approached with light, measured steps.

"I've got to hand it to you, Dr Gar, you've got the constitution of an ox."

Dahlra tried to resist, but another sharp, stinging pinch at his neck sent him back into the darkness.

Sydney could not be sure, but it felt like only a few minutes had passed before Silas returned to the study. He was carrying the large carver chair from Elwess' dining room.

"I've had an idea!" He spoke in that falsely cheerful voice used by cruise ship activity directors and movie psychopaths. He sat the chair down with a thump, and took a moment to catch his breath. "I'd planned to do you, then have a little fun with your Minder, but I'd hate for you to miss out on the main event. Besides, all good things come to those who wait."

He hooked his hands beneath her arms and hauled her limp body into the chair. He hummed to himself as he ran a length of rope beneath her armpits, binding her chest to the carver's back to prevent her from slumping. For good measure, he secured her ankles and wrists to the arms and legs of the chair with long white zip ties, the kind police use to cuff suspects. He cinched them up until they dug into her skin.

"In the meantime, I've been longing to do this ever since that night in The Library." With a yanking, jerking motion, he wrenched the engagement ring from her finger with enough force to dislocate it. "We'll call this your down payment, seeing as you won't be needing it anymore."

Sitting upright with the rope wound tightly over her chest, Sydney's head swam from lack of oxygen. As she dragged as much air as she could into her protesting lungs, she stared at the monitor, where the man she loved lay unconscious on the floor of the Chine. Silas leaned down, peering into her eyes.

His expression was child-like in its earnestness. "You see, true fear is more than just experiencing the pain. It's knowing the pain is coming. That is the most erotic sensation on earth, I find. Especially if it's happening to someone else. Someone you truly care about."

He stepped back to admire his handiwork. "Now you can watch me play with your precious Dahlra Gar. And when I'm done with him, it'll be your turn. It's nothing personal, you understand." He paused a beat, then threw back his head and laughed heartily. "What am I saying? Of course it's personal! But explaining it would take far too long."

He opened his coat to reveal an obvious erection. "Well, look what I've found. Hard already. I hope your Dahlra likes taking it up the arse. Does he? I mean, do he and Elwess let you watch, or is that a private activity for just the two of them?"

A splash of frigid water shocked Dahlra, bringing him to the surface choking and spluttering. "Wake up, you lazy bastard!" Silas laughed, setting a stainless steel ice bucket on the table. He sharply slapped Dahlra's face to bring him fully conscious. "I've gone to all this trouble for you, and you're sleeping through the opening ceremonies."

Silas had switched on the sodium vapour overheads, flooding the room with harsh, unnatural light. It pierced Dahlra's pepper-burned eyes like lasers. Blinking furiously, he turned his head, trying to get his bearings, and immediately regretted it. A wave of nausea overtook him as his equilibrium tipped back and forth, setting the room spinning like a top. He breathed deeply through his clogged nose, fighting the urge to vomit.

He was naked, bound facing inward on Elwess' fancy new St Andrews Cross. He was stretched to his limit, each limb pulled in opposing directions, his hands and feet held firmly in place with leather straps.

When his eyes finally focused on Silas, adrenaline and anger cleared his head a little. "What the fuck are you doing?" He hated the thin, desperate sound of his own voice. "Are you insane? Aside from the fact that kidnapping is a criminal offense—"

"Only if one gets caught, Dr Gar."

Dahlra took several quick, deep breaths, calling to mind all his Agency training, all the fast-track instructions he had endured in those two mind-bending months before he entered the Cell. He had been afraid then; now he was furious. He closed his eyes and told himself to calm the hell down. *Sydney will be home any moment. She'll call out the cavalry.* "You're barking mad."

"Oh, we're all mad here!" Silas walked around the cross until they were face to face. "And I must say, you're remarkably calm for a man tied to a cross, at my mercy. Let me guess: you think your Miss Chapin will be coming to your rescue at any moment, don't you? She won't, you know."

Dahlra's stomach twisted into a knot. "Why—what do you mean?"

Silas gave him a look of profound sympathy. "Oh, my dear chap. I'm so sorry." He held up his hand. From his pinkie finger, Sydney's engagement ring gleamed in the bright lights. "You see, I'm afraid Agent Chapin is an ex-parrot."

Dahlra's entire body flushed, first hot, then cold, and again his stomach rolled sickeningly. Seeing his grandmother's ring winking at him from Silas' hand filled him with rage, burning the last of the sedative out of his system. With all his strength, he tried to break away. He strained against his bonds. "What have you done to her? God help me, if you've hurt her—"

"God help me, if you've hurt her!" Silas shouted back, his voice high-pitched and mocking. "Pathetic. At least *she* didn't die whining like a baby."

"I don't believe you." Dahlra kicked against the cross in helpless frustration. "There's no way a piece of shit like you got the drop on her."

Silas gazed back at him solemnly, and in that deep pool of silence, the anger bled from Dahlra's heart and mind. "She can't be." He could not allow himself to believe it. The mere thought of her in the past tense drove a spear of anguish into his chest, and tears pricked his eyes like acid.

This seemed to please Silas to no end. "It's time to man up, Dahlra. By the time I'm done, you're not even going to remember her name." As he spoke, Silas removed several hypodermic needles from his pocket, chose one, and injected its contents into Dahlra's hip.

The needle puncture stung like the angry bee at his shoulder earlier. "What are you giving me?"

"Oh, just a little livener. It's called Sparklers, and I predict you're going to see why in a few seconds." He tossed the spent hypo onto the nearby table. "Crazy little drug. Very boutique. A good friend of mine designed it. It's all the rage in the clubs now." He massaged the injection site, and Dahlra hissed and tried fruitlessly to avoid his touch. "You see, in small doses, it's a lovely mood enhancer. It will make you extremely open to suggestion, not to mention very sensitive to touch. But in larger doses..."

He ran a slender, pale finger down Dahlra's arm, scoring it with his nail. It felt like a heated wire being dragged over his flesh. As the drug slithered through his system, leaving a trail of fire in its wake, Dahlra actually saw his skin turn red and crack open like rotten wood. Little worms crawled out and started roaming over his arm. "Jesus," he gasped, struggling to get away from them.

"I'm no chemist, but they tell me it has something called DMT in it. Makes you see all sorts of things. But my friend altered the chemical footprint somewhat. Apparently this particular batch has some extra features the standard model doesn't. I've been dying to test drive it on someone, just to see what it does. Or rather, what it can make *you* do."

Silas laughed, and the sound came at Dahlra in large visible waves, widening like smoke rings with sharp canine teeth. He shook his head, fervently trying to clear it. He knew he was starting to panic, and if he could not control it, he would be ridden by it into a ragged grave. "Why are you doing this?"

"Why?" Silas gave him a look of contempt. "Maybe it's because Silverbirch doesn't like Lightoller's witch hunt. Maybe it's revenge. Or maybe it's because you got to Elwess before I did." He shrugged. "Who knows? Who cares? Maybe it's just because I love to inflict pain. You saw how much I enjoyed making Kofryna Urbonienė suffer."

Silas stroked Dahlra's cheek, smirking as he recoiled from the touch. "Oh, yes, Dahlra Gar. I'm going to enjoy getting inside that head of yours."

Dahlra could feel Silas' hands sinking into his skull, taking his brain and squeezing it between his fingers. "Fuck off!" he growled. "I won't let you."

"You don't have a choice, Dahlra."

The way Silas spoke his name made his skin crawl, and he told himself it was *not* actually crawling. "It's not real. It's none of it real."

"Isn't it, Doctor?" Silas chuckled. "I think it's very real. Can't you feel it? Can't you see it?"

Silas' face transformed into a red-eyed demon with barbed teeth and a tongue that lolled obscenely over his thick lips. The panic pulsed against Dahlra's skin with each rapid heartbeat, and it inflated like a balloon with each breath he took. He coughed hard to dispel it. Sydney had taught him that trick. Silas words hit him broadside again. *At least she didn't die whining. Oh, God, Sydney...*

Silas loomed in close. "I can hurt you in many, many ways, Dahlra. And I'm going to. By the time your guests arrive, all they will find are your corpses. I was never all that interested in playing with your whore, but this..." Silas caressed Dahlra's buttocks in a way that made him thrash against the cross. "This, I'm very interested in exploring."

As he spoke, Silas' voice grew louder and louder, until it was like booming cannon fire. It burst Dahlra's eardrums, and even though he *told* himself it was an hallucination, he could feel blood running warmly from his ears. A cold ball of anger and vengeance settled in the pit of his stomach. *I can live through it. I have to. I have to make him pay...*

It was no good. Terror and grief washed over him, and he blinked back his tears. He turned so that Silas would not see them.

"You're very strong, Dr Gar." Silas caressed his back, his hand gentle. "But I specialise in making strong men scream."

"I won't scream." He would bite off his own tongue before he gave Silas the satisfaction.

The hand on his back slid lower, until it cupped his sac. Silas' mouth was so close to his ear he felt the lips against his flesh. As his hand tightened, he chuckled. "So very brave, Doctor. As brave as you were when you were sent to rescue Agent Chapin. You were so frightened, weren't you? All alone, with no one to help you in case you blew your cover."

In spite of the drugs racing through his system, Dahlra stared at him, shocked into speaking. "How do you know—"

"So frightened," Silas' voice, smooth and low, was the very sound of commiseration. "Lightoller abandoned you there, with no one but an agent who hated your guts. You nearly gave yourself away, didn't you? You were so scared they could smell it on you, couldn't they?"

"Who told you about—"

"Then again, I suppose your guilt still eats at you. That terrible beating you witnessed. She begged you to kill her, didn't she? I suppose, in a way, you did. It just took until today to do it."

"Stop—"

"She begged you, didn't she? Remember how she pleaded with you to kill her? She hated you for letting her take that beating. She never forgave you, you know. She died cursing your name!"

"Shut up." To his left, Dahlra saw Sydney hanging from the ceiling, like a slab of meat being pounded for the Sunday roast. Pieces of skin and muscle were hanging from her back like a ragged garment. He smelled blood and excrement in the air, and heard those men laughing, laughing... *Get ready, doll...*

Then he *was* Sydney, hanging there, waiting for the next killing blow, his teeth pulled out one by one. The Doctor had stood by and let them do it. Oh, God, the Doctor had allowed them to torture Sydney; what would the Doctor do to *him?*

Silas is not the Doctor. The Doctor died in a hail of bullets. Didn't he? The Doctor was lying on the stone floor near the sofa, his white coat stained with blood, and Dahlra bit back the urge to ask him. The Doctor grinned at Dahlra with what was left of his blasted face. Was that him? Was he Sydney or Dahlra? What had the Doctor done to Sydney?

"Stop it!" He had to keep his shit together. More than that, he had to shut up. If he talked, Silas would tear him to pieces without even laying a finger on him. But how did he know, how *could* he know about the Cell? "It's not real. It's not real... not real..." He whispered it over and over, desperately wanting to believe it.

Silas stroked Dahlra's damp hair. "Why would I lie? You know I'm telling the truth. You saw those scars, and knew you'd sliced each and every one on her back. You told her you would have gladly taken them in her place. Well, now you will. Think of it as your final atonement."

From the corner of his vision, Dahlra watched as Silas picked up a large black leather whip. Silver barbs tipped the ends of each strand, like the heads of serpents. It writhed and hissed at him. Silas draped the whip over Dahlra's back, the long strands of the flogger caressing his skin. The drug made the leather straps feel like razor blades, and a surge of adrenaline-fueled anger cleared Dahlra's head.

"You do whatever you like, Markham. But if you're trying to fuck my head apart, we're in for a long afternoon."

"Yes, we are, Dahlra," Silas answered, amiably. "And it's not your head I'm interested in fucking. Just remember that."

He stepped away, drawing his arm back for the first blow. "Now, this will most assuredly sting a bit. But there *is* no true pleasure without pain."

From behind came a high, swift swishing sound, and Dahlra gasped in shock as the metal barbs bit viciously into his back. They snagged in, like poisonous fangs, and he felt his skin tear as Silas pulled the whip away. Agony bloomed over his back, making way for thousands of little strands of suffering.

"That was just a warm-up. Like any athlete, I don't want to peak too early." Silas was rummaging around in one of the cabinets. "Ah, here we are." He returned with a bottle in his hands. "We mustn't allow any nasty infections to sneak in, must we?"

Agony danced over his body as the rubbing alcohol sluiced over Dahlra's bleeding back. He opened his mouth in a silent scream, straining against his bonds with such force, the cross shuddered.

"What was that, Dr Gar? Are we feeling it yet?"

A harsh, hiccoughing sound bubbled up from deep within. "You can get off all you want, but you'll do it without my help!"

To his surprise, Silas tossed the whip away. He pressed close against Dahlra's side, and injected him with another dose of Sparklers. Even as the lights burst in his vision, Dahlra noticed with some small satisfaction that Silas was no longer smiling. "As a matter of fact, I plan to get off quite a bit. And you will most certainly aid me in that aim."

Strong hands pressed against his buttocks, and he felt the ripping, tearing sensation of Silas' fingers. Dahlra had known this would happen; had known it the moment he realised he was naked and alone. *It won't change who I am. He can't break me unless I let him.*

"How lovely," Silas crooned. "It's been ages since I had a virgin."

Dahlra didn't scream. He did not make a sound.

He thought of Sydney.

Thirty feet above, tied to a heavy chair, unable to move, Sydney watched as Silas assaulted her lover—watched as Dahlra fought like a tiger to keep from crying out. Every ounce of Sydney's being screamed out for her to move, every pore sweated bitter rage and impotence. And throwing its shadow over everything was the killing, dull knowledge that Dahlra's mind and body were systematically being torn apart, and she could do nothing but watch. She could not even cry.

As the sick events unfolded in solid state circuitry perfection on El-wess' monitor, another frightening thought careened through her head like a pinball on speed: *How did Silas know about the Cell? All our personal business, for fuck's sake? And how does he even know the name 'Silver-birch'?*

If Silas knew everything about Silverbirch, then Silverbirch knew everything about the Agency.

Her heart was pounding so hard it hurt her chest. *My chest hurts. Holy shite, my chest HURTS.*

She concentrated hard, withdrawing inside herself. There it was: the pain, her old friend, itching, tickling, twinging, pinching, cramping; appearing like tiny dots on the far horizon, slowly making its hopscotching way back to her consciousness. Voluntary movement was coming back online.

Her lips moved infinitesimally. Muscles started checking in at uneven intervals. Even as the realisation registered, her dislocated ring finger twitched.

CHAPTER EIGHT

Already Gone

Time ceased to have meaning.

Stockpiled in this House of Horrors called the Chine was every implement one could wish for to finance a sadist's wet dream, and Silas applied each instrument with consummate skill. He sowed anticipation by telling Dahlra what he was going to do, and reaped fear with the follow-through. And through it all, Dahlra willed his strength to withstand this ordeal long enough to keep his taxed heart beating.

Silas reached between Dahlra's legs and viciously twisted his scrotum. Dahlra took deep rapid breaths, hoping it would allow the pain to pass through him. Instead it just took up residence in his groin, settling in for the duration.

"Why don't you scream?" Silas twisted again, and Dahlra bucked against the cross so fiercely it groaned in protest. "What's the matter, Gar? Not enough pain for you?"

Dahlra bared his teeth and growled, "Is hurting me is the only way you can get off?"

Silas hesitated, then relaxed his grip minutely. "What are you saying?"

Miraculously, the searing overstimulation and ache abated to something Dahlra could think around. "We both know you didn't bring me here to just to torture me. You wouldn't keep drugging me otherwise. You wanted something Elwess has never had."

Abruptly, Silas fisted Dahlra's hair and arched his neck back painfully. He pulled him into a punishing, open-mouthed kiss that deepened as Dahlra allowed himself to be taken.

Silas pulled away, flushed and panting. "You're really nothing but a needy slut, aren't you?" His voice was hard, but it trembled around the edges. There was a trace of lust that had less to do with power and more with his own personal desire. He reached between Dahlra's legs again, and this time found his flaccid cock. He pumped it expertly, demanding a response, and Dahlra closed his eyes and gave into it. His body answered Silas' expert manipulations, somehow, someway; he hoped it would trip the tumblers in Silas' ego.

He felt warm breath against his ear. "Look at me, Dahlra." He obeyed. "You're quite a beautiful man, you know. I know your type very well. On the surface, you're strong. But there's a part of you, deep down, that longs to bow to another man." Silas caressed Dahlra's bruised face almost tenderly. "I'm enjoying this, very much, more than I anticipated. If we had the time, there's so much more I could teach you."

He turned away. "Elwess should have been the one to give you your first real taste of submission, but he was too busy plotting to take Sydney away from you, wasn't he?"

Dahlra shook his head. "No." He could hear the doubt spiking the word, making it sound prickly in his mouth. "No, it was just sex."

"That's not what Elwess told me. If that was the case, why did Sydney come to London on her own, to be with him?" When Dahlra did not answer, Silas leaned in for the kill. "You think I wanted to break you? You're already broken, Dahlra. You were broken the day you came back to the UK with what was left of Sydney Chapin. Elwess knew it. That's why he took your woman away from you. They betrayed you."

"No. That's a lie."

"You've been betrayed by everyone you loved, haven't you? Even your father?"

"My-" At the mention of his father, Dahlra broke. His truest, darkest secret had been betrayed. He had done his best, and this final, awful knowledge that he would never be good enough crushed the last of his resolve and strength. He burst into tears.

Silas made soothing noises, shushing him. "It's alright, I know. And now, so do you, and we can move on. There is no pleasure without pain."

Watching Dahlra break was like watching a part of herself die, made even more insufferable within the prison of her own paralysed body. Sydney was exhausted, nearly deranged from her efforts to move. If she could only get free, she would make Silas suffer. After she was through with him, he would be begging her to kill him. She would make him pay a thousand different ways, while Dahlra instructed her, while he watched her exact his revenge, and it would be so sweet...

Just as her vengeance-fueled fantasies reached Geiger counter levels, Sydney's entire body exploded into life. Every inch of her skin felt jabbed with pins and needles. She bayed aloud at the awful, muscle-shredding sensation, and she rode the pain until it eventually dissipated into a dull ache.

She sagged against her bonds, sweaty and gasping in relief. A deep breath and a long exhale later, she approached something close to straight thinking. She could move again, and if she could move, she could save Dahlra.

She rocked back and forth, trying to feel any loose or weak spots in the joints of the chair, but she could detect nothing. It was a huge, gothic horror of a thing, heavy and solid. It was like shifting the rock of Gibraltar.

She growled in frustration, trying to pull her arms free, but it only drove the zip ties deeper into her wrists. If she kept this up, she would end up slicing the skin enough to peel her hands from her wrists like a couple of bloody gloves. The thought made her gag, and she fought back the urge to throw up. "Get a grip, for fuck's sake!" she shouted aloud. "This isn't a bloody Stephen King novel."

In desperation, she threw herself forward, and her spine gave an awful creak. The carver toppled forward, and she landed painfully on her knees. Her body screamed in pain; her dislocated finger struck up Stars and Stripes Forever, which only made her angrier. She rocked back, then forward, using the ends of the chair arms to pull her body forward like crutches. Her knees scraped over the carpet as she dragged herself along. There were knives in the kitchen; she could free herself.

Progress was slow. Too damn slow. She gritted her teeth, and headed toward the hallway, inch by painful inch. She hoped the chair was the only thing that would break when she threw herself down the stairs.

Dahlra knew he was being given dose after dose of this hallucinogenic drug Silas called Sparklers, but there was nothing to do but allow it to ride him. He itched and burned from head to toe; he shook uncontrollably, like a junkie. Every nerve ending shrieked.

The hallucinations grew more opaque and personal as Silas sought out and exploited his insecurities and memories. Each time he subdued one nightmare, another rose to take its place, more knowledgeable of his vulnerabilities and less concerned with the sanctity of his sanity. He could not win this war against his own demons.

Visions of Sydney and Elwess swam into the foreground, laughing, taunting him for his cowardice, and even though he told himself they were not real, the seed had been planted. Silas knew things about their personal life; did it not follow that the things he told Dahlra about Sydney's unfaithfulness were true as well? According to Silas, she was just another Caroline, using him while enjoying his friend. It all sounded so plausible, it rang true.

His hold on reality was rapidly disintegrating, slipping away like dry leaves on a dusty ground. In his final lucid moments, it occurred to Dahlra that Sydney's captors had hired the wrong man to work her over. If Silas had been there, he would have ruined both of them with no more effort than crushing the skull of a doll.

Elwess had never been happier to see the door of his flat. He was travel-worn and pissed off, not to mention starving. His leather trousers were hot as fuck and he was sweating like a Trojan, but hell, he couldn't be expected to pull off the Euro-Kinkmeister General routine in khakis and a Jim'll Fix It t-shirt, could he? His imposing figure had garnered some strange looks from his fellow travelers and he was given a wide berth as he strode from the terminal, but at least he was able to stop traffic long enough to get one of the few available cabs.

He was determined to surprise Sydney and Dahlra by arriving early. Besides which, he was fucked if he was going to squirm under Sydney's reproachful glare one more time. He had actually forgotten about the dinner party when he agreed to attend the play weekend in Amsterdam, and he had called in all sorts of last-minute favours with his travel agent to get an early flight back to London. Now, he just had time for a shower and a change of clothes before the guests arrived.

He unfolded himself out of the cab, stretching his long limbs as the cabbie changed his fifty-pound note and collected his bags from the boot. Dahlra and Sydney would be pleasantly surprised to see him when he breezed through the door, and no doubt he would benefit from their gratitude later in the evening. At the very least he could count on some good home cooking and something cold and wet to slake his flight-induced dehydration.

He opened the door with a flourish. "All right, you tarts! The party has arrived—"

Above his head, he heard a loud, hollow noise, followed by the sound of something being dragged across the floor. "Elwess! Get up here now!" Sydney sounded choked and breathless.

He flew up the stairs, following her voice, then froze at the door of his study. Sydney was tied to his dining room carver, dragging and pulling herself out of the room. When she looked up and saw him, he recoiled in horror. She had been beaten, her cheek cut, and her wrists were bleeding profusely.

"Jesus, Sydney! What the fuck is going on?"

"That!" He followed her gaze toward the computer monitor.

It took Elwess a moment to comprehend exactly what he was seeing. "Oh, Jesus." His testicles crawled up inside his body. "What is *he* doing here? How did he—"

"It doesn't matter! Cut me loose!"

Her harsh voice broke his paralysis, and he rushed to her side. She was thrashing about so wildly it took an age to right the heavy chair.

"Sydney, calm down! Stop flailing around, for Christ's sake!"

"Get a knife, scissors, something! Cut me loose, goddammit!"

He frantically searched the room, but there was nothing sharp enough to cut the ties.

Another hypo, another stinging needle. Another wave of timeless unconsciousness. When Dahlra next awoke, he was facing outward on the cross. On the table beside it was a roll of gaffer tape, a straight razor, and a box of sterile sharps. He whimpered, his fear threatening to override the few remaining scraps of himself left.

Silas smiled at him, a sick, putrid angel offering him the keys to a charnel heaven. "There is no pleasure without pain, Dahlra. Is there?"

"No, sir."

"Say it, then!" He punctuated his words with a hard slap.

"There is no pleasure without pain, Master Silas."

"That's correct, bitch." Another slap set his ears ringing. "Let's see which one you enjoy more."

Silas opened the box of sharps and began threading them one at a time through the flesh of Dahlra's chest, like a tailor hemming a garment. Dahlra's determination not to cry out had become his only reason to stay alive.

Remaining still, however, was no longer an option. He writhed and twitched, each movement its own punishment. Blood trickled over his pale skin, and Silas painted his body with it. "You look like a crucifix in a bugger's bible. Then again, you always did consider yourself the saviour type."

Dahlra greyed out, and came to just as Silas was stroking his limp cock. He watched in dawning comprehension as Silas readied the final needle.

"Please don't... don't do it..." He whimpered brokenly, shaming himself. *Weakling, weakling.* "I'll do anything you ask, just don't..."

"Oh, it's too late for begging, Dahlra. You want this. You know you do, really. Now, be very still, and don't forget to thank me." Silas carefully peeled back the foreskin and exposed the head.

Even then, he did not scream; he could not catch his breath enough to scream. He fainted again, and awoke only when Silas poured the second bottle of rubbing alcohol over his chest. Cursing and thrashing, he hyperventilated to block the pain, but it was no use. He was at the end. "No more. Please."

Silas took Dahlra's bottom lip between his teeth and bit it until it bled. "There now. I think we've made excellent progress today, don't you?"

Dahlra wept.

Sydney heard Elwess thundering back up the stairs. He appeared in the doorway, brandishing a long kitchen knife.

The pain of sawing through the zip ties nearly caused her to black out, but Sydney grimly hung onto consciousness, taking deep breaths as Elwess freed her ankles. "I have to get down there! He's killing Dahlra!"

He grabbed a towel and wrapped it around her bloody wrists, but she pushed him away, yanking the rope from around her chest. "Listen to me!" She shakily hauled herself onto her feet. Her head spun, and she swayed alarmingly, yet somehow managed to stay on her feet. "I need your help."

In spite of the amount of blood on her wrists, it was the dislocated finger that required the most attention. She grasped her injured hand by the wrist, and extended it toward Elwess. The finger stuck out at an unnatural angle, and even attempting to flex it sent a throbbing shockwave up her arm.

"Take hold of this finger with both hands, like this." She quickly showed him how to grasp it, and the pain threatened to blow her head off. "Whatever you do, don't let go. Do you hear me? Don't let go."

Elwess nodded and gingerly grasped the end of her finger. Sydney took three deep, rapid breaths, and jerked her hand away from his as hard and as quickly as she could. The finger snapped in place with a sickening jolt, and she screamed her rage and pain into the room. A wave of nausea hit her again, this time with the force of a cricket bat. She spun away from Elwess and vomited until spots flashed behind her eyes.

"Oh, God, Sydney, I'm sorry!" Elwess held on, keeping her upright, pushing her hair out of her face. "Oh, hell, I'm sorry! You told me not to let go—"

"No, no, you did good." She spat to get the foul taste out of her mouth. Gradually, her head cleared, and she flexed her hand. It was not perfect, but she could move it.

"I want you gagging on my cock. You'd like that very much, wouldn't you?" Silas' voice was thick with arousal. He placed a deep kiss on Dahlra's lacerated mouth. "Let's have a little fun with this contraption of Elwess', shall we?"

Silas reached around to the other side of the cross and depressed a lever. As he pumped the handle, the cross ponderously juddered upward on the main axis, each jolt sending another spear of pain through Dahlra's torn and punctured flesh. He sagged against his bonds, too exhausted to brace himself.

When the cross was almost two feet off the floor, Silas giggled, "Bottoms up." He slammed the lever into place and spun the entire cross like a wheel of fortune, suspending Dahlra upside down. A new rush of chemical-saturated blood rushed to his head, and the weight of his body answered the call of gravity. The needles pulled in this new direction, and fresh rills of agony rippled over his body. Blood trickled down his skin in warm rivulets, pooling in his ears and hair. He heard his laboured breath wheezing in and out of his lungs, and hated himself for it.

"Perfect."

Silas lowered his trousers and freed his cock, a long white worm that writhed and pulsed in Dahlra's drug-soaked mind. He glanced upward; Silas was staring down at him, pale eyes blazing with power, his long blond hair a white curtain. His face morphed into a skeleton, then into a demon, sick with sin. He grasped the back of Dahlra's head with his free hand.

"Kiss it with reverence, my dear." He pulled Dahlra toward him. "Worship me properly."

Dahlra hesitated, and was rewarded with a hard slap against the side of his head. "You seem to be under the mistaken impression you have a choice here, Gar. I suggest if you want to keep your own cock, you'd better get busy." He snatched the straight razor from the table and brandished it toward Dahlra's groin. "Do I need to give you a demonstration?"

"No, please! I haven't—this is the first time—"

Silas pretended surprise. "First time? Really? Well, perhaps all you need is a little incentive to remain focused on task." Silas dropped the razor, and reached for the gaffer tape. "Here's a little trick I learned in Berlin. Works wonders for your concentration."

There was a ripping sound as he tore a short strip of tape from the roll. He pressed it firmly over Dahlra's nose, sealing his nostrils completely. "Now, if you don't want to suffocate, you'll do as I say." He grabbed Dahlra by the throat and shook him. "I suggest you stop stalling."

Dahlra choked, and tears of humiliation pricked his eyes. "Yes, Master."

He closed his eyes and opened his mouth.

"Call the Agency emergency line." Sydney stumbled toward the bedroom. Her balance was all over the place; she caromed off the doorjamb, cursing as she banged her injured hand. "Give them your ID and address and tell them it's a code Alpha Poppa Victor."

"Do I—"

"They'll know what it means."

Their bag was still sitting unpacked on the bed, and Sydney yanked open the zip and upended it. Throwing aside shirts and shoes and underwear, she rummaged frantically until her fingers curled around the holster of her Glock. She grabbed the loaded clip from a side pocket, gasping against the pain in her blood-slicked hands. She slammed the clip home and loaded the chamber, then trotted unsteadily back out into the hall. Elwess was standing there, phone in hand.

"The Agency said they would be here in ten minutes. They'll be coming through the tunnel as well as topside."

"Good." She headed for the stairs. "Stay here until they arrive."

"Like hell I will!" Elwess grabbed her arm, and spun her around. His sallow face was the colour of curdled milk, but his gaze was firm and unyielding. "I'm going with you!"

"No. I need you to stay here!" She shook off his hand. "If Silas *is* armed, I don't want him to have more targets than I can cover."

He fought for every breath, but he was losing.

Dahlra desperately tried to keep his throat open, but Silas choked him, making him gag. "You're very good, for a virgin." Silas moaned in exaggerated pleasure. "Clumsy, but we can fix that with a little training."

Gradually, he released Dahlra's throat, and began to thrust hard and fast. "Just think, my pretty boy, all the lovely pain that awaits you at my hand." Dahlra whined in protest, and above him he heard Silas sigh with satisfaction.

He tried twisting his head away, but Silas threaded his hands in Dahlra's hair and forced his head backward. His chest burned, his lungs felt as if they were going to burst. The sensation of drowning set in, and with it came true panic.

Just as Dahlra was about to lose consciousness, Silas pulled out, leaving him to gasp and sputter. As he frantically pulled air into his protesting lungs, Silas leaned down and whispered conspiratorially. "You know, Dahlra. I may just keep you. It's not like you have anything to go back to, do you? Sydney and Elwess are upstairs, you know. I didn't really kill her. She and your friend are fucking while they watch us. You know what a voyeur Elwess is."

He forced himself back into Dahlra's gaping mouth with a smug laugh. "Now, let's finish what we started."

Dahlra took a last, desperate breath. *Sydney.*

He threw his head forward and clamped down with all the power left in his strained jaw. His teeth sank into flesh, and kept sinking.

Silas' high-pitched scream was loud enough to shatter glass. He staggered away from Dahlra with another wail of agony, flailing against the table. "You fucking bastard! You fucking, fucking cunt—"

Dahlra choked and gagged; he spat blood, then spat again, until his mouth was empty. He drew in great, deep draughts of pure, Silas-free air, and even though he knew he had forfeited his one chance of reprieve with that final, futile act of retaliation, he no longer cared.

Then his diaphragm bucked, and he could no longer draw air into his burning lungs. He thrashed and begged for forgiveness, his chest screaming for oxygen, but no one answered his pleas.

Cool, painless darkness descended, and Dahlra gratefully floated away.

Sydney left Elwess protesting in the hall, and headed downstairs. She quietly opened the door that led down into the Chine. She paused, considering her options. Her only advantage was the element of surprise; there was a lift, but it was as slow as it was noisy. The alternative was the staircase, though it, too, was deliberately loud. She removed her shoes and crept out onto the landing, wincing at the bite of the sharp metal rungs on her bare feet.

Instinctively, Sydney grasped the banister to steady herself. As she looked at the smooth pole that spiraled down with the steps, she knew what she had to do. Time was up. If that Jamie Oliver guy could do it, so could she.

She perched side-saddle on the bannister and started downward. She was wobbly at first, but she eventually found her center of balance, gathering speed as she descended one nauseating turn after another.

From below, a scream seemed to rise up from hell, turning her blood to ice and jacking her heart up to full throttle. Silas' voice rose above another unidentifiable sound, high pitched and furious. "You fucking bastard! You fucking, fucking cunt—"

The floor was coming at her fast, and she braced herself. She jumped at the last minute, landed badly, and fell onto her knees. Her adrenaline got her back on her feet before it even registered and she shook her head to quell the merry-go-round dizziness. Her vision snapped back to single lens, and she took in the carnage in one quick glance.

Dahlra was hanging upside down on the St Andrews cross, blood on his face and body, eerily still. Silas was clutching his groin with his right hand, while blood was running down his naked thighs, onto his lowered trousers. Something glinted in Silas' hand; it was the same cut-throat razor he had used to score her cheek.

Sydney leveled her Glock, but he was too close to Dahlra to get a clean shot. "Step away from him, Markham!"

He whirled toward her, wild-eyed and stunned. "How did you get here?" Shock and anger warred in his expression, but the rage won. "You know, what? I don't give a fuck!" His face twisted into a look of demonic madness. "You want your precious Dr Gar? Let's see who gets to him first, eh? The big, bad agent, or the man two inches away from him!" He turned back to Dahlra and switched the razor to his blood-soaked right hand. "Let's see if you've got balls enough for the both of you!"

Sydney fired as the razor slashed through the air. A bright fan of blood arced over Dahlra's groin, and for a heart-stopping moment Sydney thought she had hit him. Then Silas began screaming in earnest. He fell writhing to the floor, clutching what was left of his hand. Sydney rushed to Dahlra's side. "Shut up!" She dealt Silas a ruthless kick in the ribs. He rolled away, unconscious.

She turned to release Dahlra from the cross. "It's me, love. You're safe now." She leaned down to be at eye level. "I'll get you out of this contraption as fast as I..." Her words died in her mouth. Dahlra's nose and mouth had been sealed shut with black gaffer tape.

"God, no..." She tore the tape from his face; his eyes were closed, and he was frowning slightly. His skin was blotchy, his lips were blue and smeared with blood.

"The agents are two minutes away. I've given the paramedics the access code so they can come in from the tunnel," Elwess announced, running down the final steps. He stumbled as he took in the bloodbath before him. "Oh, no... No, he can't be—"

"He's not breathing! Get over here and help me—*now*!" Sydney frantically twisted dials and pumped handles, but could not find a way to restore the cross upright.

Elwess raced to the controls and quickly maneuvered the cross so that it lay horizontal. "Cradle his head! We've got to get him in a stable position. Help me get him on the table—"

"No need." Elwess swiftly released more levers. The arms of the cross moved inward, the *X* shape changing to an *I*. As Elwess lifted the device to the proper height, Sydney pressed her ear to Dahlra's chest. She could detect the faintest of heartbeats, but it was so slow, unbearably slow. Elwess unbuckled the restraints with fumbling, shaking hands.

Sydney placed her fingers against Dahlra's throat; she found a tiny, thready pulse. "Thank God. Elwess, I need your help." She grabbed his hand. "Put your fingers here, on his wrist. Can you feel that?"

He nodded. "It's very faint-"

"If anything changes, tell me. And start pulling those damn needles out."

Sydney gently arched Dahlra's neck, and pinched his nose closed. She blew two rapid breaths into his mouth, then released his nose and listened. His lungs deflated, but did not respond.

"His heart's still beating."

She tried again, and again no response. She glanced up at Elwess, and saw the same sick fear she felt. She pinched his nose and blew for a third time, and suddenly Dahlra fishtailed and took a huge, frantic breath that sounded as frightening as his silence. He choked as he tried to rise from the makeshift table.

Sydney gently turned him on his side, and he gagged, ghastly, retching coughs that sounded as if his lungs were being ripped out of his chest. Thick, pink-tinted foam spewed from his mouth and nose. He fell back, wheezing horribly, gulping in air, his face blood red and twisted with agony.

"Get a towel," she commanded. "And where the fuck is that ambulance?"

"Sydney..." Dahlra gasped helplessly. "Sydney—"

"I'm here, love, I'm here." She gently cleaned his face as he began to shiver. "It's alright. Everything's alright."

He grasped her hand, looking around sightlessly. "He didn't... I didn't..."

"Shhh. Don't try to talk right now, please." There were voices approaching from the tunnel entrance, and she looked up just as Elwess opened the door and two Agency paramedics raced in, wheeling a gurney between them. "He's going to need a stabiliser board and a collar."

"We're on it." They quickly slid the board in place, then hooked up an ECG and fitted Dahlra with an oxygen mask. He was now shuddering uncontrollably, and they wrapped him in thermal blankets.

As Sydney stroked his face, his eyes locked with hers. They were horribly bloodshot, the pupils blown from the drugs. As he struggled to focus, she leaned closer. "It's me, love. Try and stay as still as you can."

"Didn't... didn't make me scream." It was hard to understand him behind the mask. The grip on her hand slackened. "Not even when he told me... told me..."

"Don't talk. Just rest. You're going to be alright, I promise." Sydney choked. "You were incredible. You're my goddamn hero."

"He said you were... you were dead." He sighed, his eyes fluttering.

Sydney felt tears in the back of her throat. "I heard what he said. It was all lies, Dahlra. I'm sorry, dear heart. I'm so sorry."

"I know." He sighed again, and slipped into unconsciousness.

Sydney watched helplessly as the medics prepared him for transport. They spoke in short, clipped tones, sharp orders, tersely answered questions. As they consulted with the waiting A&E team, Sydney could tell they were concerned. "He's been seriously overdosed with an unknown substance. We've got the spent hypos here, so we can hopefully analyse it. I've given him two milligrams of Narcan—"

One of the medics tried to attend her, but she pushed him away impatiently. "Deal with me later. Take care of *him*!"

"Bloody hell, Syd. What's all this?"

She looked up just as Inigo and Pink entered from the tunnel side. Her partner's long, homely face was a bracing sight. He took in the scene in one quick, all-encompassing look. "Right, mate. What can I do?"

"I need to go with the ambulance, but my shoes are topside. Would you fetch them?"

"Sure. No worries." He brushed past Elwess, throwing him a wary look of suspicion. Inigo was silent as he glanced around, assessing the situation. His eyes fell on Silas Markham's inert form, then he swiveled his gaze back to her.

"Status report, Agent."

"I'll be more than happy to brief you as soon as I know Dahlra's alright." As far as she was concerned, Inigo could whistle for his status report. The room was warm, and the metallic tang of blood, mingling with the other sickish-sweet odours, was making her stomach roll. She turned impatiently to the paramedics. "Can't you get a move on?"

She turned toward the stairs as Pink made his clanking way down the last few rungs. He held a pair of trainers. "These were the first ones I saw. They were on the landing—" He dropped the shoes and drew his Glock in one deft movement. "Don't move, Markham!"

Sydney whirled around just as Silas lurched onto his feet, looking like hell come to call—blood-spattered hair, mutilated hand, disheveled, blood-stained clothing. His face twisted in a demonic mask of fury and loathing. With a roar of anger, he lunged at her, the cut-throat razor slashing through the air toward her face.

There was a deafening gunshot. Silas was knocked backward by the impact. He landed against the metal cabinets with a crash, his head snapping back against the edge with a sickening crunch. He slid down, staring at them in sightless accusation. There was a gaping hole in his chest; the cut-throat was still clutched in his undamaged hand.

Sydney turned toward Elwess, who was holding her discharged Glock with both hands. He was breathing hard, his whole body shaking.

Pink stepped between him and Sydney, his weapon leveled on Elwess. "Lower your weapon, Talbert!"

At the thunderous command, Elwess dropped the gun onto the table as if it were electrified. His wide, shock-filled eyes darted to Silas' still form. "He was coming at Sydney. He had a razor. I didn't know what—"

"From where I was standing it looked like you knew exactly what you were doing. All a bit drastic, innit?" Pink quickly retrieved Sydney's

Glock and released the clip. He towered over Elwess by several intimidating inches. "So what's your game, Talbert? Afraid your friend Silas might do a little grassing on you?"

Elwess stared at him, his confusion turning to defiance. "Grass—" He huffed angrily and nodded toward Sydney. "That prick was going for her! What's *your* game, Agent?"

Pink refused to be intimidated. "You could have easily disarmed—"

"Enough, all of you!" The three men looked at Sydney in surprise. "Dahlra's hanging on by a thread and all you three can do is bitch about that dead arsehole?" She shook her head. "I'm done. You can all stand around arguing, but I'm off to the hospital. Elwess can give you the rest of the details."

The paramedics raised the stretcher to waist height, and made their swift and careful way toward the Brompton Street entrance. Sydney quickly slipped her feet into her trainers and headed after them. As she approached the doorway, something on the ground caught her eye. Her engagement ring, still miraculously intact, winked from one of the severed fingers she had shot off Silas' hand. She retrieved the ring, and tossed the finger aside.

CHAPTER NINE

Aftermath

"Ms Chapin?"

Sydney quickly rose to her feet. "I'm Sydney Chapin."

A middle-aged doctor with thinning brown hair and a lumpy, kindly face proffered his hand. "Daffyd Hughes. I'm a colleague of Dr Gar's, and the physician in charge of his crisis team. I'm sorry to meet in such serious circumstances." His lilting Welsh accent gave every word a pleasant note. "We all here think very highly of Dahlra."

She did not have the patience for pleasantries. "How is he?"

Dr Hughes indicated for Sydney to follow him. "Dahlra regained consciousness a few minutes ago. He's quite agitated and his blood pressure is very high. He's disorientated and upset, as you might imagine. He's called for you, but he's also under the impression that you might be dead. We've settled him down a little, but perhaps if he could see you, it would set his mind at ease. We're still trying to identify the composition and dosage of the substance he was given."

"Is he going to be alright?"

Hughes paused outside a door. "It's a little early to tell how much damage the drugs may have done physically as well as psychologically, Ms Chapin. Right now, the priority is to get him stable enough to ensure his complete recovery."

Sydney grasped the door handle, but the physician covered her hand with his. "I understand you witnessed what happened to him."

"Yes."

"Then you know that it's not just the drugs he is fighting, Ms Chapin. He's been through a great amount of physical and psychological trauma."

Sydney forced herself to ask the question that had gnawed at her during the interminable ride to the hospital. "Dr Hughes, he was oxygen-deprived after he lost consciousness. He'd been hanging upside-down as well. What are the chances of... of lasting brain damage?"

The physician frowned. "A terrible thing, that. But you know, being upside-down might have worked in his favour. More blood flow to the brain, you see. It's too early to tell, but rest assured we'll be running every scan and test we can to determine the extent of the trauma." His kind face was grim with concern. "Once we ascertain his physical prognosis, I want to make sure we treat the emotional impact as well. These next few days will be quite difficult for him. He's very fragile right now. He's going to need all your support and patience."

Sydney's throat tightened. *I failed him. When he needed me most, I failed him.* "Whatever he needs, Dr Hughes, he'll get it."

He patted her arm. "Very good." He opened the door for her.

Dahlra had told her more than once how hard it had been to see her after their return from the Cell; now she had a better appreciation for his ability to maintain his professional composure. It took all her courage just to face him.

The first thing she noticed was that Silas had marred almost every square inch of Dahlra's beautiful face. Already, large purple and yellow bruises were blooming over his porcelain skin; tiny blood spots covered the front of his hospital gown, like flecks of rust. Dark blue smudges circled his swollen, bloodied eyes, but it was the expression in them that stopped her in her tracks. He looked like a man who had seen death and did not know quite how to come back to life.

She sat down on the bed and pulled the blanket up higher onto his chest, and tried to hitch up a smile. "Hey." She rested her hand on his arm and was shocked to find he was trembling. Her steady Dahlra was trembling.

"Hello, Sydney." His voice was stiff, completely devoid of its purling beauty.

"How are you feeling?"

With unnerving calm, he gazed past her to the door beyond. "I've been beaten and raped. How do you think I feel?"

Recrimination burned in her chest. "Oh, love, I'm so sorry." She gave his hand a gentle squeeze. He did not return the gesture. She wanted to hold him, to do something to comfort him, but he was disturbingly distant. "I've been speaking to Dr Hughes. He says you're going to be fine. Just a little TLC, and some counseling, and you'll be right as the jolly old."

"Did he?" Dahlra frowned abstractedly and looked down at his hands. "Well, then, that's brilliant. A little counseling ought to fix me right up."

"That's not what I—"

"Is it true, you saw everything?"

She was taken aback. "Yes..." The look he gave her made Sydney curse herself for being so piss-poor at comfort. "Look, I was thinking, after you've recovered and gone through the debriefing, we could just take off awhile, you know, go somewhere we've never been? I know Inigo will spring for first class and maybe we can... I thought we could..."

Her voice sputtered to a halt. He was staring ahead, breathing hard, his chest hitching. "Dahlra, should I go and get someone? Are you in a lot of pain?"

"Can I ask you something?"

"Of course, love."

He swallowed. "What do you think would have happened if we'd never met? What would you be doing right now?" Sydney tried to speak, but Dahlra went on, his eyes still far away. "I suppose *I'd* be at home watching telly, or at a bar somewhere having a drink, or in my study, reading a medical journal. Maybe I'd be cooking for a dinner party."

"I suppose. But you once told me that—"

"Of course, I'd still be in a loveless marriage. It wouldn't change the fact that my wife was cheating on me, or that she referred to me as the most uninteresting man she knew."

"I don't think this is—"

"Well I do. I'm dull, and I'm safe. And I like dull and safe things. Things that have nothing to do with the Agency, or espionage, or Silverbirch." The look in his eyes frightened her. "Or Sydney Chapin."

Her breath left her lungs; ice water had been dumped into her veins. "Dahlra—"

"I'm not like you." His expression was bleak. "I can't just turn this off. I can't just tell myself this didn't happen and go on like we were before."

"But you *will* get past it. I know that for a fact."

He looked away, a faint, stubborn line between his brows. Sydney persisted, "You have to give it time, Dahlra. It's not going to happen overnight. And I'll be with you every step of the way. Right now you just want to—"

"Right now I just want to lick my wounds and be left in peace, Sydney. But peace is not something I'm ever going to have with you, is it?

Sooner or later, you'll be right back at it, risking your life for people who don't give a damn about whether you live or die, and not giving two fucks about the one person who has tried to care for you."

"That's not true! I care about everything you do and say and think, Dahlra! Don't you see? It's not going to be that way. I'm not the same person I was—"

"Oh, I know you'll put it off for a while to pacify me, but eventually you'll go back to the Agency. And you'll tell yourself that it's to avenge what happened to me, but really it's just because you love playing I-Spy." His voice turned harsh and bitter. "You love it more than anything. More than me, at least."

"No." Her throat closed until it was hard to breathe.

Dahlra raised his gaze to her, his eyes like green ice. It was as if Silas had left something in him, had possessed her beautiful lover with his ugliness. "I won't do it. I won't tear my heart out anymore. I'm not going to sit at home, waiting like a lovesick fool, until the day Lightoller brings me your corpse. I'm not going to stick around just long enough to mourn you. I'm good enough to fuck you and feed you, but in the end, I deserve more." He held up his hands, as if to present the destruction Silas had wrought. "I deserve more than this, at least."

A strange sound escaped her; it left a metallic, ruined taste in her mouth. She started to shiver. "I know you do. You deserve the best. My best." She felt the first vestiges of panic. "And I'm going to make sure you get it. I love you more than anything on this earth. You know that."

"I don't know anything anymore, Sydney."

She closed her eyes and took a deep breath. "Dahlra, what happened to you... I know you're angry and upset, and you have every right to be, but don't let it change what we are, how you feel about me. Give me a chance."

He uttered a grim, mirthless laugh; Sydney realised he was crying. "Jesus, how many times did I say those very words to you? I groveled at your feet, begging for any little scrap you'd deign to give me, and for what? This?"

Sydney tried to take his hand but he pulled away. She felt her stomach fold in on itself. "We're engaged to be married. You love me. And I love you."

His dull eyes turned resentful, accusing. "It didn't stop you from taking another man to your bed. Letting Elwess talk me into bringing you that goddamn dungeon was one of stupidest things I've ever done. The other was believing it wouldn't make a difference."

Now the panic hit like a warhammer to her heart. "You don't know what you're saying. You don't mean it. You can't. Not with all we've been through together. I know you're hurting, but—"

"Sydney, please." He held up his hand to stop her. "Look, I'm really quite tired right now. You need to go, alright?"

Cold. She was so cold. "You don't really want me to leave, do you?"

"I want some time alone. Go and get some rest." He looked as blank as a piece of paper. "If you want to stay with Elwess, I'll understand."

"Are you— Dahlra, are you throwing me out?" Desperation and fear melded into a noxious poison that tasted like ash in her mouth. "Are you saying you don't want to be with me anymore? Just like that?"

He sighed. "Go and get some rest, Sydney. And have one of the on-calls check you over. You look terrible." He closed his eyes. "I can't help you now."

"But you're everything." The words tumbled from her in a harsh rush. If he heard them, he didn't respond. The last of her adrenaline-induced strength ebbed away, leaving Sydney weak and hurting all over. "Alright. I'll go. I don't have a choice, do I?"

A few steps from the door, she turned back, and glanced at him. He was still looking straight ahead, battling with whatever demons still occupied his thoughts.

She cashed in the last fraying strands of her courage to ask one final question. "Dahlra, do you wish we'd never met?"

For a long time, he studied the IV tubes connected into the backs of his hands.

"I don't know."

Sydney stumbled back, until she collided with the door. She left, and he let her.

I am not going to cry in front of these people. I am not going to cry in front of these people. The words became her mantra as Sydney quickly walked down the hospital corridor toward the car park. As she reached the end of the hall, she slowed, cursing to herself. She had come here in the ambulance, straight from the Chine without so much as a purse on her. Everything was still at Elwess' house. She sighed heavily, and most of her energy exited along with the air from her lungs.

It was so ironic. The last time she had been in this situation she had gone home with her tail between her legs, too embarrassed to ask for help. But help had been there. Dahlra had been waiting, worried sick and clucking around her like a mother hen.

What a difference a day makes.

The thought of going back to Elwess' was unconscionable. She would have to go to the office and call Pink. Maybe she could stay with him for a few days.

Sydney pressed her forehead against the rough wall. *I saved his life, but I killed his love*, she thought. Everything hit her at once: the attack, the trank, her throbbing hands, the various cuts and scrapes, Dahlra's goodbye... A sudden vivid image burned into her head like a photograph: Dahlra, hanging on the cross like a grisly sacrifice, his mouth and nose covered with black tape. *I failed him...*

Her vision doubled; she slid down the wall until she was doubled over on the floor. Bitter, yellow bile flooded her mouth, making her wretch. She wrapped her arms around her body, whimpering in humiliation.

"Sydney? Christ!"

She glanced up to see Elwess running toward her at a gallop. She stood with an effort, using the wall to push herself upright before he could reach her. He looked tired and worried. This infuriated her. What right did *he* have to be so upset?

Elwess put his hands on her shoulders and nodded toward the hospital. "Has something happened? Is Dahlra going to be alright? I came as soon as Lightoller let me leave the flat, but they wouldn't allow visitors."

His expression softened, and he stroked her hair from her face. "Oh, kitten, have you seen a doctor yet? Do you need help walking?" He took her arm. "Come on, love. Let's get you a cup of tea and a change of clothes, at least. Dahlra would never forgive me if I didn't take care of you—"

A red mist of anger and grief boiled up inside her so quickly she felt sick again. With a low growl, she shook off his arm. "Get your hands off me! I can take care of myself."

He recoiled away from her in shock. "Sydney, what's the matter? What have *I* done?"

"What have you *done*?" The anger within suffused her with a painful burst of strength, and she pushed him hard against the wall. "You've got some nerve asking me that question! Don't tell me you didn't bother to watch what was going on in your little House of Fun. You saw what he did to Dahlra."

Elwess' jaw tightened. "Yeah, I saw. And I'm glad I shot the bastard, even with Pinkerton breathing down my neck. Fucker deserved to die."

"Don't let's talk about getting what we deserve, Elwess." Her words came out like a weak cough, and that enraged her more. "Goddamn you! You've been nothing but trouble for us from the first moment we met."

"What are you talking about—"

"I'm talking about you treating us like your little playthings. I'm talking about your lies and your arrogance and your hidden agenda. I'm talking about what almost got Dahlra killed."

"Sydney, you're not making any sense."

"Oh, I'm making sense. I'm making pisspots of sense!" A little demon with a hot poker was jabbing at her brain, unmindful of reason or truth or the difference between them and the loss she felt. "None of this would have happened if not for you!"

"Me?" He was shocked into laughter. "How is this *my* fault?"

"How fucking dare you ask me that, after that little candid camera incident? You schemed to get us, and you've done everything in your power to pull us apart! I honestly wouldn't be surprised if you were in on this. It would be so easy to get Dahlra out of the way and then you could sweep in at the perfect moment and make the big rescue—"

"Now listen to me good, *kitten*." His dark brows rushed together. "Let's get this straight: you're talking bollocks and you know it. I am *not* trying to pull anyone apart, least of all Dahlra and you. I love you. Both of you!" He moved to hold her, but offered no resistance when she pushed him away again. "Come on, Sydney! I know you're upset, but—"

"I'm not upset, you arsehole! What I am is alone! Dahlra has thrown me out because of you!"

He could not have looked more stunned if she had kicked him in the balls. "What? Why?"

"He doesn't want me anymore." Just saying it aloud made her chest cave in on itself. "He said I wasn't worth this. Any of this. And he's right. He deserves better than to be raped and tortured in your little house of horrors, Talbert! He accused me of wanting you more than him. He told me he was..."

She forced herself to say the words, even though they cut like glass in her mouth. "He said he was sorry he'd ever met me. Do you know what that means?" Hot tears etched like acid into the cut on her cheek, and she welcomed the pain. "Do you have any idea how that feels? To know the one person you love more than anything else wishes he had never met you?"

Elwess shook his head. "I can't believe it. He couldn't have known what he was saying! Maybe you misunderstood him—"

Before she knew what she was doing, Sydney swung her arm in a roundhouse punch to Elwess' face. The impact sent a numbing shock wave from fist to shoulder and made her wrist start bleeding again. Elwess' head snapped back, and he clutched his bloody nose, his eyes wide from hurt and betrayal.

"You've caused me nothing but grief, Elwess Talbert. Trouble follows you around like a bad smell. You stay away from me, or by God, I'll fucking kill you."

She spun away, and left him staring after her as she made her unsteady way down the darkened sidewalk toward the Agency.

It was there Pink found her, dazedly wandering around in the foyer. He embraced her roughly. "Thank God, Syd! Lightoller's had the cavalry out looking for you!" He took in her battered, tearstained face, her disheveled appearance, his eyes dark with pity. He put his arm around her shoulder and pulled her close. "You *have* been in the wars. Blimey, what a day. Come on, gell."

"Are you sure you don't want me to go with you to hospital? Those wrists could use a..." Sydney glared at Pink until he got the message. "Right then, let's put the kettle on. I'll tell Basil to stand down the Red Alert. Then we'll have a good look at you."

He repaired the bandages on her bleeding wrists and immobilised her dislocated finger with surgical tape from their battered old St John's first aid tin. While he phoned Inigo, Sydney took a trip to the ladies toilets. She washed her face; she had allowed the on-call to hastily sink a few stitches in her cheek when she had first arrived at hospital, but the wound was still seeping.

She gingerly swished water around in her mouth to rid it of the foul taste. The hand soap stung her lacerated knuckles, and she wondered briefly if she had not given Elwess a couple of loose teeth in addition to his bloody nose. Then she reminded herself she was not supposed to care anymore.

She returned to the office just as Pink was putting down the phone. "Talbert's already made his statement. The cleaners are finishing with his gaff now. They're bringing Markham's body into the morgue, and they'll review the recording tomorrow." Perching on the edge of his desk, he fixed her with a keen look. "So all that's left is for you to tell me why you won't let me take you to hospital."

"I've been already. Been and gone." Sydney collapsed back on the battered sofa. "Dahlra woke up a little while ago." She closed her eyes, wishing it was as simple as opening them and finding out it had all been a dream. "I went to see him, and he... he told me this was too much to take. So he sent me away. He's through with me."

Pink looked as alarmed as Elwess. "I can't believe it. Now, before you go off on one, you gotta remember, mate, he's still circling the airport. Tomorrow he probably won't even remember—"

"It doesn't matter." Her heart was pounding in time with the start of one hellacious headache. "I let him down. He doesn't deserve the sorry, sordid shit he's just been dragged through. He certainly deserves better than me, and I've got to accept it."

"Well, that's cobblers, for a start. The man adores you, gell. Has for years. Look, you know better than most how drugs will make you say and do things you wouldn't do ordinarily." He smiled confidently. "The doc's a real diamond; he's not going to give up on you just like that. He's got staying power. Especially after all you two have been through. It's just too far off course."

"No. It doesn't seem all that far-fetched to me, Pink. What he said... there was a lot of truth in it. He might not remember saying it, but what if deep down, even where he won't admit it, he said those things *because* of the drugs, not in spite of them? Why would he say something like that if he didn't mean it?"

Misery swamped her like a wave. Maybe Dahlra's true feelings had been peeled away by Silas' mental surgery. "All he wants is a safe life, he said. And all he's ever got from associating with me is grief. That's why he doesn't want me anymore. I mean, I don't blame him for kicking me out of his life. It was the smart thing to do, wasn't it?"

The memory of Dahlra's rejection hit her again, and she did not have the pride or the strength to meet it. She looked up at her friend, willing her heart to stop breaking. "Ah, God, Pink! What am I going to do? I've lost the best thing I've ever had, and it's my fault."

Garnet quickly hopped off the desk, knelt in front of her and took her in his arms. His tenderness broke the last of her strength, and she burst into braying, heavy sobs.

Pink rocked her like a child. "Ah, mate, it's okay. You go on an' have a cry. What you two have been through today, you've earned it. Go on, have your grizzle, get it out of your system. Then you can get your head around it again." He gave her a hard, bracing hug. "There, now. It's alright. We've faced worse, ain't we? We'll get through it like always, won't we? My back to yours, yeah?"

For a long time he held on, steady and understanding, and let her bawl until exhaustion burned away the remnants of her anguish and despair. She slumped against her old friend, feeling heartsick and sad, so sad. When she felt she could let go, he released her and handed her a handkerchief.

While she blew her nose and tried to get a grip on her emotions, he made them both a cup of tea. Pink was one of those people who believed that nothing was so bad that a cuppa could not fix it. After adding a generous splash of milk and three sugars to her mug, he pressed it into her hand. She drank half of it in one go. It was strong and sweet, and it calmed her rocky stomach a little.

He joined her on the battered old sofa. They drank their tea in silence, as they had so many times in the past when faced with hard decisions, or bad nights when sleep was no longer an option. Staring into his mug, he finally spoke. "This job... it's a right pisser, innit? You don't wanna let your heart get in the way of it, so you don't do relationships, or emotions, because sometimes you see things your heart couldn't take otherwise."

Sydney nodded. She had been that soldier, just doing the job, keeping the status quo. "You just put one foot in front of the other. You get the work done, and hope you can go home in the evening and get a good night's sleep."

He took up the thread again. They had done this a lot as partners; one of them would start a thought, the other would take it up, like a duet. "Then, just when you think you've got it all sussed out, Ol' Basil Exposition springs it on you that, lo and behold, you've been rewarded this person, this Minder, who comes in and takes over your life. Suddenly you're learning how to smell the number nine and right is left and in is orange and instead of planning your next pint, you're sitting around on your leisure time actually thinking about the love of your life."

"Yeah," Sydney replied bleakly. "And pretty soon, you're wondering how you found your pants without them."

They spoke in unison. "'If you can't take a joke, you shouldn't-a joined.'"

Garnet's angular face softened. "You are what you are, Syd. And that's who he fell for. He knew all that about you before he became your Minder."

Sydney took a deep, shaky breath. She had never been one for self-actualising; you did what you did, and the chips landed where they fell. Sometimes, you just had to give it the old cosmic shrug. Of the two of them, Dahlra was the thinker, the philosophy student, as much her teacher as her Minder. He had encouraged her to dig deeper within. Sydney had always been afraid there would be nothing there to see; Dahlra had been confident she would find much more than she bargained for.

Pink fussed over their second cups of tea. "This sure isn't what we signed up for, was it? When ol' Baz tapped me from Kingston Crown Court, I thought it was gonna be all James Bond and gadgets and swish assignments and tasty birds swanning around swimming pools. Turns out it's mostly boredom and red tape, and funding meetings and PTSD— if, God forbid, you do see any real action."

As he spoke, exhaustion stole into Sydney. She needed a hot bath and a long sleep, but it was doubtful if she would get either for a while. She forced her spine to stiffen, and she drew on the singular, blunt resolve that had gotten her through every difficult situation, every frightening moment she had experienced since Inigo had tapped *her* from Quantico.

"I have to try and fix this thing with Dahlra, whatever happens," she said. "At the end of the day, this job won't be waiting for me, and it won't make an empty flat feel like home." In spite of her aching heart, she smiled. "I'm afraid he's raised my standards on that count. I've gotten too used to knowing someone was glad to see me walk through the door."

"Yeah. Me too, kid. Me, too."

His stern countenance softened, and Sydney felt a wave of affection and gratitude. By rights, he should be at home, letting his own Minder fuss over him; instead, he was here, taking care of her...

She frowned. "Hey, Pink, what are you doing here, anyway? I thought you and Celia were in Bolton this weekend."

"Oh, yeah, I was gonna call ya. Celia's mum was having one of her funny turns. Ceel's been up in Lancashire more days than not this month. I wanted to go with her, but she said I would be much happier here with you than there with her grouchy ol' mam. Said to surprise you and the doc. Said to give Dahlra her best birthday wishes. Another diamond, that gell."

Sydney felt a pang of guilt. It served as a reminder that she was not the only person in the world Pink had to worry about. She sniffed, and resisted the urge to wipe her nose on her sleeve. "Nothing serious, I hope. Her mum, I mean."

"She's been touch and go a few times. But Celia thinks—"

His phone rang. "Just let me catch this." He picked up the receiver. "Pinkerton."

He listened for a few seconds, and glanced toward Sydney. "Yeah. She's here with me. Fine. A bit cream crackered, but—" He stopped and listened. "Right. We're on the way."

He put the handset down and beckoned to her. "C'mon. That was Lightoller. We need to get back to hospital. Dahlra's in Intensive Care. He's having some kind of seizure."

Elwess stepped into the lift and pressed the Down button. He had just seen off the Agency bods, and he knew he should try and get some sleep, but he could not face climbing into bed now, not alone.

It did not seem possible that he had boarded a plane from Amsterdam that morning, eager to be home with his lovers. It felt like a hundred years had passed since he had walked into the house and heard Sydney's enraged cry for help. Images of the hideous afternoon scored across his vision; watching Silas raping Dahlra from the distant confines of his study... Sydney imploring him to hold onto her as her dislocated finger snapped sickeningly back in place... the helpless fear before Dahlra took that shuddering, gasping breath back to life... that sudden, chilling moment when he retrieved Sydney's forgotten Glock and released the safety, the cold, sure knowledge that, one way or another, Silas Markham was not leaving the Chine alive...

After the SOCO boys had finished swabbing, dusting, bagging and photographing everything, Lightoller sent in his cleaners with orders to remove all traces of his agent and her Minder. Elwess was given the silent treatment as everything from the spoiled food in the kitchen to Sydney's lipstick-stained tissues were gathered up and carried away. Nothing of theirs, not even a trace of Dahlra's cologne, remained.

Well, not *quite* nothing. Elwess ran his tongue over his split lip. He still carried the bruises from Sydney's right hook. He briefly considered numbing the pain with alcohol, but once that ache was gone, what would be left of them he could actually see or feel?

He knew Sydney would never forgive him. She had spent too much time suspicious of his intentions, wondering why he assumed an intimacy in their relationship when she had not yet allowed him to venture too far into her heart. His prospects with Dahlra were not all that promising, either. That bloody hospital would not even let him in the door. The Agency had effectively shut him out.

The lift stopped its clanking descent, and Elwess pushed back the safety cage. Under the cold overheads, the Chine was so bright and sterile, it gave him a strange, eerie sensation of walking into a morgue.

The smell of powerful disinfectant stung his nose. Nothing seemed out of place; no one would ever guess the atrocities that had occurred a few hours before. The only indication that something was amiss was the occasional missing objects here and there, and a few empty spaces on walls and shelves. No doubt some things had been taken in as evidence. He would order replacements tomorrow; the sooner things looked normal, the sooner he could get back to BAU.

Yeah, right. Everyone knows all you need to make it through any life-

altering tragedy is a brand new set of handcuffs. Somehow he figured it would take a wee bit more than a couple of purchases on Sexshop365.com to jolly him out of this mess.

It was too soon. He should not have come down to the Chine; he simply was not in the proper headspace to deal with any of this. Maybe that drink was the answer after all.

As he turned back toward the lift, Elwess spied the St Andrews cross, and his breath caught. Sudden shame and rage stunned him. He had been so damn proud of that thing. He had designed it himself, suited to his every perversion and proclivity; it had arrived from America six months before, and he never missed a chance to demonstrate its special features, calling it his 'device of exquisite torment.'

Someone had pushed it into a corner, as if to hide it away, a silent witness to what Silas had done to Dahlra Gar for the unpardonable sin of being Elwess' friend. For one sick, overwhelming moment, he felt as if he might pass out. Why on earth was it still here?

"Why didn't you take it as well?" he asked the room.

He could not seem to catch his breath. He realised he was sobbing, harsh, cawing sounds that tore his throat to shreds. Blindly, he stumbled toward a utilities cabinet near the sink. He rummaged through it feverishly, until he located his battered old toolkit. Then with a hammer and a spanner, he attacked his beautiful cross with an urgency bordering on frenzy, his cries reverberating around the Chine. "YOU TOOK EVERYTHING ELSE AWAY FROM ME—WHY DIDN'T YOU TAKE IT WITH YOU? WHY DID YOU LEAVE IT WITH ME?"

Cursing, grunting with effort, the tears and snot running unchecked down his face, he hurled himself at the apparatus like a fighter, until it was nothing but a dismantled pile of lumber and gears, levers and articulated chain. He reeled away, breathless and aching. He managed to drag himself to the lift, and stabbed the Up button, and waited for it to take him away from the hell he had made.

CHAPTER TEN

The Cure

Together Sydney and Garnet sprinted to the hospital, but when they arrived, they were not allowed in. Dahlra was delirious and convulsing.

It would be four long days before he left ICU. Those days were the worst in Sydney's life. They felt longer than her time in the Cell, longer than her time recovering from it. This time round, it was she who could do nothing but watch impotently from the sidelines as Dahlra fought for his life.

His vitals careened from alarmingly low to dangerously high, his heartbeat at times a squiggling line all over the monitor. In the first four hours alone he defibbed twice, and it became a mad rush to get his heart beating in a proper rhythm.

A revolving door of doctors and nurses came and went, barely acknowledging her, unwilling to commit themselves to any prognosis. Brody, her favourite nurse, tried to reassure her, but Sydney could tell he was more concerned than he wanted to let on. "Dr Gar is still critical, but that's not always as bad as it sounds, Ms Chapin. Why don't you try and get some rest? You know I'll let you know the moment there's any change."

During the first three days, Sydney doggedly stayed at her post, peering at Dahlra through the little window separating his room from the waiting area. She lived on the hospital's terrible coffee and the pastries Pink brought from the bakery across the street. At times, he broke off pieces and literally stuffed them into her mouth. She chewed automatically, her eyes never leaving the man lying in the bed. She counted the hours by the rhythmic rise and fall of his chest, the increasingly longer intervals of stability, the gradual return of normal colour to his skin.

Near the end of the third evening, Dr Hughes met with Sydney, Inigo and Pink to update them.

"We've been able to isolate some of the components of the substance Dahlra was given. It's quite a cocktail, very unique." He removed his glasses and rubbed his tired eyes. "I have a colleague in residence at the London. He specialises in these types of drugs and their effects. In the past six months, there have been three deaths reported where the sub-stances found in the bodies had a very similar chemical makeup to the one Dahlra was given."

Sydney spoke up. "Silas called it 'Sparklers.' He said it was... what did he call it? A boutique drug. I got the feeling that our friends were trying it out in the local fetish clubs to test its popularity."

Dr Hughes nodded. "The three victims were known to frequent nightclubs. One of the syringes hadn't been used, so we have a pure sam-ple. We've performed an undiluted chemical breakdown of it." He caught Inigo's eye. "This is dangerous stuff, Principal. If it's going into circulation, we're going to see more deaths. If it becomes readily avail-able, the street dealers will cut it with God knows what to extend the supply. Cornstarch, brick dust—"

"But how is all this affecting Dahlra?" asked Sydney. "Is he going to be alright?"

"So far, the brain scans have given us hope that he will recover, thanks to the quick response of the medical team onsite. I understand you were the one who gave him mouth-to-mouth before they arrived. You probably saved his life, you know."

It wasn't enough. "What about the other injuries?"

"He's had a lot of physical trauma, and those are, for the most part, superficial. His back has some minor contusions, but no real deep tissue bruising. He was sexually assaulted, and the injuries are comparable to those normally associated with that kind of attack. It was the time spent during suffocation and the drugs he was given that was our biggest worry." He gave Sydney a nod of encouragement. "But he's responding well to treatment."

"So why isn't he awake?"

"We have him under a mild sedative to keep him relaxed. Atropine can cause acute paranoia and delirium, among its many side effects. It's to keep him from the possibility of injuring himself."

As frightening as the potential answer might be, Sydney had to ask the question. "Dr Hughes, when Dahlra first regained consciousness, he was asking for me. He seemed lucid, but his behaviour was, um, a bit unusual."

"Oh? In what way?"

"He seemed a little... He seemed a little confused. He said some things that concerned me as being out of character for him."

The physician gave her a pitying look. "I wouldn't put too much credence on anything Dahlra said during that time. He had been through a terrible ordeal. From what I understand, his assailant attempted to brainwash him as well as assault him physically. He was oxygen deprived and extremely disorientated. The chances are he'll have more than a few missing hours from these past few days."

He patted her shoulder reassuringly. "I don't want you to worry too much about it, Ms Chapin. Right now, we need to concentrate on his recovery. There'll be plenty of time later on to help him with the more psychological aspect of his attack."

Dr Hughes excused himself, leaving her alone with Lightoller and Pink.

Inigo gave Sydney a look she knew all too well. "I know, I know," she said tiredly. "You've been patient, but you want your debrief."

"In your own time, old girl."

"Now's fine."

For the next hour, Sydney recounted the entire incident, from the moment she let herself into the flat until he and Pink arrived at the Chine. Inigo made notes on his well-used black notepad, interrupting only to ask for occasional clarification.

"Agent Gregorin isn't the only mole, Inigo. Silas Markham knew things nobody outside the Agency should know. Names, dates, confidential and private info—he even used the name 'Silverbirch.' Now, correct me if I'm wrong, but that name *was* classified at one of the highest levels in this Agency, and Silas was throwing it around like it was trending on Facebook."

Inigo looked grim. "I've suspected as much for a while now. The way they always seemed one step ahead of us. I had hoped if we gave Markham a little rope, he'd do us the favour of hanging his contact along with himself."

"Do you mean to tell me you knew where he was all along and you didn't bring him in?" Inigo's implacable stare was all the answer she needed. "Dahlra almost died, Inigo! You gave Silas enough rope to almost kill *him*!"

He placed a final, emphatic dot on his notes and closed the cover. "And I deeply regret it, as you know. But Silas isn't the general; he's a foot soldier in a much bigger war—"

"I should have learned my lesson the first time you made Dahlra your sacrificial lamb! Nothing's changed from when I first went on garden leave. Gregorin's dead, and the Agency is still hemorrhaging information. I've been thinking about it ever since you called us in to identify that poor girl, the one Silas chopped up. That could have easily been Dahlra, but all you can think about is the loss of a potential double."

Pink put a hand on her shoulder, but it was to Inigo he spoke. "If they can hurt Dahlra, all our families, our Minders, our friends are no longer safe. We need to stop this passive investigation, Inigo. You've let them call the setplays too long. Let us on the pitch. Let 'em know what it's like to go up against the Premiership."

Sydney looked gratefully up into Pink's honest, blue-eyed stare, and he nodded to her. It would not be the first time he had followed her into the belly of the beast to exact vengeance. She could almost hear him speaking the words; in every difficult situation, every time they knew they would have to draw their guns, they had recited their talisman. *My back to yours.*

Inigo opened his mouth to protest, but she stopped him. "I don't care how drugged out Dahlra was—somewhere deep inside he thinks that everything, the job, El—" She stopped. Just saying his name felt like a dance through no-man's land. "Dahlra thinks everything is more important to me than him. He wouldn't have said it otherwise. I have to show him how wrong he is. I have to show him that I'm doing this for *us*, not the job. And I can't do that in a crummy little bedsit in Oval on the rest of my garden leave. We do it my way, or I walk." She turned to leave. "And if Dahlra really wants me out of his life, at least he'll *have* a life."

Garnet caught her by the arm. "Syd, hang about. Wait a day or two after he wakes up, and he's had the chance to unravel all this. Then we can make a plan." He released her, and with a crooked grin, he added, "And no more even thinking about throwing in the towel. I mean, blimey, Syd, who's gonna help me prevent Lightoller from disappearing up his own arse for good and all?"

"May I remind you, Agent Pinkerton, I *am* in the same room," snapped Inigo.

In spite of everything, Sydney could not help but chuckle. Only Garnet could make her laugh in the middle of the worst crisis in her life.

"Okay. Deal," she said. "We'll talk later."

"Sydney."

She paused at the door and looked back at Lightoller. His tone was gentle, almost tender. "I'm glad you're with us. We need you here. *I* need you here. We'll talk soon."

Her exhaustion felt suspiciously like anger. It was one thing to suspect you were being manipulated; Inigo was not even trying to be coy about it. "And one more thing, since we're passing around the party favours. I don't want Elwess Talbert anywhere near us. He is *persona non grata,* as far as I'm concerned."

Pink looked somewhat taken aback by the sudden vehemence in her voice. His expression cooled. "Are you saying he's involved? I know you three had... something going on. Not that it's my business, but if you think he's hooky I'll have him in custody in five minutes."

"No. Not in that way, in any case. But I don't want him pestering Dahlra. Or me. Together or separately."

Inigo stood. "If you're talking favours, then here's mine: rest assured, we'll find the real power behind the throne, old thing. That's the best way you can avenge what Markham did to Dahlra."

And you'll tell yourself that it's to avenge what happened to me, but really it's just because you love playing I-Spy.

Sydney sighed impatiently. "Inigo, did you actually hear anything I just said?"

On day four, Sydney was sleeping on the atrociously uncomfortable waiting room chair when a gentle hand shook her awake. She leapt onto her feet, still half-asleep. "What's wrong? Is he—"

"He's doing fine, Ms. Chapin." Brody's kind face was wreathed in a smile. "I wanted to pass on the good news. Dr Hughes has just been in, and he's upgraded Dr Gar's condition from 'Critical' to 'Serious but Stable,' and they're moving him to a private room this morning."

Once Dahlra was moved into his own room, he was not plugged in to so many monitors; his heartbeat was steady, his blood pressure and respiratory rate nearly normal. The worst of the bruising was already fading.

Watching his peaceful, sleeping form, love and devotion washed over Sydney, leaving her weak-kneed and fearful. Of course a man like Dahlra Gar did not belong in her dangerous life. How could he? And she certainly was not equipped to handle the kind of scorching, passionate all-or-nothing love that Dahlra had promised her. Maybe that was the problem. Had she expected too much of him, once she realised how much he meant to her?

Not for the first time, Sydney wished she still believed in some divine being she could pray to. She had been raised a good Southern Baptist girl, but a career with the Agency had quickly cured her of any religious affiliation with the concept of a Loving Creator. She had seen too much to think otherwise.

And yet, in this place, looking down at the only man she had ever loved, she wanted to bargain with Someone or Something on Dahlra's behalf. *Let him wake up and be okay. If that means he doesn't want me anymore, fine, you win. I'll happily get out of his life as long as you give him a decent one to live. Just please, please let him wake up and be okay...*

To fill the long, awful silence, Sydney read the newspaper aloud, cover to cover. She sang his favourite songs, rubbed his lips with ice chips and gently kissed his cool forehead. She talked to him as if he were awake. "Garnet was here earlier, love. He wants to know if you would like tickets to the UEFA Championships in Lisbon. We can stay in Baixa and Celia and I can go shopping while you boys cheer yourselves hoarse. We'll be ladies wot lunch." She felt the false smile trembling on her lips. "Dahlra, open your eyes. Open them, please."

She hesitated, then continued her News At Ten update. "It's hot as hell outside. The papers are doing their, 'Phew what a scorcher' routine. BBC News reported the heat wave is so bad a lot of people are actually cutting their holidays short and returning to work because their homes aren't air conditioned and their workplaces are. I wish we were at Maidenvine. I'll bet it's ten degrees cooler in Windsor..."

Her words died in her throat. Dahlra was looking at her, his eyes glassy and unfocused. Sydney took his hand. "Dahlra? Love, can you hear me?"

He blinked slowly and nodded. With what looked like supreme effort, he managed a slow, slurred whisper. "Sydney? Are you really alive?"

"Yes! I'm alive. It's me! It's Sydney!" Before she could finish, he slipped back into unconsciousness. Running out into the hall, Sydney grabbed Dr Hughes and dragged him into the room. "He was awake! He spoke to me. That's good, isn't it?"

Dr Hughes tested Dahlra's pupils and read his latest vitals on the chart meticulously. "I think the worst is over physically, that's true enough. We'll monitor him and allow him to wake on his own. Then we'll run some more tests, to make sure the brain scans haven't changed."

He removed his reading glasses and looked at her keenly. "Ms Chapin, with all due respect, I strongly suggest that you get some rest of your own. Your exhaustion is obvious. If you were on active duty, I could and would pull rank and put you on forced leave. But since I can't, I will only speak as a friend, and a physician." He put a hand on her shoulder. "Dahlra's recovery is only just beginning. You'll need to meet it with a show of strength, and you are not capable of that right now."

Sydney nodded. "Soon. I promise." She was honest enough with herself to admit most of her strength was gnawed down to the cartilage, but she felt renewed hope wrestling with her fatigue. As long as there was still a slim chance Dahlra might be glad to see her when he opened his eyes.

Two days after the attack, Elwess was summoned to Lightoller's plush office, where he was informed he was now suspended, pending an investigation. Killing Silas had been his biggest mistake; if the wanker was still alive they would not be treating him like Jack Ruby. Elwess explained until he was hoarse: he had not planned on killing Silas; if the safety had been on, Silas would have slit Sydney's throat, but at least he would still be in the clear. Why did every good idea hinge on the execution of a tragedy? *Trouble follows you around like a bad smell.*

He gingerly touched the bridge of his nose; it still hurt, along with two of his front teeth. He poured himself a glass of very dark, very potent rum for a bit of self-medication. He toed off his shoes and flopped onto the sofa, taking a long pull of the fiery liquor. He thought about spliffing up, since nothing and no one was expecting him, but he could not be arsed.

His phone went off with a vibrating dance on the table. He sprang forward to pick it up, then fell back against the sofa. There were only two people he wanted to talk to, and it was not going to be either of them. Listlessly, he looked at the screen; it was a number he did not recognise. He pressed 'Accept.'

"Yes?"

A man answered pleasantly. "Hello Master Elwess. We understand you're in a bit of a bind with Inigo Lightoller. Something about a little altercation with Silas Markham."

Elwess sat up, his heart thudding hard in his chest. "Who is this?"

The voice was neutral, a Home Counties accent with no regional inflection. "Let's just say that we're an organisation which appreciates the value of men with special talents such as yours. We're hoping that we can come to a mutually beneficial arrangement. After all, you dispatched Markham, and Lightoller has dispatched you. Even Sydney Chapin and Dahlra Gar have cut you loose."

"Who are you? And how do you know all this?"

"Does it matter? I tell you this so you'll understand that Lightoller's Agency is not the only dreadnought in these waters. As for who I represent, please don't insult my intelligence. You know who we are."

"I have a fairly good idea."

The false bonhomie continued. "You see, we believe in rewarding a man for his initiative, not destroying his career. Why not give Lightoller a taste of his own medicine? We can provide a scope for your abilities and pleasures far beyond anything he could ever understand."

Elwess rose to his feet and slowly walked toward the window in the front room. "How do I know you aren't one of Lightoller's men, trying to set me up?" He parted the blinds and peered out; there seemed nothing amiss outside, no unusual cars or people on the street. "How do I know you are who you say you are?"

The man chuckled. "Yes, I agree, that sounds like something he would do. So let me set your mind at ease. I'd like you to visit one of our properties. Have a look around, sample some of the opportunities we have on offer. You need a new job, and we need a man like you—a man not afraid to take what is rightfully his. Interested?"

He was not surprised at the icy tone of his own voice. "Yeah. I'm interested."

"Good. Amateur Hour is over, Elwess. So the real question is: do you have what it takes to go pro?"

"If you know me as well as you say, you already know the answer to that."

Another dark chuckle. "You'll have to bring your A-game."

Elwess smiled for the first time since he had arrived back home from Holland. "It's the only game I've got, mate. Let's talk terms."

CHAPTER ELEVEN

Family

"Agent Pinkerton! A moment, if you please."

Garnet turned to see Dr Hughes trundling down the hall toward him. "Oh, hiya, Doc. What's up?"

Hughes was puffing with exertion, but his toothy smile stayed in place. "It's just that Dahlra has regained consciousness, and I promised to let Miss Chapin know. I've been trying her phone, but she isn't picking up."

"Yeah, she's attending the Markham autopsy. Probably has her mobile switched off. Tell you what, I'm heading that way. I'll track her down for ya."

"Very good. Thank you, Agent."

"No worries." Garnet waited until Dr Hughes turned the corner, then continued down the hall to Dahlra's room. Syd could wait a few extra minutes.

He paused at the door, then knocked. "Come in." Dahlra's voice still sounded muffled and hoarse, but otherwise okay.

The lighting in the room was dimmed almost to darkness—something to do with the Doc's eyes. As his own eyes adjusted, Garnet could see the fading bruises on Dahlra's face. Even more worrisome was the dull, ground-down fatigue in his eyes.

"It's me, Garnet. I come bearing gifts." He held up a Marks and Sparks bag. "Brought you some posh grapes. Syd said you liked these. I get the shits from 'em, meself, but everybody's got different tastes."

"Thank you, Garnet."

Garnet sat down, and leaned forward, elbows on his knees. "That Welsh twat, is he your doctor?"

That produced a thin smile. "I'm afraid so." Dahlra sobered. "Where is Sydney? Is she alright?"

Garnet pondered for a second how exactly to answer the question. On the surface, Dahlra's enquiry sounded more polite than concerned, but Garnet had ever been a student of body language and vocal inflection. He kept his voice breezy, nonchalant. "She's in the office. Doing a bit of research. Markham's autopsy is about to start. She's scheduled to attend it. Never one to be squeamish, is our Syd.

"As for being alright, no, quite frankly, she ain't. Still, what do you expect? The girl practically saws her hands off to try and rescue her Minder, and he thanks her by sending her packing. So, in answer to your question: no, she's a right mess."

He waited for an answer, but Dahlra simply stared at him in confusion. Garnet decided he had made the right decision. Sometimes you had to do what was right for people in spite of themselves.

"You know, Doc, her and me, we bickered like cats and dogs when Basil first partnered us up."

"I know. She told me."

"Yeah, I suppose she woulda. She was piece of work, and no mistake. I never quite knew what she was thinking in them days. Played it all close to the chest. A cracking operative, no doubt, and good to have on your side in the old argy bargy, but not the easiest person to get to know."

It was true that Garnet had always respected Sydney. From their first meeting, she was a disconcerting package of slender, tough beauty and cool-eyed ruthlessness, never revealing that soft core, in case it betrayed her. She was a woman you did not get on the wrong side of, and she rarely made mistakes, which was why they were so catastrophic when she did.

"Well, you know how her parents died, yeah?"

"They were killed in a fire. She doesn't—she won't talk about it."

"Nah, she wouldn't, would she? You see, it weren't a fire what killed 'em. They were murdered."

The Doc's eyes widened. "But why didn't she—"

"Y'see, we busted this big drug cartel out of Mexico. It was our first serious assignment, and we'd spent months working on it. We went to Mexico City ourselves to make the bust, and we was just coming back to the UK. We worked hard on it, and we were ready for a bit of R&R, and Syd thought she was safe. Back then, you did, didn't ya?"

Did they ever. They were both high from their success, still young and ambitious with all the arrogance of youth—maybe everybody has to die, but you might live forever because you were just that little bit more special.

That all changed, though.

"Pardon?"

He looked up at Dahlra, who was staring at him intently. Garnet realised he had spoken aloud. "I was just reminiscing. You know, you always think you're safe, but all that can change in a flash."

Dahlra made a hollow sound that almost resembled a laugh. "Yeah." His voice was bitter with irony. Garnet chose to ignore him.

"I'll never forget it: Lightoller met us at Heathrow, and right away we knew something weren't right. He never did that kind of thing. He didn't try and break it gently, or soft-soap it. He just said, 'Agent Chapin, I've just got word from my opposite number in the CIA. Last night, at around nine p.m., your parents were killed in a house fire. They are treating their deaths as suspicious.'

"Syd turned white as a sheet, but she didn't fall apart or cry. She just said, 'Munoz. He killed them?'

"Old Baz just nodded. He says to me, 'I want you to return to the States with Agent Chapin. Lend a hand in any legal and formal matters.' Well, Syd just turns to him cool as ice as says, 'I don't need a babysitter.'"

Garnet sighed. "You know, I like to think of myself as pretty even-keeled, but I won't lie, I was a little repulsed by her. I thought she was the coldest-blooded woman I'd even seen. Like she wasn't really human. Just standing there, knowing her parents were dead, and not a tear, not the least bit of reaction. Now, if that had been me, I would've been screamin' the place down, looking for somebody to kill."

Dahlra opened his mouth to speak, but Garnet smoothly continued. "We turned right around in the airport, and boarded a plane to the States. I don't think we probably spoke ten words to each other on the flight over.

"We're met at the airport by this Federal Agent, who's supposed to be our liaison, but before has the chance to introduce himself, Syd tells him she wants to see the house. Now, me, I didn't really see the point. Forensics had already been through there, but she digs in her heels, you know how she does, so off we go."

By now, Dahlra was hanging on his every word. Garnet went on. "He takes us to this little town her parents are from. It's nice, you know— real Americana. White picket fences, kids playing in the front gardens, crickets chirping—looks like something we used to see on the telly and think was just a movie set.

"We drive down this street, and there it is. It was a lovely house, before they torched it—two-storied, manicured lawn, long front porch. Her parents had been pretty well to do, you know. I think her dad was some kind of doctor himself—"

"Pedodontist. He was a dentist for children."

"Was he? Oh, yeah. Well, you would know better than me." Garnet painted just the right shade of innocence into his tone. "Anyways, Munoz' men killed them, you see, then set fire to the house to cover it up. But it's a big brick house, you see? Most of the walls were intact, and to be honest, a lot of it was still standing.

"Well, Syd gets out of the car and starts walking toward it. There's a local Old Bill standing guard there, and he steps between her and house. He says, 'oh, Miss, you can't go in there. It's too dangerous.' This fat, grey copper is giving Sydney Chapin the, 'now look here, young lady, this is for your own good' speech." Garnet laughed. "I can still see the look on his face when she told him, 'I'm going into my house, and if you try and stop me, I'll tear off your head and piss down your throat, you hear me?'"

He chanced a look at Dahlra; his expression was soft, absorbed. But underneath, where perhaps it counted the most, was another emotion. It was borne of affection and pride, and that kept Garnet talking.

"I followed her in, but I kept me distance. The place was a mess, as you can imagine. It's all charred and water damaged, and she's just walking around from room to room, not saying a word. And I'm following her, feeling like a right tit, and thinking, 'what's she playing at?'

"Finally, we come this little room in the back. It's like a sitting room, and the fire's hardly touched it. Old Syd stops by this little group of about ten china figurines sitting on a shelf. It's all these little delicate things, like gells in big dresses and shepherds and shit. Dresden, like. What strikes me is how neat and orderly they looked. Not so much as a smudge of soot on them, like they got no idea the house has burned up all around them. Spooky, that.

"Syd picks one of them up and says, 'my mother collects these.' It's the first words she's said since we walked in the house, and she says it like her mum's going to walk through the door any second.

"I'm just about to ask if she wants to pack them up and take them with us, when she throws it against the wall. It smashes to smithereens.

The she picks up another, and then another, and she's lobbin' 'em fast as you like. Every one of 'em's hitting the same place. I tell ya, she could give cricket bowlers a run for their money. Her aim is pukka.

"And I'm too busy watching them little china dolls hittin' the wall to notice that beside me, Syd's crying and hyperventilating, like she's going to pass out."

Garnet shook his head. "Well, I didn't know what to do, did I? Here was the Ice Queen of the Agency, coming apart. And then she turns to me, those eyes of hers full of tears, and starts calling for her mummy." He paused, and rubbed his burning eyes.

"I tell ya, it broke my heart. Over ten years past that was, and even now it breaks it a little still." He sniffed, and rubbed his nose.

"So I just put me arms around her, and she's crying like a baby for her mum and dad. I can't tell you how long we stood there, in the middle of this burned-out house, but eventually she calmed down. And finally, she looks up at me and says, 'Will you be my family now?'"

He paused and cleared his throat. He had never told anyone this story. Even after all those years, the memory of her stricken voice still had the power to reach right in and squeeze his heart. "I said, 'yeah, al-right, we're family now. I'll be your bruvva, and you'll be my sister. And I'll fight with ya, my back to your back, and we'll get them bastards what killed your mum and dad.' And she just nodded and said, 'Yeah, Pink. My back to yours.' It was the first time she'd ever called me 'Pink'. The first person I ever *let* call me 'Pink'."

What he did not, what he *could not* tell Dahlra, was that after the funeral, they took an unscheduled, month-long side trip before returning to England. Without sanction or authorisation, they went after Munoz and hit him, hard. Driven by a bloodlust neither could fully understand nor quell, they descended on his world, Keyser Söze style.

They took out his captains, his foot soldiers, his contacts and his mules. No one was spared; his wife, his children, his brothers and sisters and their families—even his little old granny. They killed his cook, his driver... they killed his fucking dogs, for Chrissake.

Sydney's thirst for revenge had been unslakable, and her shadow fell on her victims like the Angel of Death. No plea, no circumstance, no individual could sway her. Syd Vicious, Garnet privately called her, never to her face. Instead, he allowed himself to get caught up in this

relentless purge; together they scythed through the bodies of the righteous and the wicked alike, and emerged from the slaughter neither
condemned nor cleansed.

Munoz himself they saved for last. His personal bodyguard sold him
out to Sydney in a plea bargain, but she killed him anyway. By the time
they had finished with Munoz, he was begging for a bullet. In thirty days,
his organisation all but disappeared from the face of the earth forever.
Many of the bodies were never located, and the ones that were—well,
they were *meant* to be found.

In that theatre of fire, the last of their innocence was burned away,
but so was any remnants of fear. They were closer than brother and sister now, and would never doubt one another's loyalties or motives
again. Nothing was too great to forgive or accept.

When he and Syd returned home, Lightoller gave them both the
skunk-eye, but did not say a fucking word. They had gone far past the
remit of 'lawfully audacious,' but who was going to stop them? And so
they went on with their jobs, and eventually learned to deal with what
they had done. But no matter how much they bathed in vengeance, they
had spilled innocent blood as well, and that would never wash away.
*And you wonder why she doesn't talk about her parents? Would you burden
someone you loved with that knowledge?*

Dahlra might not believe it, but Garnet was certain he would have
recoiled from that woman who emerged from the wreckage of her parents' ruined house, frosted with anger and killing vengeance in her
heart.

In time, Dahlra had softened her; but so had Garnet, or so he hoped.
And so had Sydney herself; even she realised she could not live the rest
of her life trying to right every wrong, purge every corruption, justify
every action, and she mellowed enough to earn a man like Dahlra's devotion and regard.

What Syd never seemed to grasp was that Lightoller had instigated
the whole Minder thing especially for agents like herself; someone who
needed a partner outside the job, helping them claw back a bit of their
lost humanity. That Lightoller's Agency had stolen that humanity in the
first place was inconsequential in the long run.

Garnet realised he had stopped talking, and was staring moodily into
the past. He risked a glance at Dahlra, who was looking down at his

hands, his face devoid of expression. For some reason that pissed Garnet off. "Look, Doc, you think I'm meddling, and I guess I am. So I'll leave you to rest. But before I do, just give this a little thought: Sydney's my mate, and my partner. When she says 'my back to yours,' she means it. She'll take down anyone who hurts someone she loves. She'll put her feet in buckets of cement and throw herself in the river before she betrays anyone she cares about. And don't think it hasn't killed her to know that you've been hurt, because of her.

"Yeah, I know this is a shit life. Celia feels it too. And it's no place for innocents. I don't blame you for being hurt and scared, and angry. In fact, that's good; shows you're getting better."

He stood up and turned to leave, then glanced back. Dahlra's face was pale and he still looked confused, and Garnet wondered if his brains had not been a bit toasted after all.

Finally, he looked up. "Why are you telling me all this?"

"I think that's obvious, innit? Blaming Syd for what happened to you, that way lies madness. She loves ya. It took you a long time to win her trust, and you destroyed it in a matter of seconds."

Dahlra once again opened his mouth to speak, but Garnet pressed on. "I just wanted to say one more thing before you down tools for good. When you walk away, she'll survive; she might even find someone else, eventually. Sydney's not one of those women who'll waste away, pining for ya. Once she realises she has to live without you, she will. She'll go on, and she'll fight until everyone involved in hurting you has paid the price. I know; I've seen her do it.

"But she won't forget ya, and why you threw her over. And she'll never forgive herself either. She'll walk on that broken glass for the rest of her life, but believe me, she *will* keep walking."

Pink headed for the door; as he reached for the handle, he heard a soft voice behind him. "Garnet?"

He turned back to Dahlra, and saw the misery in the other man's face. "Yeah, Doc?"

"Would you... would you do me a favour?"

"I'll tell her you're awake."

Dahlra's shoulders sagged, and he bowed his head. "Thank you."

"Sure thing, Doc. Enjoy the grapes."

Will you be my family now?

Yeah, Syd. You know it.

CHAPTER TWELVE

Awake

When Sydney first joined The Agency, a stout chef named Walter Schmidt ruled the staff canteen with a Teutonic, iron fist. And while they would never earn any Michelin stars, his daily lunch specials had at least been edible. Now that Herr Schmidt had moved on to pastures anew, most of Sydney's fellow agents considered risking their lives at the hot bar more dangerous than a tour of duty in Syria.

Sydney passed over the usual grim selections on offer, and settled for a pot of tea, hoping it might be the one thing Chef Rodney could not balls up.

Silas Markham's autopsy had just concluded, and while there was some bittersweet justice in seeing his pale worm of a body on the slab, autopsies always left her feeling jaded and delicate. It did not help that her individual contusions and bruises each played their own little tune over her body. Dahlra's present condition was a different song entirely. He had yet to regain consciousness, and Dr Hughes continued to urge patience like it was the only game in town.

She rolled her neck, trying to stretch out some of the kinks. It had been a bad night. She had slept in the office she once shared with Pink. In the old days, it had been her home away from home, but she had forgotten just how lumpy and uncomfortable the sofa was. She had woken up at 3 a.m., drowning in a nightmare, feeling feeble and impotent and more alone than she had ever felt in her life. Where sleep was concerned, Sydney had a feeling she was on short rations until further notice.

The tea looked strong enough to strip paint, but potable. She added three sugars and a generous splash of milk, and downed the hot liquid in one gulp, wincing as it burned her mouth.

"You tossed that back like you were wishing it was straight scotch," said a bemused voice. Sydney glanced up toward its owner, and started with surprise.

"M-Master Brian?" Some strange reflex brought her to her feet. "What the hell—sorry, what on earth are you doing here?"

"No, please don't get up. I didn't mean to interrupt you." He kissed her proffered hand. "But in answer to your question, I'm here for the same reason as you."

Brian Collins was every bit as handsome and charismatic as she remembered from Valentine's Day in The Library. His dark charcoal suit was well-tailored. He had eschewed a tie and wore his shirt open-necked. His cropped, salt-and-pepper hair was immaculately barbered, and his grey eyes were warm and kind. In the brighter lights of the canteen, she noticed that his front teeth were slightly crooked, which added more to the overall package than it detracted.

Brian silently indicated the vacant chair beside her, his eyebrows raised in question. Sydney nodded. "I'm sorry, I'm forgetting my manners. Please have a seat."

He sat down with easy, relaxed grace. "I must say, it's lovely to see you again, Miss Chapin. Even if the circumstances are less than ideal." He took a quick glance around the room, clocking everything in one eagle-keen look. "I was so very sorry to hear about what happened to Dahlra. It was a terrible thing. I had hoped to see him while I was here, but I understand he's not yet allowed visitors. I take it he's improving, though."

"He is." Sydney busied herself with pouring another cup of tea. Thinking about Dahlra was hard enough without having to make any true confessions. That kind of post-mortem was much tougher to stomach. "I'm sorry, you said something about being here for...?"

"I was asked to give a corroborating statement regarding Silas Markham and the events that took place on Valentine's Day. I wanted to lend my support."

"Support?"

"I understand Elwess was the one who put Silas down like the rabid dog he was." He lowered his voice discreetly as a server placed a tray of sandwiches on the table. "Please join me. I hope you'll forgive me for saying it, but you look as if you could use a bit of feeding up. Besides, I hate eating alone." He took her silence for acquiescence, loaded another plate with a variety of sandwiches, and passed them on to Sydney.

She took them, more to be polite than from any real hunger, and dutifully took a bite. The stale bread stuck like glue to the roof of her mouth. She managed to wash it down with several more gulps of tea. "So you came here today to give a statement on Elwess' behalf?"

Brian filled his plate, and sat back, his shrewd eyes boring into hers. "Actually, I'm here as a favour to your Senior Principal."

"Oh, yeah, I think I remember Inigo mentioning you two went to the same college at Cambridge."

"I was a few years older, of course." His words were accompanied with an easy smile.

"I'm sure both Inigo and Elwess appreciate any help you can give, then."

"I'm not sure I can add anything to the picture, but it's the least I could do. I still know the law. I can still provide resources in a hurry. As with most professions, in this business who you know is just as important as what you know. In any case, we're hoping this will give Inigo the ammunition he needs to get Silverbirch back on the table at last."

The conversation lost steam, and the silence stretched beyond awkward to uncomfortable. Sydney could see the questions in his eyes, and decided to head them off at the pass. "You know, you could have knocked me over with a feather that night in The Library."

"I'm very flattered you actually knew who I was."

"Are you kidding? It's not every day you find yourself face to face with one of the prosecuting attorneys of your most important case, smack dab in the middle of London's kinkiest nightclub."

"And it's not every day you find yourself face to face with an agent of your calibre. Especially when she's the most beautiful and gorgeously corseted woman in London's kinkiest nightclub."

This was not exactly the direction she had hoped the conversation would take, but she accepted his compliment with as much grace as she could muster. "I suppose that explains why you were so knowledgeable about the fet side of Britain."

He nodded, like a teacher with a good student. With the easy confidence of a career barrister, he proffered, "Of course, the details of my preferred lifestyle weren't in the public domain. It's not something to be bandied about in chambers. Retirement from public office has been deliciously... liberating." For the first time since he arrived, there was a whisper of sensuality in his smile. "It has certainly been more enjoyable."

As he spoke, he kept his eyes locked onto hers, making it difficult for Sydney to look away. With her attention fully engaged, he reached for her and gently stroked her cheek. Sydney winced as his thumb brushed across the healing wound, unnerved at both the physical sting and the intimacy of his actions. His eyes, however, were full of sympathy that appeared sincere. "Dear heart, what a nightmare this has been for you." His frown deepened. "Damn Silas Markham. Damn them all."

Now the conversation was seriously straying from safe, sane and consensual. Sydney was not about to let Brian Collins take charge of it, Dom or no Dom. "Well, in any case, retirement suits you, I'd say. At least, the midnight feedings and nappy changes don't seem to have left you any the worse for wear."

"Not sure I follow." He looked at her in confusion for a second, then threw his head back and laughed. "Oh, I get it now. Yes, Kay had a boy in April. Mother and son are doing fine, as far as I know."

"As far as you know? I don't understand."

"It's not like I see her now, do I? Kay isn't my wife." He rewarded her surprise with a crooked, charming smile. "I'm her Dominant, not her husband."

"Well hell... Sorry. I, uh, I guess being the sub of a barrister teaches one to be secretive as well."

"One could say that, couldn't one? I'm going to let you in on a little secret. Kay's husband knows. She is my submissive with his full acceptance. My role isn't just to command Kay, but to champion her as well. And so now, she's at home, taking care of her family, very happy being a mum. And I'm happy for her."

He leaned in confidentially. "It's a rare man who understands himself and is secure enough in his own skin to allow his wife the freedom to seek out what she needs. Kay's husband is such a man. A former colleague of mine, in fact."

Sydney stared at him blankly, until Brian laughed. "Oh, my dear, the look on your face! I suppose our exotic little world can seem incredibly bizarre and incestuous to you and Dahlra at times. "

"I *suppose* I've never really given too much thought to it. I always thought Dahlra and I were a fairly typical couple."

Brian sobered. "I'm afraid you're very much mistaken, Sydney. In this lifestyle, there is no 'typical,' nor should there be. And even if there was, you and Dahlra are a distinctly singular and rare couple. Sadly, I'm not as fortunate as Dahlra, to live with such a devoted and lovely companion."

Sydney was assaulted with a fresh wave of hurt that had nothing to do with her injuries. Brian quietly put his hand over hers, and gave it a gentle, encouraging squeeze. Slowly, as if sounding her out, he added, "I have a confession to make. I had another reason for coming here today. Elwess is a good friend of mine, and I was hoping I could have a word with Inigo on his behalf. Principal Lightoller is, shall we say, less than pleased with Elwess. He has a dead man on his hands rather than a live suspect."

Stubbornly, Sydney looked away. "I don't think I can help with that."

"Please don't misunderstand me. Elwess is terribly worried about you." Brian paused, then added delicately, "I understand that Dahlra is experiencing a bit of difficulty in recovering from his ordeal. Elwess mentioned in passing that there's been a rift between the two of you. Now, please don't be angry with him," he added hastily. "He is very concerned about Dahlra. As am I."

Sydney looked down at her bandaged wrists, and squeezed her eyes shut, until she could feel the stitches tugging at her cheek. No. She was damned if she was going to talk about Dahlra. If she did, she would start crying again, and she would jab her eyes out before she fell apart in the Agency canteen.

"It's been my experience that talking with an impartial observer can give you a better perspective," said Brian.

"You're leading the witness."

He shrugged modestly. "Once a barrister. I'm only saying if you want to talk, I'm a good listener."

"Thank you. I'm not sure I can take you up on your offer, but I appreciate it all the same."

Brian smiled at her, and picked up his sandwich. He took a bite, grimaced, then pushed his plate away. "If this is indicative of the food here, no wonder you look half-starved." He dabbed at his mouth with the cheap paper napkin, then tossed it in the ring as well. "Why don't I take you out for some proper food? Please say yes. You look like could use some fresh air, and I could simply murder a ruby."

Now that her stomach had settled a bit, Sydney felt surprisingly hungry. Warily, she asked, "You buying?"

He nodded solemnly. "And I don't share my curry with just anyone.

You can ask Inigo."

"I'll spring for poppadums and raita."

"Ah, that's plea bargaining, Agent. My treat. I insist." When she did not reply, he sighed in mock surrender. "Alright. But I will tell you, it may be one of the very few times I'll allow you the last word."

Sydney smiled in spite of herself, and for the first time since she walked out of Dahlra's hospital room, she did not feel as if she were breathing in razor blades.

Not wanting to stray too far from the hospital, she suggested they order from a local takeaway. The delivery boy brought it right into the Agency lobby. They sat down in her old office and pried the lids from the foil containers. The aroma of the rich spices flooded her nostrils, and her stomach growled audibly.

Brian did most of the talking as they tucked into their Tandoori King Prawn Masala and Lamb Biryani. Sydney learned he had retired strongly on the basis of the original Silverbirch fiasco. "I got angry. As a barrister, I'm used to spending my time among the sinners and thieves, but that level of corruption was beyond the pale."

"Why did you get involved in the first place?"

"The truth? I thought I could win." He chewed thoughtfully. "I was a good lawyer. And I still believe in the power of the justice system, even when I lose."

Sydney nodded. Once the case was closed, she had made herself stop re-reading the memos and emails and reluctantly moved on. Not exactly out of sight, out of mind; more like forcing herself away from that third slice of cake that she knew would taste good, but made her sick afterward for overindulging herself.

"I nearly left as well. It was so bloody unfair. I thought to myself, 'these bastards have been caught red-handed, they'll get what they deserve.' Instead, we got told to change the subject or else." She placed her fork on the plate, too full to eat any more. "Then I thought, 'screw it, I'll get another chance. It's worth fighting for.'"

She stopped, and closed her eyes. *Well, there's your ah-ha moment, isn't it? So what are you doing here talking to Brian Collins when your arse needs to be at that hospital, sitting with Dahlra?*

"I can't eat another bite. Thank you for a great meal. I needed that. And now I really need to get back to the hospital." They gathered up their takeaway boxes and binned the rubbish without further comment. At the door, she turned to him. "Thank you for lunch. And for the friendly ear." As she rose on tiptoe to kiss his cheek, his arm slid around her waist, and he pulled her close.

"I realise right now you're going through a difficult time, but I hope you'll call on me if there is any way I can help." His voice was low and soft in her ear. "I'd very much like to see you again, just to make sure you're alright." She stiffened slightly, but his body felt strong and solid against hers. For a treacherous moment, the temptation to pour her heart out to him, to confess her failings and her fears, was almost greater than she could withstand.

He sensed her weakness, like a shark smelling blood in the water. "You don't have to be strong, Sydney." He placed a very soft kiss on her temple. "And you don't have to blame yourself. It's alright, love, I understand."

In spite of herself, Sydney closed her eyes and steadied herself against him. She knew she was being played, but she felt too heartsick and weak to resist it. Brian understood it too, and crooned, "Why don't we go somewhere a little more private?" He smiled as if he had won a battle only she was fighting. "I'm sure I could help you feel better."

The impact of what he was saying hit her like Thor's hammer. She knew that he was offering her more than sex. He was offering her a blank slate, a chance to hit the reset button and start over again with none of the baggage weighing her down.

It was all that Dom/sub stuff Elwess had been talking about, of being cleaned out, and given the chance to fill up with something new, something not-yet-understood about herself. It would be about learning a different way of looking in the mirror, without the image of the Cell behind her, without Elwess' dark shadow looming in the corner of her eye, without, without—

Without love.

No, Brian Collins would not ensnare her with the sticky, insoluble strands of obsession and devotion. What he was tacitly offering would be cleaner, the boundaries better defined, the expectations clear and feasible. But there would be none of that soaring, life-changing, groundshaking adoration she had known with Dahlra Gar. She would just be the next sub in line.

She pictured Dahlra, the quiet, unassuming doctor who had loved her with the singularity of a zealot. He had waited long enough for her to get it through her thick skull that they had something special. How could she even remotely consider settling for anything less?

A rush of sick shame flooded her, and her curry almost came back up. Of course Brian would think of her as a discarded toy, waiting to be picked up and played with again. And who could blame him? She had more or less acted like one.

"Syd?"

At the sound of Garnet's voice, Sydney pushed away from Brian guiltily. Just outside the door, Pink was watching her warily, his expression unreadable to most, but most certainly not to her. "Garnet, I'd like you to meet a friend of mine. Brian—"

"Collins, yeah, we've met." It was on the tip of her tongue to ask him how long he had been standing there, but she knew the answer: long enough. *Oh fuck it all, what a mess.*

"We were just finishing lunch," said Brian, with the easy grace of a master. "I've been warning Sydney she needs to keep up her strength."

"Good advice." Garnet focused his cool gaze on her. "Dahlra's awake, Syd. He's asking for you."

Her heart started clipping along in double-time.

"That's fantastic news, Sydney." Brian sounded sincerely glad, but both she and Garnet ignored him.

"Is he okay?" Sydney began to shiver, but whether from nerves or guilt, she could not say.

"He was when he said he wanted to see you." Garnet looked from Sydney to Brian, and something changed. His voice and bearing relaxed a little. "He seemed a bit better."

Sydney's shivering eased. If Pink was going to give her the benefit of the doubt, she was going to grab it with both hands and not look back. She had uglier demons to wrestle with than worrying about what Pink saw or thought he saw.

"At any rate, I'm off. I'll catch up with you later, yeah?" He nodded to Brian. "Mr Collins."

"Agent Pinkerton."

They both watched Garnet's retreating figure. "I have to go to him." Sydney turned away, hating herself and her stupidity and her weakness. "Whatever and however he feels for me right now, I owe Dahlra more than to fall at the first hurdle."

Brian made no further moves toward her, but watched her as she gathered up her things. As she headed for the door, he placed his hand on her shoulder. "I owe you an apology. I attempted a familiarity that was tactless and inappropriate. I hope you'll forgive me."

Sydney felt a little better knowing she was not the only one. "It's okay. You're not exactly seeing me at my best, either."

"I want you to do something for me."

Not trusting herself to speak, she nodded. "I want you to try and be patient with Dahlra. Men like us don't like being afraid; it shuts us down, makes us look for something or someone to blame. That doesn't make us bad men. It just makes us human."

"Look, I don't know if he can get past what happened, but I've got try and help him through it. I love him."

"Then give him time. And if, in the end, being with you is too much to ask, nothing you do will change his mind." He gave her that winning smile. "But he would be a fool, and that's something I don't think he is, except perhaps where you are concerned." He shrugged. "Look how quickly I made myself one over you."

"We'll call it a draw, then. Apology accepted." She held out her hand, and this time he shook it, equal to equal.

"Good." Brian released her hand, his eyes still locked with hers. "But the offer still stands."

Dahlra took a deep, unencumbered breath and released it with a slow sigh. After Garnet had left, he had struggled to stay awake, but the undertow of sleep had been too seductive to fight.

He opened his eyes, then quickly shut them again. The faint light coming from the edges of the curtained windows flared in his vision, like an overexposed photograph. He squinted until he could just make out the murky landmarks of the small, clinical room. His other senses filled in the rest: the sterile and somewhat rough texture of the sheets on his bed, the odourless yet stale air, the sighs and ticks of the various monitors and mechanisms harmonising around him like a familiar refrain.

He sat up slowly and stretched until his limbs trembled. With his eyes still closed, he performed an internal diagnostic. There were still a few blank spots in his memory, to be sure, but his mental processes felt almost normal. So his brains had not been given a permanent scramble, in any case.

He turned toward a soft noise and pried open one fluttering eye. Sydney was sitting up in a chair, her hands tucked in her lap, her head tilted to the side. She was fast asleep.

Keeping his eyes open was a painful thing, but he forced himself to take a good look at her. A frown line deeply furrowed the space between her brows. There was a stitched cut on her cheek. She had bruising on her face and neck. Her wrists were bandaged, and something was wrong with her left hand. Her clothing was clean but mismatched, giving her the look of a wayward urchin.

The very fact she was there made him feel safe. Even slumped in exhausted sleep, she was guarding him. He knew she would be on her feet at the first unexpected noise, Glock in hand, ready to cut down anyone she perceived as a threat. *How did you do it, little girl? How did you make sure the Cell didn't win? Do I have your fighting spirit?* He was not sure, but if anyone could teach him how to find it, it was Sydney.

He relaxed back onto his pillows and allowed his thoughts to sift themselves into some semblance of order. The deleted scenes in his memory troubled him. He worried at them, trying to reconnect the dots and see the entire picture again. They danced just out of reach, like a dream that seems so vivid but dissipates like smoke upon waking. It was hard to distinguish delirium from reality.

The memories that he did manage to piece together made him shudder. He recalled vividly the feeling of being suspended upside down, the taste of blood in his mouth, Silas' roar of pain and anger. That awful moment when all his breathing holes had been sealed shut, the feeling of desperate panic, trying to suck in air, and nothing happening. The burning fire in his lungs and the mind-warping fear he was going to die, then the nothingness...

Shame, anger, guilt, confusion, and self-recrimination flared in him like rockets, and his limbs locked in a cramping rictus of panic that threatened to drown him. He remembered a smiling man with blond hair and a white physician's coat. *He* was the Doctor, not this hatefully grinning ghoul with the icy glare.

He saw Sydney's mangled, beaten body, rotating lazily as it hung suspended from a hook in the ceiling. His love was dying right before his eyes, and her screams, her feverish pleas, echoed in his mind. He stood there, impassive, uninterested, while all he wanted to do was weep and cover his ears to muffle her cries for mercy. "Kill me...kill me..." morphed into an even more insidious plea: "Don't send me away... You said you loved me... Marry me... Are you sorry you ever met me?"

What was she doing? She was blowing his cover, *her* cover, she was going to get them both killed. Didn't she understand that pushing her away was the only way to keep her safe? Once again, Dahlra was forced to play the despicable role of the enemy, hurting her in order to keep her alive at all costs. He had to stop her before the Doctor discovered their secret. She had seen through his pitiful mask back then, why not now—

He shook his head angrily. His memory was pinwheeling into something that had never happened; it was a trick of the drugs and his own oxygen-starved brain. Sydney was sleeping peacefully just a few feet away from him, and he was alive and safe. Beaten and sore, undeniably, but alive. The sterling realisation he had survived went a long way toward negating some of the anxiety and fear.

He made himself take deep, slow breaths. With each exhale, the terror receded a little more. *Physician, heal thyself.*

With a sharp intake of breath, Sydney woke abruptly. Her wide eyes took him in, and she leapt to her feet. "Dahlra! Oh, thank God, you're awake!"

Even as her face lit up with joy, she caught herself, and a look of horrible doubt drove any happiness from her expression. Dahlra felt his own relief grow cold as she protectively crossed her arms in front of her chest. Sydney, who had never been afraid of him, even in the Cell, looked frightened of him now.

"Do you—do you need anything? Do you want me to call Dr Hughes? Are you in any pain?"

Before he could stammer out an answer, a picture took shape in his mind, and the feathery edges of a memory fluttered into focus. His last conversation with Sydney; Garnet's ominous visit. They had been neither dreams nor hallucinations. In his pain and anger and terrified delirium, caught in that mental loop of keeping his long-ago promise to keep her alive, no matter the outcome, he had said some awful, hurtful things to the one person he loved more than anything else in the world. And he had meant them at the time. Oh God, he had been so angry, so humiliated, and he had wanted someone to pay for it.

He tried to speak, but his voice caught on his dry throat, and his reply was nothing more than a garbled squawk. Sydney quickly poured him a cupful of water from a pitcher on the bedside table. "Little sips. Don't want you to choke."

It tasted like nectar sliding down his parched throat. After a dozen greedy swallows, he lay back with a nod of thanks. He cleared his throat, feeling ten times more human. And still, she looked at him as if she expected to be hurt—again.

He held out his arms. "Come closer, please? My eyes aren't working too well." She hesitated, and he grasped her hand. Her reticence unnerved him. "Sydney, love, come to me."

The entreaty in his voice broke her reluctance, and she sat down on the bed. He pulled her warm body close. She held herself so tightly she felt foreign in his arms. "Dahlra." His name sounded like an anguished prayer. "Dahlra..."

"Oh, my darling, darling girl." He crushed her against his chest with all the assurance his strained arms could provide. He dug down deep, and found the strength he needed—the strength *she* needed. "It's alright. Everything's going to be alright."

She melted against him with a harsh, grieving sound. "I thought," she gasped, "I—I saw you hanging on that cross and I thought you were dead. And then you said...you said you didn't—"

Her voice caught as he rubbed her back in apology. "I was scared, and out of my mind on whatever Silas had given me. I didn't even know where I was." They began talking together at once.

"I should never have left you. I didn't protect you. I let that bastard get the drop on me—"

"He told me you were dead. He was wearing your engagement ring. He told me you and Elwess—"

"I'm so sorry. He tranked me. I couldn't move."

"I know. You've nothing to be sorry for, Sydney."

"But you told me—"

"I was being an idiot," he insisted firmly, rocking her in his arms. "Sydney, you must believe me. I didn't mean it!"

She pulled away from him, her eyes bleak. "He made me watch. I had no choice. I was paralysed." She slumped, remorse etched into her face. "I keep seeing it when I close my eyes. He tore you apart, and all I could do was sit there and watch him do it."

All the blood-stained shards of the puzzle snapped into place, and Dahlra remembered everything, in gruesome Technicolour. Another round of panic hit him, and he shuddered as if palsied. His eyes burned with tears. "Oh, God, he did it, didn't he?" He coughed, and his body racked in a spasm of grief. "He raped me. He suffocated me." Humiliation twisted through him, cramping his bowels and churning in his stomach like rancid meat. "And I fucking let him! Oh, God, I was such a coward!"

"Dahlra Gar, stop talking bollocks right now!" He could barely hear her over the over-modulating wave of self-recrimination cresting in his head. "You didn't let him. You *fought* him. You fought him like a maniac. You bit off half his cock, for fuck's sweet sake!"

Sydney held onto him, allowing him to fall apart, and he fell willingly, knowing she was there, knowing she would catch him and hold him together. "You have nothing to be ashamed of. I'm so proud of you. And I love you like burning." Her voice was ragged with emotion. "Listen to me, love. We're going home to Maidenvine and no one is ever going to hurt you again. I promise. I swear on my life."

She held up her bruised, swollen hand. Even in the dim light, he saw the diamond flash like a beacon. "I told you the night you gave this to me that you were everything to me. Please give me a chance to prove that nothing, especially not this place, is going to pull rank on that."

Her weary strength and unquenchable resolve went straight to his head like a tonic. She meant business. He felt laughter well up in his chest, and it felt damn good. "Surely, little girl, you know by now that I'm not going to let anything drive me away from you. You're mine, Sydney. Do you honestly think anything could trump that?"

She met his ruined eyes with her own, and burst into defiant tears. "You just *try* and get rid of me."

There was a commotion outside in the hallway. Suddenly Dr Hughes and his nurse raced into the room and switched on the overheads lights.

Dahlra gave a sharp cry of distress and pressed his face against Sydney's collarbone. "Turn off that bloody light!" she barked, shielding his eyes.

The light was quickly dimmed. "I'm very sorry to disturb you." Hughes sounded cheerfully contrite. "I was afraid Dr Gar was either having another seizure, or all the monitors had gone mad." He took in the little drama in the bed, from Sydney's tearstained outrage to Dahlra, his face still buried against her shoulder. "Alright, then. As long as you're awake, let's take a few vitals, shall we?"

Hughes checked his BP and shone a penlight into Dahlra's sensitive eyes, earning another heartfelt curse. "Blood pressure is normal, heart rate is slightly elevated but nothing out of the ordinary. Your pupils are still a little more dilated from the photophobia than I would like, but they have contracted since yesterday. I'm going to set up another round of tests for tomorrow. Just to be on the safe side, you understand." He wrote the finishing touches on his notes. "I'm over the moon with how you've responded to the oxytocin. So I think we can safely say the worst is behind you, except for your eyesight. Rest will take care of that in no time."

He fixed Sydney with an admonishing look. "Ms Chapin, I stand by my earlier advice. I strongly suggest that you get some rest of your own. And try not to get your man too agitated, my dear. There will be plenty of time for all of that when you go home, you see."

Once they were alone again, Dahlra gradually relaxed, and the anxiety that had clutched at Sydney's chest loosened a bit as well. At his insistence, she moved closer, seeking his warmth. They lay together on his narrow hospital bed as she filled in the last few days, beginning with their disastrous conversation after he arrived in hospital, and ending with Brian Collins' none-too-subtle attempt to carpe diem.

"I didn't blame you for being angry. Even though it nearly killed me to admit it, I couldn't blame you for wanting out of this, either. I kept thinking that as long as you were okay, I'd stay away, if that's what you wanted."

There was not so much as a second of hesitation. "I think you'll agree that staying away from me is the last thing I want you to do."

Sydney tried to trust the relief she felt, but her unease would not let go. "Don't get me wrong, love. This was my best case scenario. But there was a lot of truth in what you said. And there's a big part of me that's still afraid you feel that way, deep down."

He silenced her with a gentle kiss. "Shh." His lips were sweet and loving against hers. "I'm not hiding anything, Sydney. Least of all from myself."

She rushed on before he could wreck her resolve with another kiss. "But it *wasn't* fair, dragging you into all this. You've always taken such good care of me, and your payment was getting beaten and..."

"Sydney, look at me."

She turned in his arms to face him. Even in the semi-darkness, she could see the love and intelligence in his gaze. His voice quietly rolled over her. "I know what I said. Listen to me *now.*

"I won't deny that some of those things *are* true. The reality of what you do isn't pretty. But I knew who and what you were long before the Cell."

"Funny, that's what Pink said."

"Wise man." He touched her injured cheek with all the tenderness of a loving parent. "Perhaps how we came together *is* mad to anyone on the outside looking in. But that's not where *we* are." He took her hand, and pressed it over his heart. She could feel it beating steadily against his chest. "We're in here. And it has always made sense *in here.*"

His voice grew more guarded, less sure. "I know we never really talked about some of the things that... happened in the Cell, even when we attended those counseling sessions. I avoided it because I had hoped it was no longer necessary.

"But when I first woke up in the hospital, I thought we were still there." He was breathing hard, and Sydney nestled closer, trying to soothe him. "I tried so hard to fight Silas, and the drugs, and his head games, and I lost. I thought if I could make him think you weren't important to me, he would concentrate on me and you could escape. I had this screwed-up idea if I could make you leave, he couldn't find you and hurt you."

It was the same deadly game he had played in the Cell, and once again, she was not privy to the rules. That fucking cell, the birthplace of their first twisted communion. Two years on, it was a crucible of guilt and blood and torment that still threatened to undermine their lives.

And yet, she could not chide him for something she had avoided herself. She had discussed a lot of things with the Agency's ace psychologist, but she had never revealed the desperate intimacy she and

Dahlra had shared in her prison; it was something they never talked about, even with one another. At first, she had been too wrapped up in her entitlement of PTSD to even consider Dahlra might need a little help with his own.

"I should've helped you exorcise it, instead of assuming you could handle it yourself." She looked into his careworn face. "We did it all wrong, didn't we?"

"I thought if we never felt the need to dissect it in depth, I would never have to own it." He looked at her with such misery in his eyes, her own filled with tears. "That night, that night when you... you touched yourself for me..." His voice grew hoarse with shame. "I always felt I'd have to answer for that night more than all the rest put together."

Sydney watched helplessly as he struggled with his moral equilibrium, and felt sadder than she ever had in her life. This fine man, who loved her so much, who had done the best, the *only* thing he could in the hideous situation he had volunteered for, had used Silas' attack to atone for her in the Cell.

She stroked his face, dark with stubble, and he leaned his cheek into her touch. "No, Dahlra. I don't blame you, and I never will. And you didn't deserve what he did to make up for that damned Cell."

She took his head in her hands. "I swear, you and me, we have to tear that thing down, Dahlra. Rip the door off the hinges, burn the lands around it and sow it with salt. Until we do, it'll always be there, waiting for someone like Silas to come along and lock us up again."

"We won't allow that." It shook her to be the recipient of his resolute gaze. "I know I'm not going to get over this overnight. It's going to take time. But it will happen." He kissed her forehead passionately. "My brave soldier. My warrior. We're our own army now. You and me."

They held onto one another as close as they humanly could, until their burst of righteous conviction faded like fireworks, until they were only two tiny specks in the universe, huddled together in a hospital bed.

"Sydney?"

"Hmm?"

"Where is he, anyhow?" There was a layer of frost on his words, but underneath fear seeped from a deeper pocket. "Where is Silas right now?"

"Well, if there's any fairness in the universe, he's currently being butt-fucked by Beelzebub." He looked at her in puzzlement, and she smiled as she brushed a lock of hair from his forehead. "My dear, you don't ever have to worry about him again. He is very, very dead."

"You killed him." It was not a question, and Sydney wished she could just lie about it, but she could not make herself.

"Actually, Elwess killed him."

"Elwess?"

"Yep. He shot him. That's why Silas is currently wandering around in hell, hiding his angry inch."

Dahlra's expressive brows rose in surprise. "Angry in—what you said earlier—did I really...?"

"Oh, you really did." He rewarded her with a surprisingly wolfish smile. It filled her with a sense of pride. "You most certainly did. Clod, meet Pebble. Riiiight."

He closed his eyes, lay back on his pillow and truly laughed. It sounded like sweet music, and felt like sunshine filling the room. Sydney kissed his warm, laughing mouth, and he responded with a smiling kiss of his own.

The room gradually grew darker, until they were lying in the hushed blackness, with only the hissing monitors as foley. Dahlra was silent, his limbs growing slack around her, until Sydney thought he had drifted off.

His deep voice startled her. "'Extinguish my eyes, I'll go on seeing you. Seal my ears, I'll go on hearing you. And without feet I can make my way to you, without a mouth I can swear your name.'" He paused. "I can't remember the rest."

Sydney's heart felt as if it would burst. Her throat was so tight she could hardly speak. "It's beautiful."

"It's Rilke." He idly stroked her head, his fingers combing through her hair. "Our own army, Sydney," he repeated, and his voice had a tone of finality to it, like an angel sealing up the tomb of a monster.

Gradually, he drifted off, while Sydney curled against his side, praying he would still mean those beautiful words when he woke again.

CHAPTER THIRTEEN

Meetings

"The second series of scans show no permanent physical damage," Dr Hughes declared two days later. "No signs of any anomalies, hemorrhaging, concussion—you, my friend, are a very lucky man."

Dahlra nodded, but did not answer. He was too busy tucking into the biggest Big Boy breakfast the Kennington Lane Cafe could deliver: eggs and rashers, sausages, beans and mushrooms, chips, tomatoes and toast. After almost a week of being fed via IV and hospital rations, he was ravenous. The fact he was chowing down with such relish was testament to his recovery.

Dr Hughes continued. "Now, we'll still want to follow-up with you, but I want to kick you out of the hospital this afternoon, so do me the favour of staying healthy and well until then."

Dahlra washed down his final piece of toast with a pint of milk, then sat back with a most un-Dahlra-like belch. "Had enough?" Sydney asked, bemused. He nodded, sated and unrepentant.

By three o'clock, they were in the car, heading up the M25 toward Windsor. Sydney drove as fast as traffic would allow, while Dahlra, looking very fashionisto in his silk shirt, grey slacks and dark shades, dozed in the passenger's seat. He was still paler than normal, and moved with a stiffness unlike his usual grace. No matter. Sydney knew a few days of fresh air, good food and Maidenvine's peace would have him back to fighting fit.

A warm hand slid over her thigh, and she smiled. "Alright, love?"

With a yawn and a stretch, he sat up straighter, and adjusted his seat belt. "I'll be fine. I know doctors have a reputation of playing fast and loose with their own health, but I'm not that reckless." He settled back in his seat. "I've got too many reasons to keep my mental health intact."

Sydney nodded, her eyes on the road. "I know you'll want some private counseling with Ted, but I'll be with you anytime you want."

He stroked her thigh again. "That's my girl. We'll be fine." They drove in silence for several minutes. "It's odd, though."

"What's odd?" She impatiently passed a lorry who had decided to slow down for no apparent frikkin' reason... Then Dahlra rattled her so much she almost ran off the road.

"Elwess hasn't been by or called. That's not like him at all." She could sense him watching her. "Sydney, is he alright? Was he injured during all this?"

She felt the stubborn anger kindling in her stomach again. "To be honest, I sent him packing. I told him to leave us alone."

He actually laughed. "What? Why on earth would you do that?"

"It's sort of complicated."

"Perhaps you'd better explain it to me, then."

Sydney downshifted and signaled to change lanes. She pulled into a motorway services facility and stopped the car.

Dahlra listened quietly as Sydney told him her side of that awful afternoon. He knew her well enough to know that she was downplaying it, hiding the horror behind the bland, unembellished truth. His testicles crawled at the thought of how she had nearly sawed her wrists to the tendons, trying to free herself. Her dislocated finger was still swollen and bruised, but she stubbornly refused to remove her engagement ring. He would get an ice pack on it the moment they got home.

Elwess' part in all of this left him with more questions than Sydney seemed willing to answer. "I still don't understand, love. If he was the one to set you free, why—"

"I don't know, really." Her brows puckered in frustration. "I just feel like all roads lead back to him. *He* made the recording; he left it out so that anybody could find it. *He* was the one who picked that fight in The Library. He's the reason Silas and his little Silverbirch gang killed that poor girl, Kofry. He was gone to Amsterdam when we needed him, he killed Silas before we could question him." She was breathing as if she had been running.

Dahlra touched her cheek, and reluctantly she faced him. "Sydney, what's the *real* reason? The one that made you angry enough to cast him out?"

She dropped her eyes. "He came between us. You thought I preferred him to you."

"Sydney."

"Elwess fulfilled his role, and he's surplus to requirements now." She sounded mulish and guilty. "He almost got you killed. If we're going to be part of the war on Silverbirch, he doesn't have a place in our lives."

"*Silas* was the one who almost killed me. Darling, you're transferring all your anger and guilt onto Elwess, because you know I don't blame you. And I don't blame him, either. If he hadn't come home and untied you, you wouldn't have been able to resuscitate me, because I would have already been dead. And then *you* would have died, my love, because Silas came to that flat to kill us both. Regardless of what Elwess has done in the past, he saved our lives that day."

"I know." There was an impatient, obstinate edge to her voice. "Okay, *maybe* I'm being unfair about it. But I just feel like he wants too much from us. And I'm afraid he'll try and come between us again."

"He probably *does* want too much from us," he admitted. "But he can never take any more than we're willing to give. And that includes me as well as you."

"But you said—"

"A lot of stuff I do not subscribe to. Sydney, I don't want us reheating this every morning for breakfast. What you will *not* do is walk on eggshells around me. As far as the status quo, nothing between us has changed. I will not give any credence to the delirious babble of a drugged and injured man. We have been and will always be straight with one another, and that is how we will proceed. No insinuations, no hidden meanings, no secrets. End of."

She glanced at him sideways, a smile teasing the corners of her mouth. "You're awfully bolshy for a guy who just got out of hospital after a near-brush with death."

"A near-death experience will do that to a chap. Once you recover, you feel strangely invincible." He detuned his voice down a semitone. "And I'm your Dominant, remember. I'm entitled to be a little bolshy."

They sat quietly for a moment, watching cars trundle down the off ramp. Sydney looked contrite, and Dahlra knew this was not something that would be gone by the time they reached Windsor. With a sigh, he said, "Well, it's too bad. Elwess was a much better kisser than Silas."

Sydney gaped at him in shock. "That's not funny! Dahlra, fuck's sake, stop laughing!" Her own laughter bubbled to the surface. "You wicked thing! How on earth can you joke about something like that?"

"Because that's how I choose to deal with it." Now that it was freed, the laughter welled up in his chest, and it felt good to release it. "I'm alive, Sydney. I'm beat all to hell, and I'll probably have LSD flashbacks like the 60's, and I haven't a clue when my libido might eventually raise its head from the parapet, but I'm so damn glad to be alive—"

Sydney twisted in the driver's seat and threw herself at him. Her foot landed on the horn, startling them both and nearly sending them catapulting into the back seat. He continued laughing as she covered his face in frantic kisses. He hugged her so hard she grunted, and this time they both laughed. He enveloped her body in his arms, giddy with the guilt-free pleasure of just breathing.

He gave her a smacking kiss on the lips, then an equally loud smack on her gorgeous arse with the flat of his hand. "Alright, my girl, start the car. Let's go home." He placed a tender kiss on her injured hand, and she gave him the first truly unguarded smile since he had awoken from his long sleep. She unfolded herself from his side and obediently started the car.

As they continued on their way, it occurred to him she had never really finished resolving the Elwess issue—nor the Brian Collins issue. God, these career Doms. Collecting scalps like bounty hunters, not caring if the wounds left behind healed or not. He was especially displeased with Brian right now—talk about kicking a chap when he was down—but he dismissed it as an opportunistic incident. Elwess was another, more serious matter.

Suddenly Dahlra could not wait to see Maidenvine again. There, they could not be touched by the taint of Silverbirch, or the Agency or even Elwess. At Maidenvine, they were safe. He knew they would eventually have to face it—they had learned a hard lesson regarding avoiding issues to their detriment. Tomorrow, maybe.

In the weeks that followed the attack, Dahlra forced himself to do the textbook Right Thing. If Sydney's ordeal in the Cell had taught him anything, it was that you had to fight the urge to internalise it all. True, she was the first to admit she had never been one to crawl inside her own head and suffocate under a blanket of introspection, but Dahlra privately thought it took more than simply a lack of imagination to beat the bad guy within. Sydney's answer had always been to *do* something. She played the piano; she ran laps around the length of the estate, she lined up empty tins on a fence for target practice with her Glock.

Dahlra decided to take a leaf out of her book; he allowed himself time to heal, then exercised to build his stamina. He ran with Sydney each morning, and he lifted weights in their makeshift gym. He worked on their late summer garden and cooked fabulous meals. They invited friends around, and sent them home full and loaded down with tomatoes and cress.

Under Sydney's expert tutelage, he learned to lock, load, aim the Glock and take six out of twelve cans off the wall in under thirty seconds. She proudly pronounced him a crack shot without the tiniest hint of patronisation, which he appreciated.

And in between, he regularly checked in with Daffyd Hughes for his physical progress, and he attended counseling with Dr Ted Browning to keep his head from melting under the heat lamp of Silas' mind games. Gradually, the poison leached out of his system, and he felt whole and comfortable again, in all aspects but one.

Sex with Sydney had always been a sensuous, erotic dream, but lately their attempts at intimacy edged into the territory of nightmare. Each time he tried to summon his arousal, it would easily spark into life, only to sputter out and disappear. He understood and accepted the emotional restrictions placed on his physicality, but it was galling. He had given himself the allotted time for his body and mind to heal, yet his libido had yet to come up for air. It was the first time since they had become lovers that he could not perform.

Sydney, of course, understood immediately. On that first disastrous morning they had tried to make love, she had even made him laugh about it. "Well, I'm not going to tell you that it's okay and that everything will be fine." She had held him, and stroked his hair, and he had felt like a failure. "But you know how this goes. It takes time. Just relax, don't obsess about it, and pretty soon nature will take over again. If you'll recall, we were together almost six months before I was even remotely interested in sex."

He knew she was right, but it did not help. Standing in front of the toilet, trying to piss around a morning erection, all he could think about was sliding back into bed next to his warm, sleepy lover and waking her up in grand style. But the moment he finished emptying his bladder, the erection would go south. After almost two weeks of this self-imposed cock-blocking, Dahlra consulted with Daffyd Hughes, just in case some physical problem had developed as a result of the attack, but all that jovial Welsh numpty would say was, "There is nothing wrong with your plumbing, my friend. All you need is a little time."

Dahlra did not want time. He wanted to make love to his beautiful fiancée, and he was damned if Silas was going to get in the way of getting it up. True, he had not lost the use of his tongue or his hands, but the inability to remain aroused nullified his desire. It felt wrong to try and fire up something he was not capable of finishing. It made him feel useless, like a neutered tomcat. And worse, he found it very disgruntling that something as seemingly unimportant as his lack of a sex drive dented his confidence so much.

"What you need is a reminder of how much fun we used to have before we left DeVere Gardens." Sydney nuzzled affectionately against his throat. "You're just as fascinating to me *in* your clothes as you are out of them, you know."

Dahlra's mobile rang, but both he and Sydney ignored it. They were locked in mortal combat, and he was winning. He could see the tension and frustration in her eyes, but he had learned his lessons well. This was not the time to show leniency.

With more aplomb than even Lightoller could feign, he headed for the 'G' in Sydney's downward S-I-N-G, and placed 'O-B-O-S' across. He didn't bother to hide his triumph.

Sydney huffed and swore under her breath. "Gobos. Wouldn't you bloody know it?"

"That's eight in total with—" he checked under the 'B,' "—a triple word for twenty-four points and that's me out."

"That's you out every time." She pushed her Scrabble easel away. "I had Q, R and C. There's fourteen more points to add to your score." She pouted prettily. "I don't know why I play this game with you. I never stand a chance. Okay, how about the best two out of three?"

Flushed and mellow with victory and half a bottle of wine, Dahlra sighed contentedly and held out his hand. "How about coming here and sitting on my lap?"

The look of surprised pleasure on her face threatened to make him feel guilty, but he brushed away that toxic thought as she climbed onto his lap and straddled his hips.

"What exactly do you have in mind?" There was an excited shiver in her voice that slid right into his groin. "After all, I'm the defeated foe. Completely at your mercy."

He eased his hands around her waist, his touch light and teasing. "Perhaps I should pour oil on the troubled waters." Beneath his feather-light touch, her smooth skin pebbled with goose bumps, and she almost, but not quite suppressed a soft mewling plea. He caressed her throat, and her eyes fluttered closed.

As he ghosted his fingertips over the swell of her breasts, she trembled, and a sigh of longing slipped from her lips like silk. Dahlra felt his desire balance with love, and meld into the perfect storm. He pulled her to him almost roughly, a little fearfully.

His kiss felt clumsy and over-eager, but the moment the soft pillow of her bottom lip suckled against his, his erection roared to life, and he surged against her, feeling her heat and arousal burning against his lap. She ground against him, making his head spin with desire.

She broke the kiss, trailing her lips over his jaw, her soft mouth teasing him in that way that had driven him mad since their first night together. His hands worried open the buttons of her blouse, finding the satiny, cool skin beneath.

Through her sheer bra he teased her tight aureoles, encircling her nipples but not quite touching them. She moaned his name, sending heat sparking in his balls. He roughly yanked the cups of her bra downward, pushing her breasts over the fabric, and feasted on her tight, enticing nipples. Her fingers threaded into his hair, impatiently pulling him away from this sumptuous banquet of flesh, bringing his mouth to hers.

They tore the clothes from their bodies, their mouths fused to one another's. She scrabbled at his shirt, her nimble fingers exposing his skin one button at a time. She leaned back only for a moment, to unbuckle his belt and open his trousers, and he lifted his hips to help her ease his trousers down, aching to feel her tight core melt around his cock...

But the moment her hand slipped over his erection, his lust wavered, then toppled over. He fought to keep the fire going, but his body was not having any of it. He pounded his fist against the arm of the sofa. "No. Fuck, not again." It took every ounce of his self-control not to push her off, run out of the house and just get in the car and drive until he was so far away from it all he could perhaps deal with it. His patience was as frayed as his sex drive.

Instead, he scrubbed his face with his hands, unable to meet her eyes. Swallowing the last of his humiliation, he forced himself to look up at her. She was still sexed up and panting, still wanting him, and he took feeble comfort in that, at least. She also looked disappointed, but resolute nonetheless.

"It's not the end of the world." She kissed his forehead, and silently buttoned his shirt. "I'm not trying to patronise you, okay? But it's not the end of our sex life. You'll get your groove back, I promise."

"And what if I don't?" He hated the self-pitying tone that coated every word. "I know it takes time, but it's not fair." He felt guilt's insidious fingers creeping around his throat. "I love you. I want to make love to you. Dammit, I want to fuck you."

"Well, I believe you will, eventually." With reluctance, she pulled away from him. "Hey, you don't want anyone else, do you?"

In spite of her teasing tone, something about the question made Dahlra's stomach fold in on itself. It was in these moments of failure that she relived that horrible moment of rejection in the hospital. Her tightly locked-down insecurity hurt worse than his impotence. "You know there's no one on this earth but you, Sydney." Christ, he was sick of himself. "I just hate feeling so broken."

She rose from his lap and curled up beside him on the sofa. He put his arms around her. "Remember when I said I loved what was between your ears as much as I loved what was between your legs?"

He could not help but chuckle, but it was a painful thing to laugh at. "I remember we'd just had fantastic sex before you said it."

She graced him with one of her steady, uncompromising looks. "You make love to me every single day. In hundreds of ways. Give yourself time. You were more than content to wait for me. Ration out some of that patience for yourself, love."

Dahlra's mobile rang again. This time he glanced at the display. "It's Inigo."

"What the hell does he want?" Sydney sat up with a sigh of resignation. "You might as well answer. He'll drive us mad until you do."

He put it on speaker. "Hello, Inigo."

"Dahlra, old chap." Lightoller's voice oozed out of the phone like olive oil. "Caught you at last. How are you? Fully recovered, I hope? No lingering effects?"

He sounded about as concerned over Dahlra's health as he would an injured pheasant. "I'm quite well, thank you."

"Excellent, excellent. And Sydney? In fine fettle?"

"Quite. But of course you'd know that, simply by checking our progress reports at the hospital."

"True, but that's not very personable, is it? Not like going straight to the source, as it were."

Dahlra glanced at Sydney, who was frowning at his phone. Since their return to Maidenvine, they had not really discussed work, though she still kept her daily phone appointment with Garnet. This could not be news to Lightoller. As the silence stretched on, Dahlra huffed in exasperation. "Is there anything we can actually do for you, Inigo, or is this simply a fact-finding mission?"

"One, nil. Actually, old cock, I was wondering if I could pin you down on when you next plan to visit London. We would love to have you both round for dinner."

"Hey, less of the 'old cock' routine, if you don't mind. That's *my* Minder, you know. What's this all about, Inigo?"

"Sydney, old horse! What ho! So lovely to hear your voice. As I was just saying, it's about meeting up with friends. It's about my dear lady wife being worried about you both and missing her luncheon companion." There was a beat. "It's about wanting to talk with you."

Judging from the death-ray glower she was giving his phone, Sydney was dying to tell the smarmy git where to stuff his invitation. Dahlra waved his hand to gain her attention, then shook his head. He pitched his voice to be every bit as oily as Lightoller's. "Well, that's very kind of you, Inigo. What day do you have in mind?"

The look Sydney gave him was part shock, part betrayal. He stroked her cheek and mouthed, *Trust me.*

Elwess was met at Morden Tube Station by a broad-shouldered, bullet-headed, navy-suited goon, charming as a mutt. He was then escorted to an elegant black BMW640. It was an impressive motor, even for someone generally indifferent to cars. The windows were tinted the same midnight black as the rest of the vehicle; as they drove in the encroaching darkness, Elwess could see nothing on either side of the road. It was claustrophobic, but he forced himself to appear nonchalant. He could see his driver eyeing him in the rear-view mirror almost as much as he watched the road. Elwess' one and only attempt to engage him in conversation was met with blunt silence.

They drove around in a confusing and pointless pattern, presumably to ensure they were not being followed. As the first slow hour slid into the second, Elwess grew increasingly restless and unnerved. It was all starting to feel a bit too much like The Long Good Friday for his taste.

Finally, the car pulled onto gravel that sprayed against the undercarriage, and Elwess' stomach gave a lurch as they came to a sudden stop. The driver got out and opened Elwess' door. "Mr. Talbert, if you please," he said, in a rumbling Bolton accent. Elwess stepped out cautiously and looked down the gravel drive, but it disappeared in the copse of trees far down the lane.

They were parked in front of a manor house. It was smaller than either Maidenvine or Ramcat, but had the same clean, Georgian lines as those two venerable old piles. The heat of London's lingering summer had not quite made it to wherever *here* was, and a cool breeze rippled his shirt against his skin. A shiver flashed over him which he suspected had little to do with the actual temperature.

Just as he reached the front door and lifted his hand to knock, it swung open. A stunning redhead stood in the entrance, with a smile of welcome on her flawlessly made-up face. A red silk and black lace corset pulled her waist into nothing, and pushed her breasts up into perfect, silky globes. Pert, red nipples peeked from just beneath the corset's edge. Mesh stockings slithered over her long legs, tapering down to slim ankles, perched atop gravity-defying stilettos.

Like a teenaged boys' wet dream, she was slender and perfectly proportioned, but dressed so obviously textbook porn mag she was almost a cliché. Kink-by-the-numbers, certainly, but built for speed, with a mouth that looked capable of sucking his balls dry.

She made a perfect bow. "Good evening, Master Elwess." Her voice was throaty and pitched to seduce. She sounded more posh than she probably was. "May I take your coat?"

"I'll keep it, thank you, Miss...?"

"Helena, sir. Just Helena."

"Thank you, Helena."

She held out her arm. "Please come with me. My master has been so looking forward to your visit. As have I." She led him into a large paneled room, what Dahlra would have called the drawing room. It was decorated like a hunting lodge: expensive-looking paintings, deer heads, gun racks—the full To The Manor Born vibe. Everything looked bought from various estate sales, as though it should be featured in an *Architectural Digest* article entitled, 'How To Bring The *Downton Abbey* Look Into Your Home.'

"If I may be so bold, it's such an honour to finally meet you," Helena was saying, with a demure fluttering of her lashes. Her eyes were bright blue, and frank with invitation. "I was the envy of all my friends when I told them I would be serving here tonight."

"I'm very flattered." He followed her to a long sofa, covered in deep burgundy velvet, and she gestured for him to sit.

"May I get you something to drink? Wine, rum, whisky?"

"Rum, please."

"Of course."

She presented a tumbler of rum, in the proper way, holding it delicately with one hand, balancing it from the underside of the glass with the other. He accepted it with a nod. As he leaned back on the seat, she knelt in front of him. "My master will be here shortly. A matter of business has detained him." Her hands, small and agile, tipped with finely manicured nails, slid up the inside of his thighs, urging them apart. She leaned in between his legs. With an impish smile on her crimson lips, she added, "I'm here to keep you entertained until he returns."

"Of course you are."

Her hands drifted toward his crotch and reached for his belt buckle. Elwess caught her wrists and gently pushed them away. "Business before pleasure, Helena." He took the sting out of his words by giving her a long, promising look, starting with her thighs and sweeping upward to her face. He patted the sofa invitingly. "Why don't you sit with me and tell me all about yourself?"

Her composure slipped only for a moment, then her smile returned. She sat down beside him, crossed her shapely legs and placed her hands in her lap, like a deb at a garden party. "We can talk about whatever you please, Master Elwess. I'm all yours."

They passed a pleasant but essentially uninformative few minutes, during which Helena chatted without actually telling him anything of importance about herself or her 'master.' Elwess kept his drink in hand, and gestured with it, but never actually drank it. He knew he was being watched; there was no fooling a voyeur. Too many surfaces and tchotchkes which cameras could hide on or behind, too many shadowy corners from which he could be observed. He let the conversation gradually wind down, then surreptitiously looked at his watch.

As if on cue, the door opened and a short, stocky man in his late fifties strode into the room. His thinning hair was silver, his brown eyes the colour of old pennies. He carried himself like he worked out. "Master Elwess!" he boomed, his hands outstretched in greeting. "Forgive me for the delay. I trust that Helena has kept you from growing bored."

"She's been a charming hostess. Quite a credit to you." Elwess rose to his feet, and shook hands with his host, who then gestured for him to sit again. "You have a lovely home, Master—"

"The name's John Walters, Master Elwess. Scotch, Helena."

There was a faint trace of impatience as Walters waited for the girl to pour his Glenfiddich. She held the drink out to him, smiling nervously, almost pleadingly. He snatched the glass from her hands, swallowing half its contents in one go with all the swagger of a born bully.

He spied Elwess' glass and favoured him with a sly look. "Do you not care for your rum? I understand you're quite a fan of Neisson Reserve Speciale."

It was the 'I know you better than you think' challenge in his voice which identified Walters as the man who had called him after he had killed Silas. With deliberate gentleness, Elwess placed the glass on the table. "With all due respect, Master John, I was asked to come here and discuss business. I prefer to do that with a clear head. Wouldn't you agree?"

His deliberate arrogance was like fluttering a red rag at a bull, and Walters' eyes flashed with anger. To his credit, though, he recovered quickly. "Right to the point, I see! I'd heard that about you, as well."

"It seems like you've heard a great many things about me, Master John. If you know which hand I use to scratch my arse, I'm going to go home and tear my house apart."

Walters laughed, but did not contradict him. "You don't disappoint, Master Elwess." He drained the rest of his drink and sat back. Helena refilled his glass, then knelt by his side. He stroked her hair while they talked.

"As I mentioned when we spoke on the phone, we owe you a great deal for taking care of the Silas situation."

Elwess glanced from Walters to the girl and back. "I'm not sure this conversation is suitable for delicate ears."

"Oh, I assure you, my pet is the soul of discretion." Walters pinched her earlobe fondly. His arrogance surrounded him like a visible aura. "She's quite well-trained, you see."

Conditioned to be scared shitless, you mean. "Well, you know as well I do that Silas was a bloody nuisance. Brawling, public drunkenness, entering my home uninvited, damaging my toys."

Walters nodded sagely and took another drink. "Silas had grown increasingly unstable. Drug addiction, among his other habits, such as taking what he wanted without asking. Lorcan had given him several warnings regarding his behaviour."

"Lorcan?"

"Our controller. He had already decided it was time for Silas to move on, but fortunately you saved us a great deal of time and palaver. Lorcan is very grateful." His smirk faded. "It's a pity Inigo Lightoller couldn't lower himself to show a little gratitude for your bravery, wouldn't you agree?"

Elwess noted they had lapsed into a kind of boilerplate doublespeak that implied much and said little. He did not have to manufacture the resentment in his reply. "I wasn't thinking in those terms at the time, but now that you mention it, I suppose it wasn't asking too much to expect a little appreciation. From all parties involved."

His eyes drifted toward the preening sub. "Forgive me, Master John, but I'm very curious. Exactly how did you acquire this information?"

Walters gave Elwess a calculating look, then handed his empty glass to Helena. She immediately rose and poured him another. "I'm going to come straight to the point. You know why you're here. We are quite well aware of our notoriety. Our business carries a high degree of risk. But we have very powerful friends, Master Elwess. Friends who are willing to use their influence in order to keep us abreast of any possible threat to our operations. There isn't much that happens in Lightoller's Agency we don't know about.

"So it should come as no surprise that we are very aware of you, and your reputation in the kinkster world. Lorcan has been following you for some time now, but naturally your ties with the Agency and certain persons therein made you a *persona non grata* to us."

"But, it is an ill wind that blows the changes." Elwess had meant to sound flippant, but his words sounded as bitter as they tasted in his mouth.

Walters leaned closer, dropping his one-mastodon-to-another routine "Allow me to be candid, Talbert. You had the ear of Inigo Lightoller. Several of your pets are well known in their attempts to disrupt our operations. You've got a reputation as being incorruptible, and that made you a potential threat. You knew enough to get a few of our old guard into trouble, had you chosen to do so. But until now, you've kept your mouth shut and refused to take a side."

He took a long pull of scotch. "You no longer have that luxury. You blotted your copybook when you put a bullet through Markham's gut."

Elwess scoffed. "You could say that. It cost me my job and my future with the Agency. Not to mention two very enjoyable slaves."

"And that's why you're here. We were fortunate enough to use our political influence to shut Lightoller down the first time. We made mistakes, we admit that. But we're learning. As you say, changes have been made on both sides. And we've engaged in a restructuring process, as all good organisations must do from time to time. When Lorcan took over, he crafted a new mission statement. One that ultimately called for fresh legs."

"You make it sound like a Fortune 500 company."

Walters laughed. "You're not far from wrong." He toasted Elwess with his drink. "And we're looking for men like you. Strong, confident men who know what they want and how to get it. You have skills that a man like Inigo Lightoller can't possibly appreciate. And you have charisma, and credibility throughout Europe. You're welcome in any fet community as one of the best and the most notorious. You should have been rewarded for what you did—not cast aside. That was short-sighted of them. We think we can do you better."

"And what exactly would I be expected to do in this organisation of yours?"

"Whatever you wish. PR, training, exhibiting, punishment, pleasure. We provide very valuable, discreet services to people who pay us very handsomely for your kind of expertise. With your reputation and eye for talent, you could name your own price. We can provide you with a future that not only allows you to do what you do best, but gives you the freedom to do it however you please... with whomever you please."

Which tells me precisely nothing.

Walters nodded to Helena, who rose and left the room, her high heels clicking on the burnished hardwood floor. Once the door closed behind her, Walters continued. "I will tell you this. Silverbirch, as you call it, doesn't have to seek men out. They come to *us*. The controller has had his eye on you for a long time, as I said, and now that your situation has changed, he wants to strike while the iron's hot. That's how special you are to us, Master Elwess."

Walters stood, and Elwess stood with him. "Lightoller has us all wrong, you know. He thinks it's about human trafficking, guns, technology, drugs." Together they walked toward the door. "Those are merely currency. Toys to play with. This is about being a king among the peasants. Men love getting their hands dirty. We give them the mud to roll around in. Let the human dregs go on, fighting and fucking and using themselves up. We'll sit back and reap the rewards. Then we walk over their carcasses on the way to our castles."

He paused, his hand on the door latch, and glanced around the room. "Do you think I was born to this? My father was a fishmonger. I grew up in a shitty little terrace flat in Poplar, not far from your patch, in fact.

"But I wanted more. So I worked hard, and this is my reward. Men like you and me, we were *born* to be kings. And Silverbirch will place the crown on your head. You deserve the best, and nothing will be denied you here. In fact, allow me to give you a sample."

Elwess followed Walters down a long corridor. As they strolled, Walters rattled on, clearly reveling in his own rhetoric, revealing nothing of real value, just a lot of innuendo and flash. Elwess recognised this type of Dom very well. Brian Collins once referred to it as ASN Syndrome: Acquired Situational Narcissism. The very epitome of kinkster *noblesse oblige.* They believed in the formalities, the hierarchies of ownership, the almost courtly way of talking—one top dog to another. Either Walters had bought into it lock, stock and barrel, or he was faking a great deal.

They came at last to the end of the hall and stopped at a small door. Walters produced a key and unlocked it. "Welcome to *my* dungeon." He indicated for Elwess to enter first. "Please feel free to play all you like."

Elwess had expected a makeshift mélange of ropes, cinder blocks, pulleys and stocks in a damp, brick-lined, cement-floored hovel. What he saw was enough to make any Dom salivate. Mahogany paneling gleamed on the walls. The floor was painted to look like polished marble. The area was large, cool, and lit with recessed spots that highlighted an array of state-of-the-art equipment and implements. Chrome, glass, leather, rubber, hemp, PVC, wood; every piece of the highest quality, every pleasure catered to and indulged.

"Well? What do you think?" Walters turned to Elwess, his smug self-importance as overpowering as his cologne. "Go on, admit it, Talbert. Even the legendary Chine isn't this well-equipped."

Elwess chose not to call him on the Chine slip. He made a mental note to completely overhaul his security system the moment he got home. He nodded appreciatively. "Impressive, Master John. You have some very tasty gear."

"Only the best, Master Elwess. Custom shop all the way." He patted Elwess' shoulder with just a bit too much bonhomie. "And speaking of tasty gear, allow me to whet your appetite."

He gestured toward a lean, olive-skinned woman wearing a black PVC catsuit. She was buckling a naked and sweating Helena onto the last arm of a highly polished St Andrews Cross. When the woman was finished, she bowed silently to Elwess and placed a palm-sized square mirror in Walters' hand. It sported several lines of white powder and a small straw.

Walters went first, hitting the coke aggressively. He passed the mirror to Elwess, who took a leisurely hit. He noted that the straw was a rolled-up fifty-pound note.

The coke did two things: it gave him the courage to do what he knew was expected of him, and took away some of the jaded knowledge that he would probably enjoy it more than he wanted to.

Without warning, Walters slapped the bound girl sharply in the face. She moaned deliriously. "Helena loves pain, don't you, my dirty little whore? I want you to show Master Elwess just how much you love it." He backed away, breathing heavily. "Nothing moistens her cunt like torture."

Catwoman offered Elwess a leather flail. It was a fine instrument, the ends tipped with silver. "Very nice." She stared at him, her eyes unreadable. By contrast, Helena's face was incandescent with anticipation. She was deep into subspace and her eyes followed Elwess' every movement as he casually draped the flail over his shoulder and paused to consider his options.

Finally, he stepped up to the shaking girl, leaning in close enough to see the pulse beating swiftly in her throat. He brushed his fingers over her cheek. "You are a very pretty little slut." His voice was low, and pitched with such seductive velvet she shivered rapturously. "Are you all mine, to do with as I please?"

"Yes, Master Elwess. I'm all yours. Please, hurt me."

Elwess felt dark, greasy lust slide into his veins like rancid oil. The arousal she was throwing his way was sharp and open, and the coke fueled his desire to give her a little bad cop, worse cop action. "It would be a pity to deny you, wouldn't it?"

He swiftly stepped back, and the whip sang through the air. It landed with perfect accuracy; he was, after all, a man well versed in the art of inflicting pain. It was all too easy to vent his frustration and trepidation on her welcoming, lily-white flesh. Soon red welts striped her breasts, her belly, even the tops of her thighs, like evenly-drawn lines on white paper.

Elwess turned to the attendant and tossed the flail into her hands. He caught her unaware, but she managed to catch it before it hit the floor. "Lovely. But not, I think, quite to my tastes. Bring me a birch cane rod." He smiled as his voice dropped to a low growl. "And turn her around. I want to stripe that pretty little arse before I fuck it."

By the time he had had enough, Elwess had broken three canes, and Helena's arse was a roadmap of crisscrossed welts. Blood beaded the deepest blows. The tears tracking through the girl's smeared makeup were genuine and ceaseless. When Elwess finally released her from the cross, she crawled toward him, still sobbing and begging for mercy.

"Poor little thing," he crooned in a menacing, baby-talking way that made her shudder and whimper. Each time she reached for his boots, he stepped back, forcing her to crawl across the rough floor. She moved with exaggerated, long strides, showing off her body, her eagerness to debase herself.

He knew her little show was for his benefit, and he knew better than to lie to himself; he was looking forward to reaping the rewards of it. He sat down on a throne-like chair and patted his thigh. As she crawled into his lap, he sneered, "Does my pretty little slut want a little relief?"

"Oh, yes, Master Elwess, please," she whined, writhing over him.

"Sorry baby, but relief is not on the cards right now." He managed a nasty, sinister laugh as he brought his hand down hard on her raw backside. He struck her over and over, without pity or reprieve, and the more he spanked her, the more she wailed and the wetter she became. "I do... love... spanking... a screamer." He emphasised each word with a merciless slap to her quivering arse.

This time, when she fell to her knees before him, he did not push her frantic hands away. The smell of her arousal mixed with her perfume created a new scent that both excited and repulsed him. It was a heady, dirty/wrong combination that made his cock as hard as stone, and he refused to question it too deeply. Better to let the girl and the coke do the work for him.

She made short work of unbuttoning his trousers, then stuffed his cock into her smeared, red mouth. He sat back, like a king, drinking his rum as she sucked him. He wrapped her long hair around his fist and used it like a handle. "That's it, sweetheart, let me fuck that pretty mouth..."

In spite of her obvious skill, Elwess could not let go. He grunted in frustration and thrust harder, making her gag, but he simply could not find the tipping point into an orgasm. Finally, he pushed her away with a curse. Helena glanced from him to her Master, and Elwess saw a flash of something that had little to do with BDSM or erotic humiliation. Elwess *must* find her pleasing; if he did not, Walters' would view it as failure, and the consequences for the girl would not be pleasant. He thought of Kofry's mutilated body...

Elwess rose to his feet. "I think your arse needs to be fucked."

"Oh, yes, sir, yes, please." Helena swayed as if in the grip of religious fervor. "Fuck me, please come inside me—"

"You haven't earned the right to my come. Bring me a condom." He impatiently tapped the birch cane against his leg as she slid the condom into place. "Turn around and bend over. Let's see if that arse is any tighter than your mouth."

He spat directly onto her entrance, and she gasped as he used his cold spittle to lubricate her. He breached her without finesse or care, sneering, "Gotta love that pop," as he plunged into her. He relentlessly fucked her arse, his thrusts hard and angry. As he pounded away on the poor girl, trying to get off, Elwess allowed himself to picture Sydney, pressed against his bedroom mirror, the scent of her leather corset and delicious sex short-circuiting his reason and his good judgment.

It was the one thing he had sworn he would not do; the most disgusting dereliction of respect. Behind his slitted, unfocused eyes, he pretended the long hair entwined in his fist was not red, but chestnut, and her back was not pale and flawless, but scored with strong, deep scars. He fantasised that the man in the room was not the cruel, greedy-eyed Walters, but Dahlra, watching him pleasure his lover.

A layer of ice covered his heart, so cold it burned, but not cold enough to freeze the memories away. *Kitten. Lovely kitten... Such a baby sweet little arse... Come into the dark with me, Sydney... Sydney—*

He came, hating himself and the part he was playing. He pushed the girl off his cock almost the moment he was done, and she quickly turned around and kissed the tops of his Chelsea boots with desperate reverence. And just to show what a complete and utter bastard he was, he tossed the spent condom in her face. He did not fail to clock the hard, bright power in Walter's eyes as he sneered down at her.

Elwess stepped away from the girl's grasping hands and zipped his fly. As he buckled his belt, he surreptitiously caught the eye of the lean Amazon in the catsuit. Her dark eyes flicked from the weeping girl back to him, and when he raised his brow, she gave him a slight nod of understanding. That tiny gesture of promise was the only thing that kept his dinner in his stomach.

He turned and followed his host out the door without a backward glance. Walters led them back to the drawing room. There was a self-satisfied strut to his walk that made Elwess want to punch him. "You're a handy man with the cane, Master Elwess. Then again, Helena doesn't count it a good session unless she needs a trip to A&E afterward."

Elwess smiled knowingly. "I could always go back and make sure."

Walters seemed pleased with his remark. He retrieved a manila envelope from his desk and handed it to Elwess. "Our controller would very much like to meet with you. He's spending the season in the Far East, and he's asked me to extend the invitation for you to join him in Japan. He wants to discuss the possibilities of what we can do for you."

He nodded toward the envelope. "Everything you need is in there, including my number. Call me anytime." As he walked Elwess to the door, he said, "Oh, and by the way; Helena is one of our special girls. She truly belongs to the organisation. No family, no home. No one to miss her. If you enjoyed her, she's yours to do with as you please." He gave Elwess a look that made his skin crawl. "*Anything* you please. Think of her as a 'welcome wagon' gift."

"Perhaps when I return from Japan, Master John." He managed a chilling smile. "In the meantime, I would hate to deprive you of such charming company."

Elwess sauntered to the car, barely acknowledging the driver, and got in. They drove down the long lane, and Elwess refused to allow himself to look out the back window. The coke had burned out of his system, leaving his balls aching and his head logy. He felt dirty, and for the first time in a long time, disgusted with himself and what he did for a living.

Oh, he had clients who paid him dearly for that kind of treatment, and he knew how to give them exactly what they wanted. But a session of out-and-out sadism without aftercare had never been his go-to kink. He did not get his jollies off training subs with that level of masochism, either. He did not trust that potential for instability.

For years he had preached safe, sane and consensual as his true gospel. He felt soiled by what he had done to Helena; more to the point, he had soiled *her* with his actions. Consensual? Yes. Well, probably. But safe, sane?

He was supposed to be a Dom who instructed subs; what had he just taught Helena? A sub should want to please her Dominant, not be so frightened of his wrath that she could not concentrate on her own self-development. *Oh, just great, Talbert. Working on your psyche skills, are we? Dr Phil must be sweating it right now.*

Rather petulantly, he reminded himself he did not want to be responsible for fucking a sub's head past the point of repair. Leave that kind of pain-washed power trip to someone who either knew how to deal with it, or didn't give a damn in the first place. Like Silas. *Or perhaps like you?* The voice in his head sounded suspiciously like Sydney's.

He was driven around for over an hour, until the car swerved to a stop. "We're back, sir." Elwess stepped onto the kerb and watched the car pull out into the traffic until it was just another set of winking lights curving through the roundabout. He memorised the registration number, but it would probably be a rental. Still...

He was back at Morden Station, and a long way from home. What he needed was a bit of Queen's Jazz album and some quality alcohol to wash a new coat of paint over the memory of the past two hours. What he *wanted* was to tuck into a large ramekin of Dahlra's famous crème brûlée while listening to that sweet, sad song Sydney played the last time he was at Maidenvine. *Black is the colour of my true love's hair...*

Elwess swore under his breath. Time to change the channel; that show has been cancelled. Screw it. He would grab a black cab and head back to the city; he was fucked before he would take the Tube—

"Mr Talbert?"

He spun around to see two men walking toward him. They were dressed in almost identical dark suits, and were as inconspicuous as a scream in a chapel. One of them, a lean younger man with close-cropped ginger hair, asked pleasantly, "Will you come with us, please?"

Elwess glanced around. He was alone, and dangerously vulnerable. "Identify yourself."

"Principal Lightoller is waiting."

Inigo Lightoller was sitting behind a flaking, grey metal desk. Even here, in this anonymous Tube station office, the bastard was as immaculate and cool as a Saville Row dressmaker's dummy. Elwess flopped down in the hard plastic chair opposite the desk, his every move a two-fingered salute to the dapper man seated across from him. Some little demon of defiance held Elwess' tongue, wanting Lightoller to speak first. They fronted one another out until Lightoller tired of the game.

"Well?"

Elwess withdrew the envelope from his coat and carelessly tossed it onto the desk. "Tickets, false ID, passport, credit card, money, and the address of the resort in Tokyo where they want to meet. Apparently I'm 'exactly what they're looking for.' Quite the catch, I gather."

"Apparently." Lightoller wrinkled his nose. "Have you been drinking?"

Toff. "Yes," he replied with a sneer. "I've been doing coke and fucking too, in case you're interested. You told me to slot myself in, play the part, be the spy. Besides, I don't turn down free pussy or Niesson for anyone—not even you, Lightoller."

"Careful, Talbert." From behind him, Garnet Pinkerton stepped out of the shadows, his tall, rangy figure looming over them like a vulture.

Elwess shrugged. "He asked, I volunteered information. Full disclosure, eh, Inigo? Isn't that what this little operation is about?"

Lightoller was too well-bred to rise to the bait, but Pinkerton bristled with pure East End swagger. Elwess looked up at the agent with all the disdain he could conjure; the night had left him spoiling for a fight. "I could draw you a picture if that would help, Agent."

"I'm getting good and tired of your mouth." Pinkerton took a step closer, and Elwess rose to his feet in one smooth movement until they were standing almost chest to chest.

"Are you now? Well, I've never had any complaints before. Sounds a little like jealousy talking, Agent. If your Celia's been complaining, I could give you a few lessons—"

Pinkerton snarled and shot forward at the same time Lightoller rose to his feet. "Enough! Put your handbags away, and stand down, the pair of you."

The two men glared at one another; Pinkerton had the advantage of age and height and a slow burn dislike that had finally tipped into full-blown disgust. His skin flushed an ugly red. "What you want is a good kicking, Talbert—"

"If I were you, I'd listen to your master's voice, *Pink*. If it's an argy-bargy you're looking for—"

"I said stand down!" Lightoller's voice rang with cold authority. Pinkerton, still fuming, took several steps back, and Elwess sat down with a huff.

"I will not tolerate this level of unprofessionalism from either of you." Lightoller resumed his seat. "It's not necessary that you send one another birthday cards, but you *will* work together, and you *will* be civil.

Now, Elwess, I would like a status report that consists of facts, not posturing, if you please."

Elwess, his eyes darting occasionally in Pinkerton's direction, described the little party at the manor house. "While I was there, I was wined and dined and given a sample of some of the, shall we say, *benefits* their organisation is willing to offer for my services. I was told their controller, a man named Lorcan, would like for me to meet him in Tokyo in six weeks' time to discuss my possible role in Silverbirch. Walters' words, not mine."

Lightoller nodded. "I would assume this chap's name is no more 'Lorcan' than yours is Talbert."

Elwess felt a sudden urge to slap the superiority right off Lightoller's face. "Probably not. Regardless of who he really is, he knows plenty. Judging from what I was told, your operation is completely compromised. 'Nothing goes on in Lightoller's Agency we don't know about,' Walters said. He didn't feel the need to be coy about quoting chapter and verse in front of a fucking sub, either. As far as they're concerned, they're bulletproof. Hell, they even call *themselves* Silverbirch, like it's the name of some poncy gentlemen's club. You and your Agency have given them brand identity, Principal."

He knew he was twisting the knife, but it was the only satisfaction Elwess would get from this meeting. Tonight he had been forced to relive his old wheelhouse; a seedy, dreary kink world that had been part of a lifestyle he had grown to despise. For all intents and purposes, Lightoller had already shot the messenger. "I'd say you've got someone inside hemorrhaging information faster than you can make it up."

"Which is why you and I are meeting in this squalid little Tube Station office with only Agent Pinkerton for company."

"What about the Men in Black downstairs?"

"Met Police detectives," Pinkerton interjected. "Old mates of mine."

Elwess scoffed. "It must be bad if you're depping outsiders for security."

"It's bad enough." Lightoller stood and buttoned his jacket, his customary signal that the meeting was over. He produced an iPhone from his pocket and gave it to Elwess. "Stop using your personal phone for anything more confidential than ordering take-away. It's too easy for your calls to be intercepted. You can trust this one. I'll stay in touch. Meanwhile, you will continue to sit at home, sulking over your loss of both situation and friends. Your resentment will increase as the days go by, and your need for revenge will consume you. Plenty of time and impetus to plan your trip to Tokyo."

Elwess felt his stomach shrivel. "You don't actually expect me to go through with this, do you?"

"That is precisely what I expect you to do. But don't worry, old man. You won't be alone." He swept out the door with Pinkerton in his wake. "I trust you can find your way home, *Master* Elwess."

CHAPTER FOURTEEN

An Intimate Affair

Since the Lightollers' dinner party called for something more formal than her daily uniform of yoga pants and Dahlra's cast-off Chelsea t-shirts, Sydney decided on a black Chanel dress she had bought on impulse in the January sales. It was slim-lined and sleek, made of dull matte silk that felt buttery to the touch, and fit like a glove. She teetered a bit on the matching black stilettos; it had been ages since she had worn anything quite this high.

She hummed to herself as she put the finishing touches on her makeup and brushed her hair. The white streak that started at her crown and flowed down the right side of her head was wider now than it had been two months before. There was nothing for it; she was going to colour it. Yes, she and L'Oréal were going to become special friends. She pushed a sultry pout toward the mirror like a television model. "Because you're worth it."

"You most certainly are."

Dahlra, in a black Armani suit, stood in the doorway, looking like every good girl's Christmas wish and every bad girl's fantasy. His silk tie was peacock blue, brightening the colour of his emerald eyes. He smiled lazily, as his eyes roamed over her body with frank and honest appreciation. "You look beautiful."

"So do you, Dr Gar." Blimey, did he ever. Six weeks of fresh air, working out and gardening had toned his waist and shoulders, enhancing a figure that had not exactly been hard on the eyes to begin with. The haunted, haggard look had gradually faded, and his porcelain skin glowed with good health. True, there was a little more silver at the temples, but all that TLC was starting to pay dividends, like the way he looked tonight. *Tall, dark and handsome, and all mine.*

She closed the space between them and grasped the edges of his coat. "Allow me." When she pushed the last button through, he adjusted the coat minutely, shot his cuffs, then presented himself for inspection.

"Will I do?" His voice was soft and intimate.

"Oh, yeah, I think so. Although you do realise I'm going to spend the majority of the evening scheming how to get you *out* of that suit."

The Bentley was waiting in Maidenvine's drive. "I thought it would be more enjoyable if neither of us had to be the designated driver." Dahlra popped the cork on the split of icy Moët that had been thoughtfully provided. "Here's to liquid sustenance." They clinked their glasses.

The days had already grown cooler in the country, but London was apparently the last to know. As Dahlra helped her from the car, Sydney gasped; the air was dense and sticky. In the short space between the air-conditioned car and the Lightollers' front gate, she wilted like a carnation.

As they walked up the steps, they saw no minion manning the door, heard no tasteful music drifting onto the Square. "Must be a small affair tonight," remarked Dahlra.

"Yeah. Only forty or so."

To Sydney's surprise, Inigo himself opened the door. He shook Dahlra's hand and kissed her cheek. "You look absolutely lovely. And perfect timing as usual. Do come in."

They entered the mausoleum-quiet home. "Um, Inigo, we didn't get the date wrong, did we?"

"Of course not, old thing. I've just knocked up a pitcher of Pimms. You must be parched in this bally heat."

"Where is everyone?" Sydney had a growing feeling they were being royally stitched up.

"Oh, it's just us. As I said, I wanted you to come round for dinner. How about that drink? We've a few minutes before the food's ready. I hope you're hungry."

They followed him into the front room, where Sydney's worst suspicions were confirmed. Sitting on the sofa, looking like he would rather be anywhere else, sat Elwess Talbert. He was dressed in vintage Elwess style: black suit, with a charcoal-grey silk shirt. A deeper grey tie with a faint pink pinstripe completed the look. She did not have to look at his feet to know his Hermes boots were immaculate. His hair was a little longer and shaggier than she remembered.

Trust Inigo to play all the ends against the middle. She glanced up at Dahlra to gauge his reaction. He appeared completely unruffled by Inigo's ruse. He was one cool customer when he needed to be.

Elwess rose to his feet, equally calm. "Dahlra. Good to see you. Are you well?"

"I am, Elwess. Thank you." He shook Elwess' hand. "I must say this is unexpected." He cut his eyes toward Inigo, who looked as innocent as a choirboy. "Although, given our host, I suppose it shouldn't be."

Elwess turned to Sydney. "You're looking lovely as always, Agent."

"Did you know we were coming?" she demanded.

His eyes seemed to drill into hers. "You know very well if I had, I wouldn't be here. I couldn't risk earning your wrath, after all." His tone was just this side of rude.

For a moment, Sydney considered just turning on her heel and walking out. As if he could read her mind, Dahlra squeezed her hand, a silent request to put the arrow back in the quiver and stand down. The gesture was not lost on Elwess; he gave Dahlra a sour smile, and Sydney did not like what she saw in it.

Inigo placed a silver tray on the coffee table; four highball glasses, and a tall, sweating pitcher of mint leaves, strawberries, orange slices and cucumbers, floating in amber liquid. Pimms had always struck Sydney as an overblown, pretentious production. It had never been a favourite of hers and Inigo knew it, which only irritated her more. They were all silent as he filled their glasses.

"I'm afraid it's just the four of us this evening. Phillipa was called away to Devonshire this weekend. A sick aunt." Inigo saluted them with his glass. "I'd like to propose a toast, if I may. To friendship."

Sydney took a cautious swallow, decided it was not as bad as she remembered, then took another drink. "Inigo, what exactly is going on?"

He looked mildly surprised. "I would think it's obvious, old thing. I'm attempting to get the band back together as it were, and I've chosen these delightful cocktails and the lobster dinner I've had shipped in from La Veranda in Carshalton as my primary means of persuasion." He smiled beatifically to his three guests. "How am I doing so far?"

Dahlra and Inigo chatted amicably throughout the uncomfortable dinner, two public-school swots well-versed in the art of bullshitting with grace. Sydney had no such upbringing; neither had Elwess. They both ate in restive silence, and though they answered when Dahlra or Inigo asked questions, they did not speak to one another at all. After the dishes were cleared, Inigo served dessert and coffee. "It just so happens that a colleague sent me a box of excellent Goldwin Louixs last week. Perfect for sharing with friends. And I've got an exceptional armagnac-"

"Enough, Inigo," growled Sydney.

"I'm sure I don't know what you mean, old girl. Do try the tiramisu. It's from Harrod's."

Under the table, Dahlra squeezed Sydney's hand again. "Thank you, Inigo. Thank you for inviting us over. Thank you for the lovely meal. It was good to see you and Elwess, of course. But before you break out the brandy and cigars, I think it's past time you told us exactly what this little play is all about."

"Snap." Elwess tossed his napkin onto the table. "This was bloody unfair, Lightoller."

Inigo dropped the *bon viveur* façade. "Alright then, to business." He looked from Dahlra to Sydney. "Elwess has been headhunted by Silverbirch. They see him as disenfranchised from this Agency and my protection, and they wish him to join them." He sipped his coffee while they digested this news. "He's been asked to meet with their controller in Tokyo in three weeks' time, and I want you to go with him."

"Sydney has not returned from garden leave."

"She is still listed as an agent of this organisation, and you are still listed as her Minder."

"Alright, Inigo, you've had your fun, but—"

"Sydney, dearest, if I may." Dahlra turned to Inigo, and his voice dropped to an icy pitch. "You really do love playing puppet master, don't you?"

Inigo met his eyes with equal cool. "Would it surprise you to know that I do not? My organisation is rotting from the inside because of this Silverbirch business. I will not let this deviant gang of hoodlums destroy everything I've worked for."

Sydney scoffed. "You're starting to sound like a 1940's melodrama, Inigo."

"I don't know who my mole is!" Inigo shot back. He pushed his plate away with a grimace. His usual unflappable manner was gone, and in its place was a man who looked frustrated, irate and humiliated. "I am looking at the only three people I actually trust at the moment. I have no other choice but to ask this of you, and we all know that if necessary, I could compel you to help me. I don't wish to go down that route." His voice softened. "Not with you, Sydney."

So there it was at last. "Surely you must trust Pink."

He inhaled sharply, but his sigh of resignation seemed to go on forever. "I trust no one but the people in this room."

Dahlra raised his hand in a conciliatory gesture. "You've never struck me as the paranoid type, Inigo. If you can't trust anyone but us, I believe you."

That seemed to mollify Lightoller. He took another sip of coffee. "I want... no, I *need* to end this. Silverbirch has rubbed my nose in its filth since the Prime Minister stood us down the first time they appeared on the radar. The credibility of the entire Agency is compromised. Because of that, one of my best operatives is captured and almost killed."

He looked at Dahlra as if daring him to speak. "I admit it. Too many mistakes were made the last go round. This time, we dismantle it brick by brick, but to do that I need my own man inside. It's the surest way to sniff out this mole of theirs."

And have them suffer the same fate as the previous one, mused Sydney. There is no forgiveness for betrayal.

"And you have no idea who your mole might be? You're not just saying that to manipulate us?"

Inigo gave Dahlra a wry look. "The problem with training your people to be the best is that they often outgrow you." There was more bitter humanity in those words than Sydney had ever heard coming from him. "This establishment does its job all too well."

In the silence that stretched from Inigo's grim confession, Sydney watched her guv'nor carefully. RADA had lost a great actor when Inigo joined the Agency, and anyone who knew him well could never be sure if he was telling the pure truth, or, as Dahlra said, manipulating it to serve his purpose. Garnet Pinkerton was, to her mind, incorruptible, and yet Inigo had tacitly admitted that he no longer trusted his top man. That was not only potentially catastrophic for the Agency, but gave Sydney a sick feeling in her stomach that did not complement the lobster.

And there was Elwess to consider. Sydney glanced his way; the cold hunger in his eyes had nothing to do with the food. She knew he still wanted her, still wanted Dahlra. Beyond that, she was not going to study her own wants too deeply. And while she knew Dahlra would ever be more forgiving on the subject, it felt wrong-guilty and foolish and *wrong*, to still feel desire for him. All he had ever offered them was smoke and mirrors and the false economy of pleasure. That she and Dahlra were all that stood between Elwess and the gluttonous maw of Silverbirch was a heavy burden to shoulder.

Dahlra turned to Elwess, who had weathered Inigo's outburst in stony silence. "And how do you feel about this?"

"Oh, peachy." Elwess turned to Inigo, anger flashing in his black eyes. "It's a shit plan, but I'm too compromised to say no. And you two are supposed to run interference?" He laughed mirthlessly. "Agent Chapin made it very clear the last time we spoke that she blamed me for everything that happened to Dahlra. I believe her exact words were, 'stay away from us or I'll kill you.'"

Inigo pursed his lips. "People under duress say a lot of things they don't mean."

"Bollocks. She meant it then, and judging from the way she's staring daggers into me now, she hasn't changed her mind."

Sydney bristled. "Don't talk about me as if I'm not here—"

"If I go to Tokyo, I'm as good as dead. Why don't you just give Agent Chapin here a gun and save yourself some airfare? I'm sure she'd be more than accommodating."

"Now listen here, you great—"

"I hardly think this is the time for insults, old thing—"

"All of you, stop. Now." Dahlra's voice rose above the others, firmly in charge. "This isn't helping anything or anyone." He stood, and turned to Sydney. "My dear, excuse me, but I would like to speak with Elwess alone." Before Sydney could protest, he gave her a quick, firm shake of his head. "Inigo, where can we talk in private?"

"I think the sitting room would suit your needs. Take your time."

"Thank you." Dahlra nodded regally. "Elwess, to me, now."

Dahlra ushered Elwess into Lightoller's tasteful sitting room, closing the door behind them. He sat down in the centre of a finely brocaded sofa; Elwess slouched into a leather chair to his left.

The entire situation reminded Dahlra of the many times he had been summoned into his father's study for a 'little chat.' He had been made to stand, sometimes for hours, while Peter Gar held court seated comfortably behind his massive desk. Dahlra had despised those patronising talks.

Following the usual opening admonishments to tuck his shirt in and stand up straight, his father would hold forth on the wide variety of ways in which his son was letting the side down, from junior school grades (*I'm sure we can do better in Chemistry than this, Dahlra; after all, I chose your name to look good on a Medical degree, not a barber's license'*) to career choices (*'Stop this cooking nonsense—if you need money to buy food, call me, for heaven's sake! What would our friends think if they saw you slaving away behind the counter at that builder's caff?'*), to suitable relationship decisions (*'I don't understand why you're dragging your heels about this. Caroline will make an excellent wife—with a pedigree like hers, you'll never have to worry about a mismanaged household. In any case, her father's got his heart set on you as a son-in-law'*).

When Silas had taunted him about his father, he had been frightened and under the influence of mind-altering drugs. In those moments, he had been so close to owning his father's disappointment in him. In the clear light of day, healed and clean, those memories no longer had the power to twist his emotions and his self-esteem.

And he was himself now a father of sorts, the titular head of this family of three. He was going to have to have a little chat of his own with Elwess, and he hoped he would not screw it up. One thing his father had never appreciated was how dangerous it was to underestimate those he cared about.

"I'm sorry we've been out of touch for so long," Dahlra began. "We've been a bit buried up at Maidenvine. I'd like to hear your side of this situation."

"You have a lovely bedside manner, Dr Gar. It almost sounds sincere." Elwess glared sullenly into the distance. "A lot happened while you were 'buried.' So, which situation would you care to address first? What happened after your little dance of death with Silas, or my imminent departure, courtesy of Air Silverbirch?"

"I've been very concerned—"

"Oh, have you?" His eyes flicked over to Dahlra like twin switchblades. "All that radio silence made it pretty clear just how many fucks you give. One phone call. That would have been enough."

Elwess rose from his chair and began to pace. His voice was low and tarry and spitting with contempt. "'So, how've you been, Elwess?' Oh, let's see: I come back from Amsterdam on your birthday to find out Silas Markham has ambushed and raped you. I show up to that little soiree just as Madame in there is sawing her wrists off to get to you.

"After I manage to free her and get the Agency to pull their fingers out, I arrive in time to see her trying to get your lifeless body breathing again. And just when the cavalry arrives, that blond cunt Silas tries to slit her throat, so I get the bright idea to save her life by shooting him. Unfortunately, my aim is so shite I end up killing him instead."

He barked a mirthless laugh. "Apparently that was a mistake, since the next time I saw Sydney, she was giving me her best Henry Cooper imitation and knocking my front teeth loose. Then for the grand finale, Lightoller calls me into his office and informs me the whole clusterfuck is somehow *my* fault, and suspends me.

"So Silverbirch decides that since no one else wants to touch me with a barge pole, they'll just reach out and snatch me up to play in their little sandpit. And foolish me, I inform our fearless leader, thinking I'm doing my bit to redeem myself. He happily orders me to go along with them because it just might 'make up for almost getting Dahlra killed.' So I put my head on the chopping block."

After a moment, Elwess continued. "I can never admit this to anyone but you. Silverbirch is very alluring. There's a lot on offer. It's quite an ego trip once you get used to the beautiful women begging you to degrade them." He gave Dahlra a hard smile. "They've got it all: quality gear, plenty of willing flesh to play with. I got to show off my skill set by whipping some poor girl into A&E, and proving just what a nasty bastard I can be. Sex, drugs and rock 'n' roll, all wrapped up in a tidy no-win situation. I can't wait to get my merit badge in whips and chains—"

"Enough!" Dahlra's voice sounded sharp and loud to his own ears. Getting Elwess to talk was one thing, allowing him to wind them both up was another. "Just answer me one question: Are you tempted?"

Elwess' head snapped back, and he stared at him for so long Dahlra thought he had seriously misjudged the situation. "You're actually asking me if I thought about defecting for real? How fucking dare you! In case you've forgotten, these people raped and chopped up a girl like she was a side of beef on some sick, online game show. One of them nearly destroyed you! Fuck's sake, Dahlra, give me some credit."

There was something dangerously off-kilter about Elwess at that moment. It was more than just the darkness Dahlra had always sensed deep within the man. Most of the time, it manifested itself in very small doses; flashing from the corners of his eyes in sinuously revealed secrets; looming in his louche posture over the figure of a sub awaiting her punishment. Dahlra knew if he could not prevent it spilling over the edges, it would finally crest this self-imposed levee of Elwess' personality, and stain everything in its path with indelible damage.

In a deadly quiet voice, he went on. "I killed a man because he was going to hurt Sydney, because he had hurt you. That man belonged to Silverbirch. So I hope you understand why I'm not in that big a hurry to sell my soul to them just because I can't join in any reindeer games with you and Sydney anymore. If you honestly think I am, then you don't know me at all."

He turned on his heel and headed for the door. Dahlra intercepted him, gripping Elwess' bicep. He played his last card. "Do you still call me Dominant?"

The question derailed Elwess as completely as Dahlra had hoped it would. "What?"

"Do you still consider me your Dominant, Elwess, and I'd think very carefully about the next words out of your mouth."

Elwess tried to outstare him, but in the end, he slumped in resignation. "I want to." A ghost of a smile made his mouth twitch at the corners. "Sir."

"Then sit down. I'll have no more outbursts."

To Dahlra's unbounded relief, Elwess obeyed. He resumed his own seat. "I 'fucking dared,' as you put it, because I needed to know where your head was, and you were too busy with the bullshit and histrionics to tell me. I still consider you my submissive, and one that I have neglected while I was recovering. That was not your fault, and I'm truly sorry for letting you down. It. Won't. Happen. Again." He said the last four words like individual sentences, and in a way, they were.

Elwess sagged back into the chair. He kept shaking his head, as if trying to negate everything. "I went along because those were my orders. I felt like shit afterward. It was about as enjoyable as masturbating into a toilet. I kept thinking about you and Sydney. How glad I was that you weren't there to see what I did." He scrubbed his face with his hands.

"Dammit, Dahlra, I needed to talk to you, to show you—"

"Then show me now. I'm not going anywhere. Now, here is the truth as I see it. Silverbirch thinks you want what they have. Whoever this controller is, he's gone to a lot of trouble to court you.

"They don't want or need another mole to tell them what the Agency is doing; they want you to join *them*. Don't you see? For this 'Lorcan' chap, that would be Lightoller's ultimate failure. This could be the perfect opportunity to plant a bug, set up a sting operation, or whatever these Spy vs. Spy types can think of to infiltrate the organisation. You're the best chance they have of doing it. And Sydney and I will be there with you."

"Are you sure that's safe? What if they figure out you're there?"

"Then you'll tell them Lightoller sent us to spy on *you*." Dahlra smiled. "You're still in his bad books, but we're still enthralled by you enough to defy Inigo and seek you out for reconciliation away from his home turf. Another spit in his eye."

"So you're asking me to—"

"I'm asking you to trust me."

Time seemed to stand still in the coldly tasteful room. Just as Dahlra was about to admit defeat, Elwess pulled himself out of the chair and knelt at his feet, hands on thighs, head down. The perfect submissive's pose.

"I feel like everything I ever did or was is slipping away, and I can't stop the landslide." His voice was tired. "I don't know how to write my own story anymore. And I've got too little confidence in this to know if I'm going in the right direction. But, yeah, I trust you, Dahlra." He looked up into Dahlra's face with haunted eyes. "A man without a Master is just a fool on his knees. I'm tired of feeling like a fool."

Dahlra leaned forward and placed one hand on the back of Elwess' neck. He felt tension knotted beneath his fingers, and he rubbed the tight muscles soothingly. "I'll be there for you. Just like you were there for me all those times. I promise: you will get your pride back." Gradually, the taut muscles relaxed.

He took out his phone and tapped in a quick message. A few seconds later, Sydney opened the sitting room door. She took in Elwess' kneeling form, then looked back at Dahlra, her large eyes full of questions. He held out his hand to her and she stepped in and closed the door behind her, allowing him to draw her down next to him. She eyed Elwess warily, and he returned her gaze with impassive defiance, as if to say, *I have a right to be here. I gave this submission willingly.*

Dahlra knew he had about ten seconds to compose the right words. He had to establish equilibrium between the three of them, or they would lose it forever. And even as upset as Sydney had been, Dahlra did not think she wanted that, either.

"Sydney, you and I stood together in the Chine months ago, while Elwess accepted his punishment in perfect submission. Do you remember what I asked him, about forgiveness?"

From the corner of his eye, Dahlra saw Elwess nod in unison with Sydney. There was reluctance in her voice, but he knew she would answer honestly. "You asked him if he thought we were so fickle that we couldn't forgive him, or make him face Inigo on his own."

"Yes, my love. You and I retreated to Maidenvine to heal, not to become hermits. And neither of us are the kind of people who throw the ones we love under the bus. I will not forsake Elwess, and neither will you. Now, it isn't in me to deny you anything, but I need you on board, love. And you need to be honest with yourself. It isn't a sin for you to want Elwess."

Her eyes widened. "But I didn't—"

Dahlra put a finger over her lips. "Shh. It's alright." He leaned in close, keeping his voice for her ears alone. "That first time I brought you to the Chine, you knew we weren't going to Grandma's house. You stayed because you *wanted* the big bad wolf, just as much as he wanted to play with the little girl in red. There is no shame in admitting that."

He stroked her cheek. "I will not allow you to self-flagellate with your own guilt, especially if you've convinced yourself Elwess holds the whip. So I tell you now: you cannot, you will not, remain angry at one another for protecting me in the heat of battle, because the truth is you love one another. And the three of us have to own that, one hundred percent."

At last, Sydney nodded, her head bowed in acceptance. She slipped down from the sofa, sinking gracefully to her knees opposite Elwess. Across the seemingly fathomless gulf between them, she reached out.

"I was so scared," she said hesitantly, "and I *did* feel guilty, and responsible. And Silas was dead, and Dahlra said..." She glanced up at him, then sighed. "Well, it doesn't really matter what he said. The fact is, I just wanted to blame someone, to make someone hurt as much as I was hurting."

She looked up at Elwess then, her lovely eyes bleak and sorrowful. She took his hand and kissed it. "Tell me that what we had isn't broken beyond repair."

Elwess was quiet for a long time. Finally, he favoured her with a smile that carried the tiniest trace of his old, sardonic smirk. "You've got a mean right hook, kitten. Now, come here." He gently drew her into his arms. "I've missed you. Hit me as often as you like, just don't shut me out again."

"I won't." Gratefully, he pulled her into a tighter embrace. "Things are going to be different from now on."

Between them, Dahlra felt all the allegiances shift into their proper positions. The restless inertia of the past weeks faded into the background, leaving him with a clarity of focus he had not felt for a long time. He envisioned days of discussion, nights of negotiation. Whether Sydney resumed the Silverbirch investigation, or moved on after they returned from Japan, Dahlra pictured them happily planning her future, and setting the next phase of their lives in motion, together.

A strange sensation started in his shoulders, and fanned outward, toward his arms, his chest, his solar plexus and beyond. Not exactly weightlessness; it was more complex and infinitely more exciting than that. It was not so much dropping a heavy burden; it was the feeling of shouldering the proper one. For the first time since the attack, he felt his skin riding easier on his bones. He felt very alert, and eager—he felt in control.

A lifetime ago, Sydney had said spoken to him about training the hawk to come to the fist. These two hawks of his, both proud and pitiless in their own way, had surrendered to the force of his will. Relief loosened the stress in his back and, he felt proud, not just of himself, but all of them.

Everything he had ever planned or dreamed or fought for came down to that crystalline point: this was what it meant to be the Master, the Dominant, the *Daddy*. It meant this brilliant surge of power and responsibility. He embraced it, saluted it with his fist and his brains and his heart and his body, and pledged his troth to it. He suspected it had always been within his grasp; he had just never truly understood it until the moment they both knelt at his feet, and swore themselves to him and one another. *A Daddy is for life. Ray Winston, eat your heart out.*

Eventually, Elwess helped Sydney to her feet and they sat beside Dahlra on the sofa. "Okay, I'll do it. I'll go into the belly of the beast. But not for Inigo. So, where do we go from here?"

"You forget, we've been here before," replied Sydney. "Inigo's not above playing dirty, but he usually sends in the cavalry on time."

"We knew, we've *always* known that you were too sweet a carrot for them to resist," Dahlra added. "They were going to recruit you; it was just a matter of when. We had hoped to have more time, but Silas put paid to that."

"Time to do what?"

Dahlra kissed Sydney's forehead and rose to his feet. "Time to put all our conditions into place, of course. We hold more cards than you think, Elwess. Now, if you two will excuse me, Lightoller and I are going to discuss those conditions in private. Then Sydney and I are going home."

"You could stay in London." Elwess looked slightly abashed. "I'm not an idiot. You can't wait to get your hands on one another. I could always sleep downstairs."

"Thank you, Elwess. But I have something else in mind, if you don't mind being a little flexible. There might even be a cooked breakfast in it for you as well."

As he turned, Dahlra felt Elwess' large hand on his shoulder. "I just want to tell you—" he began, then perversely grew quiet.

"Go ahead."

"I... I just want to say that you are ten times the Dominant I ever was."

"You don't have to flatter me."

"I'm not trying to. I'm just saying. I'm a service top and I always will be." He smirked. "Perhaps I need to start training with *you.*"

Dahlra could not help but pity him at that moment. Like Sydney, Elwess had never been comfortable with self-analysis. It must have been hell for the man to start questioning himself this far down the road. His self-confidence, the arrogance that rode like blood in his veins, had deflated, leaving only a scared balloon behind. As his Dominant, it was another thing Dahlra would have to rebuild.

"You *are* a service top, *and* a Dominant, and a damn good one. And I'm going to be in need of that. Perhaps soon."

Elwess' eyes flicked over to Sydney. "Are you sure?"

Dahlra made himself wait a beat before answering, a trick taught to him by none other than Elwess himself. "You know, when things settle down, we really need to have a little chat about this tendency of yours to question me, Elwess. We'll take care of it when you come to Maidenvine. I want you to live with us until further notice." He turned away, but not before he saw Elwess' jaw drop open. "Your flat isn't secure. You'll be safer with us." He paused at the door and turned to face Elwess. "Will you agree to this?"

"Of course."

Sydney was looking at Dahlra with a mixture of admiration and respect that was so powerful it made his head spin. "Maidenvine *is* much safer than London. We can take care of ourselves there. If there's any fallout, we could tuck him away until things blow over."

For the first time, Elwess seemed to understand the implications of Dahlra's offer. "Do you think it would actually come to that?"

Sydney shrugged. "Hope for the best, expect the worst and you won't be disappointed."

"I was sort of hoping for, 'Of course not, Elwess, everything will be sweetness and light, we're just planning for every contingency.'"

"You want the truth, or what makes you feel good?" Sydney sweetened her words with a wry smile.

"I'll take both with a shot of Neisson's." He looked from one to the other. "So, Master Dahlra, are you planning on at least cluing me in as to what you're going to do?"

"Of course. After I've had a word with Inigo."

Dahlra left Sydney and Elwess in the sitting room, knowing they would make cautious but sure headway toward rebuilding their friendship. He headed back to Lightoller's dining room, where he found their host sitting at the table where he had left him, musing over tiramisu and a snifter of brandy. He looked up at Dahlra when he entered the room. "Well?"

"I have conditions."

"I expected you might." He gestured for Dahlra to sit. "We might as well hammer them out now."

"No hammering. They're met, or the three of us walk."

"Elwess—"

"I speak for Elwess." Dahlra poured himself a brandy, and joined him. "He's my family, and as head of this family, I speak for us all."

Lightoller favoured him with a sour look. "So now you're his Minder, too?"

"If it makes you more comfortable thinking that way." Dahlra took a sip of the excellent brandy. "Before we start, I want it duly noted that I think you're allowing Silverbirch too much control over the situation. You're letting them call the shots, and you're pushing Elwess into something he isn't prepared for." Dryly, he added, "You may recall my own situation in the field was not dissimilar."

Lightoller studied his glass with maddening nonchalance. "With all due respect, Dr Gar, I think I am perfectly capable of knowing how to control this situation quite well, thank you."

"This trip is nothing more than one big, feckin' Hail Mary, and they're going to see it as such. Make them wait. Sniff out the mole first. At the very least, locate Silas Markham's residence—"

"You seem to be under the assumption I have unlimited time and resource."

"Don't you?"

Lightoller drained the last of the brandy from his glass. "I have superiors, you know. I have to answer to them, and they are not as patient as you or I, Dahlra." He closed his eyes for a moment. "Elwess will go to Japan. You will go with him, and I have every confidence that when he returns, he will have the answers I need."

"And what if he doesn't? You start an internal inquisition? You interrogate every agent? You grow even more paranoid until you lock yourself in your precious Agency and summon an exorcist?"

"Enough, Dahlra. You've made your point."

There was something in his eyes Dahlra did not recognise or understand. Later he would tell himself it was the result of too much brandy. "What are you not telling me, Inigo?"

Lightoller looked away. "Nothing that will make any difference now."

"I hope you're right."

It took surprisingly little fuss to map out their plan, and Inigo agreed to all conditions. He even made suggestions to improve them. For the first time, Dahlra allowed himself to feel sorry for Lightoller. The man was watching his Agency being eroded from the inside out, and if the only three people he could trust had their own agenda, what could he do about it?

Dahlra stood. "Well, now that's done, and I cannot dissuade you from this course, we'll be going. We have very little time, and a lot of preparation. I'll be in touch."

Inigo called out just as he reached the door. "Dahlra?"

"Yes?"

Inigo's expression was one of abject puzzlement. "One 'big, fecking Hail Mary'?"

He scoffed. "And you call yourself a football fan? Look it up." He went to fetch his lover, leaving Lightoller to his brandy and cigar, alone as always.

The night air had finally grown cool. Compared to the drop in temperature outside, the closed compartment of the Bentley was warm, and carried the mouth-watering scent of Dahlra's cologne like incense. He sat at one end of the long seat, draping his arm across the back. He had requested she sit at the opposite end. "So I can look at you." Now his eyes drifted over her body like a slow-burn, teasing caress; his handsome, unsmiling face was spectral in the dark space.

The combination of too many Pimms and the soft, cozy interior conspired to make Sydney a bit sleepy; Dahlra looked about as far from tired as you could get. In spite of his casual demeanour, there was nothing indolent or languorous about him. He thrummed with pent-up energy. It seemed to build, like an impending lightning strike, growing brighter and more seductive as the Bentley brought them ever closer to Maidenvine. "We've another hour or so before we reach home."

"Home." That was a good word. "I think home is wherever you are."

"It's also where I get you naked. Would you like that, little girl?"

Thoughts of napping were forgotten. Sydney felt as if something warm had been placed in her lap, and she knew without looking her nipples were hard enough to be visible from space. She swallowed around a dry throat. "I want you to make me scream."

"I'm not going to do that."

"No?"

"No." His eyes met hers. "I'm going to make you forget how."

The warmth between her thighs ratcheted into a humming ache. "Oh, God." When she attempted to move closer, he shook his head. She obeyed him as if he held her still by will alone. "Dahlra, please—"

"Oh, you'll beg. You'll beg, and perhaps I'll give you what you beg for."

She was on him almost the moment they walked through the door, grinding against him like a teenager. He allowed her to maul him, indulging her artless eagerness, her frantic hands tangling in the folds of his coat. "I've neglected you too long, my girl. Shall I make amends?"

"Yes, now, please." She pulled at him, trying to urge him up the stairs.

"Go on, then. Get undressed and lie on our bed. I'll be right there." He looked down at her for the briefest moment, then grasped the back of her neck and lowered his head to hers. It was a kiss that moved against her slowly, taking her over, full of dark, sensual promise. He devoured her mouth as if drinking from the sweetest draught, until she was breathless and panting and still he mined this deep vein of passion as if he could pull it from her bloodstream.

The kiss ended so abruptly she almost stumbled, and when she looked up at his face he was flushed and stern. "Will you go now?"

"Yes, sir."

"Will you do as I say?"

"I'll do anything you want—"

"Oh, yes, Ms Chapin. You will." He gave her one of those slow, knicker-wetting smiles, as his fingertips ghosted over her kiss-swollen lips. "Take a deep breath, little girl. While you still remember how."

She left him on unsteady legs, her heart pounding. He had made love to her in so many ways and played through so many fantasies, but in all that time, they had never consciously tried to re-enact that first, forbidden time. As she heard his soft tread following her up the stairs, her excitement became unbearable. She practically sprinted to the bed, so that he would find her as he had instructed.

Dahlra leaned against one of the large bed posts and gazed down at her, his expression full of longing and desire. His voice slid over her like silk. "Do you know how beautiful you are? How much I want you?"

"You want to watch, Doctor?" Her voice slurred with arousal, and she shivered as the balance of power between them rolled from one to the other. "Then so do I." She touched herself as a soft moan of longing escaped his lips. "Undress for me."

He obeyed her instantly, never taking his eyes off her. He was so beautiful; masculine and strong, like the quiet romance that was at the very core of his nature. It called to her, commanded her and humbled her all at once.

He was righteously hard, and they both gasped as he grasped his cock and gave it a slow, teasing stroke. His expression grew taut. "Oh, fuck, I don't want to play this game anymore."

She reached for him. "Neither do I."

He rolled her over until she was beneath him, pinned by his weight. She grasped his face in her hands and kissed him feverishly until he relented and gave in to her. His kisses were thrilling and suffocating and left her gasping. He finally released her, and whispered, "I am so in love with you."

There was such clean, unabashed love in his eyes, and Sydney was overwhelmed by it all over again. She uttered a soft cry of wonder, and Dahlra closed his eyes for a moment, as if he wanted to commit that particular sound to memory. "I'm going to find every inch of your body that makes you cry like that." His voice was barely above a whisper; just consonants on a breath. "Tonight isn't going to be nearly long enough."

He made love to her inch by inch, with his hands, his body, his mouth, his voice. His lips were soft and warm as they glided over her skin, placing tickling, suckling kisses down her arms, over her throat, against her belly. Sydney grasped the headboard, arching her back up to his irresistible mouth, moaning as his lips pursed over her nipple and sucked hard. It was exquisite, and all the more so because of the evident pleasure he took in doing it. His large hand urged her thighs apart, his fingers teasing her with a maddeningly light touch.

Her hips rocked against his hand of their own accord, and she grasped his wrist, pleading for more. With agonising languor, he brought her to the edge, then backed up, only to ease her toward the breaking point again. She writhed and undulated against him, desperately trying to move his fingers where she could get her satisfaction.

His feathery kisses made their way down, until he settled between her parted thighs. With a mischievous smile, he licked the seam with leisurely enjoyment, and her hips bucked impatiently. He held her down easily, opening her to him with his characteristic mixture of precision and gentleness, and, oh God, his mouth... His long tongue found the ripe, distended bud, and curled around it as if taking ownership. The last of her higher reasoning processes narrowed down to that one tiny scrap of flesh, the mouth currently suckling it, the fingers easing in and out of her slick core, and the man attached to them.

He sought out that tiny spot within and tormented it until it pulsed in an unrelieved cycle of burning heat. She was hurtling toward an exquisite peak of pleasure, pushing her those last precious inches toward his goal until she could not catch her breath—

It was like being hurled from a great height, and when she fell, she did it gratefully. He pushed her onward, mapping out every place that felt good and every place that was too much, sending her racing through her climax with the glory of a shooting star.

Gradually, his touch gentled; the talented mouth eased back, placing tender kisses on her thighs. Dizzily, she pulled at his hair, his arms, forcing him to join her face to face, and he surrendered to her grasping hands.

For several moments they merely held on to one another. She kissed him deeply, tasting herself in his mouth, and stroked down his firm chest, carding her fingers through the dark trail that led to the nest of wiry hair cradling his erection. It was not going anywhere.

She could feel the heat from it even as her hand closed over his cock. She glanced up into his face, and saw the feral certainty blazing in his eyes. A thrill of joy ran through her and she gave it a deep, twisting stroke.

Dahlra obviously had other plans. He rolled her onto her back and had her at his mercy in seconds. She was so primed and ready for him he speared her in one swift, delicious movement, and his face dissolved into an expression of utter ecstasy. A low growl, twinned with a breathless moan, escaped his lips. It was the richest, most erotic sound she had ever heard, and she clenched around him, earning a heartfelt curse. "Ah, you wicked, wicked thing. How do you expect me to last if you do that?"

Enthralled by that vein of hedonism he kept closely guarded and only displayed for her, Sydney was determined to make him let go, to give in to his own formidable passions. She curled her thighs around his waist as he rocked his hips against hers with hypnotic, slow circles, finding every sweet spot, and even this was not enough.

Soon the slow ride was over; he was finished with the pretense of control, and she held on, meeting his thrusts with her own, pistoning against him, loving the ache spreading through her loins as he filled her, the dragging, glorious friction as he withdrew, rolling their hips together and apart, each thrust bringing her closer and closer. He caught her mouth in a possessive, frantic kiss, his thrusts pumping into her in counterpoint.

Though she had already come twice with no thought of climaxing again, all bets were off with Dahlra Gar driving her to the tune of his engine. She was so close, close enough that no command could hold it back. Looking up into his face, abandoned, lost in that golden moment between tension and release, Sydney slipped the lead.

He rose onto his arms and fucked her with relentless power, his hips crashing against hers faster and deeper, melting her with white-hot heat. He gave a feral cry, and his rhythm broke with his climax. He drove into her once, twice, three times, and her own orgasm imploded around him, wrecking her with crippling, overwhelming ecstasy. She clutched at him, aftershocks of pleasure rippling through her, dragging him inward as if to hold him inside her forever. He fell limply against her, panting like a runner, his heart thumping wildly against her chest.

She held him as his breathing slowed, his sweat-slicked body a priceless weight on top of her, until he eased over onto his side. She curled up on his chest, and he threw a lazy arm around her.

Her body was still singing, even as exhaustion tried to wade in and claim her. "That was..." She tried to laugh, but it came out as a very inelegant snort.

A low chuckle rumbled in his chest, tickling her. "You took the words right out of my mouth." He sounded spent and sheepish, but underneath, very happy. "Are you alright? I wasn't too rough, was I?"

"I'm fine." She reached up and planted a soft kiss on his cheek. "Have I mentioned how gorgeous you are when you come?"

"Not today, but do feel free."

"You're incredibly gorgeous when you come."

With no more effort than moving a pillow, he lifted her until she was on top of him, straddling his hips. He put his arms around her and drew her close. "You are incredible. Full stop." As his warm palms cupped her breasts, he purred, "I plan on giving you a lot of gorgeous tonight."

Sydney had learned early on to never doubt his word, and for good reason. He had been right. The night would not be long enough.

CHAPTER FIFTEEN

Coming Home

A week later, two agents in a nondescript van pulled up to the kerb in front of Elwess' flat. Their job was to make sure he arrived in Windsor without incident. Yeah, it was official: he now merited babysitters. Elwess tried not to feel like too much of a pussy about being grateful.

While they waited, he dug out his suitcases. The rasp of the zip was loud in the quiet flat, and he glanced around, feeling observed and exposed. Lightoller's men had assured him his home was bug-free, but he could not shake the itchy feeling that he was being watched.

For a moment, he simply stared into the open bags, as if the meaning of life could be found hiding in the compartment he reserved for his pants. *Want to find the God particle, my old China? Try your shaving kit. Freudian slips? Stowed away in your gym bag, of course. Unless you left them in the medicine cabinet along with the dark matter.*

"Jeez, you're completely mental, Talbert," he muttered aloud, rubbing his temples. It was hard to focus; he could not grab any thought quickly enough to stop the cyclone in his head. It came as no surprise that they always blew in the same direction.

He sat down on his bed, feeling wearier than he had a right to be. He knew the cause, but it did not make him feel any better about it. It only made him feel even more of a coward. "Oh, fuck it." He abandoned any pretense of packing. He went downstairs, put the kettle on, and waited for it to boil, trying not to think too much about that little Guess Who's Coming To Dinner episode at Lightoller's gaff.

It was no hardship to admit he had always appreciated and respected Sydney. She had a fearsome rep and the stats to back it up. The hell she had suffered and survived confirmed the calibre of BAMF she was. And who could forget that hellish day she had almost cold-cocked him? Elwess had been frightened enough of her before she hit him. If she cared enough about him to fight in his corner, he pitied Silverbirch.

But Dahlra—man, that had been a supersized dose of what-the-fuck, hadn't it?

If anyone had asked him as recently as a fortnight ago, he would have stated unequivocally that he knew Dahlra Gar very well. And he would be the first to admit he had initially dismissed Dahlra as the archetypal upper middle-class toff, all stiff upper lip and repressed sexuality, too afraid of his own dick to take free pussy when it was on offer.

Still, their friendship had grown over the past seven years, and while he had always treated Dahlra with affectionate, albeit somewhat patronising regard, their relationship had evolved into something uncanny. Elwess respected and loved him. And he knew him. After all, he had seen Dahlra vulnerable, miserable, frightened, joyful, exhausted, powerful, howling in pleasure and broken on his cross like a martyr.

But really know him? He had been wrong about a lot of things in his lifetime, but never as wrong about anything as he had been about Dahlra Gar. With cold clarity he realised that no one, even Sydney, truly knew the depths of the man.

"Trust in me." The naïve, idealistic GP Elwess had met all those years ago was still there, but the man who had striped his arse in the Chine, the man who faced him down in Lightoller's sitting room with high-octane Dominance... This was someone Elwess had never seen before. Now he knew how Lois Lane felt the first time she saw mild-mannered Clark Kent do the Superman phone-box strip tease. He still could not quite make his mind up whether he was afraid or jealous of the smooth bastard.

All he knew for certain was that Dahlra had emerged from his talk and told Elwess to pack as much of his life as he could and move to Maidenvine to live with them until further notice. "Think of it as an extended pyjama party," he had quipped, as he and Sydney were leaving.

Pyjama party, my arse, he thought. Dahlra could tart it up all he wanted, but it all added up to Elwess walking the plank for the Agency. There was no backing down now. Shit had gotten real. From now, until this whole Magical Mystery Tour of the Far East was over, he would first be under the Agency's protection, then under Maidenvine's—providing he did not screw everything up in Japan.

Dahlra had gambled against the house, but they all knew Elwess was the hundred thousand-pound chip he had used to place his bet. He would probably never know all the things Lightoller and Dahlra had negotiated, but he was left with the feeling that neither man was one hundred percent happy with the resolution. At this point, anything that pissed off Inigo Lightoller would, in all likelihood, buy him a few more hours of breathing

Elwess went to the kitchen and retrieved the box of Yorkshire Gold. He made himself a cup of strong builder's brew, then took down two more mugs. Might as well make something for the babysitters as well. *Wow. Empathy. My, how you've grown.*

As he stirred the sugar and milk into their mugs, he reflected on said newfound empathy. Apparently it had not kicked in enough to use it when it could have done some good. He should have manned up. After he killed Silas, he should have gone to Maidenvine and beaten the door down, demanded to talk to Dahlra. He could have helped him; at the very least, he could have served him up a man-sized portion of misery loves company.

It takes one, as they say, to know one, and Elwess knew better than most that some things never healed; you just learned to live with yourself by refusing to stew in it. *Fake it 'til you make it, and all those other nuggets of wisdom. Jesus; next I'll be quoting the old 'what doesn't kill you makes you stronger' chestnut.*

He had never really talked about what had happened to him, because talking about it did not necessarily help. He did not think he could ever make himself confess the whole story, not even if Dahlra asked him point-blank. He would simply look straight into those sharp, green eyes and lie his head off.

What had happened to him had been about payback as well; there were days when he thought he might have even deserved it.

He had been living in Amsterdam with a Domme named Marta. She thought she was getting the quintessential diamond in the rough; in reality, he was just another cocky little toerag looking to get his dick wet. It was never going to be a Bogie and Bacall situation, in any case. They were always scrapping like alley cats both in public and in private, and he was not always discreet or subtle in how he clocked in his spite work. He had played his role of the bad boy too much and too well once too often, and Marta was not the forgiving type.

In a fit of pique, she sold him out to a group of bully boys who had spent one memorable evening having as much fun with him as two thousand guilders could buy. During that endless night, they had passed him around like a party favour. If he allowed himself, he could still recall the burning, humiliating terror of being violated in every vicious way they could think of. As a parting gift, they had beaten him unconscious and left him for dead, dumping his naked, broken body in the back alley of a nightclub in the middle of a rainstorm.

He was hospitalised for pneumonia, and he pissed blood for a week. He probably would have died, too, had it not been for Roland Devereaux, the owner of the nightclub and a Dominant Elwess knew well. Devereaux had been the one to discover him in that alley, had taken him to hospital, then welcomed him into his home as a guest while his devoted subs nursed Elwess back to health. Elwess had never told them what really happened either, but of course they suspected.

Eventually, the physical scars had faded, but it had taken quite a lot of damn good TLC before he could stand for anyone to even look at his prick, much less touch it. Rape was not about sex; it was about power and humiliation, and when your power was taken away in such a degrading, painful manner, the sex drive went with it. The spirit might have been willing, but the flesh was too freaked out to perform.

It had taken a few cranks of the motor before his damaged mojo roared back to life, but when it finally, blessedly did, the sex had been more satisfying than any he had ever had before. Of course, once the seal had been broken, Elwess fucked more women in those following weeks than he had in these last five years. He would eventually develop a more discriminating palate, but at the time he was just glad to get it up and keep it up. After that, he wasted no time in topping up his quota.

As he healed and matured, he stopped blaming himself. It had been the first of many crossroads he would face, and the most important: he could choose to cherish submission, or punish it. The seeds of pure sadism found some fertile ground in his anger and bitterness toward Marta. It would have been so easy to burn off the impotence in vengeance fucking and cruelty.

Devereaux, a true Dominant's Dominant, had seen the warning signs and, to his credit, had decided that Elwess was worth the bother. *You can so easily become the type of person who nearly destroyed you, Elwess,* Devereaux had said over and over, *but isn't that just letting them win? Aren't you made for better things?* With patience and encouragement, Devereaux had shown him how to grasp his true potential—and learn to prize submission as its own reward.

He had not brooded over those days in a long time. Maybe he should.

After scrounging up a packet of biscuits and taking the impromptu refreshments to his babysitters, it took a surprisingly long time for Elwess to pack. He filled suitcase after suitcase with clothes, embarrassed at just how much schmutter he actually possessed. He owned a lot of black.

Looking around the flat he had occupied for the past ten years, he realised just how impersonal it was. It was just a place where he ate, slept and fucked. There was precious little he wanted to take with him. Everything important was waiting for him at Maidenvine. He found he could not think beyond the next two weeks; perhaps that was for the best.

He did not need a crystal ball to tell him Dahlra's own dry spell was over. It was as obvious as the look in Sydney's eyes when they left. Unlike his own story, Dahlra would not break his duck with another Dom's plaything, oh no. He was taking his own woman, his beautiful woman. If Elwess' experience was anything to go on, Dahlra would feast on her, trying to wreck the bed they lay in and some part of himself in the trying. He would find out just how many times and how many ways they could make one another come before they both passed out or went mad with it or died from it.

And there he would be, the gooseberry in the middle of the crème brûlée. Moving in was a good idea, sure, as long as he could pretend they were not having sex. That, he noticed, was not one of the activities mentioned in the great pyjama game.

Unsurprisingly, it was raining on the afternoon Elwess arrived. Watching from the upstairs window, Sydney was troubled. This was not the Elwess Talbert who had last visited Maidenvine. He made his slow way up the steps, with none of his usual, bounding impatience. His ever-restless black eyes were dull, and carried a lot of sleepless nights in their depths. She saw with approval that his escorts saw him safely to the door, had a private word with Dahlra, then bid Elwess farewell.

His eyes widened when he first caught sight of her; she had cut almost eight inches off her hair, and now sported an auburn pageboy. She could not help but laugh at his desperate attempt at not looking shocked.

"Look, no more Lily Munster!" She framed her hair with her hands and batted her lashes flirtatiously. "Well, what do you think?"

"I think I could get used to it. Is this your cunning disguise?"

"I prefer to think of it as camo. Disrupting the pattern, if you catch my drift."

Not to be outdone, Dahlra was sporting the beginnings of a rather dashing salt-and-pepper beard. The jury was still out on it, though; Sydney thought it scratched like hell.

Elwess regarded it thoughtfully but did not comment on it. "I just hope I'm not going to be in the way." His tone was carefully neutral.

"Don't be daft, you dozy prat," replied Dahlra bemusedly. "You're always in the way."

"We'll bear the strain with grace." Sydney's quip was teasing in its tone, but Elwess' searching look left her feeling guilty. She took his hand. "If you must know, we're really glad you're here. Dahlra's killed the fatted calf for your return. Well, the fatted goose. After all, it will be home for the time being..." Her jabbering commentary toppled, then fell over.

Elwess looked down on her from his great height with uncertainty. "Am I really in danger, or is this just Lightoller's way of scaring me into doing what he wants? I'm driving over here with an armed escort and suddenly I can actually *feel* the target on my back."

Sydney honestly did not know how to answer. And more disquieting was the fact that she was not sure how to deal with this sepia-toned version of Elwess. She knew the change could not be blamed solely on Silas, as much as she would have liked to. Her own actions and decisions following Silas' death had been just as instrumental in driving Elwess out of the Agency's good books and onto Silverbirch's radar.

She answered him as truthfully as she could. "I don't want to scare you, Elwess. The truth is, I don't know exactly how scared you *should* be. I only know that we can provide protection here if you need it."

He was silent for a moment, then scoffed. "Big bad Dom, huh? Running to hide behind his friends." It was a bitter sound, made even more desolate because he blew this particular kiss toward himself.

"I'm just glad you still consider me a friend to hide behind."

The two men brought Elwess' things into the house and staggered up the stairs under the weight of four massive, trunk-sized suitcases. Dahlra arrived in Elwess' room with a case in each hand. He dropped them just inside the door, and they landed with a loud thump that shook the floor. Flexing his strained arms, he groused, "What's in here, for fuck's sake? Your *entire* collection of whips and chains?"

Fiddling with the lock on one of the cases, Elwess replied evasively, "Just some clothes. You don't realise just how much crap you have until you start murdering your darlings."

"Need any help unpacking?"

He stopped and looked up at Sydney, and something like his old smile settled in place; a little sadder, but full of East End cheek. "Nah, kitten. I'll do it later." He straightened and ushered them out of the room. "Can we put the kettle on? I'm gasping for a cuppa."

Even British Doms, thought Sydney, *think everything can be made better with a cup of tea.*

Down in the kitchen Elwess settled in with his brew, while Dahlra finished preparing the welcome home dinner.

"How about a little—"

"No, I don't need any help." Dahlra fixed them both with a warning look. "What I need is for the two of you to get yourselves back to normal. I want a concerted effort on your parts to forget the past few weeks and remember how to be a family again."

Left to their own devices, Sydney discovered that getting back to normal was easier said than done. It was odd: she and Elwess had seen one another in every stage of dress and undress, and in every sexual position reasonably flexible adults could assume. Nevertheless, without the soothing emollient of Dahlra's presence to diffuse the static between them, the afternoon was as awkward as a disgraced MP's garden party. They talked too much; they suffered through long, dismal silences, they had difficulty meeting one another's eyes. During dinner, they managed to restore some equilibrium, but only because Dahlra ran interference.

It was a far cry from that long-ago February weekend at Elwess' flat, with him fussing around her new corset and then clumsily trying to entice her into going to bed with him. Even after she had called him on it, they had at least been able to face one another. Their conversations had been effortless and real, their feelings for one another easy to manage. Now, they could not even muster the courage to admit how badly they were failing at being friends.

Later, as they parted to retire to their respective bedrooms, Sydney reached up to give Elwess a peck on the cheek. He instinctively flinched away from her, as if he expected her to punch him again.

Sydney recoiled, humiliated. "I suppose I deserved that." She turned away, nursing a small ache in the middle of her chest. "I'll say goodnight, then."

As she walked away, she heard him sigh. "Sydney."

She stopped at the door, but could not make herself face him. "Yes?"

He walked over and pulled her into a crushing embrace. She felt his rapidly galloping heartbeat telegraphing his anxiety against her chest. "That was a crap move on my part. Especially after all you and Dahlra have done." He rested his chin on the top of her head. "I'm scared shit-less, girl, and I don't know how to behave."

Before she could reply, he touched his lips to hers and gave her a brittle smile. "Goodnight, kitten." He entered his room without looking back.

Later, as they lay in one another's arms, Dahlra told her, "Of course he's frightened. And fear makes you feel out of control, and a man like Elwess isn't used to being anything but master of all he surveys." He lazily scored her back with his nails. "He doesn't like to be reminded he's just as human as the rest of us. We need to help him get his confidence back, or he'll be of no use to anyone."

"The really disturbing thing is that I think we're going to have to go to him. He's so prickly. You'd think I was going to twat him again when I tried to kiss him goodnight. Perhaps he doesn't want me anymore." Even as the words left her lips, Sydney realised how sad she would be if that were true, and how uncomfortable it made her to admit it.

Dahlra chuckled and kissed her hair, his new beard rasping gently against her forehead. "Oh, he wants you, *kitten*. He just doesn't want us to catch him following you around the room with his eyes." Mischievously, he added, "Besides, he once told me he had a thing for gingers."

Gary 'Gazza' Chapman was already running late when he picked up the motor. He had wanted to run it through the car wash before he got home, but of course, the damn place was packed when he got there. Jules had warned him if he was late again for dinner, and *this* dinner in particular, he could kiss sex goodbye for at least a fortnight.

He was not too worried, though. He had bought this Mercedes two weeks before, but the bloke had been more than willing to hold it until their anniversary. Gaz had kept it a complete secret, even from the lads at work. Every day he had meticulously rehearsed how he was going to present it to her, had pictured it so much in his mind, he could see it happening like a YouTube video.

He would swing it into their street, and call her on his mobile. "Hello love, can you come out and gis a hand with the shopping?" She would huff and complain that she was tired and why couldn't he bring in his own fookin' shopping, but she would nevertheless be waiting for him at the door of the flat. Then he would hand her the keys and say, "Happy Anniversary, love!"

She would throw her arms around him and he would be the hero. Gaz smiled as he pictured the look of total rapturous happiness on her face. Nothing would be too good for him. It would be his Get Out of Jail Free card for at least a year. He was inordinately proud of himself.

The Merc was a few years old, but it was in perfect nick, from its Arctic White paint job to its pukka leather upholstery. It was plush and ran like a dream and was loaded to the eyeballs with all mod cons, including one of those all singing, all dancing stereos that looked more like the cockpit of an aeroplane and boasted a bass tube that made the windscreen pulse in time with the beat. It had come taxed and MOT'd for a year, and anyone could see the guy was practically giving it away. It even had a great registration: MY13 JUL. Thirteen was Jules' lucky number at the Bingo.

"Nothin' too good for m' Julie," Gaz sing-songed to himself, in what he considered a very credible imitation of Allie G. Jules hated when he did that, but after tonight, she would not care. In fact, Gazza bet himself she would brag to her girlfriends about it.

He was too busy enjoying his dreams of glory and trying to tune in to Smooth Radio to really notice the slowing traffic ahead. He turned the corner just as the blues-and-twos finished barricading the road.

He cursed under his breath. "Fookin' Dibble, checking every fookin' innocent bloke in Manchester City Centre for fookin' drink driving when they should really be out rounding up the gangs of fookin' criminals too busy shooting each other and selling drugs to stay off the dole—

"

Gaz slowed to a stop as he reached the sign marked 'Driver Check-point.' Thank fook he had all his papers in order and only put away one pint at lunch.

One of Greater Manchester's finest, a great lardo of a bloke, approached the car. Gaz fumbled around the unfamiliar armrest buttons until he found the one to lower his window. As it disappeared into the pocket of the Merc's door with a quiet, motorised hum, the PC leaned down and peered into the car. "Evening, sir. May I see your insurance documents and driving license, please?"

Wordlessly, Gazza handed the man his documents and waited. The PC gave his license a quick, practiced glance. "Thank you, Mr... Chapman. I'll be right back."

While he waited, Gaz turned his attention back to trying to fathom his car stereo; he could get some stations, but Smooth Radio was turning out to be elusive. BBC One and Four came in loud and clear, but he could not stand either one. He flipped through the owner's manual, still neatly housed in its leather book cover in the glove box, but it was no help, either. Even his old banger could get Smooth from time to time. *Oh, well, you can't have everything*, he mused.

It occurred to Gaz that the Bill was taking an exceedingly long time. He switched off the stereo and fumbled for his mobile. He had just passed from very late to what Jules referred to as 'start calling the hospitals' late, and pressie or no, he would have to call home and face her wrath.

Dibble tapped on the window, startling him. "Mr Chapman, would you step out of the car, please?"

"Sure, Constable. Is there anything wrong?" It was on the tip of his tongue to show a little impatience to hurry things along; he was a model citizen, after all, and they knew it. But he also knew if he showed too much strop they might just park him for the hell of it and Jules would use his bollocks for a door knocker no matter how many new cars he gave her.

He exited the car, and any demands he had intended to make died in his mouth. Face to face, the PC was not the fat Dib Gazza had originally thought; he was built like a brick shithouse and had the face of a friendly but determined bulldog.

"Mr Chapman, I am arresting you for motor vehicle theft with intent to defraud. You do not have to say anything—"

"What the fook—" Gazza jerked as his hands were brought behind his back and secured with zip ties. He sputtered and choked, "I haven't done owt wrong! You saw the papers—it's legit! You can't just arrest me! I bought this car two weeks ago—I just picked it up today! I'll call my motherfookin' lawyer!"

Dispassionately, the Dibble continued. "You do not have to say anything. But it may harm your defense if you do not mention when questioned something which you later rely on in court. Anything you do or say may be given in evidence. Do you understand, Mr Chapman?"

Protesting, Gaz was led to a waiting police car. He yammered his innocence all the way to Northampton Road, where he spent his anniversary objecting to being fingerprinted, processed and jailed, courtesy of the Greater Manchester Police.

It looked like this present was not going to meet with Jules' approval after all.

Her mobile rang. Sydney glanced at it, then answered. "Hello, Inigo."

"Ah. Hello, Sydney. I was wondering if I might be permitted to drop by sometime?"

"Sure. What day would you like to come?"

"Well, as I'm in Windsor now, I was thinking in about ten minutes, if it's not too inconvenient."

Trust Inigo to ask if he could come round for a visit whilst parked in their driveway. Dahlra headed for the kitchen, muttering something about tea and biscuits while she and Elwess scurryfunged around the front sitting room, snatching up mugs and plumping pillows.

Exactly ten minutes later, Sydney opened the door to her Principal just as he raced up the steps, getting soaked in the few feet from his car to the door. "Ghastly weather up here in the country, what?" He brushed the rain from his Gieves and Hawkes raincoat in his fastidious, fussy manner. "I forget just how long that drive is up to the house. Do put the kettle on, won't you? I'm parched."

"It's on." She tossed his coat onto the hall tree. "And if I'd known you were coming, I'd have turned off the rain. Showing up unannounced isn't like you, Inigo. What's up?"

"What do you mean, 'unannounced'? I gave you ten minutes. As to why I'm here, I thought you all might enjoy an update, my dear. We've had some recent developments. Oh, and by the way, I like the hair. Very Louise Brooks."

Inigo still did not have any news on the mole, which he admitted while making a great business of preparing his tea. "But I do have an item of worth. Since Urbonienė was discovered, we've liaised with several of the larger constabularies throughout the country. They've provided us with local CIUs to assist with the case. Saves us a lot of manpower and provides good relations with law enforcement."

"Ever the philanthropist," Dahlra interjected dryly, passing a plate of homemade biscuits.

Inigo ignored the remark as he chose a digestive. "Manchester's unit has confiscated the car that picked her up from her flat on the day she disappeared."

"I thought you checked that out back in April, when the girl's body was found."

"I'm afraid it was a case of forests and trees. We focused all our attention to what happened to her *after* she caught the train to Luton. CCTV showed her getting on the train, getting off, and walking down the street from the station. We trawled through Luton Council's tapes for a few weeks. Cameras captured her walking down the street, and as Sod's Law would have it, the next section of the street's tapes were erased back in March."

"Why would they do that?" asked Elwess.

"A lot of monitoring systems only keep their tapes for a limited time," Sydney explained. "They don't have the storage space or the resources to back up everything they monitor."

Inigo confirmed this with a nod. "Unfortunately. When we started this investigation, we questioned Urbonienė's former roommates and asked them to recall the day in mid-February she moved out. According to them, she called a cab to take her to the train station. Stu Palermo traced the number she dialed from her deactivated phone, but it came back listed as 'no subscriber.'

"We spoke to the roommates again two weeks ago. It transpires that none of the girls actually *saw* the bally car; they just assumed she left in a black cab. We ran through all the checks with the cab offices and found nothing, so we started looking at the mini-cab services, Uber and the like. We had one possible lead, which turned out to be a hoax.

"Then we went back to the neighbourhood and knocked on doors again, asking locals. As luck would have it, an elderly neighbour remembered seeing her get into a black Mercedes. He even waved goodbye to her. He was in hospital the first time the detectives came round in April, but he remembered it because he said it was such a very 'posh motor for that neighbourhood.'"

Inigo sipped his tea. "Now we had something to track on CCTV, and sure enough, we found it. We even got a good read on the registration. It turns out the car was registered under a false name, and all attempts to locate the car met with a dead end. It had gone to ground."

Elwess shifted. "I assume we're getting to a point sometime before we get back from Japan?"

Inigo pursed his lips primly. "Allow me my one vindication, if you don't mind. Actually, I can't even claim that. What happened next was pure happenstance.

"Two nights ago, police pulled in a white convertible Mercedes in Manchester City Centre during a routine drink driving sweep. Registration came up clean, but lo and behold, the VIN was the exact match of the black Mercedes."

"At least we know what it was up to during its absence."

"Precisely, old girl. The driver is currently being held in Manchester, and the car was confiscated. Our men have taken it apart piece by piece."

Dahlra shook his head, marveling. "You only hear of coincidences like that on CSI."

"It happens more often than you'd imagine." Inigo looked rather smug, which, given the circumstances, Sydney did not feel was strictly warranted. "Whoever chopped it did a good job; new seats, new carpets. It looked like a new car. If they hadn't been so careless when filing off the VIN, it would have never been recognised."

"Oh, come on, Inigo!" Elwess huffed. "Quit drawing this out! We're not waiting for the next advert break."

"Fine. Ruin it for the rest of us." He took a deep breath, as if savouring his words. "The forensics team found several strands of hair wedged under the back seat footwell. Luminol revealed the boot had been scoured, but minute blood drops were found, along with traces of saliva. They both belonged to Kofryna Urbonienė."

Elwess whistled softly. "Shit."

Inigo inclined his head, as if taking a bow. "The hair, on the other hand, belonged to none other than Silas Markham."

Now that *was* worth waiting for the slow buildup. "So what about the driver?" asked Sydney. "Any connection with Silverbirch?"

"None we can ascertain. The chap claims to have bought the car two weeks ago in Clayton. The seller was a man by the name of Nick Red-dihoff. I'll give you three guesses as to Mr Reddihoff's town of residency."

"Luton," said Dahlra.

"In one. It's a bogus address, of course but it's too much of a coincidence to ignore." Inigo sat back in his chair. Earning his nickname, Sydney observed, seemed to have drained him of energy. "If we can just find Markham's place, we might learn more—even discover the mole. I had hoped to be able to come to you with that information, but..."

Dahlra chewed his bottom lip thoughtfully. "This car business is very secret squirrel for someone as unstable as Silas."

"My thoughts exactly," replied Inigo. "He was involved in her death, most assuredly, but I can't help but wonder if the same person who organised Urbonienė's disappearance ran Silas' life as well."

The four of them digested this thought along with their biscuits. Sydney knew they were all thinking the same thing: *Lorcan.*

Inigo turned to Elwess. "In any case, Friday, you will be flying to Japan. I expect this to be a fact-finding mission and nothing else. Come to the Agency on Thursday for your final briefing." He brightened. "We'll lunch at the King Bill. Some nice fish and chips to see you through two weeks of sashimi." His nose wrinkled in that middle-class disdain that so many of his ilk affected when faced with something decidedly un-British.

He stood. "And now, I really must go. My night driving isn't what it was, and it's quite dark out here in the country. Thank you for the tea."

Inigo shook Dahlra's hand, kissed Sydney, then turned to Elwess. "A word, if you don't mind. Walk me out to my car."

Sydney slipped her arm around Dahlra's waist as they watched the two men leave. "Now that *is* odd."

"What?"

"Inigo never drives himself anywhere. And I'll just bet no one knows where he is, either. Something else is going on. This isn't just common-or-garden paranoia." Sydney released her breath with an irritated huff. "I hate getting pushed around on Inigo's chessboard." She nodded toward the door. "And I wonder what all that's about as well."

Dahlra draped his arm loosely around her shoulders. "We'll winkle it out of Elwess." He placed a warm kiss on her forehead. "Tonight."

Elwess followed Lightoller out onto the front steps. The rain had stopped, and the wind was dispatching the clouds, sending them scudding across the sky like boats pushed by impatient gondoliers. The full moon finally made her appearance, casting everything in a ghostly, bluish light. The two men gazed out into the glum beauty of the moonlit meadows; through the encroaching mist, Elwess could make out the tiny lights of the nearby village. They danced like St Elmo's fire.

"What's on your mind, Ini—"

"Elwess, I've always been rather lenient where you're concerned." Lightoller's public-school, jolly-hockey-sticks manner dropped like a tattered scrim. "I've allowed you to tailor the Minder training programme to your louche specifications. I've given you plenty of freedom to drop tools whenever you attended one of your dirty weekends abroad. I've even allowed you to manipulate and fuck my Agents. I'd say I've been a very generous 'guv'nor', wouldn't you agree?"

Elwess shifted uncomfortably. "I suppose that would depend on why you're mentioning all this in the first place, Inigo. Are you trolling for compliments, or are you setting me up for an arse-reaming?"

"I'm asking you, you smug son of a bitch, because I'm trying to keep your worthless carcass alive, and I need to know if you are being one hundred-percent honest with me!"

Elwess recoiled at the vitriol in Lightoller's voice. "Honest about what? You've had your watch dogs sniffing around my hole ever since this whole Silverbirch fiasco went down three years ago."

"Careful, Talbert."

"You're the one that dragged me out here! If you've got something to tell me, then say it, and stop quoting chapter and verse just to make a point."

Lightoller regarded Elwess with narrow-eyed suspicion. "A former lover of yours washes up in the Channel after literally being on ice for months. A rival of yours with links to Silverbirch suddenly goes around picking fights and nearly murders my Agent and her Minder.

"Why them and not you? You were the one who assaulted Markham in that den of iniquity of yours. You were his rival. Why did he turn his wrath on Dahlra instead of you?"

Elwess' heart shifted into a higher gear. "Silas was a nutter—everyone knew that. He knew it would hurt me more to have a go at someone I care about. It's always been personal with him. He's never mentioned Silverbirch to me."

"And is Silverbirch personal? Have you done anything, anyone, in your seedy, sordid past that connects you to Silverbirch?"

Elwess made himself look him in the eye without flinching. "No."

Lightoller looked at him with such cold scrutiny it was all Elwess could do to remain still. "I think you're lying."

"Sorry you think so."

"If I discover you are withholding any information from me, I swear before God—"

"Fine!" Elwess exploded. "Swear all you want, but if we're going to stand out here playing my dad's bigger than your dad, at least let me go in and get a coat. I'm not going to catch cold just for the privilege of listening to you yammering on about what a cunt I am for not telling you something I don't actually know."

Lightoller grabbed his arm. "I am sending two good people into an unknown situation to protect you. I could make you go alone, but they would never forgive me." His expression left Elwess in no doubt of his contempt. "For reasons known only to themselves, they care enough about you to risk their own lives. *Don't* make me regret indulging them."

Elwess jerked his arm away. Lightoller adjusted his cuffs, pulling himself back into his polished, impenetrable shell, then left without another word. Long after the car disappeared down the drive, Elwess stood on the steps, staring out into the cold darkness.

Dahlra and Sydney had already headed for bed; the downstairs was quiet and dark. As Elwess passed the massive oak door to their bedroom, Dahlra called his name. He paused in their doorway, drinking in the sight, his heart beating in his chest like a primal drum, his anger and resentment forgotten.

Illuminated only by the fire in the grate, they lay curled together on the bed. Petals of the same dark flower, they looked gilded in gold and copper, idols to be venerated and worshipped. Dahlra was sitting up, pillowed against the huge iron-scrolled headboard; Sydney lay resting against his chest, her eyes closed, her face soft and relaxed. He was massaging her shoulders; the soft whisper of oil gave her flawless skin a pearly sheen in the firelight.

His hands floated deftly over Sydney's creamy flesh, palms ghosting over her erect nipples. He pinched and flicked them, and she whimpered and writhed against him. Her legs scissored apart, and Elwess caught the glimmer of a different, more enticing lustre. Sydney opened her eyes, and the desire he saw in that sloe-eyed stare made his mouth water.

Dahlra caught his eye. "Like what you see?"

Elwess nodded, his raging, stupid lust so great he could not even articulate an answer. Dahlra cupped Sydney firm, rounded breasts and offered them like ripe fruit. His arched brow was both a challenge and an invitation. "Well, are you going to stand there and watch, or come here and give my girl what she needs?"

In that moment, facing the man he had knelt to and called Master, Elwess remembered who he was: that arrogant son of a gypsy, a king of his kind. When one king offered another such a generous gift, how could he refuse? He would take it and enjoy it like revenge, and her lush body would be just as rich and sumptuous. He felt his lips curling into a sneer of power. "I'll be glad to give her exactly what she needs, Master Dahlra."

He undressed as he walked into the room, leaving his clothes where they fell. He crawled onto the bed from the end. Sydney reached for him, but he batted her hands away. Dahlra captured them above her head, forcing her breasts to stand proud, her reddened nipples like sweet cherries to be plucked. Elwess took one in his mouth and sucked it hard, drawing it tighter and tighter.

She mewled and pressed her thighs together, rocking her hips, trying to find that elusive sweet spot. He pressed against her belly with a firm, uncompromising hand. She resisted him, and he punished her recklessness by nipping her luscious tit with his teeth. She cursed in surprise and pain, and the sound was like the sharp strike of a flint. She looked down at him with the intensity of all dangerous animals, waiting for the spark to catch.

He laughed. "You can glare all you want, sweetheart. But you issued that invitation." The glint in her eye turned dark and dangerous, and it called him home like a familiar song. "Spread your legs. Yeah, just like that, nice and wide." He peeled her open with slow, dirty deliberation. "Playtime's begun. Let's see that sunshine."

With their eyes locked together, he lowered his head and lapped at her warm, delicious flesh. At his touch she gasped, and the sound disconnected his body from his worry and fear.

He knew how to make a woman come; that was a given. And he knew *this* woman's body, knew which switches and dials to manipulate to get her off quickly. But it had been a long time, and she had made him wait. She had made him wait for months. Tomorrow, he might use the finer instruments of sex, like cherishing and making love and savouring, but tonight, he would use her with all the sledgehammer force the word 'fuck' implied.

A fox screamed into the night, jerking Elwess awake. He hated that human-like shriek that sliced through the night air. Dahlra would have probably said it sounded like the anguished wail of a condemned soul. Elwess thought it sounded like the kind of irritating ratbag that loved to freak the hell out of city boys like him. He rolled over onto his back and willed his heart to calm the hell down. *Fucking nature. Never a moment's peace.*

Sydney snuggled up against him, soft and warm, her breasts pressed invitingly against his chest. "You okay?"

"Fox." He sat up and stretched. "Be right back."

He stumbled in the dark on the way to the loo. His hands, his face, his cock were saturated in that distilled aroma of sex: a citrusy, musky odour that never failed to turn him on. He caught his reflection in the mirror as he washed his hands; a tall, pale man with messy hair, stubbled jaw and snow-pissholed eyes, more asleep than awake.

While he was gone, Dahlra had rolled over and spooned against Sydney. Together, they were beautiful; Dahlra, pale and silvery like the moon, Sydney, warm and golden as the sun. His own personal galaxy.

Elwess tried to recall how many times he had slept with anyone other than these two. Had sex, yes. Fucked, played, hell, sometimes had even made love with other women, but woke up with them in his arms? Rarely. And rarer still, awoke in their arms. Dahlra nuzzled sleepily against Sydney, a smile of contentment on his handsome face. *Have I ever dared to trust anyone that much? How many have ever given me reason to?*

That thought brought him fully awake. Tonight had been good; rough and tender, dirty, passionate and vital. The sex had held an aching tenderness; it was not just fucking now, in spite of his urgency and lust. There had been a *newness* to it. They were not back to where they had been before Dahlra had been attacked, but it was the best kind of olive branch. They loved him, and tonight they had tried hard to prove it.

And I love you. Am I prepared to show them just how much? Before he could fuck everything up by overthinking, he crawled in bed beside Dahlra, who awoke at once.

"Budge over." Dahlra looked a bit nonplussed, but complied. Elwess pressed at his shoulder until Dahlra was lying on his back. Without thought or consideration or even a pause to take his next breath, he closed his hand over Dahlra's flaccid cock and gave it a firm stroke.

Dahlra jerked, wide awake. "What do you—"

"Hush."

"Elwess, what—"

"I don't know. But it's okay." His hand slid over the smooth flesh, and it quickened under his touch.

Dahlra was watching him with a mixture of uncertainty and unasked-for arousal. His voice sounded scratchy and breathless. "You don't have to do this. I don't...I'm not—"

"Neither am I, but I want to. Sydney understands."

Dahlra turned to look at Sydney, who was watching them closely. She nodded. "I do understand." She and Dahlra shared a slow, deep kiss, languid and extravagant. He made a soft sound of surrender, and she drank it down, stroking his cheek. His cock, fully erect now, pulsed in Elwess' hand, and with less surprise than he would have expected, Elwess discovered he was equally as hard.

Sydney's kiss left Dahlra breathless. His eyes were luminous in the dim light, glazed and lust-ridden. He pulled her higher up the bed until she lay over him. He wrapped his arm around her waist, and captured her velvety nipple in his mouth with exquisite gentleness. A light sheen of sweat bloomed on his skin; Elwess could feel the beat of Dahlra's heart pulsing in the veins of his cock.

Sydney lay back against the pillow, watching the two men raptly. Dahlra slipped his hand between her parted thighs and found *that* sweet spot. She rocked against him with a sigh of pure bliss. He moved in unison with her, matching his rhythm to hers. Elwess was completely in their thrall, never taking his eyes from Dahlra, pumping his cock with deep, steady strokes.

Dahlra's orgasm was already straining at the lead; his balls were heavy and tight, and Elwess felt pride that he could pull such pleasure from this special man, who had never asked anything from him but friendship and faithfulness.

Then a warm, strong hand closed around his own cock and gave it a shy, almost tentative stroke. "Oh, fuck." He buried his face against Dahlra's shoulder. "I'm... you don't have to—"

"I know." Dahlra's laughter turned into to a soft moan. His hand was large and sure, and when it grasped him and pumped hard, Elwess saw stars and his own balls drew tight and hard against his groin.

Dahlra was fucking Elwess' hand now, his hips bucking rhythmically, his cock blisteringly hot. The three of them became a moving, living wave, awash in this intoxicating, intense madness.

Suddenly, the hand on Elwess' cock tightened unbearably, and he drove his final, jerking thrusts against it. He gave into the liquid fire melting in his gut, chained to the realisation that *this* was right, his Dominant was giving him what he needed. This was all he was; this was all he wanted to be, living in this powerful circle they had forged with their passion.

Elwess' orgasm rose from his burning thighs and through his prick, engulfing him in pleasure so intense he nearly blacked out from it. Dahlra's climax grew too big for his body to bear; he made a last growling, uncontrolled sound of ecstasy just as Sydney, too, found her frantic, beautiful release. They came in a wild, gasping rush, their bodies locked in this electric current, fusing them together, melting them like wax so that one ended where the other began.

The three of them fell back, breathless, panting like animals, their bodies still undulating against one another. Elwess' hand had totally seized up; he flexed and shook it to release the cramp. The tendons of his arm ached. "Damn, Dahlra, you have a really big dick."

They all laughed, and suddenly, just like that, they were *together*, friends and lovers again. It was the most natural thing in the world to roll over and press his lips against Dahlra's. It was a kiss given in love and tenderness, and Dahlra accepted it with the same bashful grace that had accompanied the unexpected hand job. When it ended, Dahlra looked up at him with a mixture of affection and puzzlement.

Elwess felt a silly grin slip over his face. "Long time listener, first time caller."

Dahlra laughed, then glanced down at his sticky abdomen. "I'm a mess."

"I'll get something to clean us up." It took herculean effort for Elwess to sit up. He unfolded himself out of bed and headed toward the loo again on unsteady feet. "Back in two ticks."

He dropped a flannel into the sink and turned on the hot water full blast. It gushed butt-munchingly cold from the tap, but he did not mind waiting on it. He needed a few minutes alone to collect himself. In the short space between the bed and the bathroom, his energy had flatlined. His balls hummed with a familiar, pleasant ache; his old feller felt as if it had been in a rock crusher. He could smell the clean scent of Sydney, and the richer, darker aroma of Dahlra blending with his own musky smell. He was marked by them both now.

His knee-jerk feeling was that he needed to examine his head about what had just happened, but after a moment's consideration, he could not be arsed. Did he want sex with men? No. Not even a flicker of interest. Sex with Dahlra? Well, different beast entirely.

He reached for the soaked flannel and pulled his hand away with a hiss of pain. While he was playing Ask Dr Freud, the water had heated to such a blister-inducing temperature it had fogged the mirror. *As words of wisdom go, 'keep up the introspection shit and you'll end up boiling your cock off' is not as concise as 'sometimes a cigar is just a cigar,' but what it lacks in eloquence... I think I may be suffering post-coital delirium.*

He managed to tame the temp to something he could handle, gave himself a perfunctory going over, then took a wet flannel back to the bed. His lovers were dozing in the hazy glow of aftercare. Dahlra's head was cradled on Sydney's breast; she held him in her arms, one draped over his shoulders, the other caressing his head. It amused Elwess that

Sydney was absolutely sparko. She could wake at the sound of a gerbil farting, but with Dahlra slumbering in her arms she let sleep take her with the abandonment of a child.

Elwess touched Dahlra's shoulder; his eyes opened and he quirked a questioning eyebrow. Elwess held out the flannel. "No, this isn't Groundhog Day. I'm willing to concede the occasional homoerotic moment, but it doesn't come with valet service. You're cleaning your own tackle."

Dahlra took the cloth, but before he saw to his own needs, he turned to Sydney. He bathed her with such gentle tenderness she barely stirred. Finally he turned the flannel on himself, washing away the results of Elwess' impromptu gay porn scene. "I'm not sure what kind of moment that was." He looked pensive, as if the subject merited some serious thought. "It was different. Pleasant, but different."

He lay back, and placed a hand behind his head. His free hand stroked Sydney's hip absently. "Then again, I have a strange, sneaking suspicion that it was just a very bizarre, erotic dream. One of those dreams all middle class English boys have but tell themselves they don't." He glanced up at Elwess with that same no-nonsense expression he had worn the night he asked him to accept his Dominance. "And what was it for you?"

Elwess was too tired to formulate a snarky reply. They were past the locker room excuses. "I suppose at the end of the day, I don't want you to associate pain with a man's touch. And maybe... Blimey, Dahlra. No one has ever come to bat for me like you and Sydney."

"I had rather hoped it was because you found my masculine charms irresistible, and not for some misplaced idea that you owe me." While his words were flippant, there was a cooler undertone to his words that rocked Elwess back a bit.

"No, I didn't mean it that way—not at all. I didn't think of it as some kind of protection money," he replied emphatically. "And it wasn't about paying the rent, either." Under Dahlra's uncompromising gaze, Elwess grimaced. "Well, maybe just a little." An unbidden laugh escaped his lips. "And you know full well you're a bit of top totty."

Sydney stirred. "Are you two done?" She squinted up at him and sighed grumpily. "Fuck's sake, Elwess. Tie and knot in it and go to sleep."

Both men laughed, and Dahlra pulled her into his embrace. "We are, darling girl. Everything's alright."

Sleepily, she sighed and drifted off again as Elwess climbed into bed behind her. He settled into his favourite position, with his dozy cock nestled between the velvety cheeks of her bum. He pressed his chest against her scarred back, and for the first time since June, he fell asleep without hearing the sword of Damocles swishing inches above his head.

CHAPTER SIXTEEN

Come Fly With Me

Sydney's first weapons instructor, Glen Kilkenny, an ex-RAF officer with a toothbrush moustache and thinning hair, taught her the fifty-four steps to breaking down, cleaning and reassembling a Glock 17 nine-millimeter pistol. According to Kilks, it should be done each time the weapon was discharged, and every step must be followed in order to safely ensure a properly cleaned and workable firearm.

The first few times Sydney performed the entire procedure, it had taken her forty-five minutes from start to finish. As her respect and usage of the gun increased, she became more economical with her movements. Fifteen years and four Glocks later, the muscle memory in her fingers was so deeply ingrained, a thorough cleaning took around fifteen minutes. Once, she had managed eight, but that had only been for show. Afterward, she had broken it back down and cleaned it again. She believed in cutting time, not corners—hence the reason she was meticulously making sure their weapons were in good order at half-eleven at night.

This was both prelude and postlude to action; the preparation of mind, body and metal. She thought of it as a kind of meditation, a seemingly contradictory combination of Zen and cold precision. It always left her feeling relaxed and alert, even if she was just giving her gun a once over after target practice.

Knowing what she knew about *bushido*, she supposed she understood why. Battle lust always produced an elated state of readiness, a chilling commitment to the gun that was both primal and calculated. In the right situation, this heightened state of awareness tuned her reflexes tripwire-sensitive, enabling her to load, aim and find her target with blinding speed. Before she and Dahlra became lovers, it was the most visceral thrill she could achieve on her own. She had long ago stopped questioning the pleasure of it, and had finally stopped feeling guilty for missing it.

Eject the clip, remove the slide and recoil spring, remove the barrel from the slide; clean the bore, the barrel, the spring, the slide, the frame, oil the slide rails; reassemble, function check.

"Am I the only one turned on by this?" Elwess was watching her with open fascination. "You look like you could do that in your sleep blind-folded."

"I can, and I have." Sydney zoned out again, focusing on her task with almost mesmeric concentration. She pulled the trigger, pulled the slide back, locked it, pressed the release, then pulled the trigger again. The hammer fell with a positive, confident click. She wiped the exterior down with a cloth, loaded one of the mags and slid it home with another satisfying click. Now that the gun was whole again, she merely held it for a moment. It was a good, reliable weapon with a smooth and rapid action, the weight and balance perfect for her hand.

She and this Glock were old friends—a medal-winner at every shoot-ing contest the Agency had held during her career, and more importantly, a welcome ally in a firefight. Together they made a fine unit, a single, deadly instrument perfectly suited to their lethal purpose. She had saved lives with it (at the memory of the handsome doctor ask-ing her if she needed paracetamol for her cramps, she smiled), but she had taken even more. Her job at the Agency had always been as much about elimination as protection.

She checked and loaded extra clips, verified the safety was on, and snugged the loaded weapon into its shoulder holster with the ease of long practice. She was now as ready as she would ever be for any even-tuality within her control; anything beyond that stayed in the lap of the gods.

Dahlra had insisted they eat a light meal before leaving for Gatwick Airport, but Elwess picked at his unenthusiastically, looking as if the next bite would bring the previous one back up again. His eyes were narrowed and tense, his face the colour of dirty linen. "You're packing a lot of heat for what's supposed to be a routine flight."

Sydney shrugged. "Hope for the best, expect the worse."

He pushed the rest of his meal away.

They were scheduled to depart around four in the morning, when the airport was at its quietest. Just after midnight, two black cabs ar-rived, both with Met Police drivers behind the wheel. Elwess would leave first; Dahlra and Sydney would follow shortly. Though they were taking the same flight, they planned to arrive at the airport a few minutes behind him. As far as Elwess or anyone else should be concerned, the older gentleman with the greying beard and his auburn-haired companion had nothing to do with him.

After Elwess kissed her goodbye, Sydney watched the cab pull away while Dahlra and their driver finished loading their bags. Remembering Elwess' pale, serious face, Sydney was overcome with affection for him, followed closely by a sick sort of intuition, like she might never see him again. It was just pre-mission jitters—everyone got them, and if they said they did not, they were lying—but her frustration with the entire operation made them worse.

She could not shake the feeling that, in his increasingly obsessive desire to beat Silverbirch at their own game, Inigo had not thought the situation through with his usual deliberation. There were too many variables to consider, too many vulnerable spots that could be exploited. Sydney had prepared the three of them as best she could, but it did not seem to be enough.

Added to that was the nagging feeling that her holiday away from full-time fieldwork was going to bite her in the arse. A perfunctory fitness regime and unsatisfying sim tests in the Agency's famous Black Box training facility had confirmed she was out of practice and sluggish. Inigo had been correct about one thing; two years of good food, good sex and good love had made her pudgy and indolent. The old Sydney would never have let an amateur like Silas get the drop on her, and the stakes had grown only higher.

The feeling of growing anxiety was so pervasive, she phoned Elwess as soon as they were on their way to Gatwick. "Everything alright?" Amid the sounds of the cab's diesel engine and faint music in the background, his deep voice sounded queerly disjointed.

"Look, I know we said we'd meet at the gate, but I've changed my mind. Wait on us in the terminal, and when we finish going through security, I want you to fall in behind us, okay?"

There was the briefest pause. "Don't tell me you have some spidey sense."

"Not at all," she lied. "It just makes more sense to allow us to lead. And watch out for anything unusual. Just keep alert and pay attention. Don't discount anything as not being important."

Her phone buzzed to indicate an incoming call; it was Inigo. "Listen, I have to take this call, but don't forget. Fall in behind us before we start for the gate. And if you see anything, or hear anything strange, remember what we discussed."

"Okay, Sydney, I will." His voice sounded serious enough to placate her, but it did not really make her feel any better.

She answered the other line. "Hey, Inigo."

He sounded incredibly ebullient for the middle of the night. "Good morning. I thought you'd like to know we've just located Silas Markham's flat."

Her feeling of unease ramped up. It seemed just too much of a coincidence that it would happen now. Sydney replied with more enthusiasm than she actually felt, "Well done. How did you do it?"

"After you return from the Far East, I shall regale you with the feats of derring-do your fellow agents committed to find it, but for now, just know that we're inside and it's being searched."

"So you still want us to go to Japan? You don't want to see what your search of the flat might uncover first?"

"Of course you must go, old thing." Judging from his admonishing tone, Sydney was clearly raining on his parade. "For the first time in ages, we know something Silverbirch doesn't. Strike while the iron's hot, I say." The connection ended, leaving Sydney feeling more uneasy than ever.

"Well, hell."

"What did he want?"

Sydney quickly filled him in. Dahlra ingested Inigo's news about Silas Markham's flat with an almost preternatural calm, but in the end he, too, felt they had no choice but to play out the plan as it unfolded. "Inigo sounds like our Generals ordering the troops over the top in the Somme while he ponders his maps in dear old Blighty. Damn the landmines, full steam ahead, and all that. He's so keen for this to work, he's stopped hearing any dissenting opinion."

At two am, Gatwick airport was as busy as if it were ten o'clock in the morning: a noisy, bustling wave of different nationalities, complexions and languages. A non-stop flow of cars, taxis and buses made their continuous loops from Departures to car park; the air around them was thick with diesel fumes and the scraping rumble of luggage wheels crossing the tarmac.

As they unloaded their bags at the drop off, Sydney leaned in close to Dahlra. "I'm not trying to be melodramatic, but if things go pear-shaped at any time, please promise me that you won't try to play hero. Will you do that?"

"I'm torn between feeling like a coward and making that promise, and wanting to protect you should anything happen."

"Go ahead and feel like a coward, but just do what I'm asking. I'm sure it's going to be a routine flight and I'm being overly paranoid, but..." She took his hand. "Promise me. I'll be able to do my job better, knowing I won't have to worry about you so much."

He was looking down at her from a face that seemed so foreign behind the beard. He had donned a black fedora, which also added to the stranger danger vibe. But his eyes were all his, and would forever look at her with that clear, clean honesty she trusted more than anything else on earth. He put his hand on his heart. "I promise, *Hayabusa-san*."

Sydney snorted. "Peregrine, right. More like chicken." He laughed, and a couple turned their way and stared at him searchingly. Sydney realised with the trendy hat, beard and rich, plummy voice, Dahlra looked and sounded like an actor, and they were probably trying to identify him.

Once they were out of earshot, she added, "You don't have to be brave to do this job, love. You just have to not shit yourself long enough to get the job done. After that, all bets are off."

Every precaution had been taken to get them out of the country without incident; hence the separate cars and semi-disguises. Gatwick no longer flew intercontinental; they would fly British Airways to Venice, then catch an Alitalia flight to Tokyo's Narita Airport. Inigo had been very dicey about his choice to use Gatwick instead of Heathrow, which boasted several non-stop flights. Sydney assumed he was hoping they would lose any tail that might follow, but if he had another agenda, he was playing that one close to the vest. It was just another reason the entire mission felt like a hack job.

As they walked into the terminal, Sydney spotted Elwess placing his bag on the scale at the BA check-in station. He was handing the clerk his passport and documents, saying something that made the young woman duck her head and fluff up her hair. Only Elwess could pull at a time like this.

They watched him give the clerk a final, rakish smile, toss his coat over his arm and stalk away toward the security scans. The clerk watched him go, then said something to her colleague which made them both giggle like school girls. They leaned far over the desk, watching him walk away. *Bloody typical.*

As their passports were scanned and their bags were checked, Sydney looked around, feigning the world-weary countenance of the inveterate globetrotter, while checking the exit points. She saw the usual departing passengers trundling toward the security scanners, fishing out plastic baggies filled with toiletries, like collections of mini-bottles confiscated at a frat party. Sleepy, travel-knackered passengers suddenly appeared head-first from the lower ground escalators, like newly evicted zombies. They shuffled toward the baggage carousels, carrying shopping bags bulging with their limit of duty-free cigarettes and clinking with cheap booze.

Nothing seemed amiss. She and Dahlra joined the queue to pass through security; she was still unable to shake the nagging sensation that they had missed something.

Lightoller's phone sounded again, and he picked up before the second ring. He listened without interrupting Agent Whitner for two minutes, his face growing darker with every passing second. Anger washed over him, but he made his voice sound as normal as possible. "Right. Bring him in. Wake him up, *truss* him up if you have to, and bring him round immediately."

"We've already dispatched a team to his flat, guv'nor."

"Well done. Phone me the moment you—"

"I'm afraid there's something else, sir."

"Yes?"

"We've found a second set of identifiable fingerprints at Markham's flat."

After a brief moment in the private security rooms, during which they confirmed their identification and verified that Principal Inigo Lightoller had cleared them for special onboard privileges, Sydney and

Dahlra entered the no-man's land of the concourse. As they reached the long spiral walk toward Gate 59, they caught up with Elwess, who had been idly studying the Arrival/Departure screens overhead. After they passed, he waited a beat, then started following a few feet behind them. The three of them joined a growing number of passengers all heading for the departure terminal, until they were engulfed in a small, flowing sea of people.

They entered the final corridor that led down toward the International gates, and Sydney tensed. To someone who habitually marked every landscape with regards to its escape route, this was quite possibly the worst place she had ever seen. It was a narrow passage, only about forty feet across. The floor sloped downward like a swimming pool, ending with a set of double doors that led into the gate area. It certainly gave Sydney a greater appreciation of how fish in a barrel must feel.

There was a small cluster of office furniture shoved up tight against the wall to her right, probably some makeshift checkpoint set up during the busy holiday season that someone had never got around to removing. Gatwick always looked like Earl's Court two days after the Ideal Home Show closed up shop.

The sides of the walls remained at their original height, forming a rising balcony almost thirty feet above them on either side of the corridor. Glass panels under the railings prevented anyone or anything from accidentally falling through. Four wide, concrete pillars about thirty inches across held up the ceiling above, two on each side of the passage.

Above her, on the left, she noticed a member of Gatwick's maintenance staff leaning on the balcony rail. He was idly watching the departing passengers herding down the slope, like cattle through a run. He was nondescript, walking beige, almost deliberately so. It would be difficult to pick him out of a police lineup. Another employee, short and balding, approached him, pushing a cleaning trolley. As he passed, their eyes met, and they nodded at each other almost imperceptibly.

The hair on the nape of her neck prickled, every fibre on high alert. Sydney glanced around, not bothering to try for inconspicuous. Suddenly she could not wait to be on that plane, and away from this box canyon of a corridor.

Lightoller had just received the confirmation call that Sydney, Dahlra and Elwess had passed through airport security when his phone rang.

"Give me some good news, Garnet."

"I can't. The flat is empty." He paused, and Lightoller could hear him breathing hard over the phone. "Sir, I found a message—"

Lightoller listened for perhaps ten seconds, and felt his heart sink into his stomach.

"Goddammit! Meet me at Gatwick North. Now!"

He ended the call before Pinkerton could reply. "John, how far are we to Gatwick?"

His driver glanced back at Inigo in the rearview mirror. "At least twenty minutes, sir."

"I need to be there in ten, John."

"Yes, sir."

It was time to abort. He dialed Sydney's number. His heart was beating so hard it made his chest ache. Sydney's phone rang until it went into answer phone. As did Dahlra's.

As did Elwess'.

About fifteen feet in front of them, a Skycap came through the double doors, then turned and closed them. A family of three, mother, father and daughter, approached him, and the father asked him something Sydney could not understand; his accent was very thick. The porter ignored them and continued walking. The adults apparently thought he wanted them to follow him, so after a brief consultation, they turned and tagged along. Sydney had only time to think, *what's a Skycap doing here?* when her phone rang.

The Skycap whirled around to face her, his hand reaching for something in his pocket. Adrenaline kicked in like ice water beneath her skin. By the time the Skycap extricated his gun, Sydney's Glock was in her hand. "Drop your weapon! Everybody, get down!"

He was still on the move when he fired, so his shot missed her by a mile and hit the father, who staggered back with a shout of pain, clutching his arm. The mother and daughter, frozen in shock, stood between Sydney and the gunman in the middle of the corridor. The two females stared at her blankly, wearing matching expressions of stunned disbelief. "Get out of the way!" Sydney shouted.

Just as the mother came out of her daze and moved to help her fallen husband, the Skycap feinted to the right and fired again. The bullet caught the woman squarely in the chest. As she dropped at her husband's feet, Sydney fired a single shot, and the porter fell, clutching his throat. He made a horrific gurgling sound, aspirating his life's blood as he died.

Before she could reach the wailing, hysterical daughter, Sydney heard hoarse shouting, and turned to see five men, including the two men she had seen on the balcony, thundering down the corridor toward the doors. They were firing into the crowd as they came, harvesting chaos and confusion in their wake. Passengers stampeded in a blind panic, racing toward the open ends of the concourse.

Those who headed for the double doors crashed against it, but it was locked. Those who tried to run back found themselves facing the incoming gunmen. The air grew thick with the sounds of shouts and gunfire. An alarm claxon started braying throughout the airport, its warbling shriek adding to the hysteria.

Dahlra and Elwess were to her right and slightly behind; Sydney whipped around and ordered, "Get behind that stuff in the corner, both of you!" Dahlra nodded grimly, then darted away. Elwess hesitated, but when she shouted, "Do as I say! Now go!" he fled for shelter as well.

From the concourse, Gatwick Airport police approached the area, slowed down by the hordes of people plowing around them. Sydney eased around to the other side of one of the pillars, firing as she moved. The closest gunman, Mister Beige, who had been paying more attention to the upper balcony than where he was going, almost ran straight into her. He had just enough time to glance up at her, registering his surprise with an almost theatrical double-take, when she fired. A small round hole appeared in the middle of his forehead, and most of his brains exited out the opposite side. His legs collapsed beneath him.

A second attacker ran past her, a younger male with shaggy blond dreads and a shiny, silver revolver that looked like a cheap Smith and Wesson knock-off. He managed to fire several shots, wounding one of the police officers before getting pinned into the corner. Within seconds, both the gunman and the officer were dead, but Sydney would not know or understand the implications of this until later.

A single shot spun her around to the right and slammed her against the pillar. A sharp, burning pain blazed across her right bicep. The older man who had nodded to Mister Beige ran toward her, cursing, his gun raised, when a heavy report from behind her took him off his feet. His weapon flew from his hand, and Sydney moved away from her shield to kick it out of reach. She turned to see Dahlra duck back behind the forgotten pile of the furniture in the corner.

She put the pain aside and rolled around to the back side of the column, searching for her next target. Two gunmen tried to flank the crowd, moving in a pincer formation, firing as they moved. The one to her right was a heavy set man with what looked like a sawed-off shotgun; he was sweating profusely in the humid air, and looked terrified.

Sydney shouted, "Throw it down, Haystacks, and I'll let you walk!" He looked uncertain, then dropped the sawed-off like it was a game of Hot Potato.

A harsh coughing sound stuttered in the room, like machine gun fire, and Sawed-off screamed as a series of black and red holes appeared in his plump middle, like gory swiss cheese. Sydney turned back to Dahlra. "Do you see where that's coming from?" He shook his head.

"Dahlra! To your left!" Elwess shouted.

The last gunman standing held up his hands in surrender. He was the youngest of the bunch, a skinny boy with a surprisingly pretty face. He was weeping with fear. "Don't shoot! Don't kill me please—"

Another rapid burst of gunfire rattled. Pretty Boy stared down at what was left of his chest cavity in shock, then fell forward on his face. Sydney looked around frantically. Two Gatwick officers were wounded, and three more were down; the others were busy trying to herd the passengers out of the area.

Who had killed these guys?

A glance to her right revealed Elwess standing motionless behind the other column. He was spattered with blood.

"Are you alright?"

White-faced, he nodded briefly. "It's not my blood." His expression changed from shock to horror as he spotted her bleeding arm. "God, Sydney, you're wounded!" Before she could answer, another stuttering, flat blast of gunfire sprayed the carpet in front of the exit, driving back the few remaining passengers trapped with them in the corridor. A bullet sang past Sydney's head so close it sounded like ripping fabric. She dove back behind the column as the rapid bursts of gunfire blasted the plaster from its surface.

"Everybody shut up and get back along the wall!" Sydney bellowed. "There's another shooter! And somebody shut off that fucking alarm!"

Another ten long seconds passed, then the braying claxon abruptly ceased in mid-scream. The silence seemed to lift some of the tension from Sydney's chest. She glanced up at the balcony behind them; there was a red line of light sweeping across the glass, reflecting from the balcony on the other side—a laser sight. She followed the line of the beam back into the shadows of the opposite balcony, and saw the gunman. He was shouldering a standard army-issue M4A1.

"This is Special Agent Sydney Chapin. Identify yourself, gunman." She knew there would be no answer, but at least he would know—

"I would've thought you'd already guessed by now, Sydney. Maybe Lightoller was right. You *are* soft."

Sydney's stomach took a swooping dive as she recognised the voice. "Sonofabitch. I don't believe it." Her cold battle lust was heated by sudden, swift anger. "Are you shitting me? *You're* the fucking mole?"

Chips of plaster flew around Sydney as the bullets chewed up the pillar's façade, and she curled herself into the smallest target possible. The shooting eventually stopped; she could hear the soft pinging sounds of the spent casings raining down onto the corridor.

He only became an agent because he accidentally shot himself in the foot with what was supposed to be an unloaded gun, and they gave him the job for spotting the difference, Garnet often quipped. *I wouldn't trust him not to trip over his feet in a proper dust-up, but he's awwight, basically.*

Ross Bullard. The guy who looked as if he dressed himself by taking a superglue shower and running through his closet. The bloke everyone primarily liked, in a dismissive kind of way, but thought either too lazy or too dull or too gormless to make much mischief. It had never occurred to any of them to suspect the quiet, feckless, accident-prone buffoon who managed to injure himself at least once on every mission.

Along with the sick sense of betrayal on Inigo Lightoller's behalf, Sydney felt personally grassed. She had worked with Ross for years, had *helped* him rise in the Agency.

With grudging admiration, she realised that Ross had picked the perfect place to stage his ambush. He had let his foot soldiers incite the panic, then positioned himself in a dark corner to take his sniper shots. From his vantage point, no one could sneak up behind him, and he had a panoramic view of the entire area. If it had not been for the first gunman bugging out early and the pillars they now hid behind, it really *would* have been like shooting fish in a barrel.

"You and your boys are sitting ducks, Sydney," Bullard shouted down to her. "All I want is that murdering cunt."

Sydney caught Dahlra's eye, and he shook his head and shrugged as if to say, *I don't have a clue.* Keeping her voice calm and reasonable, she replied, "You're going to have to be a little more specific than that, Ross. Who you talking about?"

"That cocksucker, Elwess Talbert!" His voice was hard and angry. "Give me Talbert, and I swear I won't hurt another soul."

Elwess shot her a look of terrified confusion. Sydney's own uncertainty burned away with the fuel of her anger. "Do you mean to tell me that you came here to take out an *Agency* man for them? Whatever they're paying you, I hope it's enough to cover your funeral expenses!"

"Shut up!" There was a tinge of panic in Ross' voice. "Silverbirch didn't send me. I just want the shit who killed my Silas!"

"*Your—*" The penny dropped. "Oh, I see. So all this time, you've been kissing arse with Silverbirch because you're Silas' bitch?"

"I have never been—"

"Then, your fuckbuddy Silas gets popped, and your friends at Silverbirch congratulate Elwess for getting rid of him. Now he's their golden boy, so you're trying to kill him." She forced herself laugh at him; it was an ugly sound. "I really wouldn't want to be in your shoes when either Lightoller *or* Silverbirch catch up with you. The Agency ransacked Markham's house last night, Ross. By now, Lightoller and the cavalry are on their way." At least, she fervently hoped so. "If you want a snowball's chance in hell of walking out of here this morning, drop your weapon now."

"You know that's not going to happen, Sydney. We both know I'm not leaving here alive." He sounded as if the thought had just occurred to him. His voice hitched, as if he were fighting tears.

"You don't know for certain! But I can guarantee you that Silverbirch won't give you a hero's welcome for this, and Inigo's not going to feel too charitable if you don't stop trying to kill us."

A shot pinged off an overhead arc light, spraying glass. "I didn't shoot to kill you, you know that. And I don't *want* to kill you, Sydney." His voice sounded almost plaintive.

She put a reasonable, sympathetic tone back in her voice. "I know that, Ross. If you'd wanted me dead, you had plenty of chances." She frantically cast about for the right thing to say. "Now I'm giving *you* a chance, which is more than Silas gave Kofry, isn't it? You *do* remember Kofry, don't you?"

"That was Talbert's fault! It was payback! Silas said we could do anything with her—"

"Silas got bored with her and threw her away. You must have seen the photos. They chopped her to pieces! What do you think Silas would've done when he got bored with *you*?"

"You don't know anything! He cherished me! He never treated me like a joke, which is more than I can say for you and Pinkerton, and you were supposed to be my mates! He was everything." Bullard was crying now, his voice the anguished, whining plea of a boy. "And that scum killed him like a dog!"

"He was nothing *but* a dog, you fucking gimp!" Elwess shouted over his shoulder. "And I'd shoot him again, Bullard, because that what you do to rabid dogs—you put them down!"

"Shut your everfucking mouth!" Another series of three-round bursts blasted a suitcase into rags and chewed more of the pillar away. Plaster rained down on her and Elwess, and Sydney wondered how long it would take Ross to whittle away at the pillars until they were nothing more than apple cores, exposing them to however many bullets he had left.

"Elwess! Not. Helping," Sydney hissed. She raised her voice. "Ross, listen to me. Put down your weapon, and let this Silas thing go. He was taken out because he was attacking us, and it was either him or me."

She could hear him weeping; it made her want to kill him for being such a whinging little shit. She tried on her most 'I'm-being-patient-but-you-need-to-listen-to-me' voice. "This isn't the Wild West, Ross. There is no 'eye for an eye.' Remember, Silverbirch wanted Silas eliminated as well. You can't run back to them and say sorry. Not after this. Now, Lightoller's on his way, and when he gets here, he'll want to talk to you.

He doesn't want a dead Agent. Your knowledge is very valuable to him. Let's talk to him together."

The room was deathly quiet, as if everyone was waiting for his answer. *Maybe he's actually bought it,* Sydney thought. *If he'll just put down the M4 and I can wing him—*

A woman who had been crouched and whimpering in the corner directly beneath Bullard's position broke cover like a quail. She ran toward the main terminal, a moaning, tearing sound juddering from her in step with her heavy tread. The M4 coughed its deadly message into her broad back. Her companions screamed her name (*"Cynthia!! Oh, God, no, Cynthia!"*), and Sydney watched impotently as the unfortunate Cynthia threw her arms wide and made a sharp, surprised *"Hai!"* sound. She actually took three more running steps, as if rushing forward to embrace a friend, then crashed to the ground. She lay in that hideous, still way that all dead things lay. A spreading pool of red stained the carpet beneath her.

The stark silence was ripped open by the wails of fright, and a lower, moaning sound of grief. This time, when Bullard spoke, he sounded flat and cold. "I may not be in your league as an Agent, Sydney, but I know bullshit when I hear it. Lightoller isn't interested in saving me, and I don't give a fuck about Silverbirch. I never have. All I ever cared about was Silas, and now I'm going to kill the bastard who murdered him."

"Why now?" Elwess demanded. "It's no secret where I live. Why didn't you just ring my doorbell and blow me away when I opened the door?"

"Enough!" Bullard took a deep breath, and Sydney recognised that as well; the long intake of someone who has set their course, and has no intention of deviating from it. "I'm not interested in hearing what you're going to do, Sydney. Here's what *I'm* going to do. I'm giving you thirty seconds. If Talbert doesn't show his ugly face, I'll kill every man, woman and child in this concourse."

Sydney glanced toward the desk Dahlra was crouching behind; it was eclipsed by the same column that sheltered Elwess, and not within Bullard's sightline. While he was not a target, Dahlra had no line of fire to take Ross out, either.

She turned toward Elwess, and their eyes met. "Can he do it?" His expression changed from frightened to a blank, heavy resignation.

"How many more people can he kill before he runs out of bullets?"

"Inigo—"

"Lightoller isn't coming to the rescue and we all know it." Elwess sounded angry and accusatory. He was breathing heavily. "At least, not in time enough to save all these people."

"No, Elwess," Sydney growled warningly, but he had already closed his eyes and was starting to move. A powerful shard of fear stabbed her in the chest. "Wait, for fuck's sake!"

He was panting like a wounded animal. "Ross, if I come out, will you promise—"

"You're not fucking going anywhere!" Even as Elwess moved away from his hiding place, Sydney lunged toward him. Gunfire blasted all around her as she pushed Elwess back into hiding. A screaming meteor slammed into her right side, knocking the breath from her lungs and sending her heart into Megadeath tempo. She felt a hideous crunch against her ribcage as she and Elwess landed back behind the pillar.

With each breath scorching her like inhaled fire, Sydney whipped around the far side of the column, aiming from memory. From behind, she heard Dahlra's gun in duet with her own; a sweet, gunslinger's symphony singing death to their enemies.

The glass wall in front of Bullard shattered, raining down on the civilians below. Ross looked down at his shirt in dazed disbelief as two bright red blooms appeared—one over his collarbone, and one on his upper arm.

Sydney dropped her clip with one hand, frantically fishing out the spare, and prepared to reload, when another series of shots bellowed through the corridor. A third flower blossomed over Bullard's side, near the liver, and a fourth caught him directly in his throat. He made a hideous sound that might have been a name, then coughed, spraying the air with red mist. His eyes clouded, and he fell backwards. The rifle slipped from his fingers, and fell the twenty feet to the floor with a loud, metallic clatter.

The silence was like death itself.

A strong set of hands gripped Sydney's shoulder and dragged her behind the pillar again. She looked up into Dahlra's worried face. Beside him, Elwess held on to her, his expression one of absolute terror. "Oh, God, you've been shot, Sydney—"

"I'm fine." There was a dull ache in her side that felt like it went all the way to China. She caught Elwess' arm and hissed, "Get behind the desk. Do it, Elwess!"

She winced as Dahlra swiftly removed her coat. He was breathing hard, his face pale and sweaty. He looked disheveled and badly shook up, but otherwise unharmed.

He quickly felt against her ribs, and she hissed at his cursory examination. When his fingers found the flattened bullet, he sagged with relief, his voice shaking, "Oh, thank Christ."

"Thank Kevlar." She chuckled, then moaned in pain. "By the way, Tex, fine shootin'. I'm impressed—"

Dahlra's hand closed over her mouth. "That wasn't me. I only shot him in the chest." His eyes darted around as he spoke. "There's someone else in here."

For a moment, they stared at one another. Quietly, she murmured, "Help me up." Dahlra caught her under her arms, and slowly helped her to stand. She bit back a grunt of pain; it hurt to breathe.

Elwess was staring at a point over Sydney's shoulder, his eyes wide with recognition and confusion. "Bloody hell! What are *you* doing here?"

Sydney whirled around, following his gaze, and the entire flying circus went from Monty Python to full-on, League of Gentleman, Poppa Lazarou shit.

"Celia?"

Garnet's Minder was standing alone, several yards away from them. In her hands she held a very similar Glock to Sydney's own; one of the standard Agency-issued weapons, and it was aimed squarely at Sydney's forehead. If Celia decided to shoot again, all the Kevlar in the world would not help.

Moreover, something was distinctly wrong with Celia. Gone was the happy woman Sydney had last seen by Garnet's side. Her eyes were wide and wild; her bright, manic smile looked as if it had been etched on her face with acid. Moreover, she did not look strictly sane.

Sydney put up her hands, still holding her own weapon. "Hey, Ceel." She tried to sound friendly, but she could hear the strain of tension in her own voice. "I have to say I'm really glad you helped me out, but you want to put that gun down? The way you're shaking, it might accidentally go off, yanno?"

Celia shook her head. "I don't want to hurt anyone. I didn't want to hurt Ross. But once I realised what he was planning..." She made a pathetic gesture, as if to say, *a girl's gotta do what a girl's gotta do, right?*

"What are you doing here, Celia? Is Garnet with you?"

"No." Her hands began to shake more noticeably. "Garnet never had *anything* to do with this. I want that made clear. You tell Inigo that Garnet is innocent, Sydney, you *hear* me?" Her voice joined her hands in the shakes department. Christ, she was going to rattle herself apart.

There was a commotion near the mouth of the corridor; Sydney heard a cacophony of familiar voices rising in volume as they approached. With relief, she spotted Inigo and Garnet running toward the area, accompanied by what looked like the rest of the airport security staff and half the Agency. Celia trained the gun toward the entrance to the corridor, and adopted a textbook-perfect stance. "Stay back!" She swiveled the barrel back toward Sydney before she could move. "I don't want to hurt anyone, but I don't want you coming any further."

Garnet skidded to a halt, his homely face confused and alarmed. "Celia? What the hell are you doing? I come home and find this note about—"

"Stay back, Garnet!" Celia seemed to crumple inwardly at the site of his anguished face, but the gun never strayed from its target.

Dahlra's voice, measured but firm, rang out in the corridor. "Everyone, do as she says! That means you as well, Garnet." One by one, they retreated, until Celia and Sydney stood alone.

Now that the fight-or-flight urge had dissipated, Sydney's wounded arm throbbed; each breath hurt to the point of agony. "Look, Ceel, I don't want to be a pussy about this, love, but I really to get my injured ass to hospital. Why don't you let Dahlra and Elwess and me go, okay? Garnet's here now. He can take care of everything."

"No, he can't!" Her eyes narrowed. "I don't care where you and Dahlra go. You can go to hell for all I care." Her eyes flicked to Elwess. "*He* is going to Japan." The gun moved from her to Dahlra. "And *you* are going to stay out of this, or I'll kill you both. I wouldn't want to, you understand. But I will."

"Celia..." Garnet's voice was a harsh moan of grief. It almost shamed Sydney to hear it. "What in God's name is going on, gell?"

"I can do it, too. I'm a good shot." There was twisted note of pride in Celia's voice. "Aren't I, Garnet? As good as Sydney, you said. Didn't you?"

"Why didn't you come to me first, Celia?" Garnet edged closer. "You didn't have to do this—"

"Stop, Garnet, please!" Celia screeched, and he stopped. "I have to make sure Elwess Talbert arrives in Japan. After that..."

"But why you, Ceel?"

Celia nodded toward Elwess. "I've had to be with Ross almost every moment since Silas Markham died to keep him from hunting Talbert down. They thought he was too afraid to do this, not in public. But I knew. I knew he was going to try, today. I had to make sure he didn't, don't you see? You understand, don't you, Sydney?" A hopeful, pleading look slicked over her face.

Sydney shook her head. This was making less sense with every word Celia uttered.

"Celia." Elwess inched closer. His voice was low and soft, and he held his hands up in a gesture of surrender. "Thank you. I'm grateful you saved my life—"

"I don't give a tup'ny fuck about your life!" she cried, breathing hard.

"Then why go through this charade just to make sure Elwess goes to Japan?" From behind Celia, Sydney watched as Garnet and two other agents edged toward her. Celia looked around, her eyes those of a cornered animal, crazed and desperate.

"You don't know what they're like! They showed me the photos of that girl they chopped up—"

"Celia, I would never let anyone do that to you!" Garnet sounded near tears. His gaunt face was as white as parchment. He held out his hands entreatingly. "Whatever they said or threatened you with to make you do this—"

"They have my sister!"

Celia's words echoed like screeching birds, silencing everyone around them. She gave Sydney a pleading look. "I don't want to say what they told me they'd do to her. But they sounded like they were looking forward to it."

She gulped, as if her words were physically hard to swallow. "They promised to send her back alive and well as long as I made sure Elwess Talbert went to Tokyo. When I told them what Ross was planning here, they told me to get rid of him. But he got away from me last night."

She mastered her nerves, choking them down like bad medicine.

When she spoke, her voice was stronger. "I don't know why it's so important that you have to go to Japan, and I don't give a damn about what happens to you when you get there."

Her face lost some of its intensity. "I suppose I don't care what happens to me, either. But my sister is innocent in all this." She shot Elwess a look of pure hatred. "If they want to chop somebody up, let it be him, not our Debbie." She turned back to Sydney. "I'm giving him ten seconds to start walking toward that gate, or I do Sydney. Lightoller?"

A dreadfully long pause weighed down the silence. "Yes?" His voice was death itself.

"Tell them to unlock those doors and give the airport clearance to let him fly. I'll surrender to you as soon as the plane takes off." Celia rapturously closed her eyes, like a child making a wish. "And then I can have my sister back."

"And you honestly think Silverbirch will just release your sister because you forced Elwess onto that plane?"

"It's a simple hostage negotiation, Sydney." The hands holding the gun were steady now. "My sister's life for his."

"Stop all this bollocks! This is insane. I'm going!" A cry of distress rose from the edges of the hall as Elwess strode into Celia's line of sight. He picked up his discarded coat and bag, his face infused with anger. "Fuck this for a game of soldiers." He threw on his coat. "You can piss about all you want playing Mexican standoff, but I'm going to Japan."

"Didn't you just hear what she said? Don't you get it?"

"Don't *you* get it, Sydney? I can't hide behind a bloody column for the rest of my life. Kofry died because of me. People have died here *today* because of me. Hell, Ross Fucking Bullard died because of me." He shook his head. "I'm not going to add you and Dahlra to that list."

He turned to Celia, his expression hard and resolute. "I'll go. But I want your word you'll give yourself up the moment the plane takes off. You hurt one hair on their heads, and all the agents in the world won't keep you *or* your sister safe. I'll bloody well make sure of that."

"I said I will, and I will." Celia sounded coldly calm, now that she was having her way.

Sydney turned to look at Dahlra, but he and Elwess were staring at one another, a silent, dark communion of which she had no part. Anger and helplessness warred in her gut, and glancing at Inigo and Garnet, she saw the same feelings mirrored in their grim, tight faces. "Elwess, please—"

He held up his hand to silence her, but it was to Celia he spoke. "At least let me tell her goodbye."

After a moment, Celia nodded. "First, drop your weapon, Sydney. Put it on the floor and kick it away."

Sydney complied, hating herself. She had never had to relinquish her weapon in a firefight, and the humiliation of it burned worse than the gunshot wound on her arm.

Elwess turned to her. "It's been fun, kitten."

"No. You can't do it. Not like this."

To her surprise, he laughed. "Are you kidding me, girl? Remember what I told you about dark loving dark? I'll be greeted like a hero." He leaned closer, and the cruel, ugly look of triumph on his face actually made her recoil. "I'll bring you back some souvenirs, kitten."

He turned to Inigo, his haughty, arrogant posture firmly nailed back in place. "Tell British Airways I'll be waiting at the gate until they resume the flight. See you when I get back, kids."

He started toward the double doors, head held high, not looking back. Dahlra stepped up beside Sydney. "You're going nowhere, Elwess."

He leveled his gun at Elwess' broad back. The shot was so close Sydney was momentarily deafened. Elwess staggered forward, still clutching the handle of his luggage. As he sank to his knees and collapsed, Celia's scream of rage echoed through the concourse.

"No! Debbie! Debbie!" Garnet grabbed Celia's wrist and wrenched the gun from her grasp. She fought and screamed like a madwoman, even as Garnet wrapped his long arms around her and tried to calm her. "They'll kill her, Garnet! They'll kill my Debbie!"

She turned to Dahlra, her tear-streaked eyes wild and full of spitting fury. "Why? Why didn't you let him go? My sister is dead! You've killed her!" Her voice dissolved into sobbing, wailing screams.

Dahlra looked first at her, then Garnet. His eyes were as hard as flint, his voice was the soft rattle before the strike. "I'm sorry, Celia, but you backed the wrong organisation. Elwess belonged to me, and they can't have him."

He retrieved Sydney's gun, and together they approached Elwess' prone figure. Dahlra knelt beside him. "Looks like it's just not your day to travel, Elwess."

In that split second, when he did not move, Sydney thought, *Oh, shit. Something went wrong. He's really—*

With a groan, Elwess pulled himself up into a sitting position, and Sydney breathed a sigh of relief. "Great fall, Olivier," she said, with a shaky laugh. "For a minute there I thought it was real."

He looked up at them, wincing and rubbing his knee. "I think I jarred every bone in my body."

"That's method acting for you." She turned to Dahlra, and kissed him in a flurry of love and respect. "And congratulations on *your* BAFTA-winning performance. 'He belonged to me, and they can't have him.'" She shook her head, marveling. "You are such a badass."

Elwess grinned up at Dahlra. "Ah, man, when you gave me that nod and told me to start walking, I gotta tell you, I really didn't think that Mission: Impossible shit was gonna fly."

During the previous week, while they discussed worse-case eventualities, faking someone's death had been one of their possible scenarios. As Sydney had quipped, "Well, it had worked once..."

The 'Mission: Impossible shit,' as Elwess had so eloquently called it, had been the last scenario on earth Sydney thought they would ever need to deploy. None of them had ever imagined it would take place on British soil, against one of their own. That it worked was due more to Celia's naiveté than any actual feasibility. As desperate acts went, it was right up there between the sublime and the ridiculous.

Elwess rose to his feet. "I always said you two would be the death of me." He wrapped them in a bear hug that made Sydney's bullet-bruised ribs scream High C. At that moment, she was so proud of both men, she really did not mind the pain all that much.

From over Elwess' shoulder, she spotted Celia and Garnet. Celia had wrapped her arms around her body, as if cradling it. She was weeping more quietly now, and Sydney could hear Garnet's gentle voice as he tried to comfort her. He glanced up and caught Sydney's eye, and gave the three of them a look that was almost as deadly as his aim. He was angry at them all, and she understood, although it hurt to admit it. This was far more serious than the school playground animosity between him and Elwess, worse than the unspoken question of finding her in Brian Collins' arms while her lover fought for his life in hospital. Far, far worse even than the bloodbath they now waded in.

Celia had become the centre of Garnet's life; they shared a bond that went beyond sex, beyond friendship, beyond partnership. *There is no forgiveness for betrayal.* The trouble was, it ran in so many directions from so many sources. Who was actually the betrayer, and who was the betrayed?

As if he could read her thoughts, Garnet shook his head and turned away. There was something final and awful about that singularly nullifying gesture. Sydney realised it would be a long time, if ever, before Garnet truly forgave them for the part they had played in Celia's self-destruct. And as far as her sister was concerned—was her blood on their hands as well?

Dahlra touched her shoulder. "Love, I'm going to have a word with Lightoller and find my bag." He glanced at Elwess. "Keep an eye on her and give me a shout if she grows dizzy or her colour changes."

Together, she and Elwess watched Dahlra as he approached Inigo. The hard plating of battle lust flaked away, leaving Sydney feeling drained and exhausted. Elwess was quiet, but his body thrummed like an engine. She rubbed his back briskly, trying to shake him out of it. "Blimey, Elwess, you are so much more trouble than you're worth sometimes."

He gave her a look that tried to turn into a smile, but it cost too much to manufacture the real thing. "Nothing new, eh? Jesus. You couldn't make this shit up if you tried."

"Well, it's going to be a long time before Gatwick will trust us with their airport again." Sydney looked around the abattoir of a concourse. God, what a mess. The St Johns paramedics arrived, and were making their way amidst the walking wounded. The dead gunmen and their victims were already being bagged and tagged, their families whisked away to private rooms and hospitals.

For a moment, Elwess seemed to sag against her. "Thank you for saving my life. I don't know what going through my mind when I told Ross—"

"I thought that was when you and Dahlra decided to-"

"I wasn't even *thinking* about faking my death at that point. I had totally forgotten about anything but how fucking scared I was. I was just ready to give up."

Sydney rubbed his back soothingly. "It's alright. I understand. Just giving up and giving in, because you can't see any other resolution. I've seen it happen before. It's like that book, you know—Watership Down? The rabbits called it 'going tharn.'"

She touched his sweaty face. "We'll ask for the family discount at our next counseling session with Ted Browning. He's a good man to talk to about a bad situation. It'll help, I promise."

Elwess embraced her tightly, gripping her arm right at ground zero. Sydney cursed, the pain sending her reeling, and he pulled away with a hiss. "Ah, fuck, Sydney, I'm sorry!" He brought his hand away, sticky and red. "Dahlra, she's really bleeding here." His voice was almost accusatory.

"She's *been* bleeding, you prat." Dahlra glanced around the room, his eyes full of conflict. "Under any other circumstance, I'd send you on to hospital with Elwess. It doesn't feel right, leaving all these wounded people behind. They need a doctor.

"But I want to get those ribs x-rayed as soon as possible. If one has broken near a lung, we'll need to get you immobilised. And I'm still concerned about the possibility of shock."

He retrieved his physician's bag and led them over to the desk. "Inigo has taken over the cleanup. He wants us out of here." He cut away Sydney's bloody sleeve, examining the wound, then cleaning it with saline. She tried to be tough about it, but could not hold back her growl of pain.

"Damn! That hurts worse than being shot. Stop digging for gold in there."

"This won't take long. Be brave."

"Alright, but there better be recompense. A lolly isn't going to cut it this time, Doctor Evil."

"It looks like the bullet only grazed your bicep." Dahlra was talking in that faintly distant voice doctors use when having too much fun rooting around in your anatomy. "You've bled a bit, but the wound is clean." He bound her arm with gauze and surgical tape. "A few stitches and you'll be right as the jolly old. Now aren't you glad I insisted we get tetanus jabs last spring?"

Then he gave her one of those looks that both jazzed her up and made her feel like Wonder Woman. "You were amazing." He took her face in his hands and kissed her very gently. "But fun and games will have to wait."

As he spoke, a fresh fleet of St John's paramedics arrived, wheeling in gurneys to transport the wounded and the dead. This seemed to mollify him somewhat. "Elwess, give us a hand while I call for a car. It's going to take an age to get out of here as it is."

Together they rounded up their scattered belongings, sorting their baggage from the heaps of suitcases that had been abandoned and damaged in the melee. Sydney glanced around tiredly. Inigo was conferring with a man who had to be Gatwick's security chief; she could spot retired Old Bill anywhere.

Being the Agency person she was, Sydney found herself wondering how Inigo would spin this for damage limitation. If she was a betting person, she would wager that every phone and camera in Gatwick North was being checked for incriminating photos right now, and even as she sat there, the media was being ushered into a room somewhere for the biggest bullshit Press Conference that Inigo could manufacture.

The area had taken on the gruesome unreality of a film set. The room was a shambles; police, Agency men and airport security were swarming everywhere, questioning civilians draped in blankets, sipping cups of tea. At the thought of a big ceramic mug, filled with Yorkshire gold and three sugars, Sydney sighed wistfully. The Brits got a lot of things right, and hearty, strong tea with milk and sugar was one of them. At that moment, it sounded like the best medicine imaginable.

Her emotions flatlined as the pain of her injuries spiked, and the dull melancholy that always followed a firefight settled in her bones like old lead. One of her fellow agents was dead; her partner of ten years would never fully trust her again. She had been given a choice, and she had chosen Elwess. In all likelihood, Garnet would never forgive her for it, either. That hurt almost as much as her cracked ribs. After all they had been through, she wished things could have played out differently, but at the moment, she had no idea how to fix it.

Grinding fatigue pressed down on her like a steamroller. *In a few days*, she told herself, *you'll feel a little depressed, but that just means the shock's wearing off.* She always used that line on the civvies; it was as good advice as any.

Across the corridor, Garnet stood talking to Celia. He was looking down at her with all the loving gentleness of a parent trying to comfort a hurting child. Inigo beckoned to him, and he reluctantly left Celia's side. She raised her miserable eyes and met Sydney's; she looked small and forlorn and alone. For a moment the two women simply stared at one another—each hurting, each sorrowful.

Then Celia raised her eyes to the balcony above, and her expression turned to pleading. She gave an almost imperceptible shake of her head, and mouthed an emphatic, beseeching, "No." Tears welled in her eyes, and in them Sydney could see dull, bottomless acceptance. Ross Bullard had worn that same expression; so had Elwess. It was the look of someone who had given everything, and it was not enough. *Going tharn*, Sydney thought tiredly, then, with dawning horror, her heart revved up to hyperspeed. *Going tharn!*

She looked around frantically, following Celia's line of sight up to the people lining the railings on the upper balcony, their morbid curiosity drawing them to the horror show below. Among them was a short, dumpy, middle-aged woman with coarse, black hair and olive skin. She wore a Gatwick maintenance uniform, a cleaner's cart by her side. She was gazing down at the wreckage below without a flicker of interest. As Sydney watched, she reached into her pocket, and retrieved a small flat, square device.

Celia must have seen it, too. Her expression dissolved into one of panic and terror. She stumbled back, her arms outstretched in surrender. "No don't! Please, I did everything you asked—"

Her pain forgotten, Sydney leapt to her feet. "Move, everybody, move! Dahlra, get down—"

The explosives strapped to Celia's midsection detonated, and the blast threw Sydney back several feet, slamming her into a row of discarded chairs. The glass balcony shattered, raining down shards on all the luckless souls still in the vicinity.

Sydney was dimly aware of the rubble falling around her, and the coppery scent of blood in her nostrils. She opened her burning eyes, but all the colours were reversed, like a negative of a photograph. She saw a ball of weirdly-coloured fire in the spot where Celia had stood. *Connnncusssssion!* she thought, and in her mind the word was sludgy and warped.

The world became a silent film of hell; Sydney could hear nothing but a high-pitched, distant whine. She tried to rise, but a boulder was holding her down. She was breathing lungfuls of acrid smoke, and each breath brought a new agony worse than the one before. She moved her head, and caught the grisly sight of a severed limb, smoldering and bloody, some six feet away from her face. Nearby, a discarded shoe was lying on its side.

Something about that shoe worried at her. Sydney made the super-human effort to focus her eyes and think. It was black, a Hermes Chelsea boot made of fine leather, covered in dark, sticky blood. Recognition dawned, and it ripped consciousness away from her body, just as the blast had torn Dahlra's shoe from his.

CHAPTER SEVENTEEN

Goodnight, Sweetheart

Sydney walked into the bedroom, her gait slow and stiff. She paused by the dresser mirror and caught a glimpse of herself. The tiny nicks and cuts on her face were fading, and her wounded arm in its sling already carried the maddening itch of healing deep within its tissues. Her eyes were still faintly bloodshot, their expression dull and flat. She looked and felt mobile enough to be grateful for being alive, and banged up enough to feel good and sorry for herself. Her hearing was still muffled, but she had been assured her ears would fully recover from the blast.

She crossed the room over to the oak wardrobe that took pride of place in the corner. It was a massive, dignified sarcophagus of a thing, a family heirloom heavily carved and redolent with the smells of age and old money. As she pushed it open it gave a low, protesting creak; her broken ribs answered in painful harmony.

Listlessly, she sifted through her wardrobe. She was surprisingly spoiled for choice. How many black dresses did one woman need? The long-sleeved gabardine was too big for her now. The empire-waisted crepe was never her type. The wool one made her itch if she wore it for more than an hour. The fourth was horrifically dated, New Romantic all the way, complete with a high, stiff collar and shoulder pads. Why the hell had she kept that one all these years?

Pausing at the fifth and final one, Sydney ran her fingers over the bodice. It was the little black silk she had last worn to Inigo's house the night they reconciled with Elwess. A shame it was sleeveless; too summery for September. It would not be appropriate.

And today, of all days, it was important to wear the right thing, to *do* the right thing. Her mind fretted and worried around the decision, circling it over and over like a needle on a skipping record. *Life is pretty messed up when you can't even decide what to wear.*

She tried to clear her head of its nagging, looping and ultimately pointless dilemma, when she spied Dahlra's long coat. It hung at the far end of the wardrobe, straight and formal, as if standing to attention. It was made of fine wool; so black it made her black dresses look charcoal grey. *This* garment looked right at home in the Narnia wardrobe; it was elegant and classy, like its owner, as if it had every right to be here. As if it, too, understood the importance of Doing The Right Thing.

She grasped the coat, pressing her face against the rich fabric. She could smell the lovely scent of him, could almost feel the warmth of his body, as if the coat held a part of him in reserve. God, Sydney loved that black coat...

Her eyes widened and she clutched at the arms like a child grasping for her father's hands. Black coat. Black dress. Funeral. It was as if her mind had been tucking all this away, hiding it, and now it was back with a vengeance, bringing with it all her guilt and unhappiness. She had to attend the funeral of a friend.

God, that sounded so bloodless and superficial. All that time spent together—was that all it added up to—friend? And was that what she was to him? Did downgrading herself to 'friend' make it any easier to live with?

We did the right thing we had to make her drop the gun we couldn't let Elwess on that plane after all that had happened I failed I'm sorry about her sister I failed I'm sorry I failed I'm so fucking sorry—

"Shut up," she whispered to herself. *People die, and those that love them have to be brave enough to go through this ghoulish ceremony to show their respect. And if you have one shred of self-worth, you'll put him in his proper place, girl.*

Sydney's stomach gave a lurch, and for a moment she was sure she was going to be sick. She quickly closed the wardrobe door and leaned against it until her nausea finally passed. She wheeled away and groped for the bed, breathing so heavily her broken ribs flared and prodded her with their insistent, dull ache. She half sat, half fell onto the mattress, earning another jarring, breath-stealing wrench of pain, and waited for her emotions to flood her heart and finally spill over. She desperately needed to vent and rant and plead and grieve and weep, but the emotions bled away into nothingness.

Either her shock was one deep, long trench, or she had not quite started on her journey yet. While the occasional flashback jumped out at her from around whatever crazy angle her head was currently travelling, none of them had the power to loosen her emotional release valve. She was tired, so tired she felt as if she could sleep for centuries, but that would not happen any time soon, either. Sleep had been a bit of a wash lately, to be honest.

In her thin dreams, she kept reliving that awful morning in Gatwick. She kept seeing Pink, meeting her eyes from across the corridor, his face hard with betrayal and anger and hurt. Sydney knew he had understood what she and Dahlra had done for their friend and lover; hell, he would have done the same thing in their place.

But the short rations of grudging acceptance could never fill the belly like the truer, richer feast of forgiveness, and now she could nourish herself with neither. When that anonymous cleaner pressed the button on that little black detonator, she had taken more than lives that day. She had taken Sydney's redemption.

She sensed movement before she actually saw it, and glanced up as Dahlra entered the room. He, too looked bruised and battered, but thankfully, wonderfully alive. He was tired and dispirited, and more than once, they had sat up all night together, unable, perhaps unwilling, to go to sleep. He had attended six funerals in five days, though, and the strain was starting to show. His clean-shaven face was still too pale; his hair, which had been black at the beginning of summer, now showed startling amounts of silver, especially around the temples.

Silently, Sydney held out her one good arm to him. *Come here to me, Dahlra Gar*, she thought. *You're the doctor; heal me, like you have over and over.*

Wordlessly, he crossed to the bed and sat down beside her. With solemn tenderness, he cupped her face and kissed her. "Is it the pain, sweet girl?"

The loving words warmed her, tried to melt that solid ball of ice in her heart, and it strained to break free from its sterile prison. She wanted to tell him that she felt like a ship, locked in a frozen sea, unable to move or navigate, but that sounded so melodramatic and naff she could not make herself utter the words. With renewed frustration she realised that even Dahlra's deep, abiding sweetness was not enough to pull her tears from their wasteland. They only served as a reminder of what she was not able to cry over. Maybe she *had* cleaned house a little too well; maybe nothing was left.

"I'm fine, love." Her voice still sounded hollow and internal to her damaged ears. He looked dubious, but he did not challenge her. Instead he took her hand, checking her pulse. She tried to sit up, but the strained muscles banding her ribs protested, and she gasped unwillingly. "But I'm sick of not being able to move without groaning like an old woman."

"Give it time. You're healthy and strong. It won't be long before you're as good as new. But for now, you have to be careful. Doctor's orders." He kissed the tip of her nose and smiled down at her. "In the meantime, I don't minding giving you a lift." With the long practice and ease of working with fragile patients, he gently slid his arms beneath hers, hooked his hands around her back, and pulled her upright. Wearily, she laid her head against his shoulder, and he held her close. His arms were safe and solid and she wanted to stay there forever.

"I wish you would tell me how I can help." His warm lips nuzzled soothingly against her neck. Even with only partial hearing, Sydney could hear the sadness and concern in his voice, but it only fueled that feeling of failure.

"You could help me find something to wear. I've been staring at the wardrobe, hoping the right thing would jump out and dress me, but nothing is cooperating."

"How rude of them." He gave her a smile. "I'll have a word with the wardrobe fairy at the earliest opportunity."

He eschewed the many black choices, and instead picked a hunter green Lanvin with long sleeves and a modest neckline. He helped her dress with quiet efficiency, straightening a hem here, smoothing a seam there. It was a deeply personal and benevolent act, and required no action on her part other than to just stand there and let him clothe her.

As she stepped into a pair of heels, he placed his warm hands on her shoulders and gently turned her toward him. His smile was tender. "There. You look lovely. My brave girl." The respect and love and surety of this fine man staggered her with bleak gratitude. He had been through so much because of her, yet still thought her worthy of his constant, deep love.

He swept his thumb across her cheek, as if to wipe away a tear. "You don't have to do this, you know."

"I know I don't. But I do, really." She looked into his eyes and found the understanding she sought so desperately.

"Yes. I suppose, at the end of the day, you do. Just remember, I'm here."

His words reverberated in her mind like a prayer, and once again she had the sudden feeling beneath her ribs that he had at last tripped the tumblers that would end this strange emotional paralysis. And once again, the feeling ebbed away before she could grasp it.

Dahlra's here. "I wish I was," she whispered, and leaned against him.

He stayed with her, steady and patient, until she felt strong enough to go on.

In so many ways, they had been very lucky.

There had been perhaps three or four seconds between Sydney's shout of warning and the moment the explosives strapped around Celia's waist actually detonated. The forward blast killed ten first responders; counted among them were Gatwick Security Police, St John's Ambulance paramedics and Agency men. Sydney could not recall how many civilians had been killed or wounded. This troubled her; she had always been careful to remember and honour those who had died on her watch.

She had been heading toward the desk Dahlra had used during the firefight, when a large, warm hand of air gave her a mighty shove, crashing her into the row of chairs. She received a concussion and a collapsed lung. So she was lucky.

Dahlra had been the farthest away from Celia. At Sydney's cry of alarm, he had instinctively dove behind the desk. He consequently suffered only minor injuries from flying debris; he too had been extremely lucky.

Elwess was standing closer to Celia, but he was also on the run when the blast knocked him off his feet and hurled him into the back of the descending end of the concourse. A flying chunk of the pillar which, ironically, had been his shield during the initial attack, caught his foot literally while in midair, breaking the ankle in three places. It had been his boot Sydney had seen lying on the floor, the ones just like Dahlra's, which Elwess had so admired and later purchased for himself.

Inigo had also been close to the explosion, but had reacted with a speed that only the truly self-preserving can produce. He was thrown sideways by a St John's paramedic caught in the forward momentum of the blast, and suffered a compound fracture of his left forearm. Sydney had been unconscious and therefore was mercifully spared Inigo's scream of pain as Dahlra pushed the splintered bone back under the skin. Inigo's quick reflexes had saved his life and that had been lucky. Sadly, the same could not be said for his human shield.

All of them had been temporarily deafened, but everyone's hearing was coming back online.

Garnet had reacted to Sydney's warning with the speed and timing of a true hero. Witnesses reported that, rather than running away, he had thrown his arms around Celia, around certain death. Pink, who would never have been at the airport at all that morning, except that his Minder's fingerprints had been found at Markham's flat, and her note of confession in theirs, had probably saved them all from being killed. He and Celia had later been identified by dental records.

Acting as representatives of the Agency, Dahlra and Inigo, the two least injured in the explosion, attended all the funerals of the victims. Today's would mark the last.

Inigo had done a chillingly good job of collateral damage control, blaming the bombing on that convenient bugbear 'Domestic Terrorism,' and scattering the seeds of recrimination in so many directions, it had taken days for the press to realise they were chasing leads that did not even exist. Sydney had seen him do it before, but it still made her feel sick to watch him manipulate and massage the facts with such consummate skill. Not for the first time she was glad Lightoller had no interest in throwing his hat into the political ring. God help them all if he ever decided to run for office.

It had been Inigo who had used the phrases 'incredibly fortunate' and 'could have been much, much worse' over and over, mainly in relation to the ease in turning the entire incident into something that had nothing to do with his Agency and everything to do with Silverbirch.

Later, during the confidential debriefing, Inigo had revealed that both Ross Bullard's and Celia's fingerprints had been found in Silas' house, along with a series of horrific trophy photos implicating Silas and Bullard in Kofryna Urbonienė's murder. All but one of Ross' accomplices had been two-bit hustlers he had hired from various anarchist-based internet chat rooms. They were amateur, weekend warrior-types with delusions of sensationalistic glory.

The last was a disgruntled former Gatwick employee with more grudge than brains. He had stolen the security codes than had enabled them all to enter the airport undetected. They had only been ballast; Bullard had never meant for any of them to leave Gatwick alive. There was no one in the Gatwick maintenance department fitting the description of the cleaner Sydney had seen with the detonator. She was a truly unknown quantity; no one could remember seeing her enter or leave the airport.

In their own debriefing, Inigo pressed the dossier into her hands. "Ross' involvement with Markham doesn't make for pleasant reading. Disturbing at best, pathetic at worst. Perhaps it will help you understand what happened." He grimaced. "I had always known Ross wasn't the most sterling of agents, but as God is my witness, I never suspected he was the mole. I never gave him credit for being intelligent enough. There was even a time when I suspected..."

"Don't say it. Don't even think it, Inigo." A quick flash of anger made Sydney's injuries harmonise like a choir of the damned. "Not after this."

"No. Not now." Inigo gave Sydney a look that mirrored her own miserable feeling of helplessness. "I think I'm getting too old for this game, old girl."

After listening to the song and dance Inigo had played for the spin doctors, Sydney found she did not have the stomach to indulge his self-pitying bullshit. "Fight your own demons, Inigo. I've only just finished killing off the last batch you saddled me with."

He glanced at Dahlra, but did not quite meet his eyes. "I know." He indicated the file. "Keep it. Put it away for now. There will come a day when you will want to know why this happened. When you will *need* to know."

Sydney did not reply. She did not care. As far as she was concerned, Silas and his fuck buddy Ross Bullard had killed Garnet and Celia as surely as if they had detonated the explosives themselves. If her own finger was on the button as well, she would have to answer for it sometime in the future.

But she could not do it now.

They entered the courtyard of All Saints Church in Carshalton in the late afternoon. Autumn leaves drifted down around them, but the sun managed a weak appearance, dappling the tiny graveyard with soft light.

Dahlra quietly propelled her toward the arched doorway.

Just ahead, they saw Inigo and Pip Lightoller entering the church; as they disappeared into the shadows inside, Inigo put his uninjured arm around his wife, and she leaned against him. Sydney and Dahlra joined them, sitting beside them on one of the church's pews. Pip, ever soft-hearted and caring, accepted Dahlra's kiss on her cheek, and took Sydney's hand.

"My darling, I don't have the words. I know how much you and Garnet meant to one another. Such a fine man. And poor, poor Celia." She dabbed at her eyes with a linen handkerchief in a vain effort to control her emotions. "I've just come from visiting Garnet's mother. The poor dear simply collapsed at the news. Her doctor forbade her to come to the funeral. Can you imagine it, Sydney dear? Having to bury your own child."

"I can't, Pip," replied Sydney, dry-eyed.

"She was always so terribly proud of him. Proud of you both. She's absolutely devastated, but bless her, she was asking after you. I promised her you and I would stop round next week and visit with her. I know it would comfort her. She's such a lovely woman."

"Yes, she is." She wondered what Pip would say if she told her she would rather eat her Glock than look Garnet's mum in the eye and explain the part she had played in his death. No, she envied Ma Pinkerton, the ease in which she immersed herself in her grief. Sydney was starting to worry that something was fundamentally wrong; perhaps the concussion had shuffled her brains like a deck of cards, and one had fallen out of the pack. There had to be some rational explanation for this lack of emotion. There *had* to be.

Somewhere in the small congregation, Sydney could hear the sound of weeping. Her throat was dry, so dry she could barely swallow. She glanced up at Dahlra, who squeezed her hand. "Hold on, my love. It will be over soon."

"Will it?" Her whisper sounded harsh to her own muffled ears.

At the front of the church, a small box sat on the bier, surrounded by flowers. Beside it was a colour photo of Garnet as a smiling young man in his late twenties, carelessly leaning over the railing in front of the old shell grotto in Carshalton Park. He was wearing a black suit that managed to look both too large and too short for his long, lanky frame. *I'm like Tommy flippin' Cooper here*, he had bemoaned.

It was the day they had received their first commendation from the Agency. Pink had been as good as his word; she was family now. His parents had taken them out for lunch at the local Harvester to celebrate, and it had taken forever to get him to stop clowning around long enough for his dad to take that photo.

It was painful to recall those halcyon days, when they were dangerous young gunslingers, high on adrenaline and convinced they would live forever. Pink had been more than her partner, and that had been her privilege. They had made a pact, long ago, sealed in the blood of the righteous and wicked alike. For his sake, Sydney would own the part she had played in this dirtiest of all endgames.

A plump vicar approached the bier and gazed out into the congregation. "My dear friends, on behalf of the family, I want to thank you for being here on this saddest of days. To all of us who knew and loved Garnet best, I hope you will remember him as a man who personified the words 'loyalty' and 'duty.' A man who loved very deeply, and whom he loved, he protected at all costs. He was a hero, who made the ultimate sacrifice, doing what he did best: keeping safe those he loved, the only way he knew how."

He looked down at the photo, then to the box beside it, as if they all needed reminding its contents were all that was left of that smiling, gangly boy in Carshalton Park.

"I would like to tell you my favourite story about Garnet. I was speaking to him at his grandmother's funeral some years back. The talk turned to the afterlife, and Garnet said, 'Vicar, do you think heaven is really full of angels flapping around, playing those little harps and people prancing on clouds? Because I think I'll give that heaven a miss.

"Heaven should be like your local that never closes, and every time you go in, all your friends are there, laughing and drinking and telling jokes. The sun's always shining in the beer garden, and we can watch the footie all day long on a big screen telly. Oh, and Chelsea always wins the Premiership.'"

This brought a round of bittersweet laughter. Garnet's loyalty to Chelsea Football Club was legendary.

The vicar continued, "So, this afternoon, when you meet to raise a glass to Garnet Pinkerton, I want you to picture him in that great heavenly Local, holding court in the beer garden, where the sun is always shining, cheering at the footy, and waiting for all of us to join him."

Sydney glanced up at Dahlra, who stared ahead, unsmiling. This moment was between him and Pink, a place where she could not follow. Still, she knew what he was thinking: there would be no more boisterous, laughter-and-lager-fueled Match of the Day afternoons, cheering on The Blues with Garnet.

The vicar looked down at Sydney with a little nod. She rose and slowly walked toward the front of the church.

As she faced the congregation, she thought, *Oh, Pink, I don't think I can do this. Not even for you.* She focused on Dahlra's handsome face, looking back at her from the sea of mourners. His eyes were swimming with unshed tears, but even so, she sensed his pride in her.

It all came back to Doing The Right Thing, did it not? Other than to watch his back, this was the only favour Garnet had ever really asked of her.

"I like hearing you sing, Syd. I want you to sing at me funeral."

"Yeah, right. And how will you know if I don't?"

"Oh, I'll know, mate. I'll know. And if you don't, me ol' china, I'll come back an' haunt ya."

Vintage Garnet, that was; hyper and full of bad jokes and football chants when off duty, focused and cool when engaged. So loyal and alive and vital and tough...

And gone.

"My back to yours, Pink," she whispered hoarsely. "My back to yours." Yes, she would honour him, this final time, in the only way that she could. Last time counts for all, as her dad used to say.

From somewhere above, the dignified strains of organ music rose in the air, as familiar and comforting as a child's lullaby. Sydney faced the congregation and sang her final gift to Garnet Pinkerton.

"Amazing grace, how sweet the sound, that saved a wretch like me,
I once was lost, but now I'm found, 'twas blind, but now I see....

"T'was grace that taught my heart to fear, and grace my fears relieved,
How precious did that grace appear, the hour I first believed.

"Through many dangers, toils and snares, I have already come,

T'was grace that brought me safe thus far, and grace will lead me home..."

Her voice faltered. *My grace has been taken away. I didn't have your back. I couldn't protect you from the dangers we had to face. And in the end, I couldn't have saved you, because I loved Elwess too much to sacrifice him.*

It's not fair, Pink, she thought miserably. *I'm singing your song, and you're haunting me anyway.*

For Dahlra, it had been a terrible ordeal of pain and loss, and he felt a weariness deep down in his bones. He was honest enough with himself to call it what it was: an exhaustion of the spirit, a deep sorrow of the soul. He did not have many close personal friends, and today he had bid farewell to one of the best of them. In the early days of his Mindership, Garnet had sometimes acted as a buffer between Dahlra's duty and Sydney's mistrust. Later, they shared a comradeship outside their mutual love for Sydney; it was a bond he shared with no one else, even Elwess.

And as sad as Dahlra was, he was more worried about Sydney. The funeral was the culmination of this protracted period of grief, and he hoped that she would find her own way out of the numbed box that had closed around her. He could see the emotions simmering deep within, like a pressure cooker ready to explode, but her inability to release them was both unnatural and unhealthy.

It was a dilemma that would cause him many sleepless nights. It would also eventually lead to an altercation that would change everything as they knew it, and forge an alliance that would both strengthen them and place them in mortal danger.

Beside the church was a tiny little pub called The Woodman. It was the Pinkerton family local, and today it was full of solemn, quiet people paying their last respects. At one of the tables, Dahlra saw Lightoller lean down to say something to his wife, who nodded and headed toward Sydney. Lightoller approached him, holding a drink of what appeared to be whisky.

"How's the arm, Inigo?"

"Bally uncomfortable, as you well know. Thankfully I'm well medicated." He took a drink, grimacing at the burn. "Dahlra, I realise this isn't exactly the time and place, but I wanted to fill you in a bit."

"You're right, Inigo. It *isn't* the time or the place."

"I know that Sydney doesn't want to discuss Silverbirch—"

"We've discussed it, Inigo. But at the present time, my job is to make sure she is healthy and happy, and she is currently neither."

Lightoller looked away tensely, and Dahlra decided to take pity on him. "I haven't discouraged her from returning, if that's what you wish to know. There's a lot of unfinished business between Elwess and Silverbirch. We both want to see it to its conclusion."

"We dealt them a blow."

"We only squared the pitch. And even then, the cost was too great." Lightoller took another drink. "I know."

"Tell me something, Inigo, and try to tell the truth. Do you have any idea just how much Silverbirch knows?"

"No." Something in his glum tone convinced Dahlra to believe him. "But I will tell you this. I was going to explain it all when you returned from Japan:

"You may remember me saying that we received an incident report from a minicab driver while we were investigating the Urbonienė murder."

"The one you said was a hoax?"

"That was what we originally believed. The driver had been dispatched to courier what he was told was a mannequin from Croydon to North London."

"A mannequin?"

"One of those sex dolls, I believe. It was covered head to toe in PVC." Inigo's face creased with disdain. "On route, this doll, mannequin, what have you, apparently came alive. It was choking, foaming at the mouth, and consequently fell unconscious just as the driver arrived at his destination. It was taken from his cab, and he was paid rather handsomely to keep his mouth shut."

"Did it not occur to him that this person might need a doctor?"

"The driver thought the whole incident was one big April fool prank. It was only later, when we questioned the minicab office the second time, that he came forward, realising he may have been involved in Kofry Urbonienė's disappearance."

"What an idiot!"

"Most minicab drivers are not hired for their intellect, Dahlra. At any rate, both the pickup and drop-off addresses were cleaned out by the time we arrived. Forensics found DNA in both flats and the cab, but it didn't match Urbonienė's, nor any other missing persons on file. And since there was no *corpus delicti*, we considered that it may well have been a prank."

He took a sip of his whisky. "Celia White's sister Debra was abducted from her home on March 28th. The timing of her disappearance correlates the driver's testimony, and we have since verified the DNA match as hers, based on the sample from Celia's Agency file."

"Was Debra still alive when he dropped her off?"

"The cabbie thought so."

"So Debra White goes missing from her mother's home in Bolton and ends up down south. Then Silverbirch uses Celia as insurance in case Elwess needs a bit of persuasion to meet them in Japan. She's given further incentive to succeed by forcing her to wear explosives. If she fails, everyone dies..."

It was like looking at the seven disparate Scrabble tiles on the tray. Nothing made sense at first; then the word was there, all along, if one only moved the letters in the right order. Understanding hit Dahlra with the force of a sledgehammer. "You knew. You knew about Celia's sister all along. You knew the minute you got her DNA sample."

Inigo sighed. "I confronted Celia with the information. Silverbirch had already contacted her. She agreed to work for me as well. I thought I had *my* mole at last."

"You heartless bastard!" It took all of Dahlra's self-control not to punch Inigo's perfect veneers down his throat. "So you told her to play double with Silverbirch. That's why you didn't bring Garnet in. You wanted to keep her blind, in case they turned her. And lo and behold, they did."

Inigo nodded. "I instructed Celia to tell Garnet her mother was ill, and she was needed to care for her. She was absent from their home quite a bit during the past few months. I thought she was gathering information and sniffing out the mole. Instead, Silverbirch was using her to keep both Bullard hidden from me and Elwess in line. That is, until they caught wind of Bullard's vendetta. In addition to threatening her with her sister, they made Celia blackmail Ross should he attempt to harm Elwess in any way. She stated all of this in her note of confession.

"Of course, when Ross found out I was sending Elwess to Japan to meet with their Controller, he saw it as his opportunity to kill him." Inigo waved his hand with dismissive contempt. "He had no intention of surviving the attack. Celia followed him to Gatwick. She was told to stop him, and at the same time make sure Elwess got on the plane."

"But she didn't tell you any of this, did she?"

Inigo's tone was as dull as ash. "Of course, we had no way of knowing all this until Garnet found her confession. She wrote it after they forced her to wear the explosives. Had she trusted me, perhaps she and Garnet would still be alive."

He sniffed. "Such a waste of a keen operative. Look how she kept all those plates spinning right under our noses! She could have been such an asset as a double."

Dahlra's already-fragile respect for Lightoller frayed down to a single thread. "And her sister? Do you know if she's still alive?"

"Afraid not."

"Now that you've lost your mole, you don't really care, do you?"

"Of course I do!" Lightoller's eyes flashed with real anger.

I'll just bet you do. "What about Elwess? Is he still in danger?"

"I'm not entirely convinced he ever was. But I will admit you were right, old man. Upon sober reflection, I agree sending you to Tokyo was, what did you call it? A 'Hail Mary?' I should have listened to you."

Dahlra turned his back to Sydney, lest she spot him and clock the anger that blazed into his chest like a hot spear. His words dripped from his tongue with all the acid he could muster. "Well, I must say that *is* a relief to be able to say, 'I told you so', Principal. I'm sure Elwess would have welcomed that bit of good news when he was staring down Ross Bullard's crosshairs—not to mention running for his life from Celia, the suicide bomber. And we haven't even touched on all those innocent people who never walked out of Gatwick alive. They must be as relieved as I am. All that needless worry for nothing."

"You make it sound as if I planned all this!"

"Didn't you? You can't give someone enough rope to hang themselves and then act surprised when you see the noose swinging—"

Dahlra paused. This cross and double-cross business was giving him a headache. "Have you been looking at this all wrong, Inigo? Have you confused cause with effect?"

"What do you mean?"

"By the time Celia's sister was taken, Silas was already a liability. We know Bullard had been his creature for a long time, perhaps as long as he was a mole for Silverbirch. Odds are Silas was the *reason* he became the mole."

All the Scrabble tiles were falling into place now. "Elwess actually asked Ross why he had chosen such a public place to kill him. Why he hadn't just knocked on his front door and blown him away, and Bullard didn't answer. This was a suicide mission. He said as much. Maybe he thought Silverbirch's controller was planning on killing Elwess himself. He would have told them he planned to revenge Silas. Maybe he thought he was saving them the trouble." He stopped. Was his logic just traveling in a circle?

What little colour remained in Lightoller's face drained away, until he looked ill. "Celia wasn't there just to make sure Elwess got on the plane." He turned his bleak eyes away. "She must have thought they would spare her and her sister. Why else would she have trusted them and not me? But this Lorcan fellow must have realised Bullard and Celia were close to cracking. And once Elwess was on the plane, she became surplus to requirements."

Dahlra pinched the bridge of his nose. His headache was ratcheting up exponentially. "None of us were supposed to leave Gatwick alive. Not even Elwess. Well, congratulations, Inigo. You not only lost the chance to turn one mole, but you managed to create another one. This Lorcan fellow must be laughing loud enough to be heard in China. Bravo, for doing Silverbirch's dirty work for them."

Dahlra did not bother to hide his anger now. "And you still think we were never really in danger? You and this Lorcan character are just as cold-blooded as one another."

When Lightoller did not reply, Dahlra pressed on. "And what about Garnet? Did he know you betrayed him?"

"I was protecting him!"

"Potato, potahto. Did. He. Know?"

Lightoller drained his glass; he looked as if he could really use another. "I don't know. I think he might have suspected. Near the end. I don't know."

"And let me guess: you'd prefer me to keep this sordid little fable from Sydney as well? Because it wouldn't do, seeing her Principal in such weak light, now, would it?"

Lightoller stared stonily down at the floor. His voice was tight with angry resignation. "What do you want of me, Dahlra?"

"Oh, I've got a list, Inigo."

"While I'm feeling generous, then."

"I want you to send your top surveillance team to Windsor. There, they will install the best security system the Agency's blood money can buy. I want Maidenvine so buttoned down, no one, even you, can consider entering without at least ten trusted people knowing about it. I want to live in a fortress where I can keep Sydney and Elwess safe."

"You do realise they will have to leave there eventually. You'll have to do some shopping now and then."

"Look me in the eye and tell me Silverbirch isn't a potential threat to my family, Inigo. And try to at least *sound* sincere."

Lightoller briefly met his gaze, but could not hold it. "Alright. You shall have your fortress. It's a large estate; it will probably take two weeks to finish."

"You have one."

"I'm not a miracle worker!"

Dahlra smiled coldly. "I want it done and I want it done quickly. Put more men on it if you have to, but the longer they're around, the more questions get asked. We had a deal, Inigo. I held up my side of it, and there's still the matter of Elwess and Japan, isn't there? Don't go cheap on me."

For a moment he thought he had pushed too hard, and Lightoller would just walk away without a word. Finally, he huffed in defeat. "Alright. We had an agreement, after all. A week it is." His eyelids fluttered for a moment, as if he was trying to curb his temper. "Is there anything else you want to squeeze from me while I've got out my pocketbook, old cock?"

"One or two more things, but I have other matters to attend to now. I'll call you on Friday with the particulars. In the meantime, it's getting late, and we've miles to go, *old cock*." Dahlra held out his hand. "Thank you, Inigo."

For a moment he seemed to consider not taking it. Finally he shook Dahlra's hand. "You can be a stubborn bastard when the need arises, Gar."

"When it comes to my family, I can, and I am, Inigo."

Dahlra watched as Lightoller made his way back toward his wife, then caught Sydney's eye. With a glance toward the door, he raised his brow in question. She nodded gratefully, and he fetched their coats. It did not escape his notice that Lightoller neatly sidestepped his question about Japan. From now on, Dahlra was going to pay very careful attention to Inigo's footwork.

From Carshalton, they returned to London, where they met up with a restive and irritable Elwess. He had spent the previous two weeks in the hospital, enduring the comforts of Sister Madgerton, the pug-nosed nurse who had ripped Sydney's bandages from her ravaged back during her stay at the Agency hospital.

Elwess' patience, never generous to begin with, was stripped down to the wire and showing signs of shorting out. "Christ, I'll be glad to see the back of this place," he groused, as they wheeled him toward the car. "If I had to deal with that bellend Hughes and his battle-axe nurse one more day, I think I would have offed myself and saved Silverbirch the trouble."

His broken ankle had been corrected by surgery and the aid of several screws pegging the bone together. "Or so they tell me. They could have inserted hamsters for all the competence of the place."

"Well, we can always check by attaching fridge magnets on you when we get home," Dahlra quipped.

"Why not? It can't be any more humiliating than spending quality time here. That Madgerton bitch could give all the sadists in Soho a run for their money."

Dahlra could see the tense lines around his eyes; Elwess was in pain, bitching about it made him feel better, so he let him vent. Neither he nor Sydney had been able to spend much time with him during his 'fortnight-long incarceration at that concentration camp Lightoller calls a hospital,' so his petulance was somewhat justified. Besides, they were both all too familiar with what passed for Madgerton's bedside manner.

A blade of gauzy light slanted across his face, making Dahlra blink and sneeze at the same time. He stretched, yawned until his jaw cracked, then relaxed back into the mattress. To his left, the massive bed was empty, the bedclothes pulled up over his shoulders to keep him warm. A low fire was dying in the grate, its pops and crackles providing a soothing backdrop.

He laced his fingers and hooked his hands behind his head, staring groggily up at the ceiling. He tried to remember the last time he had slept in. By habit, he was both night watchman and lamplighter, the last to fall asleep at night, the first to wake in the morning. He threw back the covers and swung his legs over the side of the bed.

His progress down the stairs slowed to a stop as the faint sound of music reached his ears. Sydney had not played the piano in ages. These past couple of weeks, she had been like a captured songbird, too dispirited to fly or sing. He did not count the funeral. That had been duty.

He recognised the plaintive melody she played, but could not recall the name of it. Now and again he heard the odd, discordant note. She was out of practice, and her playing lacked its usual fluidity and confidence. He did not care. Hearing her play after the long period of silence took him back to the day they arrived in DeVere Gardens. She had played *Maple Leaf Rag* while he cooked for her, and he had never forgotten it. It had validated something deep and fundamental in his soul.

Even now, years after those first, difficult days, Sydney's music still felt like the final forgiveness, the ultimate acceptance. Music meant she was at least trying to come back to life. Perhaps it could unlock her self-imposed, penitent mourning, and take her to that place where she could truly forgive herself.

He entered the six-sided Conservatory at the back of the house, and bit back a laugh. Elwess, wearing a pair of black track suit trousers and a faded Black Sabbath t-shirt, was stretched out on the long sofa, one arm draped across his chest, the other dangling to the floor. A cold mug of tea sat on the floor just out of reach, scummy and over-stewed. His walking cane lay beside it; he was snoring softly.

Sydney was wearing the white dress shirt he had worn the night before, and judging from her long legs and the barest peak of a shapely hip, nothing else. She glanced up and saw Dahlra's reflection in the large windows that marched around the room. Although her eyes still held the sadness she could not release, her smile was so full of happy-to-see-you, Dahlra sapped out a little.

He took a deep breath, as if he could inhale that smile along with the cool, fresh air. He tried to remember his bland, dutiful life before he met her, and just could not do it. Christ, the very thought of life without Sydney Chapin, of never knowing the thrill and rightness of real love and seismic passion and unstoppable, protective devotion, made him momentarily feel as bereft and lost as the sad little tune she played.

He sat down beside her on the piano bench and watched with a boyish sense of pride as her fingers floated over the keys, coaxing the final, sweet-sad notes of the piece. He never tired of watching her play, her deft fingers at once strong and sure, sensitive and gentle. Dahlra had always appreciated music, but the concept of creating it was exotic, akin to conjuring magic. Though he had often been told he had a lovely speaking voice, he could neither carry a tune, nor play any instrument.

Sydney ended the last chord, and turned to him for a kiss. Her face was cool, and the hands that clasped his were freezing. "You should have made that lazy wretch build the fire in here," he said, by way of greeting.

"Good morning." She snuggled closer, burrowing down into his thick robe, her fingers encircling his waist like a band of ice. He shuddered so violently her eyes widened in surprise.

"Sorry, love!" Her sheepish smile carried that helpless look of someone fighting laughter. "Cold hands much?"

"Just a bit." His voice was comically high-pitched. "Don't mind me. When my balls drop back out of my body cavity I'll be right as the jolly old." He pulled her close, ignoring the cold. "Have you been awake long?"

"About an hour or so. Elwess was already awake when I surfaced, and you were sleeping so soundly I wanted to let you have a lie-in."

"I must have needed it. How are you feeling, love?" He lay his forehead against hers. "In here?"

She caught his hand in hers, and kissed it. "You know, Pip once told me that it's better to forget and smile than remember and be sad, but I don't want to forget."

For a moment, Dahlra thought she might actually open up, really lay herself bare, but that spirit guarding the gate of her feelings stepped between them, and he knew she was not yet ready. He did not know what to do, other than be patient. They had been here before, he reminded himself. They would come through this stronger and closer. He just had to figure out how to open that gate.

With a hasty peck on the cheek, he pulled her to her feet. The psychoanalysis he would leave to those better qualified; for now, he would do what he was born to do; he would be her Minder.

"Hungry? Let's put on a Full English."

After breakfast, while Elwess lingered over coffee and the broadsheets in the dining room, Sydney followed Dahlra back into the kitchen. "I have something I want to discuss."

"I'm all ears."

She took in a bracing breath. "Alright then. Okay, here's the deal. I'm tired of trying to snag you between crises. I want you to set the date."

Dahlra managed to take a sip of coffee without choking. "As in a wedding date?"

"No, as in getting the new pig trough installed before winter. Of course, the wedding date."

Dahlra laughed and kissed the crumbs from Sydney's lips. "I couldn't agree more! When and where?"

"Yesterday, preferably, but since that's not the case, the sooner the better. As far as a venue, it could be someplace really nice, or the public loo at St. Pancras Station for all I care. Probably not a church, though." She nodded toward the dining room. "I don't want to have to explain to the insurance adjuster why the place spontaneously combusted the moment Beelzebub walked in."

Dahlra chuckled. "No excommunication factor. Check."

"Other than that, as long as I'm legally Mrs Dahlra Gar at the end of the day, any place is fine with me."

As if on cue, the sun broke through the morning clouds and flooded the bright kitchen with yellow light. Dahlra felt absurdly pleased. "Consider it done." He kissed the ring on her finger, unable to keep the silly grin off his face. "Mrs Dahlra Gar. I like the sound of that."

"Me too." Sydney's returning smile rivaled the light streaming into the windows. "I'll go tell Elwess the good news."

Dahlra busied himself with the dishes. It was hard enough not to run shouting through the rooms like a lunatic; better to keep a little dignity. But after all, it was not every day a chap got proposed to. Sydney would tease him mercilessly for being the blushing groom.

As he headed into the dining room to refill their coffee, he heard Sydney saying, "As for you, boyo, how about coming with me to London to help me find the most gorgeous wedding gown my ill-gotten gains can afford? We'll do lunch, and get matching facials and pedicures at the spa like a proper hen party. Whad'ya say? Elwess?" The smile in her voice faded, turned cold. "What is it? Elwess, what's wrong?"

Elwess was staring at the newspaper, his face frozen in an expression of alarm. Dahlra placed a hand on his shoulder. "Elwess? Is everything alright?"

He started slightly, then looked up, completely flummoxed. "Y-yeah. No. Holy shit." He passed the newspaper to Sydney. "Look at this."

Sydney bent over the paper, then glanced up at Dahlra. "'Popular Recreational Drug Linked to Two Deaths in Local Club'."

Dahlra's stomach did a slow, forward roll. "Go on."

"'A Soho nightclub has been shut down and its owner detained pending an investigation of the deaths of two young women involving a new, potentially-lethal recreational drug.

"'Ambulances were called out in the early hours of Saturday morning to the Executive, a West End nightclub known to be popular with members of London's underground fetish community.'"

She glanced up at Elwess, who nodded. "It's fairly new. A younger, more vanilla crowd than the Library, but it was getting a good rep. Until now. Keep going."

"Well, it goes on a while about the identities of the women... Oh— 'Detective Inspector Frank Morris stated police are now investigating whether both women had taken a fatal version of'—" She stopped. "Shit." She glanced up at Dahlra with haunted, troubled eyes. "'—a fatal version of the recreational drug Sparklers, laced with the powerful painkiller fentanyl. Sparklers has rapidly become the party drug of choice with clubgoers in the Capitol.'"

Sydney threw the paper down. "So, Sparklers has hit the mainstream. I think any question about Silverbirch lying low for a while just got answered." Her expression hardened for a moment. "Alright. As far as I'm concerned, they've just declared war. We're going to make sure those bastards at Silverbirch know they're in one."

Dahlra shivered, but not from the cold. "So that's what you're going to do, then? See their war, and raise them a cataclysm?"

"If necessary. And I wasn't using the royal 'we'. If we *are* going to be a team, we're going to be a real team. Are you in?"

To Dahlra's surprise, there was no fear or trepidation in his heart—only a grim, flat-bladed resolve, like a knife being honed to a razor sharpness. He was both elated and terrified at the savage excitement he felt, and he answered her with strength and confidence.

"Yes. I'm in."

The Dress

"Sydney, no."

"But-"

"It makes you look like a meringue. A definite no."

"Everything has been a 'definite no,' Elwess. There are no more gowns left in the shop!"

"Then they need to find some more. Because these aren't doing it."

Sydney gave Elwess her best Paddington stare, but he met it with maddening impassivity. She was standing in a bustier and heels on a round platform in the middle of a multi-mirrored dressing room, in one of the most exclusive dress shops in London. Elwess lounged in one of the dainty chairs like some sort of Roman Emperor, giving the thumbs-down on gown after gown, while the eager shop owner plied him with tea and cakes.

They were several hours into shopping, and Sydney regretted bringing him along. "I suppose we'll just have to find another shop, then, Mister Impossible-To-Please."

"We could go to Lo Chang's and have one made for you."

"I'm not having Low Change shoving me in some steampunk bridal corset. It'll be covered in buckles and valves and made from PVC or barbed wire or the foreskins of lemurs or some such shit." She wrinkled her nose and mimicked the Chinese seamstress. "'I hope she wurf it, Masta Elvis'.'"

Elwess threw back his head and laughed. "Oh, Sydney, you're priceless. I know; she's abrasive and strident as fuck, but she makes lovely bondage wear."

"I'm not in the market for bondage wear. I'm trying to find a suitable wedding dress."

"What's the difference?"

"How's it going?" The young shopkeeper popped her head into the dressing room. "Oh, that's a lovely gown! Don't you love it?"

Elwess turned his full attention to the fresh meat on the hoof. He zeroed his considerable focus in on her, as if out of habit. His voice was a hypnotic blend of polite command and insouciant indifference.

"Well, Jane, I think we're going to pass on trying anymore of these Barbie doll dresses."

"They're wedding gowns," Sydney reminded him. "They're *supposed* to look that way."

"Nonsense. I'm sure Jane can find something more..." He tantalised her with a slow blink. "Special?"

Jane blushed a little, then fluffed her hair. Elwess held her gaze, but his expression did not change. He rolled his walking stick slowly between his fingers, and even though Sydney knew he was doing it on purpose, it did not stop her from rolling her eyes. Smug git.

"Um, we do have some fantastic pieces in our exclusive collection," Jane offered, batting her eyes. "But most of them are special order, or reserved for other customers."

"Well, we're here, and they *aren't*."

His voice was so confidential, so manipulative, Sydney wanted to laugh in spite of her aggravation. "And all's fair in weddings and war, I suppose."

Elwess ignored her and rose to his feet, towering over the hapless shopgirl. "I'd very much like to see your...exclusive collection, Jane." His low, purring voice was pure sin. "I won't tell if you won't."

"O-okay."

Sydney smiled ruefully as the girl disappeared. "I think you've pulled."

He shrugged indifferently. "A loose thread is easy to pull."

Sydney flopped into the nearby chair and kicked off her dainty shoes. Her feet hurt and the bustier was digging into her still-sore ribs. "This was supposed to be so simple. Get in, do a quick reccie, identify the target, make the purchase, Bob's your uncle." She glanced at her watch, groaning in frustration. "We've been at this for five freakin' hours. I probably purchased my entire wardrobe in less than three, including shoes." She looked dolefully around at the foamy carnage of discarded wedding gowns. "Why is it so damn difficult to find a sodding dress?"

He gave her his patented, 'you've just asked the dumbest question on the planet' look. "Because it's your wedding, and the only one you're going to star in. And you want to look perfect. You want Dahlra to see you walking down the aisle looking like Christmas come early. You want him to fall at your feet in adoration, and remember why he's the luckiest bastard on the planet."

With a disdainful sneer, he lifted a ruffled crinoline with the end of his walking stick and tossed it aside. It landed in the corner with a sharp, girlish rustle. "And you won't do it in these monstrosities. They're nothing but royal icing. Sweet, but no substance."

Sydney glanced at the dress she had just vacated. "Royal icing? You said this one made me look like a meringue. You called the last one a bottle of milk. The one before that was too frothy. And the one before *that* looked like a marshmallow. Maybe you're just hungry."

"And maybe you're not hungry enough." He spoke each word like a triphammer. "You deserve the perfect dress. You'll just have to look a little harder."

Sydney huffed in frustration. "I'll be more than happy to lace you up in this damn bustier if you want to try on the next sixty." He seemed to be on the verge of answering, when Jane bustled in, carrying one last garment.

The moment it dropped over her shoulders, Sydney got that in-your-gut feeling that she had found the Holy Grail. The gown was made of the lightest ivory chiffon, with a trumpet-style body that hugged her slim, shapely form down to mid-thigh, where it widened out into a lush, flowing skirt. The bateau neckline highlighted her long neck and arms, and the broad lace panel at the back hid the worst of her scars. Dozens of champagne-colored silk flowers cascaded from the bodice, and pooled at the hem of the chapel-length train. It looked as if it had been made just for her.

Jane spoke with hushed reverence. "It's a Rani Zakhem. One of our most exclusive. In a class by itself, innit?"

Sydney turned to Elwess, who was nodding slowly, a smile of pure pleasure on his face. "That's the one."

She smiled at her reflection, then her elation flatlined. "What?" Elwess asked, warily. "Surely after all those rejects, you know this is It."

"No, I absolutely love it. It's perfect. But it's not mine. It's already spoken for, remember?"

Elwess waved a dismissive hand. "Oh, don't worry about that. I'm sure we can come to some arrangement."

"Oh, sure. The owner might let me borrow it the day after *her* wedding."

Elwess' dark eyes flashed. "Leave it to me, kitten. End. Of."

With a shrug, Sydney let Jane help her out of the beautiful dress again, and she retired to the dressing room to change back into her street clothes.

As they left the shop, the Bentley pulled up to the kerb. Rick hopped out and held open the door for them just as a car went past. It slowed down, and the driver studied them keenly. He was middle-aged, a little stocky, with a hard, arrogant face, and he was staring directly at Elwess.

"Who is that?" She turned to see Elwess glaring back, his bearing equally proud and arrogant. The driver then spotted her, and sped off, but not before Sydney memorised the license number. "A friend of yours?"

Elwess looked grim. "Nobody important." His voice was flat and hollow. He did not seem afraid, but rather angry. Sydney let the matter drop; Dahlra would winkle it out of him.

As they were getting into the car, a voice called out, "Mister Talbert! Mister Talbert!" Sydney whirled around to see Jane from the shop running toward them, holding a garment bag. "You forgot this!" She handed the bag to Elwess with more than a little ceremony.

"Ah, yes. Thank you, Jane." He gave her a perfunctory smile and a large tip, then tossed the bag into the back of the car.

As they settled in for the long drive, Sydney touched the garment bag. "What did the lovely Jane bring you? Something to remember her by?"

"See for yourself."

She opened the bag, revealing a man's black suit, obviously bespoke, and exquisitely tailored. It was cut exactly like Dahlra's now-legendary long frock coat, with its many buttons. This coat was black, of course, embroidered with tiny, matte black brocaded roses. The Nehru collar and the pocket were trimmed in velvet as soft as a pelt. Matching trousers and a Saville Row silk dress shirt completed the outfit.

Elwess gave her an expectant smile. "Well? Tell me now if you hate it. We probably have time to replace it."

"I—I don't know what to say. It's perfect." She ran a finger over one of the tiny roses, picturing Dahlra undoing all those buttons. That was definitely something to smile about. "He's going to look like a king in it."

Suddenly two and two equaled five. "Hang on. This didn't come from the dress shop. Elwess, what is going on here?"

"I had it made last week. When I bought your dress."

Sydney had that same disorientating feeling she had experienced the first night Dahlra brought her to Maidenvine, with most of their stuff already there ahead of them. "*You* bought my wedding gown? The gown I tried on *just now,* after about a hundred rejections? The one in the 'it's spoken for' exclusive collection?"

"You will notice Jane never actually said *who* it was spoken for."

"But why the hell did you let me try on every sodding dress in the shop?"

"Because you would never have taken my word for it. You had to see for yourself it was the best dress. I know you, kitten. Choosing a tomato at the supermarket is an hour-long affair."

Nonplussed, Sydney huffed. "You really are a pain in the arse sometimes, Elwess!" Suddenly she laughed. "Lucky for you I did love it. What would you have done if I had rejected it, too?"

His smile reminded her of that old serpent in the Garden, right before he tricked Eve into munching on a nice McIntosh. "The thought never occurred to me."

Their ride was quiet for several miles, both of them lost in thought. Finally, Sydney broke the silence. "You're planning on moving back to London, aren't you?" She stared out the window at the passing countryside. "Once we're married, you're leaving."

He put his arm around the back of the seat and drew her near. There was a jaded, tired tone to his voice; nothing tricked up or badass now. "As much as I love getting under your skirt, kitten, I can't hide behind it forever. I need to get on with my life. And you two need time alone."

"Just promise me that you'll be careful. I'm not too worried about Silverbirch attempting anything at Maidenvine, but it's open season here in London."

He nodded, and there was sadness in his eyes as well. "I will. I promise. It's not like I'm leaving tomorrow. And I won't be gone forever."

"You'd better not. I don't want you getting too attached to anyone." She shut her mouth with a snap. Where in the everfucking fuck had *that* come from?

His inner antennae, cat-whisker sensitive to any sexual vibration, must have pinged her thoughts. He burst into a rich, nasty laugh that sounded more at home in the Library than in the back of a classy motor. "So now the truth comes out. You're gonna miss me when I go. Admit it, Sydney. You think I belong to you."

Of course she did. In those days before Silverbirch overplayed their hand, she and Dahlra had schemed enough to keep him. Was it because they did not want Silverbirch to have him, or because they had wanted him more?

Sydney knew it was not a question of his body. Elwess had sex like other people had a midnight snack. But his heart? He had given that to no one but them. The idea of him taking *that* back...

She decided to let it lie. She was not about to start querying her motives too much. It would be the equivalent of questioning his loyalties, and she had put *that* to bed before the mess at Gatwick. "You *do* belong to us."

"I know that. And I accept that completely. No doubt in my mind." His long fingers caressed the back of her neck. "But don't forget. You belong to me too, kitten."

The phone chirped with Dahlra's ringtone, and Sydney answered it quickly. "Hello, love."

"Have you killed him yet?"

Sydney laughed. "No, it's been touch and go a few times, but..."

"Any luck on the dress?"

"You won't believe me when I tell you."

"I'm looking forward to it."

"Well, you'll just have to wait. It's bad luck to see the dress before the wedding day. Any luck on that front, by the way?"

"I think you'll be pleased. I'll tell you everything when you get home."

"We're on our way."

"Hurry."

She dropped her phone back into her purse, and in that moment, she wanted to see Dahlra's face so badly she had to resist the impulse to tell Rick to step on it.

She had fought so hard against the idea of a Minder, especially him. She had always been so proud of her independence, but at the end of the day, what she had actually been was afraid to give her heart away. She had not reckoned on Dahlra Gar, with his gentle obsession and his gorgeous eyes and his sexy voice, and his stubborn, mettlesome pledge to keep her alive at any cost. She had saved his life, and in return, he had given it over to her, heart and soul. And somewhere along the way, she had found the means to rediscover her own heart and her own soul.

They had come together in a hell of blood and fire and guilt and redemption. Living proof, she thought without *too* much irony, that love really *can* conquer a lot of shit and survive. God, they had come so close to losing it all. She could not even let herself wonder about the what-ifs. There were no what-ifs in life—just the reality you made, and how you cultivated it.

That fierce protectiveness welled in her chest, and once again her feelings beat at the bars of the cage, demanding to be set free. But before she could allow the door to open, they slipped through her fingers like sand, and she allowed them to ebb away. She was no fool; this was a temporary aberration, and her feelings could and probably would come back online at the worst possible moment. But Sydney also believed in playing the hand you were dealt, even if you had to bluff to stay in the game.

It did not change the fact that she still had a job to do; in many ways, it was probably a good thing. Her emotions could not get in the way of her duty if they could not overwhelm her, and she needed to be dutiful now more than ever. She had made a vow she would never allow anyone to hurt Dahlra again. It would take vigilance and strength, and she had plenty of both. In the end, they would be more than a fair exchange for what remained bottled up inside.

"Everything alright?" Elwess asked.

She looked back at him, and thought, *and here's another one. That's okay, too. Silverbirch is out there, waiting. It hasn't gone away, and it won't forget about us.*

"Yeah. Everything's fine." She leaned back and settled into the crook of his arm. "He's home, waiting."

Dahlra is waiting for me. The thought was both grounding and thrilling. Her Minder was at home—he *was* home, waiting for her, and together they would keep their world safe. *I'm strong enough to protect them both.*

And I will.

End of Book Two

ABOUT THE AUTHOR

Teddy Raye wrote her first novel at sixteen, and her first book of short stories in her early twenties. She was too shy to read them to anyone, but with encouragement of friends, she started writing fanfiction, resulting in over 250 essays, short stories and novel-length pieces. Though her first love was erotic romance, her stories grew in scope and depth, ranging from humor to horror. It was only a matter of time before the lure of writing her own characters became too strong to resist.

The evolution of the *Her Minder* series began on a Tube ride into Central London, and grew over the years from a simple story of an erotic encounter into a trilogy of suspense, intrigue and lush romance. Book Three, *Silverbirch*, is in the works. She is also currently working on a Steampulp Murder Mystery entitled *Oubliette*.

Teddy lives in South Carolina with her two cats, Sevvy and Bello.

www.ingramcontent.com/pod-product-compliance
Lightning Source LLC
Chambersburg PA
CBHW060354260626
47160CB00006B/2312